"*The Controversial Princess, told from Adeline's POV, is thick on plot, rich in character development with Kindle-melting sex and the perfect blend of twists and turns, shockers and villains!*"

~SueBee, Goodreads Reviewer

"*The Controversial Princess is an all-consuming, scorching hot, modern royal romance with twists, turns and a jaw-dropping cliff-hanger that will leave you begging for more.*"

~Mary Dube, USA Today HEA

"*The Controversial Princess provided us with the romance our hearts needed, the passion our hearts craved, with jaw dropping twists and turns that kept us guessing and eagerly flipping the pages.*"

~TotallyBooked Blog

"*A brave, cutting-edge romance . . . This is a worthwhile read.*"

~*Library Journal* on The Forbidden

"*Unpredictable and addictive.*"

~*Booklist* on The Forbidden

"*The Forbidden proves that Jodi Ellen Malpas is not only one of the romance genre's most talented authors, but also one of the bravest. In this raw and honest portrayal of forbidden love, Jodi delivers a sexy and passionate love story with characters to root for. The Forbidden is easily my favorite read of 2017!*"

~Shelly Bell, author of *At His Mercy*, on The Forbidden

His
TRUE QUEEN

ALSO BY JODI ELLEN MALPAS

The This Man Series
This Man
Beneath This Man
This Man Confessed
With This Man
All I Am—Drew's Story (A This Man Novella)

The One Night Series
One Night—Promised
One Night—Denied
One Night—Unveiled

Standalone novels
The Protector
The Forbidden

The Smoke & Mirrors Duology
The Controversial Princess (Book #1)

His
TRUE QUEEN

JODI ELLEN MALPAS

Cover design by:
Hang Le

Cover photo by:
Rafa G Catala

Model:
Chema Malavia

Edited by:
Marion Archer

Proofread by:
Karen Lawson

Interior Design & Formatting by:
Christine Borgford, Type A Formatting

To women everywhere.
Be fierce.

THE ATMOSPHERE IS eerie, the sea of people stretching as far as the eye can see. They are all silent. But I can hear them breathe. I'm sure I can hear the wings of birds flapping up above, too.

In my grieving haze, I look up to the sky. There's one bird circling, a spectator with the best view. A magpie. A single magpie. One for sorrow. Maybe it's silly, since I've never bought into old wives' tales, but I search for another. Two for joy.

There is no second magpie.

There is no joy.

I drop my eyes back down to the concrete before me, now focused on the sounds of my footsteps. Loud footsteps—footsteps that seem to bang and echo through the streets of London. The world is watching. Eyes are on us from every corner of the globe. The King of England's body is being carried on the most elaborate gun carriage, pulled by two dressed stallions. My family and I are following on foot. Quiet. Somber. Out in the open for the world to see. Our grief exposed.

Nine days on, I still feel utterly numb. I would think I was in a horrific nightmare if there weren't reminders at every turn. A silent crowd. Back-to-back TV reports and newspaper articles. Claringdon Palace swarming with officials. Almost every media outlet descending on London to soak up the grief and report the latest on the death of the King and Heir Apparent. A broken mother and wife. A bitter brother and son. A country in mourning.

I glance to my left and find Eddie staring directly forward at our father's elaborate coffin, his face expressionless, though cut with lines of resentment. I can smell the alcohol on him. Can see his poorly hidden anger like a coat of arms embellishing his chest. His suit is creased. His hair is disheveled. His face is sallow.

The Fallen Prince.

The man who will never be King.

Tears creep up on me, and I quickly divert my eyes to the ground again, willing the water back. I don't know why I'm crying anymore. For my family's loss? For the world's loss?

For my loss?

On cue, an image of Josh sweeps through my mind and takes hold, fogging my vision further. A single teardrop leaves my cheek and plummets to the concrete, forcing me to quickly brush at my face to prevent more from coming and betraying my duty to remain composed while the world looks on. *Don't show emotion. Keep it together.* Only half a mile more and we'll be within the safe walls of St Paul's. Safe? Nowhere is safe. Nowhere is private. My life-long sense of suffocation has been put to shame in light of recent events. I can't breathe, and to add to my agony, the one person that made my life bearable has gone.

My already heavy legs seem to fill with lead, putting one foot in front of the other becoming more of a slog. Never before have I needed to be held and told everything is going to be okay. Never before have I wished so hard for a man's arms to take me in them and hide me from the cruelty of this world. But only one man's arms are what I want.

And I can't have him.

I look up once again, as if I may find him amid the dense crowds. Of course, I don't, and my heart aches a little more.

The procession comes to a gradual stop, and gunfire sounds loudly, making me startle and my heart lurch. I dart my eyes to where I know Damon to be. He's unfazed, and he nods to the doors of St Paul's. I follow his eyes and find two neat lines of soldiers forming a walkway into the cathedral, their weapons pointing to the sky. Quickly gathering myself, I wait for my mother to lead before Eddie and I follow my father's coffin into the sacred building. I expected it, but the sight of the TV cameras still makes me falter in my steps toward the altar. And as I settle on the pew, surrounded by world leaders, fame, fortune, and supremacy, my grief is masked for a few moments by something else.

Something formidable in its power.

I glance over my shoulder and lose a few breaths when our eyes meet. He looks as defeated as I feel. And then he looks away, and I know it isn't because he's fearful of someone seeing us staring at each other and what that might mean. It's because he can't look me in the eye. He can't accept that our story has come to an end. He can't accept that my guilt is superseding every other emotion I possess. Guilt is a horrid emotion. My father and my brother are dead, and it is because of me. I don't deserve to be happy. I deserve all the losses that come with wearing a crown. And the biggest loss of all is losing Josh.

∞

I FINALLY BREATHE steadily for the first time today once the doors of Claringdon Palace close behind me. As soon as my legs have carried me to the Claret Lounge, I close my eyes, take hold of the sideboard, and focus only on the oxygen hitting my lungs. I feel utterly exhausted. "Your Highness," one of Claringdon's maids says tentatively, holding a tray out to me. One single glass of champagne rests atop of it, the bubbles almost hypnotizing. I look at her and find a soft smile. *Your Highness*. Not *Your Majesty*. No one knows of the scandal. No one knows my disgraceful arse has landed on the throne. The world has been waiting for Eddie to be sworn in, his devastation and unstable frame of mind being blamed for the delay. Not the fact that he's *not* the late king's son.

Returning her mild smile, I accept the glass.

"Anyone would think you are celebrating," As always, my father's sister, Victoria, the eldest of his siblings, looks at me like I'm something she's just stepped in. "It's your father's funeral, for crying out loud, and here you are disrespecting his life with your red lips, sheer stockings, and champagne."

A gentle hand lands on my forearm, and Uncle Stephan's straight lips softly warn me from attacking. I don't attack, but something deep and desperate urges me to smack her down. I take the glass and give the maid a reassuring gesture, since she's only offered what she knows I need. "You may leave," I say to Victoria, short and sharp, leaving no room for discussion.

"Excuse me?" Her indignation would make me smile if there was anything much to smile about. Of course, she doesn't know she just insulted her queen.

"Leave," Eddie says, pointing a deadly expression Victoria's way before casting his eyes around to the rest of the family.

It takes that one word from my brother, the man they believe to be King, for Victoria to put a sock in it and everyone to leave the lounge. Even the footmen heed the bitter vibes, shutting the door on their way out, leaving my mother, Eddie, and me.

Eddie flops down on the couch and pulls a hipflask from the inside pocket of his suit jacket, knocking back a good dose. "Thank God that's over," he mutters. "Can we please now tell the world I'm not King? That my mother fucked a member of household staff behind the late King's back and birthed me as a consequence?"

"Edward," I cry, horrified by his harshness. I look at my mother and find glassy eyes staring blankly at her son. "Have some respect."

"Respect?" he snorts. "I've lived a lie for thirty-three years. I've been forced to endure this life, wasted years following protocol, and all for nothing. Forgive me, but I have a life I'd finally like to start living without the constraints of this godforsaken family holding me back." Another long glug of his drink. "So when are we telling the world that they have a queen and it's their precious Adeline? I'm sure they'll be delighted." He sneers at me, and it's all I can do to stop myself from slapping his smug face. I don't like this Eddie. Where's my beloved brother, the man I've leaned on for years? Bitterness doesn't look good on him, though I realize he has every right to be angry. Yet his rage shouldn't be directed at me.

"You need to stop drinking." I look at my glass of fizz and place it on the table in front of me, suddenly turned off by the liquid I usually savor.

Eddie chuckles and takes another defiant swig. "Even as Queen, dear sister, you cannot tell me what I can and cannot do." He toasts me with his hipflask. "Your Majesty."

Queen. That word makes my skin crawl each time it's spoken. "Stop it," I warn. "Just stop it."

"Why? You going to have me beheaded?"

"Edward," I yell.

"Yes, Your Majesty?"

I rise from my seat, brushing down my skirt to busy my hands and prevent them from swiping at his face. "Just grow up."

"Enough." Mother stands abruptly, landing us both with eyes full of annoyance. "In the past few days, I have buried one of my children and my husband. You *will* have some respect."

Eddie and I both snap our mouths shut as there is a tap on the door. Mother quickly composes herself before calling for whomever it is to enter. A rather cautious-looking Sid, Claringdon's long-serving Master of the Household, clears his throat, addressing Eddie. "Your Majesty, your guests await."

"Thank you, Sid," Mother says on Edward's behalf. "We are

taking a few moments."

"Very well, ma'am." He leaves and closes the door, and Eddie struggles to his feet with the help of the arm of the Chesterfield.

"I'll be in the library," he mumbles, wobbling his way to the doors at the other end of the lounge.

Mother reaches for thin air before her. "But, Edward—"

"I will be in the library," he repeats, not turning back. "The sooner this circus is over, the better. Have fun." The door slams loudly, making Mother flinch and my eyes close hopelessly.

Just like Eddie, facing the army of mourners is the absolute last thing I feel capable of, but one look at my despairing mother unearths a duty in me I never knew existed. I can't let her face this alone. So curling my arm through hers, I lead her toward the masses of people who are ready to shower us with sympathy. "However are we going to approach this mess, Mother?" I ask quietly, knowing as soon as today is over, truths will have to be told.

"Like we've approached messes all of our lives," she answers, looking at me with a strength I'm familiar with. "Like royals." Her neck lengthens, and an air of determination carries her toward the Grand Hall as gracefully as it always does. "With smoke and mirrors."

I glance at her, a little wide-eyed, just as I'm attacked from the side by Jenny, who quickly and efficiently reapplies my red lips and dabs my cheeks with a powder brush. "I'm fine," I tell her as Mary-Ann, Mother's chief lady-in-waiting, works on Mother. "Smoke and mirrors?" I ask as we're given space once more. "Isn't it time to clear them, Mother?"

"One doesn't clear smoke and mirrors, darling. One preserves them."

Of course *one* does. I close my eyes and ask her a question I've wanted to ask for weeks. "How did you know Helen was lying?"

Her back visibly straightens. "Mother's instinct," she says simply, not giving any more than that. I sigh, shaking my head to myself, but I'm soon distracted from my mother's stoic face when the doors to the Grand I Iall are pulled open and the bustle of chatter drops like a mute button has been pressed, all attention pointing our way. The absence of Edward is obviously noted, some people looking beyond our static forms in the doorway for my brother. Their King. Mother squeezes my hand before she releases me and glides to the first of the people waiting to greet her. The Prime Minister, Bernie Abrams, a man famed for his antiquated approach to leadership, who is hanging on to his power by the skin of his teeth. My father never liked him. I could tell from the umbrage in his tone at the mere mention of the man who has run our country for the past four years. I smile on the inside, remembering my father's sheer exasperation each Wednesday morning when he'd have to endure his weekly roundup on all things political from the Prime Minister. I always found it amusing that the King thought Bernie old-fashioned in his political views. My father was a dinosaur in all things traditional where royalty was concerned.

As Mother moves onto the next in line, I brace myself to endure the Prime Minister myself. Two minutes in his company is enough to need to jump-start one's brain, his voice monotone, his personality severely lacking passion. The man is entirely boring. Watching paint dry is more interesting, and to think I will have to sit in a room with him for an hour each week and listen to him drone on about political issues. It should be one more reason for me to fight my fate with everything I have. Yet the fight in me has diminished. My fate is written. This is my punishment.

"Prime Minister," I say, letting him bow and take my hand.

"Your Highness. My deepest sympathy."

My lips straighten as I brace myself to hear those very words from every single person in the room. I should have joined Eddie, my need for a cigarette and a drink suddenly strong. Duty forces me to greet everyone with a smile and a few words, my strength waning with each person I present myself to. The faces begin to blend, their words a distant buzz in my ears. Important people, royalty from various lands, leaders from dozens of countries, cabinet members, and distant relatives, all talk at me.

But I hear only one voice. The voice that always calmed me. His voice. My American boy.

~

HOURS INTO THE unbearable scene, I feel like I could collapse, my head becoming light. It's all too much, so overwhelming, and the added knowledge that this will be my life almost every day—the duty, the fortitude, the front—is enough to make me want to stop in the middle of the room and cry. To scream at the top of my voice that I want out.

I whirl around, ready to find Eddie and join his pity party, but my path is blocked, and the heavy scent of something familiar, masculine, and primal, hits my nose and makes me dizzy. He shouldn't be here. It's only because of his father's friendship with the late King that he is. And, perhaps, so he could corner me like this.

"Your Majesty." His soft southern drawl enhances my despair, spikes flashbacks that I've fought with all my might to keep at bay. I train my eyes on his chest, afraid of eye contact. Afraid of the feelings swirling inside me getting out of control.

"You must not call me that," I whisper to my feet.

"Why? You're Queen, aren't you?"

My jaw tenses, anger creeping forward. I shall not waste my breath explaining to Josh that no one yet knows of my position. That as far as everyone is concerned, I am still *Her Highness* and not *Her Majesty*. Because he already knows that. He's simply emphasizing my royal status, reminding me, as if it had escaped me how impossible my life is now.

"Thank you for coming," I murmur, stepping to the side as I fight to keep my heartbeats steady. Josh steps with me, keeping my escape just out of reach. "If you don't mind," I breathe, "I need to excuse myself to use the bathroom."

"I do mind." His tone is cut, short and . . . angry. I can't possibly blame him. He was escorted from Claringdon on that fateful day of my father's death, and I haven't answered his calls since, have deleted every message he's sent. I can't face my further loss. Can't face . . . anything. "You can't even look at me." Taking one step closer, I virtually feel the heat of his breath on my skin.

"I'm afraid I must go." Another step to the side is once again blocked by Josh.

"Why are you doing this?"

His question stuns me, as evident in the lift of my wide eyes to his. As soon as our stares meet, the swirl of emotions in me go into overdrive, every snippet of our love affair playing through my mind like the perfect kind of torture. A reminder of how I came to be here. At my father's funeral. How I came to bury my brother only a few days ago. How, now, I am destined to be the Queen of England, and how much I hate that prospect. "My father and my brother are dead because of me. The country has lost their Sovereign because of me. My destiny has been written, a destiny I cannot bear, yet it is my own doing. It is my punishment."

His jaw, so tight it could pop, rolls in anger. "You can't blame yourself."

"Then who else can I blame?" I ask, taking a wise step back, away from him and his potency. "I can't be with you, Josh. Because every time I look at you, I think about my selfishness and the consequences of that."

"You're not the only one suffering the consequences, Adeline."

No. No, I am not. I only have to look around me to see the lives that have been turned upside down. Lifting my chin, I ignore his statement and yank down the protective barriers I'll have to depend on for the rest of my life. "You may address me as *Your Majesty*, Mr. Jameson." My tone is even and strong, albeit forced, and the result is a pang of further guilt in me and straight lips from Josh.

"Thank you for coming. Please, excuse me." I make to pass him and quickly drink in air when he seizes my wrist, holding it by his side to conceal his aggressive gesture. He doesn't look at me, and I refuse to look at him. Damon catches my eye nearby, his body twitching to come over. A mild shake of my head warns him away. I do not want a scene. Not here. Not now.

"I don't care if you're Adeline, a princess, or the Queen of fuckin' England. You will not treat me like you are superior. It doesn't suit you. We are equals. Man and woman. Lovers. Friends. *You* love *me*."

I close my eyes, forcing back the tears. Love him. I do. With everything I have. Yet I no longer own my feelings. I mustn't love him. And I don't deserve his love. Those thoughts set the anger dormant within me alight. His words are yet another reminder of my loss.

With my nostrils flaring, I yank myself free of his harsh grip. "Good day to you, Mr. Jameson." Urgently breathing in oxygen to stop me from passing out with the effort it takes me to walk away, I make my escape. Panic rises in me, people moving in from every direction ready to drown me in more sympathy. I can't talk. Can barely walk.

"Your Highness." The Prime Minister is suddenly in my way, smiling and talking. I catch the odd word as he harps on about political nonsense, how he'll miss his weekly meetings with the King, but looks forward to his first with Edward, how he thinks my brother will rule with strength and compassion. My brother won't be ruling with strength and passion. He won't be ruling at all. But how does the Prime Minister think *I* will rule?

"Ma'am?" Damon's voice is the only one I hear clearly, his tone soft and soothing, and I look up to find my head of protection gazing at me with concern. Of course, he knows of the mess I'm in. Of the lies that have been unearthed in the wake of my father's death. "Shall we get you out of here?"

My lip quivers with relief and gratitude. "Please," I croak, barely able to hold myself up any longer. He has a supporting arm around me within a second, virtually carrying me away from the crowds. People move from his path, his persona threatening anyone to try and stop me to talk. He takes me through the Claret Lounge, through the library, takes a shortcut through the kitchens, and into the garden. And the moment he closes the door behind him, he ensures I'm steady on my feet before pulling out his cigarettes and putting one between my lips. He lights it and stands back, letting me take a long, needed draw. My exhale of smoke has a sorrowful whimper stream out with it.

Damon sighs and lights his own cigarette. "Is the hopelessness due to a certain American's presence, or the fact that the Prime Minister has literally bored you to tears?"

"I can't do it, Damon," I blurt, my hand shaking as I guide the cigarette to my lips to take another pull, leaving the white stick bumping across my red lips before I manage to grip it and draw. "I can't be Queen." Pointing to the doors we just exited, I shake my head, my reality becoming more real by the second. "I mean, I'm sure everyone in that room disapproves of me. And I've never cared to furnish myself with political information. I'll have no idea what I'm talking about."

A small smile crosses Damon's lips. "Your Majesty, it has been a very long time since the Sovereign has had any say in how their country is run." He puffs out his smoke and points down the path for us to walk. "That is why you have a cabinet and a government. They do it all for you. All you have to do is listen to the Prime Minister tell you, out of courtesy, what they are doing and how they are doing it. You may need to pass the odd law here and there, too."

"That's just a formality," I mutter.

"That is how a constitutional monarchy functions, ma'am. You're a status symbol for your country. A historical institution."

I laugh. "Yes, the stable British Monarchy. The envy of every country. Respected and admired. But it's all just smoke and mirrors, Damon. You know that."

His nod is mild, but his understanding is great. "How's Eddie?"

"Drunk," I answer, taking great pleasure from flicking some cigarette ash at a solid granite cherub statue. "I'm rather jealous."

He chuckles lightly. "And your mother?"

"Ever the amazing actress." I stop at the end of the path and look toward the palace. "I don't want to go back yet, Damon. Would you walk some more with me?"

"Of course, ma'am." He leads on, our pace lazy and easy.

"Has there been any breakthroughs in the investigations?" I ask, more out of habit than curiosity. I know Damon wouldn't know, as he's not been included in any of the meetings held in the King's office. It's all just MI5 big-bods being courteous by giving us morsels of information.

"The King was piloting the helicopter."

I throw my stare his way. "What?" Damon was at Evernmore. He must have known this already. "My father hasn't operated a helicopter in years." I know he used to make time for flying in his military days, but that was years ago. What was he thinking?

His expression is blank. "I know. No pre-flight checks were performed. There was a mechanical fault midflight. An experienced pilot would have likely dealt with the issue and brought the helicopter down safely. But your father . . ." He fades off and sighs. "Your father was on a mission, Adeline." I wince. *On a mission to stop me.* "Where was the pilot?"

"Taking supper in the kitchens."

"Why didn't you tell me this before?"

"Nothing was certain. Besides, you've had enough to deal with."

I swallow hard, staring at the small stones at my feet as I continue to wander. Damon hasn't told me before now because he knows how guilty I feel already. Now? Now I feel positively wretched. "John was trying to stop him. That's why he was on the flight, too." That guilt squeezes my heart.

He hums, and we continue to walk in silence, until Damon

breaks it. "There is one thing I would like to run by you, if you don't mind." Damon reaches into his inside pocket and pulls out his phone, and I cock my head in question, prompting him to go on. "Josh's security team sent me some images."

I feel my throat tighten. "Of what?"

"Of the person possibly responsible for ransacking Mr. Jameson's hotel room the night of his premiere." He points his phone to me, and I look at the image. It's blurry, terribly blurry. I can only really make out the shape of a man exiting the elevator, the lighting dim. "Do you recognize him?"

I squint, looking closely. Whoever it is took great care to conceal themselves, a hat on his head, his chin dipped. "No, I don't, but what does it matter?" I look at Damon. "Mr. Jameson's reputation is safe now, I believe." I glance back at the palace again as Damon puts his phone away, wondering if Josh is still there. People were starting to leave. Has he? "I suppose I should be getting back before my absence is noticed."

Damon looks at the palace, too, as he flicks his cigarette onto the grass. I can't help but smile at the thought of the gardener's face when he stumbles upon something so disgraceful littering his preened lawn. "I think your absence will have already been noticed." He plucks the cigarette from my fingertips and adds it to the lawn with his.

"Would you do me a favor, please, Damon?" I ask, knowing I could only ever ask him.

His smile is knowing. "Why don't you have a few moments to yourself while I go ensure some of the guests get home safely."

God, what would I ever do without my Damon? I nod my thanks as he leaves to check that Josh has left, and I start to wander toward the entrance of the maze, coming to a stop at the threshold. Venturing into the labyrinth of greenery would be silly, yet it is the only place I can hide around here. I need to hide. To escape. I start meandering through unhurriedly, picking a few leaves from the bushes as I go. I could find my way to the center within minutes, but today I take endless wrong turns in an attempt to stretch out my walk for as long as possible.

Half an hour later, I breach the opening that brings me to the center where my grandfather's statue looms. The solid marble homage isn't the only thing I find. "Sabina?" I say to myself, watching as she stands at my grandfather's feet, staring up at him. She's lost in her thoughts, and it keeps me from disturbing her for a few moments, until I feel guilty for intruding and make my presence known. "Sabina?" She whirls around on a little gasp, and though I have seen her today, it's only now I appreciate how utterly tired she looks. "Are you okay?"

"Your Highness." She bows her head a fraction. "Yes, yes, I am fine. Just taking a moment to myself."

I know that desire all too well. Approaching her, I look at the statue. "My grandfather was quite a frightening man, don't you think?"

Turning to mirror my position, Sabina looks up, too. "He had his moments."

"Every picture I've seen of him, he looks so formidable. Of course, you knew him a lot longer than I did. Was he always so heavy-handed?"

"More so after your grandmother passed away." She looks across at me and smiles. "Before that, he could be quite the charming man."

"I don't know if I should believe you."

"I can understand that. Things in this world are sometimes very hard to believe." She cocks her arm, and I slip mine through hers, smiling when she pats it affectionately. "How are you, Adeline?"

"Still in shock, I think."

On an understanding nod of her head, she turns us, and we start to amble casually through the maze. "And Prince Edward? I haven't seen him since your return from St. Paul's."

I swallow. And so the lies begin, and I truly hate that I have to lie to Sabina. She's the only person in my life I feel I can talk freely to, and now that privilege is lost amid more secrets and deceits. "He's struggling to come to terms with it all," I reply quietly. That's not a lie, though why Sabina thinks he is struggling will be a little misleading. "I can't believe my father tried to fly the helicopter. And I cannot understand why on earth he would allow John to travel with him. Every reason for that rule to be in place has now been proven."

"David is deeply shocked, too. Apparently, they were all set to go on their hunt, rifles loaded, their hipflasks topped up."

Given what Sabina has been through herself recently, her husband passing, I can only be grateful that her son was not on the helicopter. The poor woman has had her fair share of losses, and though David is far from being my favorite person, I wouldn't wish him harm, if only for Sabina's sake.

"As I understand it, His Majesty was in quite a hurry to return to London," she says quietly. "I have no idea why."

"It's all my fault," I whisper dejectedly, not thinking, feeling my guilt beginning to overflow. I can see it now, my father marching to the royal helicopter in a blind rage. His advisors trying to stop him. John trying to stop him. I made him too mad to listen to reason. "I shouldn't have left Evernmore." Has David shared with Sabina the circumstances of my row with the King? Has he told her I was cavorting with Josh Jameson, and that is the very reason my father was on the royal helicopter? And if he has, would she ignore it like everyone else who was at Claringdon when I arrived with Josh that day? Will she pretend he was never there? Like our affair never happened? My internal questions lead to more. Does she know about Eddie? Does she know I am now Queen?

"How could it have been your fault, Adeline?" Sabina asks softly, not helping me decide whether she simply doesn't know anything, or if she's pretending she doesn't. Of course, she's been around this family for long enough to know protocol, and protocol might be telling her that if she knows, she shouldn't let on. But I don't want her to play ignorant. I want to talk to someone about my woes, someone who won't judge me, and the only person I can to talk to is her.

"Sabina—"

"It is not your fault." She cuts me off with a stern tone that's not like Sabina at all. But she's wrong. This entire mess is my fault.

"But—"

She stops and turns into me, and then does the unthinkable. She covers my mouth with her palm. "One has to be a fighter in this world, ma'am. Defeated isn't a dress you wear well."

Her words hit me hard, catapulting me back to the time when I overheard a conversation she had with my father at the stables. The resentment in her expression when the King complimented her on her strength. That she's always been a fighter.

One has to be in this world, she had replied. I take her hand and pull it away from my mouth, pondering my slowly dawning thoughts. There was another time when she told a very angry David that some secrets should never be told. I inhale a little, something slowly slotting into place. My conclusions don't tell me if she knows of my affair with Josh, but they do tell me one thing. "You knew about my mother and Davenport all along." I drift off when she recoils a little. "When you were with David at the stables, you said some secrets should never be told." I bite my lip, everything beginning to make sense. "David was angry because you knew about my mother's affair with Davenport, and you kept it a secret from him all this time. He was mad because my father was his friend and he didn't know. Only Sir Don knew." I laugh. "And you. Did my father know you knew? Does my mother?"

"Goodness, no." Her eyes close and she breathes out. "Adeline—"

"You knew Eddie wasn't the King's child. And you now know the crown will soon land on my head."

Her eyes open, glassy eyes, eyes full of regret. "I'm sorry, Your Majesty."

Your Majesty. I can see the apologies pouring from her gaze, and though part of me is so very cross, I really cannot blame Sabina for not telling me. She's never told anyone.

"How?" I ask simply.

"I've been around your family for a very long time, Your Majesty. Sometimes one sees things one isn't supposed to."

I turn away from her, hating the remorse splashed all over her tired face. "And how did David find out?"

"He overheard a conversation between his father and me shortly before he passed. He was most annoyed with the King for not confiding in him."

That would explain David's absence when his father died. He was sulking. His nose had been put out of joint. "And then my father had no choice but to tell David when the letters came back to haunt him."

"Indeed."

"Will it ever end, Sabina?" I ask. "The lies, the secrets? Will that be my job as Queen? To protect the web of deceit from ever being exposed?"

"Part of it, yes. But you already know that. You must rule with your head, not with your heart. And I know better than anyone that this will be the hardest part for you, Adeline."

More treacherous tears tumble down my cheeks, and I move before Sabina sees them. She's demanding I reach for the indifference a royal requires, but I can't. *I don't want this.* But I can't let anyone see how devastated I am. How broken. Because I am a queen, and queens are strong.

But where will I find that courage?

2

I SQUINT WHEN the curtains are whipped across, opening the gates for the blinding sunlight to flood my bedroom. I frown in my sleepy state, wondering what on earth Olive is playing at. Propping myself on my elbows, I search my room for her, finding the blurry outline of a body by the window. But once my vision has cleared, it's not Olive I see, but a stern-faced lady who I recognize from the staff at Claringdon Palace. Gert. She's old-school.

"It is ten o'clock, Your Highness." She slides a tray onto my dressing table and begins plumping a few cushions on my chaise.

"What are you doing here?" I ask as my eyes follow her around my suite, her hands fussing and faffing with anything she can lay them on. "And where is Olive?"

"I believe Olive has been redistributed to another royal household, ma'am."

"What?" I'm now awake and most furious. "Whatever do you mean, redistributed? No one from my household should be *redistributed* without at least consulting me." A horrible thought suddenly comes to me, and I dive out of bed in a panic, ignoring Gert's startled eyes as I shoot across the carpet in my lacy nightdress. If

Olive has been redistributed, then what about Damon? And Jenny and Kim and Felix?

Yanking the door open, I throw myself out of my suite and hurry across the vast landing, looking over the balustrade as I round it, searching for him. "Damon," I yell, drawing many staff members from various rooms, all coming to see what the commotion is about. "Have you seen Damon?" I ask a wary-looking maid, whose hands are full of clean bed linen.

"No, ma'am, I haven't."

"Shit," I spit, taking the stairs like a mad woman, unperturbed by my state of undress. "Damon!" I reach the front door and swing it open, searching for Damon's car. No car. My dread multiplies.

"What in God's name is going on?" Dolly asks, her hand armed with a whisk as she ventures from the kitchens. "Oh my goodness." She wobbles to a stop and takes in my scantily clad form. "Your Highness?"

"Where's Damon?" I have no time to address everyone's shock. I'm too worried. If Damon has been forced out, there will be hell to pay.

"He has gone to collect His Majesty the King."

For a second, I'm utterly confused. Then I remember who is King. Or apparently King. "And where is Edward?"

Felix appears, ushering Dolly back to the kitchens before approaching me, coming close, obviously not wanting anyone to hear. "I believe His Majesty had a private gathering at a suite in a Mayfair hotel last night."

Oh God. What has he done? The communications team will be in meltdown. And just as I think that, Felix answers his phone, looking very stressed indeed. "Do it," he hisses. "Every camera on the premises, do you hear me?" He stabs at his phone with an angry thumb and stamps off. I sag against the door, cursing Eddie in my head. He's gone off the rails, and when the world believes you are King, that is not something one should go off. At least, not publicly.

I hear the sounds of crunching gravel under tires, and I turn to find Damon rolling through the gates. Rushing down the steps, I go straight to the back door of his car and pull it open. "Oh my goodness," I cry as Eddie topples out of the car and lands at my feet. The stench of stale alcohol hits my nose as he rolls onto his back, chuckling.

"Sister," he squawks, grappling at the side of the car. "Or should I call you Your Maj—" He convulses and proceeds to throw up. I jump back, just missing the spray of vomit.

I look despairingly at Damon as he drags his big body from the driver's seat, his face a roadmap of annoyed lines. "He's going to kill himself at this rate," he mutters.

My brother, the charming, adored, handsome prince, is unrecognizable. "We should get him to his suite." I bend and push his blond mop from his eyes, staring at his pitiful form.

His drunken eyes blink open, and an uncoordinated hand feels around in midair until he finds my face. "I still love you," he slurs. His drunken words, words I know he really means, bring on a fresh batch of tears.

"I know you do, you silly fool." I look at Damon. "I should get him cleaned up."

On a roll of his eyes, Damon dips and collects Eddie, throwing him onto his shoulder and carrying him into the palace. "Why are you in your nightie?" he asks as we take the stairs, my hand holding Eddie's where it's dangling down Damon's back. His eyes are rolling now, and he quietly mumbles nonsensical words.

"I thought . . ." I drift off and shake my head. "Never mind."

With the help of a few footmen, we get Eddie into his bed, and rather than let anyone else strip him down, I ask them to leave so I can take care of him myself. His dignity is already dented enough.

As soon as one of the maids sets a bowl of warm water and a washcloth on the bedside, the room clears, and I am alone with my brother. "What am I going to do with you, Edward?" I wrestle his arms out of his suit jacket and toss it to the floor before starting on his trousers. "This is not the behavior of a prince." I laugh at myself. I'm a fine one to talk. Although, now there is *no* reason for him to behave like a prince. And there is every reason for me to behave like a princess.

Or a queen.

Starting on his shirt buttons, I unfasten them one by one until Eddie's chest is revealed. His usually well-defined torso, the result of years in the military, looks somewhat lacking in the muscle department. He's lost weight these past few weeks. He's not eaten, just drank. He's not exercised, just drank. "I will help you, Eddie." I dip and kiss his scruffy cheek. "I won't let you go down this dark path." I stroke down his cheek with my palm, ignoring the stench of vomit as I stare at him. I sigh. He's dead to the world.

Once I have him out of his shirt, leaving him in only his boxers and socks, I wring out the washcloth and start wiping his face clean of vomit. I take my time, until he's as clean as he can be without a shower. Dropping a kiss on his forehead, I tuck him in and dip to collect his suit, holding it at arm's length as I carry it from his suite, my nose wrinkled.

"Have this dry-cleaned, would you?" I ask, handing it to one of the maids outside Eddie's suite. "And please leave the pri . . . King to rest." I make my way to my private quarters, finding Gert still faffing around my suite when I enter. I'm not one to pass judgement, but I really do not like Gert. She's perhaps mid-sixties, and just by the way she is looking at me, I can tell she belongs to the camp of royal staff who are antiquated and disapprove of me. "Oh. You're still here." I sniff, wandering over to my bedside table. "Can I have some privacy, please?" I find my secret stash of cigarettes and light one, disregarding the rules *and* Gert's poorly concealed disgusted face. Knickers to her. "You may leave." I take a teaspoon and stir my coffee, blowing out a plume of smoke slowly, almost cockily. Gert doesn't appreciate it. Her old face is twisted as she leaves. "And please don't enter my private quarters without knocking again."

"Apologies, ma'am. I received a direct order from Claringdon to wake you."

"By whom?" I ask, my stirring pausing.

"The late King's chief advisor, ma'am."

"Sir Don?"

She nods, and I feel anger burn my veins. "You are to be at Claringdon by noon, Your Highness."

"That is all." I dismiss her abruptly and drop onto my dressing table chair, catching my reflection in the mirror. No wonder everyone was looking at me like I might be a monster as I ran frantically around the palace looking for Damon. Because I really do look like a monster. I reach up and pat my pale cheeks on a sigh, then take another hit of my breakfast and exhale it into my reflection.

More smoke. How very apt.

∾

I FEEL LIKE I'm being held up with foundation and headache pills. Although I know beyond all doubt that I couldn't possibly feel worse than Eddie right now. As we pull up at Claringdon, I risk a peek at him once more, if only to remind myself just how awful he looks. I'm pretty sure he's still drunk.

"What?" he asks without even the courtesy of looking at me.

"You look truly frightful." I'm honest. I can't possibly be telling him anything he doesn't already know. "And that was an entirely stupid thing for you to do," I finish, stepping out of the car when Damon opens the door. He gives me a little shake of his head, as if to remind me that whatever I say to my brother will fall on deaf ears. I know he's right, but still.

"When did you become all holier than thou?" Eddie mutters as he joins me at the bottom of the steps. Sir Don and Sid are waiting by the door at the top, and not for the first time since the crash, I miss Davenport greeting me in his usual stuffy, stoic way. We're told he handed in his resignation. I suspect that *that* resignation letter was written for him. Probably by Sir Don.

"I'm worried about you," I reply to Eddie. He seems to be in self-destruct mode, and he's going about the right way of exploding very soon.

"Don't be. Since I'm not technically a royal anymore, no one should be concerned about the way I choose to live my life."

My patience is fraying, and I turn to him, making sure he sees it. "You are still my brother," I say on a hissed whisper. "And your mother is still a Spanish princess, so you are wrong on both counts." I storm off, leaving my wayward brother with those words to rattle around in his tender skull. "Sir Don, Sid." I nod at them both as I pass, pulling my gloves off and handing them to . . ."Olive?" I say as she smiles awkwardly, doing her usual terrific job of ridding me of my outerwear. "You're here now?"

"Yes, ma'am." Nodding politely, she scampers off before I can question her further, not that she would speak. Turning my suspicious eyes toward Sir Don, I'm not surprised to find a straight, unmoving face. It was him who redistributed Olive from Kellington to Claringdon. Suddenly having Davenport on my case for all these years feels like it could have been a breeze. "Why are we here?" I ask, lifting my chin in a forced act of strength.

"This way, Your Highness." He sweeps his arm out toward the stairs that lead to the grand landing. There's only one reason why we would be taking the stairs. My father's office. I come over a little stifled, the thought of stepping in there overwhelming. I haven't seen inside the four walls of my father's private study since I left to go to Evernmore.

I move forward, looking back to find Eddie dragging his feet like a petulant child being summoned to the headmaster's office.

"Is that your phone?" Eddie asks as Sir Don follows us up the stairs. It's only with my brother's prompt that I hear the faint sound, and I riffle through my bag to find it. My steps falter when I see who's calling. "Don't tell me, it's Mr. Hollywood," Eddie says quietly.

I shoot him a glare, letting my phone ring off, and as soon as the screen clears, I see a message. My pulse quickens as I read his words.

I've received my warning. Keep my silence and keep my distance.

I shove my phone back into my bag and try not to think about who's throwing out the warnings, but when I turn and catch Sir Don's eye, that task becomes trickier. Was it him? What's also difficult is trying not to think about whether Josh will heed the warning. Because I, now more than anyone, know what this institution is capable of. And now I also suspect that even if my father didn't know of my affair with Josh before I told him, his people did, and Josh's trashed hotel room was another warning. Yet what I can't figure out is why they didn't tell the King. Because he was friendly with Senator Jameson? Because they thought they could handle it without bothering the King, knowing I'd never listen to him should he demand I stop seeing Josh?

We're shown into my father's empty office, and Sir Don leaves us alone, shutting the door behind him. Eddie immediately heads for the antique globe where my father's stash of Scotch is hidden, whereas I stand on the threshold, reluctant to venture farther inside. Something isn't right, and it takes me only a few seconds to establish what. The usual, familiar stench of cigar smoke isn't as strong. In fact, it has nearly gone completely, and never would I have thought I'd miss it.

Swirling his drink as he wanders around Father's office, Eddie seems to take in every little detail, eventually arriving at the massive portrait of the King over the fireplace. He stares up at it, throwing back his Scotch violently before mockingly toasting the oil on canvas. "Rest in peace, *Dad.*"

I don't reprimand him on his disrespect. There would be little point. Besides, the door opens before I can think more of it, and Sir Don re-enters, followed by Mother and David Sampson.

"Mother?" I question as she gracefully floats across the office and takes a seat quietly in the corner. Sir Don motions for everyone to be seated, and everyone does, except Eddie, who chooses to remain standing by the fireplace. Sir Don waits for his audience to settle before he draws breath to speak, so very serious and cold. "The people in this room are the only people who know of the situation."

Eddie snorts into his drink as he takes a sip, laughing to himself. "No, actually, I believe Daddy is missing." He isn't speaking of the late King, of course. My father. Mother's husband. "Has Davenport been warned?" Eddie asks. "Threatened?"

After my message from Josh just now, I have every faith that yes, Davenport has been warned. "Why are we here?" I cut to the chase, the atmosphere unbearable. "You obviously have a plan to fool the public and avert the scandal of Eddie's illegitimacy, so let us hear it."

Sir Don stands, pulling in the sides of his jacket. "I believe His Royal Highness Prince Edward has passed the throne to his sister due to medical issues."

I cough on nothing. "What?"

"Yes, what?" Eddie parrots. "What the hell is wrong with me?"

"As we all know, Prince Edward fought gallantly for his country, but sadly he is now suffering the consequences of his commitment."

"Are you fucking kidding me?" Eddie splutters. "I have to feign PTSD so the world doesn't know I'm a bastard?" He swings his eyes to Mother. "And you're happy with this?"

She doesn't murmur a word, her quiet state of Switzerland revisited.

"Obviously," Sir Don goes on, ignoring Eddie's questions and my shocked face, "given the circumstances of Princess Helen's pregnancy, we—"

"You mean the fact that she bedded another man to get herself pregnant in order to secure the throne for her family and the future of the Monarchy?" I clarify.

"Indeed." Sir Don nods, completely unperturbed by my sarcastic reminder of my sister-in-law's scheming. "Needless to say, an un-born Sovereign is out of the question, even with a Regent to rule in its name until the child comes of age. Therefore, the next in line is Eddie—"

"But he's battling his demons, so the throne comes to me," I finish for him.

"Quite." Sir Don takes his seat, and I laugh, because this is so bloody typical.

"How about the truth?" I suggest. "Let's lessen the burden of everyone lying and tell the world the truth." I catch Mother's wide eyes and worried expression before she corrects it.

"You will be ripped apart, Your Highness," Sir Don says frankly. "The Monarchy will be made a laughing stock. And, once more, you will still be Queen of England. Being the Queen of England is a task in itself, made easier if your people love you. Toss their illusions of your quintessentially perfect English heritage into disrepute, then I'm afraid the job will be tedious at best. And your country will not support your reign. You need their support, ma'am. You need their love."

Stunned into silence by his frankness, I cast my eyes across the room to my mother, who says nothing to refute Sir Don's claims. Neither does anyone else in the room. So that's that, then? I will rule a country built on secrets and deceptions, but my people will love me?

A piece of paper is handed to me by Sir Don, and I look at it blankly. "What is this?"

"That, ma'am, is a statement from His Royal Highness Prince Edward renouncing the throne."

What? My eyes shoot to Eddie. His jaw is tight, his eyes dark and trained on Sir Don.

"It requires your approval, ma'am."

Casting my eyes back to Sir Don, I tilt my head. "I assume these are not the words of Prince Edward."

"Approve it," Eddie hisses, knocking back the rest of his Scotch before slamming the empty tumbler on the desk and grabbing a pen. Snatching the announcement from my hand, he roughly signs it, adding an over-the-top period with a stab. "Your Majesty," he says, handing me the pen.

My heart sinks, and I give him sorry eyes that he can't possibly recognize through his haze of resentment and anger. "Eddie—"

"Sign it, Adeline." He goes back to the drinks globe and refills, knocking another Scotch back.

On a despondent sigh, I mindlessly scribble something close to my signature next to Eddie's.

"Now." Sir Don takes the announcement and clears his throat. "There is one more matter to be taken care of."

The sound of two loud clicks follows his words, and I look across to see a briefcase on my father's desk, David having popped it open. He pulls out a small black case and unzips it. "Is that a needle?" I ask, shooting forward in my chair to get a better look.

"Indeed, ma'am."

I hear Eddie chuckling over by the fireplace. "You're lucky. They shoved that thing in my arm the moment your father popped his clogs."

"Edward," Mother sighs tiredly.

"The results were swift and conclusive," Eddie rambles on, helping himself to another two fingers of Scotch. "I am a bastard." Swinging around, he grins at me. "Don't worry, it doesn't hurt." A quick glug of his drink. "Much."

"Why is this happening?" I ask, looking at Sir Don. "Do you think I might be illegitimate, too?" My eyes divert to my mother, finding her shaking her head. Is that despair, or is she telling me that I am, indeed, who I think I am?

Sir Don goes on. "Forgive me, ma'am, but given the circumstances, we need to be sure the crown is landing on the right head."

I'm astounded, but there's that little tiny part of me that hopes this blood test reveals that I am like Eddie. A bastard. If only to save me from my fate. But then another part of me, the proud part, the disgusted part, wants to prove to these arseholes that I am, in fact, the King's daughter. I could refuse. Tell them to go to hell. But I don't. *Let them have their blood test.* I viscously yank up the sleeve of my jumper, slapping my arm on the desk. "Fine, but David is not putting that needle in my arm."

"Of course." Sir Don heads for the door.

"How hard are you all wishing that I, too, am illegitimate?" I ask his back on a curled lip.

"Not at all, ma'am," he says as he swings the door open, revealing Dr. Goodridge. I'm only mildly relieved I have a professional to draw my blood. Although Dr. Goodridge is an old man and shakes somewhat terribly.

Ma'am. I notice none of them have addressed me in the true and expected way their Queen should be addressed. Your *Majesty.* I'm right. They don't want to accept I am their queen. They don't want to bow to the notoriously rebellious and reckless Princess Adeline Lockhart. Why else would they do this? They think I'll be a terrible Sovereign, and a silly part of me wants to prove them wrong, the jumped-up fools that they are. Utter fools, because if I am not Queen, the next in line is Father's sister, Aunt Victoria, and she would be absolutely unbearable with a crown on her head. God, and her husband Phillip? He'll relish it. Lord it up, throw his weight around.

I have so much more to say, but with Dr. Goodridge present, I realize I can't. The old man makes his way over, the hump on the right side of his back seeming to get worse each time I see him. He slaps the inside of my elbow, looking closely for a vein. "A small scratch, ma'am."

I wince when I feel the sharp prick, closing my eyes and breathing through the process. Within seconds, it's done and a plaster is being applied. Pulling my sleeve down, I sit and watch the vampire who has just sucked my blood put all his equipment away.

"I'll take it straight to the lab." Dr. Goodridge snaps his case shut and leaves, his old legs carrying his old body slowly. He gives Sir Don a small nod before he closes the door behind him. I bet he's been asked to rush this through and deliver the results to Sir Don without delay.

"So now I have to wait to find out my fate?" I ask.

"Your fate is sealed, Adeline." Mother speaks up, not only to me, but to everyone else in the room who may doubt her. "I assure you."

I look straight into her eyes and know she is speaking the truth. And my heart sinks further.

"If you're done with me." Eddie moves to leave, stopping at the door. "Great story, by the way," he says to Sir Don. "I mean, totally brilliant. I believe I will play the depressed, drunken ex-soldier brilliantly." He storms off, and the rest of the room empties, leaving Mother and me alone.

I wait for the door to close before I speak. "I don't want to do it, Mother," I say quietly, desperate for her to hear the devastation in my voice.

"You must, Adeline."

"Why? Why must I?"

"Because there is no one else. You are the only member of my direct family who can rule, and I refuse to let you throw that away. Everything your father worked for. Your grandfather and his father. You will not cast aside their memories by dropping the crown at the feet of that vulture sister of your father's."

I recoil, never having heard so much passion and determination in her voice. "Who cares who gets the throne?" I ask.

She stands and brushes down her skirt. "I do, Adeline. I haven't endured the past forty years to see my children hung, drawn, and quartered by the British public. I did not leave Spain for that. Don't you see? The story, the smoke and mirrors, it's to protect you and Edward." Approaching me, she strokes a soft hand down my cheek, smiling fondly at me. "Wear the crown. Be a queen. That is all you have to do." She leaves, and I am left all alone with nothing but her words stirring the guilt, the hopelessness, and the despair.

And the broken heart, because being Queen isn't *all* I have to do. Abandoning my heart comes first. Abandoning my soul.

3

POSITIVE. I NEVER doubted what the blood test results would be, not when I looked into my mother's eyes, but there was always that little part of me that hoped. For a brief second, when I realized what was transpiring in my father's office, I felt like I had a lifeline. Something that could save me. Something that would take me away from this nightmare. Alas, it wasn't to be. I am, indeed, the King's daughter. The heir to his throne. And now, Queen of England.

I tossed and turned all night, dreaming up elaborate plans to wriggle my way out of the responsibility. But, and it is alien to me, my mother's words have stuck with me, and they have stuck hard. Eddie would be ripped apart. I would be ripped apart. My dead father and brother would be ripped apart, and though she never mentioned herself, my mother would be, too. Crucified. I can't let that happen. My heart simply won't allow it, not for the sake of my selfish need to walk away. My destiny is written. My sacrifices have been made. My punishment determined.

And as if my sacrifice has heard me, my phone rings from the bedside and his name glows at me. In my current frame of mind, lost and hopeless, I shouldn't take his call. Weakness isn't a trait I should reveal to Josh, and I can't guarantee I won't crumple under the sound of his voice, won't beg him to come rescue me from my prison.

Reaching for my phone, I roll to my back and stare at the screen as it continues to ring. And then it stops. Just for a few seconds, just a few moments of relief. And then it sounds again. I silence it and drop it to the pillow, getting myself up and taking myself to the safety of my bathroom. I shut the door. Rest my back against it. Stare at myself in the mirror ahead. I don't look like a queen. I look like a lonely and lost young woman, whose hair needs brushing and whose skin looks grey and sallow. Frankly, I look unacceptable, and in a silly attempt to rectify that, a kind of self-justification plan, I start to get myself ready for my day. Whatever that may hold. What will it hold?

By the time I'm done, my makeup is perfect, if a little heavy to conceal my tiredness, my long dark hair is straightened, and my attire simply signature Adeline. A figure-hugging black pencil dress with skyscraper red stilettos.

"Oh," Jenny says when I pull the door of my private quarters open, looking me up and down with her hands full of styling tools, products, and makeup bags. "Am I late?"

"No, I'm early." I collect my purse, retrieve my phone from the pillow, and leave. "I thought I would get myself ready today."

Jenny scampers behind me, juggling the things in her hands to keep hold of them. "You should have called. I would have come earlier."

"No need," I assure her, taking the stairs to the foyer. Knowing the dinosaurs who sat in my father's office yesterday reading me my rights, they're probably expecting me to be dressed in a two-piece and pearls, *a la Mother,* now I am unofficially the Queen. No way. Over my dead, royal body. It won't be happening now, and it won't be happening when they tell the world I am now their Queen.

Glancing down at my phone as I take the stairs, I purse my lips when I see a text message from Josh. *Don't open it. Don't open it. I forbid you to open it, Adeline.*

But despite my mental mantra, my thumb takes on a mind of its own and clicks the message open. I stop abruptly at the bottom of the stairs when I come face to face with the picture he's sent, and a small, helpless whimper escapes before I can pull it back.

"What is it, Your Highness?" Jenny questions, sounding concerned.

"A dirty cheeseburger," I mumble, my eyes filling with tears. There's even an American flag speared through it. Josh's words stamp all over my mind.

Every girl needs something bad for them now and then.

I swallow and look to the bottom of the picture where he's typed three simple words.

Even the Queen.

This is a message, loud and clear. He's not giving up. He's had his warning, and he's ignoring it. Clearing my screen, I hold my phone against my chest and nibble at my bottom lip for a few thoughtful moments. He needs to stop. He needs to walk away.

"Ma'am?" Damon appears from the kitchen, looking me up and down. "Are we due to be going somewhere?"

I have no plans that I have advised him of. No arrangements have been made for my travel. And in truth, I have nowhere to go. "I don't know," I admit, gazing at him, certain he can see how lost I am.

On a sigh and ushering Jenny away, he collects me and walks me to the car. "Perhaps the stables?"

"Yes, that's a wonderful idea." I could kiss him for his genius plan. Distraction, it's what I need, and what better way to do that than in the fresh countryside air on horseback. Stan and Spearmint will think I've neglected them these past few weeks.

"Although you're hardly dressed for the stables," he says, as he opens the back door for me.

His phone rings and he reaches into his inside pocket for it while I follow his eyes to my body. "Oh my." I laugh a little. "I can barely walk in this dress, least of all ride a horse." I thrust my purse in his chest as he takes the call. "Give me two minutes while I change." I dash off up the stairs, my spirits considerably better than before.

"Your Highness," Damon calls, pulling me to a stop halfway up. "Yes, what is it?"

He holds up his phone, his face grave. "You've been summoned."

My stomach drops. "Whoever by? And whatever for?"

"I believe it is time," he says simply, his chest expanding in a deep breath that could serve both of us, and I hope it does because I've suddenly lost my ability to breathe.

"Time," I murmur. The official statement I reluctantly signed was released yesterday. The country is shocked but sympathetic toward the Fallen Prince. But Eddie still has their hearts, thank God. I take the handrail to steady myself, my eyes darting across the steps. It's time for me to fulfil my duty. It's time for the world to know. Of course, they knew the moment Eddie had renounced his position, but now it will be official. Real. "Then I suppose we should be on our way."

Just put one foot in front of the other.

Keep your back straight.

I look at my red heels, and something sick inside of me smiles. They will be horrified by my attire. Good. Let them be. I walk down the steps, shoulders back, and slip into the car. Damon says only one thing the entire drive. Looking in his rearview mirror, he gives me a crooked smile. "You may just be the most beautiful queen I've ever seen, Your Majesty."

I laugh a little. "Worried I might fire you?"

Damon shrugs, his smile still in place as he refocuses his eyes on the road. "You'd miss me too much, ma'am."

I smile and take one last breath as he pulls up to the gates. He's right. He's in my corner, and that cannot change now.

The Private Chamber is bursting at the seams with people. Old people, all quiet. There must be two hundred bodies, all eyes on me. The Accession Council. I take in the scene, all real now, when it has only ever been something built in my imagination by my mother. It really is as intimidating as it sounded, though Mother spoke of it with a certain edge of fondness. As I stand here now, my mind wanders to an easier time. A time when I was an oblivious little girl.

She entered my room and dismissed my nanny, her usual crisp skirt suit replaced with a nightdress and full-length robe. Lifting me into her arms, she carried me to my bed and tucked me in.

"Tell me a story, Mother," I begged, nestling into my pillow. These moments were rare. I would keep her with me for as long as possible.

"A story?"

"Yes, one with a happy ever after."

She laughed, bringing lines to the corners of her eyes. She'd seemed to get older in recent years, and I knew it even as a six-year-old girl. "Right then, let me see." Placing a fingertip on her chin, she looked into the distance as if deep in thought. "Ah. I have just the tale."

"What's it about?"

"The Accession Council."

I frowned. "What's that?"

"They meet all but once in a lifetime, hundreds of members of the Privy Council and many other important people. You know what the Privy Council is, don't you?"

"Yes, they help Daddy do his job right."

"Indeed. But only when a new Sovereign takes the throne is The Accession Council called, and on this day, they were all there for your father."

"Because Grandfather had died and Father was now King."

"Exactly that, little princess." She clucked my chin on a fond smile. "To welcome him. It was daunting but exciting, a happy occasion, a new era, but clouded by the loss of your grandfather. There he was, a prince,

a young man in his prime, and he was their King. The Nation's King. By the grace of God, he swore he would rule his country with all his heart. With his Queen, his two little princes, and his beautiful princess."

"That's me," I sang, making her laugh. "I am the princess."

"That you are." Settling beside me, she let me snuggle into her side. "He would uphold his duties with pride and conviction, lead by example, and he would love his people," she told me. "He would do his father proud. He would do his family proud. He would do you proud, my sweet little princess. Being King is a job of great importance and privilege, just like the job of being your daddy."

"Will I be King one day, Mother?"

She smiled. "No, my darling. You will never be King." Dipping, she rested her lips on my forehead. "But you may one day be Queen."

I blink a few times, taken aback by the flashback. Did she know this might happen? Or did she fear it? It's only now I appreciate the heart in my mother's words back then, and what she was inadvertently doing. Warning me. She was also trying to show my father in the best light. And it's only now I wonder if my father's strong arm with me all these years have been the actions of a king, or the actions of a father simply wanting the best for his daughter. Or to prepare her. His love seemed to shine less as I grew up, his authority becoming stronger. Something changed him, and I cannot help but wonder if it was my mother's betrayal. Was that why he was so hard on me? So cold? But he didn't treat Eddie with the same contempt. He didn't try to bully my brother.

Because maybe he knew Eddie would never be King.

You are an aberration, Adeline. A disgrace to the Royal Family.

A disgrace. Would he turn in his grave to know I was taking his throne? Would he write me off as a failure? Was this his worst nightmare come true? Probably. The notion makes my shoulders lift with my chin.

I gaze around the room. Everyone is still staring at me, and it takes me a few seconds to realize they're waiting. They're waiting for me to speak. My mind goes blank, and all I can think about is how old everyone standing before me is. Except me. I must be half the age of the youngest member of the Privy Council, a mere baby in their eyes. And here I am in a tight black pencil dress and red heels. Their Queen. I bet they are inwardly shouting their disapproval.

Clearing my throat, I hunt through my mind for the right words. Any that might give the impression that I know what I'm doing, when I have absolutely no idea. What do I say?

"My father was a good man," I begin, calling on the mask I've relied on for years to get me through this moment. It's only the beginning, and all I have is my heart to follow. My desire to prove my father wrong is suddenly so fierce. To show him I *can* do this. To show all of them. "His passing was premature, a shock for us all, and now his duties and responsibilities as Sovereign have fallen to me." I look around the room for any expressions that might tell me how I'm doing. Every face is straight. They're robots. "My father worked tirelessly to further the happiness and well-being of this country. He adored his people, and if I can mirror even a speck of his devotion during my reign, I will have served well. I will have made him proud." *Proved him wrong. Proved you wrong.* "I must thank you in advance for your advice and guidance in the coming years. I will lead with a strong heart and a stable mind. I will depend upon the support and loyalty of you and my people. And I will pray that God steers me right on this new and unexpected road I've found myself upon." I nod, signaling I'm finished, and then hold my breath, trying to replay every word I've spoken. And I can't help but wonder if my father would be proud. Shocked? Would he laugh?

Heads bow. Silence lingers. My eyes drop to the table in the center of the room, where various papers are laid out, an old-fashioned fountain pen set neatly to the side. Ceremonial forms. Sacred oaths to be made. My heart quickens as I'm invited forward, and for the next half hour, my life is a blur of promises made, commitments vowed, and historical papers signed, as I shakily let myself be guided through the rigorous tasks the constitution demands.

As I lay my pen down, my eyes fall to one line amid the hundreds of others.

Queen Adeline the First, by the Grace of God, Queen of this Realm and of all Her Other Realms and Territories . . .

Queen Adeline. Me. I stop breathing for a moment.

"Your Majesty?"

I look up through foggy eyes and find The Garter King of Arms smiling mildly at me. "Yes?"

"I humbly request that your most gracious declaration may be made public."

"The Accession Proclamation," I murmur, and he nods. The paper every person in this room will sign before it is read out to the public on the balcony of Claringdon Palace, following centuries of tradition.

The world will know.

I breathe in deeply and nod before walking out of the room, and as I look at my feet carrying me away, I notice for the first time that my shoes were the only splash of color in a room full of stuffy importance. And I was, in fact, the most important.

"I need to pee," I say to myself, then I laugh out loud, because the Queen should never speak such words. When I fall into the lavatory, I'm not as desperate to pee as I am to look at myself in the mirror. To stare for a second and try to comprehend what has happened. "Your Majesty," I say to myself, over and over, hoping at some point during my chant, it might start to sound right. It might begin to suit me.

An hour later, it still doesn't, and the only thing I seem to have achieved is a bursting bladder. On a long sigh, I use the toilet, wash my hands, and make my way to Damon. The stables. That is my only escape.

When I reach the top of the stairs, I pause in my tracks, looking back to the doors of the Private Chamber. I hear him. The Garter King of Arms talking, crisp and clear, shouting the Accession Proclamation from the balcony to the people below. Relaying my unprepared speech word for word to the world, following age-old tradition. That's it now. No going back.

Sadness washes over me, no matter how hard I try to stop it. I look at my phone when it chimes, though I know who it will be. He'll be watching, like every other single person in the world. His message is a simple "congratulations." Nothing more. My silly eyes sting as I take the stairs, looking up from my phone when I hear scuffling footsteps below. Coming to a stop, I'm utterly thrown by the masses of household staff all lined up neatly, all heads slightly bowed in respect.

All welcoming their new queen.

All except Damon, who is waiting by the door, his face knowing. I pass them all as quickly and as gracefully as I can muster and grab the fresh air with all I have when it meets my lungs. "Goodness me," I breathe, accepting Damon's hand when he offers it. "Thank you."

"Your Majesty," he replies as he helps me into the car. I notice two cars up front and look over my shoulder to see another two behind. And as soon as we make it to the gates, I realize why. Swarms of people and press cover the square outside the palace, all . . .

"Are they cheering?" I ask, listening hard.

"I believe they are, ma'am." Damon's smiling eyes find me in the mirror as he reaches back and hands me his phone.

"What is this?" I look at the screen, my hand meeting my mouth in shock. *Long Live the Queen*, reads one article, an official portrait of me accompanying it. *Finally a Sovereign with a pulse*, reads another. *The most beautiful queen in history*, says one more with various shots of me at various events, always in couture. And, finally, there is a picture of me at my father's funeral just days before, looking to the sky, a drop of water rolling down my cheek. I inhale, knowing such displays of emotion from a royal are unheard of and highly frowned upon. The headline reads, *Empathetic, zealous, and real. She is a queen our country will be proud of.*

I swallow and drop Damon's phone into my lap, looking out of the window as he crawls through the crowds, police cars now having joined the procession. The overwhelming sound of my name being chanted should fill me with pride.

I can't figure out why it doesn't.

≫

DAMON TOOK ME to Kellington where I suffered the same suffocation. All household staff waited in the foyer to greet me for the first time as their Queen. I couldn't bear it. I quickly changed into my riding clothes and escaped.

When we pull up at the stables, I see Sabina talking to Dr. Goodridge. Damon opens my door, and I wander over to them, remembering the last time Sabina and I spoke, how fraught and uncomfortable it was.

"Just take care of yourself, Sabina," Dr. Goodridge says, bowing his head to me as he backs away. "Your Majesty. Congratulations."

"News sure does travel fast," I mumble, returning his little nod.

"Your Majesty." Sabina steps back and curtseys, and I'm quick to pull her up.

"Sabina, really, let us not be silly," I admonish gently, needing her to know how uncomfortable she's making me. "You have known me since I was a baby."

She smiles as I offer my arm for her to link. "You should get used to it, ma'am. Many people will be falling at your feet, and you can't very well scorn them all."

We start toward the north stables together, taking our time. "I can do what I like, surely. I am Queen, after all." I flip her a wry smile that she returns as equally wry.

"You and I both know that not to be true."

"Are you okay, Sabina?" I ask, and she smiles, looking off toward

Dr. Goodridge, where he's getting into his Jaguar. "I'm fine. Just a few pills to help me sleep, is all."

"You need to take care of yourself," I say. She's taken the responsibilities of the stables all on her own since Colin passed. The stress is clearly taking its toll if she needs help sleeping. "I'm warning you," I add on a cheeky smirk.

She stops us and turns to me, taking my hands, her face serious. "And I feel it only right I warn you of something, Your Majesty."

"Oh, Sabina, will you please stop with the formalities."

"It is what's expected, and you should get used to it."

I roll my eyes, and she takes that as her cue to warn me of whatever I may need warning of. A lot, I expect.

"David," she says, giving me a moment to absorb her son's name. I force my face not to screw up in repulsion. Sabina is the sweetest lady, and Haydon, albeit a little deluded, is really rather sweet, too. So what happened to his dad? He's the furthest from sweet one could possibly be. If he thinks he can continue with his ambitious attempts to marry his son off to me, then he can think again. And I will make no bones about telling him so. He was there when I declared my love for Josh to my father. He knows, yet I know beyond doubt that he, just like Sir Don and my mother, will ignore it.

"Sabina," I begin, but my attention is pulled away from the old lady's soft expression when I hear something beyond, something I'm hoping I'm mistaken in thinking is . . ."David," I breathe, dropping Sabina's hands and stepping back. Did he follow me here?

He paces over, what seems like a genuine smile on his face as he removes his flat cap. "Your Majesty," he greets, the customary slight bow of his head executed perfectly. "How lovely to see you again."

I don't know why I do it, since all this formality is currently making me twitchy, serving only as a reminder of what has become of me, but I offer my hand and get a cheap thrill when David Sampson falters before taking it. "Very good to see you, too, David," I say as he holds my hand. I pull it away once I'm suitably satisfied at his level of squirming.

"How are you?" he asks.

"As well as can be expected during such conflicting times. Only a few days ago I buried my father, and today I am Queen of England."

"Indeed. It was a beautiful service, fit for the King he was." A sadness I've never seen in him blankets his face, and I would be lying if I said it didn't catch me off guard. David looks truly grief-stricken. "I will miss my friend terribly."

"As we all will," I reply quietly, unable to gauge his sincerity. And when Sabina reaches for David's arm and rubs gently, I get a horrible, misplaced sense of guilt creeping up on me once more.

"It's so tragic, Adeline," he whispers.

Sabina coughs, and David quickly shoots his eyes to mine. Silly and immature as it may seem, I don't give David the same leniency I did his mother, cocking my head to the side expectantly. I can't ignore how this man played a massive part in making my life miserable, and it isn't something I'll forget anytime soon.

David soon corrects his faux pas. "Ma'am." He smiles, and that seems genuine, too. "We must have supper together."

"Sounds good to me." Haydon's voice comes from behind me, and I turn to see him approaching. Well, isn't this a lovely day out at the stables for the Sampsons? "Adeline," he murmurs, taking my hand before it is offered and kissing the back. I can't bring myself to correct his error, not the touching before being invited to touch, nor the informal addressing of me. "You look sublime."

"Thank you, Haydon." I remove my hand from his with subtle force and nod to the stable block. "I really must be going. Please, excuse me."

"And supper?" David prompts, eager and not afraid to show it.

"That would be lovely." I smile with some effort. "Please let Kim know, and she'll be sure to diarize it." I turn and make my getaway, the weight of power on my shoulders nearly too much. And though I shouldn't be, I feel irritated. Because David is pretending I didn't have a secret affair with an inappropriate man. He's pretending he didn't sit in the King's office in Evernmore and bear witness to my confession. He's pretending it's not my fault the King—his friend—is dead. And I just know it's because his son is now *promised* to the Queen and not a princess. "Smoke and mirrors," I murmur to myself.

Over the next few hours, I saddle-up Spearmint, exercise him, strip him down, and clean his tack. Then I pay some needed attention to Stan, taking him out for a little hack in the open fields. Damon isn't far away while I lose myself in the fresh air, ever closer since Eddie's incident, despite the investigation now being closed. I try to clear my mind of every miserable thing tarnishing it. I try to find hope amid my turmoil. Impossible.

I slow Stan to a walk and sigh, reaching forward and rubbing his neck as he clomps along. "What do you think to this madness, boy?" I frown when his skin wrinkles under my touch. Pinching him, I twist a little and release. His skin tents, taking far too long to return to normal. "Are you thirsty, boy?" I ask, pulling him to a stop. I dismount and pull his reins over his head, taking his mouth and lifting his lip back. "You are; you're thirsty." I press on his gum and release, watching as the white flesh takes an age to return to its usual healthy pink. Looking up, I see Damon has pulled to a stop a few yards away.

"Everything okay, ma'am?" he asks out the window of the Land Rover.

"I think he may be dehydrated," I call back. "There's a stream through these trees. I'm going to walk him down and see if he'll take some water." Damon makes to get out of his car, but I put a hand up, halting him. "I'm still on royal land, Damon," I say tiredly. "There's no need for an escort."

"I believe Prince Edward was on royal land, too," he replies, and I tilt my head in impatience. He's going over the top.

"And a satisfactory outcome to that investigation was made,

was it not?"

"Very well." Damon relents and pulls his cigarettes from his inside pocket. "Do you mind?"

I shake my head in dismay and lead Stan through the trees toward the stream. "Since when have I minded if you smoke in my company, Damon?"

"Well, you're Queen now, ma'am."

"Don't remind me," I mumble, trudging through the overgrowth. "Come on, Stan. I know it's down here somewhere. And whatever is going on at the stables for you to need water so urgently?" It really isn't acceptable, but so very unlike Sabina to let the care of our horses slip. A few branches crack under my riding boots, echoing through the woodland. Of course, there has been a lot going on. I really can't blame her for being distracted.

Hooking my arm under Stan's chin, I hug my face to his. "But we can't have you being neglected, can—" My feet suddenly weld to the ground, and my heart drops into my riding boots. "What the fuck?" I blurt, blinking to make sure I'm seeing correctly.

"For the Queen of England, your mouth sure is vulgar." Josh raises his eyebrows in convincing disapproval, sliding off the back of his horse.

I kick myself and quickly send a mass apology to the heavens, to every past king and queen who has lived. "You startled me." I turn around and march away before I can get caught up in a spar with words or be forced to look at him. To face my loss. To face what I can't have.

Then I remember . . .

I glance at Stan and grit my teeth, turning back toward the stream. Toward Josh. Oh goodness, has there ever lived such a prime example of a man? "This is private property." I go on the defense. It feels like the only good move I could make. "You may only frequent royal land on authority of the King, and since he is now dead, and I am now Queen, I don't believe I have given you authority. Please leave."

"Oh," Josh pouts, his head dipping a fraction. He's not doing it out of shame or respect. Oh, no. In fact, I'm certain he's doing it so he looks like the most adorable thing on earth. He looks perfectly disheveled in old jeans and a lumberjack shirt. "I don't get ex-fuck perks?"

Ex-fuck? I'm stung, and I know my face tells him so. "This is not funny, Josh."

"I agree, Adeline." He's not smirking now, more scowling. "All this is the most *unfunny* thing that's ever fuckin' happened to me."

That's happened to *him?* "Why are you here?" I should kick myself for asking such a stupid question.

"Because I knew once you'd been forced to utter every oath they could throw at you, you would escape and find some peace in this madness. That's why."

"And?" I sniff, looking away. I hate that he knows me so very well. But it's also one of the things I love so much about him. And, worse, I hate that I appreciate it. Appreciating anything in my world is dangerous. It means you're attached. It means you can hurt when they try to take it away from you.

My obstinacy makes something in Josh click, and he kicks the leaves at his feet with a lack of anything else to kick. "*And,* fuckin' look at me," he roars, forcing me to step back warily. "You think I'm going to let you cast aside what we had as if we never had it?"

I remain silent, not asking him what else he expects me to do, maybe because I'm terrified of what that might be. So instead I say something utterly stupid. "Thumbs down," I murmur pitifully, despite Damon being well out of earshot.

"No. Never. You never get to give me a thumbs down, Adeline."

"It's *Your Majesty,*" I shout, staggering back a few feet with the force of my shout. "You will address me with the respect my position demands."

"Your position should be on your back under me," he yells. "And you should be calling me *your fuckin' king*. How does that sound, *Your fuckin' Majesty?*"

"You're a heathen. I want you off my land."

"You're a liar. I want you to stop lying."

"I'm not lying."

"Yes, you are. You're lying to me. You're lying to yourself. You're lying to every single person in this fuckin' world." Josh stomps forward, and I blindly stumble back, catching my foot on a stray branch. I lose my footing and fall to my arse in a pile of dry leaves. I don't yelp because it doesn't hurt—I'm numb to everything except Josh—but I do curse to high heaven, further cementing Josh's claim that I have a vulgar mouth. "God damn it." With my palms splattered on the muddy ground behind me, my knees bent, I look up at the man looming over me. "This is all your fault."

"I take full responsibility. For everything."

Everything? "Like what?"

"Your fall. My feelings." He offers his hand, but I ignore it, getting myself to my feet and brushing myself down of dry leaves. "For *your* feelings," he finishes softly.

My hands falter midway down my jodhpurs. "I do not have any feelings," I grate, ignoring the unrelenting . . . feelings. The warmth, the disappearance of my woes, the heady sensations of want manifesting within me. Me. Him. The potent cocktail of chemistry we create, just being in each other's presence. The woodland surrounding us is drenched in it. The atmosphere is thick.

I glance up when a few moments have passed, silent moments, and meet his eyes. The amber swirl of desire sparkles madly. My heart kicks. He licks his lips, and I follow the path of his tongue from one corner of his mouth to the other. "Stop," I whisper, to who I don't know. Him? Me?

My hands come up to my head, my fingertips pushing into my temples, as if I'm trying to force every reason why this can't happen to the front of my mind. I look for my father's words, but I find other words instead.

You will be ripped apart. Eddie will be ripped apart. Your father's and brother's memory with be tarnished.

But . . . I fell so madly in love with a man, and now I am being forced to disregard that. Can I? *Should* I?

I swivel on my boots and run. I can't trust my head to talk reason, can't promise I'll even listen to my reason if I find it, so I'm depending on my legs to take me away as quickly as they can.

"No thumbs down," he growls, snatching my wrist and yanking me to a stop, spinning me to face him. My face is grabbed with one brutal hand, and his mouth is quickly on mine. He's gone low, way below the belt, and worse still, we both know it will work. My universe seems to align, positive and negative working together, our lips glued by an invisible, highly powerful force. Then I feel his tongue sweep through my mouth and explosions of the most calming kind erupt in my soul. My keen hands find his hair and force him closer, our kiss crazed and messy, but so utterly calming and immaculate. I let him guide my backward steps, I let him spin me away from him, and I let him thrust me up against a tree trunk.

The scratchiness of the bark on my forehead doesn't faze me. I'm too blindsided by the reminder of what we share. Lips pushed into my arse, his wet mouth by my cheek, Josh holds me tightly. Possessively. Like he owns me. And I don't care. He's the only thing in this world I don't mind controlling me. "Maybe now I want to violate a queen." He reaches to my hips and slowly draws my jodhpurs over my backside. His lazy approach could be mistaken for giving me time to deny him. It's not. He's merely prolonging my agony. I want him so badly, and he knows it. His hand on my arse. His mouth all over me.

Bringing my arms up to the tree, I rest my head on them to lessen the risk of grazing my head when he strikes me.

Thwack!

As is always the way when Josh tans my backside, I don't cry out in pain, but rather moan my way through it, being carried to another world. A world where I am not *me*, but just his. And then his fingers are between my thighs and he's massaging me gently, my flesh wet and ready for him. "Some things don't change," he whispers, biting at my cheek, circling his fingers, plunging them deeply, scissoring my swollen clitoris. "Thank God. Tell me you've missed me, Adeline."

"I've missed you," I say on demand, my pleasure making it more of a labored whisper than a sure proclamation, as my pulse races and my desire for him multiplies unstoppably. I start to roll my head, my knees becoming weak. And when I reach the pinnacle of pleasure, I feel like every shitty thing in this world pours from my body with my climax, my whole being relaxed for the first time in weeks. I've needed this so much. Needed *him*.

Josh lets me take a few seconds to regulate my loud breathing, pulling my trousers back into place and turning me around. Brushing my mane from my sweaty face, he cups my cheeks with his palms and rests his forehead on mine, staring so deeply into my eyes. I can't mistake the twinkle in his for anything less than adoration.

"I'm in love with the Queen of England, Your Majesty. You need to help me find a way to be with her."

His words could make me cry, and for a second my wobbly lip gets the better of me. I mustn't cry. I mustn't. "It's impossible."

"Who says?"

"Everyone."

"Well, I don't. Nothing has changed for me."

"But everything has changed for me," I say. "We're a train wreck waiting to happen."

"My train has already crashed, and it's in fucking tatters since I left you at the palace. Nothing can feel any worse than that, Adeline."

"Trust me, Josh." I take his hands from my face. "It really can."

He looks to the sky, his Adam's apple rolling with each hard swallow he takes. He's trying to calm himself down, trying desperately to see reason like me. It pains me to see him like this, as much as it pains me to feel as I do. "You didn't even break up with me," he whispers. "You watched them escort me away, and all I could do was watch it all play out on TV. You didn't answer my calls, my messages." Dropping his eyes to mine, he circles my neck with his palms and holds me firmly in place. "I wanted to be there for you. I was waiting for the bomb to drop, the news of your succession, and now it finally has. I can see it in your eyes, Adeline. No one else can, but I see it. You don't really want this. Guilt and responsibility shouldn't dictate your heart."

"And what would you have me do? Throw my mother to the wolves? My brothers, my father, my entire family history? Just to feed my own selfish need?"

"No, to feed mine," Josh replies shortly, and I flinch at his frankness. "I'm sorry," he sighs. "I didn't mean that. Just . . ." He growls under his breath. "Just don't be hasty. Don't write us off yet."

I smile, finding his determination admirable, if a tiny bit frustrating. "You've already had your warning, Josh. Your hotel was trashed, and that was when I was a mere princess. They'll ruin you."

"They can shove their warnings up their asses." Releasing me, he stands back, scuffing the mud with his boots. "There must be a loophole somewhere. A chink in the armor of the stupid laws you royal people have to abide by. I'll find it."

There is no loophole, and if there was, it would be sewn shut pretty speedily. "It's impossible."

"No. I won't let you believe that."

I don't counter this time, because I know he won't listen. Part of me is wishing he's right, that there is a loophole, though I know there are none. We can't be together. "Josh . . ."

Looking past me, he frowns. "What's wrong with Stan?"

Oh goodness. I shoot over to my horse who looks somewhat lethargic. "I think he's dehydrated. I brought him through here to get him a drink."

"Let me see." Josh takes his head and looks Stan over. "His eyes are dry." Taking his reins, he clicks him down to the stream, and I thank heavens when my beloved horse slurps some water. "He's real thirsty. You should get him looked over."

"I will," I promise, stroking down his neck, waiting patiently for him to finish up. God, he might drink the stream dry. "I should go before Damon starts to worry."

The solemnness of Josh's face matches my own downhearted-ness as I pull Stan back toward the bridle path. "Adeline?" he calls, and I look over my shoulder. He doesn't say anything, and instead approaches me, giving me a soft kiss on the lips. "This won't be the last kiss I give you," he vows, and I inhale a little dreamily, ignoring the voice in my head that's disagreeing with him. Because I desperately wish it isn't our last kiss. "I'm leaving for South Africa tomorrow for a week. I'll be back in London as soon as I can. I'll call you, and you *will* answer."

I nod, if mildly. "Goodbye."

"For now," he adds, stroking down the bridge of my nose before stepping back and letting me walk away. "I love you, Adeline."

I swallow down the wretchedness those words evoke. Words like that shouldn't make a woman feel so utterly hopeless. They should fill her with life. But I'm no ordinary woman.

Each step I take is forcefully measured to ensure my stability, and I touch my nose to feel the heat still lingering from his touch. Oh, how I wish I didn't have to leave. That it wouldn't involve headline news, MI5, and the government if Josh took me away to a faraway land and hid me there forever.

When I breach the trees, I force myself to locate my ever-depleting mask and have it firmly in place for when I meet Damon. "I heard you shouting," he says dryly as I slip my foot into one of Stan's stirrups and pull myself up.

Once I'm settled in the saddle, I look across to him. "And you didn't come to find out why?"

Flicking away his cigarette, likely the second or third he's had since I left him, he falls into the seat of the Land Rover. "It sounded like you were handling things just fine on your own, Your Majesty."

"I was. It was just—"

"Or was the American handling *you* just fine?" His smirk is slap worthy, and my mouth falls open, my shock profound.

"I have no idea what you are talking about, Damon."

"I've heard that before."

"Drive on," I order petulantly, only making his smile widen. "This minute."

"Yes, ma'am." He starts the engine and honks the horn, pointing across the field. I'm totally mortified when I see Josh cantering away in the distance.

My lips twist, my eyes closing. "I've only been Queen for a few hours, and I've already demonstrated how utterly weak I am. I'm a terrible Monarch."

"Love doesn't change because the world does, ma'am," Damon says gently.

His statement, so profound and true, brings more wretched tears to my ever-crying eyes.

4

IT HAS TRULY been the longest week of my life, my bewildered self so completely lost amid the formalities, procedures, and being shown the ropes, if you will. I've not made it to the stables either, much to my displeasure, so I've had daily calls with Sabina who has kept me abreast of Stan's condition. He's doing better, drinking plenty, and is on steroids prescribed by the royal vet for a virus of some kind.

I'm wandering absentminded through the Picture Gallery with Sir Don, words coming at me left, right, and center. When we enter my father's office, I note two things. Firstly, the cigar stench is completely gone now. The room seems so . . . empty. As if the scent I always hated is the last thing connecting me to my father. And I truly miss it. And secondly, the huge portrait of my father that hung above the fireplace is gone. And in its place . . .

"What in heaven's name is that?" I ask, stuck on the threshold, gawking at the monstrosity that has replaced my father's portrait.

Sir Don looks in the direction of my horrified stare and straightens. "That, ma'am, is the new Queen of England," he says dryly.

I look at him like I hate him, because I think I actually do. Not only because I sense sarcasm in his tone, but because I feel like his sole purpose is to make my life miserable. Pointing at the . . . *thing* that has replaced my father's portrait, I get my ticking jaw under control. "That is not the new Queen of England," I hiss. "*That* is bloody hideous." I take another peek at the oil on canvas and cringe. I look at least thirty years older than my current thirty years, and my attire is plain awful—a civilized two-piece skirt and jacket I was forced to wear in my early twenties when meeting the Emperor of India. I can only conclude I was feeling uncharacteristically compliant that day. Of all the pictures there are of me over the years, they chose that one? "Get rid of it," I order, ready to pull it down from the wall myself. "Immediately."

"Ma'am, it is tradition for a portrait of the current Monarch to hang in that very spot."

"I am not your traditional Monarch," I spit, marching over to the wall and reaching up to the portrait, squinting to blur the hideousness. "I want my father's portrait back in its place right this minute." I struggle and curse as I try to remove the huge frame from the wall. Did they nail it here? I give up and turn to Sir Don. "I want it gone. And in future, you will consult me on all things." Goodness me, I just know they scoured the archives of pictures for one suitable to hang as tradition states, and I know they were probably losing all hope as they assessed the many *colorful* pictures of me. Until they found this monstrosity and had it depicted in oil. And rather speedily, too. It still smells freshly painted. I will never be that woman in the painting.

"As you wish, ma'am," Sir Don says flatly, clicking his fingers in indication for a footman to see to it. "I will arrange for the royal artist to sit with you and discuss something to Your Majesty's liking."

"Very good." I avoid the wall above the fireplace and make my way to my father's desk, already planning what I will wear for that portrait sitting. It won't be a dowdy skirt suit. "What is all this?" I ask, lowering to the chair, taking in the masses of envelopes on the desk, all held together neatly with string.

"That, ma'am, is correspondence from across the globe, all checked and approved."

"Were there any unapproved?" I motion to the chair for Sir Don to take, which he does, but only because I invited him.

"Much."

I raise an interested eyebrow. "Such as?"

"I don't believe Your Majesty really wants to be furnished with such information."

I actually do, but I realize my need won't be fed. "So what do we have?" I ask, pulling the string to release the pile.

"Invitations from many countries. I suggest we choose wisely."

I nod mildly as I scan the papers. An invitation from the Australian Prime Minister, the Chinese Emperor, the Premier of the British Virgin Islands. "Oh, The White House?" I muse, scanning the invitation to a state dinner in my honor.

"Yes, ma'am. That is one I suggest we accept graciously."

"And the others?"

"You are Head of the Commonwealth, ma'am. Our relationships with many of these leaders is stable and sure. America, however, we should always work diligently to maintain our friendship. They are important allies."

I push the pile of invitations across the desk toward Sir Don. "Then I guess you should separate them into piles of yeses, noes, and maybes." I smile sweetly.

"Very well." He goes to his diary. "The Earl Marshall has requested an audience to discuss your coronation."

I inhale, my heart starting to thump so much I'm sure Sir Don must see it punching out of my chest. "Already?"

"It will be one of the biggest, most anticipated events in recent history, ma'am. We cannot begin to prepare soon enough. Of course, we must leave a satisfactory length of time for the world to mourn the passing of the late King."

"How long is a satisfactory length of time?" I ask. No length of time will be enough for my family to get over this. "It's not even been three weeks." And it already feels like he's being forgotten.

"A month, maybe two."

"How generous."

"The show must go on, ma'am."

I sit back and fall into thought, my mind being blitzed with images of broken bits of a helicopter. "Can I ask you a question, Sir Don?"

He looks up from his diary and rests his pen on the page. "Of course, ma'am."

"Why was John on the helicopter with my father? It goes against everything the King stood for. You and I both know he was a stickler for tradition."

On a sigh, Sir Don begins to nod mildly. "David and I were helping Dr. Goodridge up after a rather nasty fall when we heard the helicopter blades. We were too late to stop him. We didn't know John was on board until he sent me a message fifteen minutes into their flight. He told me the King wouldn't wait for the pilot. He was about to take flight alone." Shaking his head, he breathes out heavily.

I knew it. I knew John was trying to stop him. My throat fills with remorse, making my swallow lumpy. My father acted recklessly and hastily, something he wasn't known for. But why? I will always know I am responsible for his and John's deaths, but why did he not use his many resources to find me? To deal with me. Did I finally send him over the edge of reason? Yes. Yes, I did. And I killed my brother at the same time. I can't help but think that John must hate me more in his death than he did when he was alive.

Sir Don clears his throat, pulling me back into the room. "I believe a royal statement is being drafted to reflect the conclusions of the investigation. The public want to know what happened."

I panic a little. Will the statement state *why* the King was in such a hurry? Of course it won't. "And what will this statement say?" I ask tentatively.

"I believe the King stepped away from protocol in a haze of worry when he received word that the Queen had collapsed. A result of stress after the countryside incident involving Prince Edward, I expect."

I can only stare in stunned silence. More smoke. More mirrors. Lies to protect us.

"I will have the statement ready for your approval later, ma'am," Sir Don says.

I feel shame eat me from the inside out. "I don't believe the statement will require my approval, Sir Don," I murmur.

A sharp nod, and he's back to his diary, as if he is unaware of who was actually responsible for my father's death. As if it's normal to hide such scandals. Of course, to Sir Don, it is perfectly normal to hide *such* scandals. "Now, about staff arrangements."

Staff arrangements? I don't like where this conversation is heading. "What about—" I'm cut off when my phone starts ringing, and I quickly snatch it up from the desk when I see who is calling me, hoping Sir Don didn't catch his name before I managed to hide the screen. Goodness, if Sir Don gets even a sniff of suspicion that I have seen Josh, God only knows what will be done to keep him away. I reject the call and return my attention to Sir Don, fighting to maintain my composure. I'm not sure whether his face is interested, or whether I'm being paranoid. "What about staff arrangements?"

With his eyes on my hand that is clutching my phone, he continues. "Obviously you will inherit the late King's—" This time, it's Sir Don who is cut off by my ringing phone, and my grip around it increases, hoping I'll squeeze it silent. "Does Your Majesty need to take that call?" he asks, a certain amount of inquisitiveness in his tone.

"One is in a meeting." I stab the reject button once more,

wondering why of all the times he could call me today, he chooses now. When I'm with Sir Don. I knew he would be flying back into London today; he texted me to tell me. In fact, he's texted me every single day. Each time I have told myself not to reply, to not engage with him. And failed. The opportunity to lose myself in the escape he gives me, even by exchanging messages, was too much to resist. Ignoring my feelings is harder. "Continue." I do the safest thing and turn my phone off, resting it on the desk.

"Indeed." Gathering himself and clearing his face of all questions, Sir Don scans the page of his diary again, reminding himself of where we were. "Your staff will be redistributed across other royal households, though some will remain at Kellington. We will confirm once it is established whether His Highness Prince Edward will remain in residence at Kellington." He turns his page and rambles on, while I just stare at him across the desk. "The royal suite is currently receiving a deep clean and repaint, ready for Your Majesty to take up residence here at Claringdon. A staff meeting has been called so you can—"

"I will not be residing at Claringdon." I interrupt Sir Don with no apology, and he looks up, definitely stunned. "I will also retain my staff, and Mother will remain in the royal suite indefinitely. As for Edward, he *will* remain at Kellington, and he will continue to share our staff with me."

Sir Don sits forward, looking gravely concerned. "Ma'am, Claringdon Palace is the home of the British Monarch."

"*Was* the home of the British Monarch. Now, Kellington Palace is." If he dares to argue with me . . .

"Your staff—"

"Is my staff and will remain my staff."

"Ma'am, forgive me, but the royal household staff here at Claringdon are trained and experienced in serving the Sovereign."

"They will continue to serve my mother since she will be living here."

"Kellington isn't equipped to accommodate the extra staff you require as Queen, Your Majesty. Some members of the royal household you must retain without question. If you choose to redistribute any of them, then we will have to contend with a severe drop in morale. They will believe they've been demoted."

"No one can serve me better than my current staff. They know me. They are more qualified for that reason alone, and if they don't meet your expectations, then we teach them how to." Goodness me, if I'm going to have this power, I will at least retain some of the things that keep me sane. My staff keeps me sane. They'll replace Jenny with someone who'll have me looking like a middle-aged has-been before I can blink. I won't hear of it. And Damon? Never. He's staying. They are all staying. "Damon will become head of security to the Queen. Jenny will be my chief stylist and lady-in-waiting, along with Olive. Kim will continue to serve as my private secretary."

"With all due respect, ma'am, your private secretary is far from equipped to tackle such a role. Please, I must insist."

"Davenport was my father's private secretary, but I can't have him as he's no longer in royal employment," I point out. *Because you sent him packing with threats and a stern reminder of his blood oath.*

Sir Don, obviously struggling with my defiance, taps his pen on his diary. "I don't believe Major Davenport was utilized to his fullest."

I have no doubt. Davenport always seemed to be with my father, but given what I know now, I suspect that was merely a ploy on my father's part to keep his enemy close. Everyone knows Sir Don was the man who took on the role of advisor when my father called for it, despite Davenport being more than qualified. After all, he served my grandfather before he *served* my father.

"I believe Major Davenport was not given the opportunity to express his full potential." I cock my head in silent acknowledgement of what we all know but will not speak of. I never had much time for the old stickler major, but through everything, his commitment to my father never wavered. Despite everything, his own personal torture, he was always there, following barked orders. He was underutilised. Wasted. I never thought I would feel sorry for the man who I now know to be at the center of one of the biggest royal scandals in history. But I do. I feel awfully sorry for him. He was a glorified servant, and now I suspect another reason my father didn't strip him of his position was because he didn't want to rouse questions. The King and the major were the best of friends. Everyone knew it. My father was a proud man. He wouldn't want anyone to know of the sordid affair between my mother and Davenport, but at least one person had to know. Someone had to hide the letters between the lovers. And that someone was Sir Don. "We all know the Major was more than qualified to advise the King on all matters." In a sudden flash of rebelliousness, I blurt something rather obscene but unstoppable. "Major Davenport will be reinstated, and he will serve me as my private secretary alongside Kim. I think they will work very well together, and in my very best interest."

Sir Don looks like his head could pop off. "Excuse me?"

"I do believe your hearing is perfectly fine, Sir Don."

He looks utterly stunned. "And me?"

"You will retain your position as Lord Chamberlain, and you will execute the duties required of that role." I stand. Meeting over.

"As you wish, Your Majesty." Sir Don rises from his chair and nods graciously, when I know he is feeling anything but.

"Thank you, Sir Don." I round the desk and make my way to the door, catching sight of the new portrait of the strange woman as I go. "And please do get rid of that thing."

I close the door behind me and fall against the frame, utterly exhausted after holding my own. But, at the same time, mighty proud of myself. "Take that, you miserable old bastard," I say to myself, crossing the landing to the stairs as I switch my phone back on. Endless missed calls flood my screen, and before I can even think about whether or not I'm going to return them, it rings again. A quick scope of my surroundings reveals I'm alone, so I scoot to the huge window and answer. I'm not going to feel too bad about my lack of restraint. I need a pick-me-up after this frightful week, and Josh always picks me up. "Hello," I breathe, only just stopping myself from supporting my weight by resting my head on the glass.

"When I call, answer your damn phone." He's irritated, making his southern drawl more enhanced, and, right or wrong, I smile, because the past week is forgotten with the sound of his words. Any words, as long as they are his.

"I'm really rather a busy woman, don't you know?"

"Oh, I know, but I would prefer you to be busy with me."

I smile to myself. "Why, Josh, you are more demanding than my kingdom."

"See me." It's not a request, and it soon takes my light mood to heavy and sad. His want is simple, yet the logistics surrounding it so very complicated.

"How?"

"I don't know. You are Queen of fuckin' England, for fuck's sake. Make it happen."

"Josh, I—"

"Do you want to see me?"

That's a ridiculous question. "Of course, but . . ." But what? I inwardly laugh at my own silent question. But *everything*. "You've been warned to stay away."

"I told you what they can do with their warnings. Who the hell is warning me, anyway?"

I ponder that for a second, looking over my shoulder when I hear a door open. Sir Don exits my father's office and heads in the other direction, missing me by the window. "The institution," I answer. "The dinosaurs who have supported the Monarchy for decades. Those who live and breathe for the royals. And probably a few politicians, too."

"You need to get your people under control," Josh retorts, and I roll my eyes.

"Don't you get it yet?" I ask, calling on my mother's words that one time when she was trying to appease me over my father's demands. "My title symbolizes status, not power."

"It's bullshit."

I turn when I hear approaching footsteps, finding Damon across the landing. His thumb waves between up and down. I give him a thumbs up on a small smile before indicating with a finger that I'll be with him in one minute. "I need to go."

"I'm at Hotel Café Royal. The Royal Suite." He hangs up, and I gawk down the line. The Royal Suite? My gawk turns into a suspicious pout, tapping the corner of my mobile on my chin. The scoundrel. I can't possibly rock up to the Regent Street hotel and swagger across the pavement and through the doors. What is the fool thinking? I dial him back, taking air, ready to tell him just that, but he gets in first.

"The Royal Suite," he reiterates. Then he hangs up again.

"Well," I huff, completely slighted by his rudeness. But then I'm smiling, because isn't that what I loved about him in the first instance? His complete disregard for who I am. Or was. Because, of course, I am someone different now, someone even less attainable.

And he still doesn't give a flying hoot.

My smile widens, and then it drops like a stone when I remember how impossible it would be to see him.

"Ma'am?" Damon says, appearing at my side. "Should I ask?"

"Definitely not," I sigh, turning my phone in my hand. "Please, take me back to Kellington. I've had a bellyful of this place."

We head for the stairs together, getting stopped by Sir Don as we take the first steps. "Ma'am."

"What is it, Sir Don?"

"I have just got off the telephone with Major Davenport. I'm afraid he has declined your offer."

I'm surprised, but at the same time not surprised. And I bet Sir Don didn't offer the job with grace and encouragement. "Very well,"

I say dismissively, taking the stairs down to the foyer.

Damon is soon close on my heels. "May I ask what job?"

"You may," I say on a sideways smile.

"What job?"

"Private secretary to the Queen."

Damon isn't one for showing facial reactions, but he can't hide this one. "Can I ask why?"

"You may," I reply on another tilt of my lips.

"Why?"

"Because though it pains me to admit Sir Don is right, Kim isn't qualified. Davenport never really fulfilled his duties with my father, and you and I know why that was."

Damon lightly snorts his agreement and opens the door once we make it through the foyer. "We do." He looks back up the stairs. "I've had a polite reminder to keep my mouth shut."

"You, too?" I ask, once again wondering why the hell I'm surprised. Everyone who knows anything of such scandal around here receives polite warnings. "From whom?" I follow his eyes and find them watching Sir Don coming down the stairs. "He just tried to redistribute all my staff," I whisper.

"Doesn't surprise me. I knew I was on death row. How long have I got you for?"

"You didn't hear me. I said *tried*." I walk to the car. "I told him where to stick it."

Damon laughs and helps me into the car. "So I'm stuck with you?"

"Afraid so," I reply on an impish grin. "Damon, I would like to go somewhere. Will you take me?"

His tilted head screams nervous as he holds the car door. "Where would you like to go, ma'am?"

I don't answer, but instead call someone who can give me the address of where I need to be. Felix sounds rather shocked to hear from me. "Your Majesty?"

"Yes." Damon shuts the door. "Please send me Major Davenport's address without delay."

"Certainly, ma'am."

I smile and hang up as Damon gets comfortable at the wheel. That was a lot easier than I thought it would be. The moment the address lands, I pass my phone to Damon so he can see the screen. And he rolls his eyes, starting the car and pulling away. "Please explain your logic," he says, holding a hand up to the gateman before checking the cars up front and tailing are in place. "You really want Major Davenport as your private secretary?"

I sit back, looking out of the window. "Something tells me he is the best man to serve me." I can't explain it, really. I have the pick of the bunch, could choose anyone to be my right-hand man, but something is telling me to choose him. I just have to convince him, and though it's probably immoral, I feel like a plea from the heart will work. The Major has never felt needed, and if I have to use my mother as a weapon, I will.

He loves her. And I know she loves him.

And two people who love each other should be together. Even if it is in secret to prevent the risk of public skinning.

My eyes drop to my lap and dart. It's like a lightbulb moment for me. Everything clear.

Secrets. Lies. The Royals have always been protected by smoke and mirrors.

Why change the habit of a lifetime? I can still protect my mother, and she can still have Davenport. Because he'll be working for me.

Maybe I'll be a good queen after all.

5

THE WHITE STACCATO-FRONT building is beautiful and cute, but a little unassuming. All these years I've known Major Davenport, I never once imagined where he lived. Now I'm looking at his home, I would never have painted this in my mind. It's quaint, pretty. Nothing like Davenport. I look down the narrow, cobbled backstreet where I'm standing, a street that is now blocked with cars. All mine. Damon is twitching beside me, his eyes taking in every inch of the area, low and high. I realize it's making him uncomfortable while I stand here taking my time to absorb what's before me, and maybe build a little courage, too.

"Right, then." I walk up the brick pathway of the tiny front garden and take hold of the shiny gold doorknocker, tapping it firmly once before standing back and straightening my shoulders. Long seconds pass, and I peek at the window to my right. The net curtains prevent me from seeing inside. "I don't think he's home," I say, looking up to the first floor.

"Then we should go before you attract any attention."

"Relax, Damon," I sigh, looking up and down the street. "It's deserted." I hear something from beyond the door, a few mutters of a grumpy, stern voice I recognize.

"Stay," Davenport orders, pulling the door open, his body bent to hold the collar of a dog. I recoil, surprised, as does Major Davenport. "Your Majesty?" His years of service has him mirroring Damon, scanning the street.

I smile, a little nervous. "Good afternoon, Major." The dog wrestles and wriggles in Davenport's hold, and eventually breaks free. It runs right at me. "Oh my goodness." I take a backward step, feeling Damon's hand land in the small of my back just in time for the dog to launch at me. Its big paws land on my thighs, its tail wagging so fast it's a blur.

"Cathy!" Davenport stomps down the path and seizes the dog, pulling it back toward the house. "You are an embarrassment."

I stand in shock, but not because I've just been ambushed by a dog. "Cathy?" I question, and Davenport pauses at the door. He named his dog after my mother?

He stands tall and turns toward me, giving my protection team the once-over. "You had better come in before the whole of London finds out you are here and I have streams of reporters on my doorstep." He opens up the way. "My home won't accommodate everyone."

Probably just as well, since no one can hear what I want to say. Glancing at Damon, I give him a small nod before making my way into Davenport's tiny little house. "Thank you."

"The lounge is to your right." He shuts the door and follows me through to the charming room, where two old leather rollback couches virtually take up the entire space. "Would you like tea?"

"That would be lovely." I perch on the edge of one of the cushions and put my hands in my lap while Davenport leaves the room. I soon hear the sounds of cups chinking and cupboards opening and closing, and only a few minutes later, he's back with a tray. As I watch him serve, I ponder what to say, how to kick off our conversation, all the while marveling at how he looks so less intimidating when he's not dressed from head to toe in his crisp suit. His trousers are still rather formal, but his jumper not so much. "Thank you." I smile when he hands me a cup and saucer. "How are you, Major?" That seems like the obvious start.

"Very well, ma'am." That's it. That's all he says, and that is plain habit rather than truth. He looks old today. Tired. His hair is still perfect, as is his moustache, but . . .

I search my mind for another conversation leader, anything to prevent the awkward silence I know is coming. "I didn't know you had a dog." I look across to the fluffy thing that's now past the excitement of a visitor and curled up in her basket by the fire. The Major worked ungodly hours, surely not ideal when you have a dog. "Who took care of her while you were at work?"

"I only recently acquired her," he says as he stirs his tea. "A little companionship during retirement can't hurt."

My lips purse, my fingertips squeezing the china handle of my cup. Only recently, and he named her Cathy. "I'm sure." I take a small sip, and the awkward silence I was trying to avoid descends.

Until Davenport breaks it. "Forgive me, ma'am, but why are you here?"

I sigh and slip my saucer onto the wooden table before me. "You declined my offer to reinstate you."

"Correct," he replies flatly, making me pull back.

"But why?"

"I am an old man. There comes a time when one must admit defeat."

My heart breaks, because something is telling me he is not talking about being too old to work, but more being too old to fight for my mother. "You were forced out. You did not admit defeat, you simply had no choice *but* to."

Major Davenport gives me high eyebrows over his cup. "And why is this any concern of yours?"

Oh, no he doesn't. "Major, you can cut the curtness," I retort firmly. "I know it's all a front. Besides, I don't think I need remind you of who you are being curt to." I collect my saucer, if only for something to do with my hands other than twiddle my fingers nervously in my lap. His surprise can't be hidden, and neither can his ironic smile. "I offered you a job. I would like you to accept it."

Sitting back in his chair and crossing one leg over the other, Davenport suddenly looks like the stern, high-handed major I always perceived him to be. I never dreamed I would be pleased to see the sight. "Your Majesty," he breathes, resting his palms on the arms of his high-backed chair. "With all due respect, you cannot force me into employment."

I stare at him defiantly, my back teeth aching from the force of my bite. "Then what the hell *can* I do as Queen, because so far I'm not seeing any benefits, only disadvantages?"

His smile widens, and it's truly a sight to behold in my turmoil. "I see weakness," he says. "Never show weakness or vulnerability, ma'am. They will skin you alive. That is your first lesson. Lead with assertion and heart, but do not mistake your title as anything more than the highest of privileges. You cannot have an opinion. An opinion opens you up to criticism, and you mustn't be criticized. When you smile or frown on public engagements, it is being analyzed. Did she like it? Did she hate it? Is that an opinion she is expressing? No matter if you disagree with your cabinet, you cannot stop them from doing what they are going to do. You can only warn and advise. You cannot *tell*. The best rulers listen. They keep their political opinion to themselves. They observe. The Royal Family is an institution, ma'am. One that is loved and envied across the globe. Your job, first and foremost, is to uphold the status of the Monarchy. To be a national treasure. It has been many years since the Sovereign wielded any true power." His eyes never once leave mine, and I'm pretty sure he's relishing in my stunned silence. "That was lesson two to"—his hand waves through the air—"however many. Your father struggled with the concept of a constitutional monarchy. He also struggled to make his country love him. The conflict between his duty as a father and a husband, and of being King, truly played havoc with his mind. He didn't know how to be all three."

I remain quiet, hoping for more, but by the look on Davenport's face, he thinks he's already said too much. "And so my mother fell into your arms," I say quietly.

"He wasn't King when your mother and I fell in love. He was a prince, being groomed to rule. He was barely nineteen when he married your mother, and your mother was barely eighteen. Just kids. John came that very year, the boy your father so hoped for. It cemented his future. Your mother felt like she had served her purpose. Your father gallivanted off around the world on royal tours, and stories of his shenanigans reached England. I was your grandfather's private secretary before I was your father's, as you know, and watching the beautiful Spanish princess crawl further into her shell each day was truly a saddening sight." Davenport looks out of the window, thoughtful. "I found her in the library one evening. Researching British history and polishing her language skills. She really wanted to be the best she could be for your father." Finding my eyes again, he clears his throat. "I'll let you conclude the result of that meeting."

"Love?" I ask, relaxed for the first time since I arrived. I never expected any of this, truly I didn't, but it is very much welcomed, even if he is delivering his heartfelt story in a somewhat detached tone.

Davenport sighs and glances away, as if not quite believing he's saying these things, least of all to me, but not being able to stop either. "She felt wanted, and, trust me, she was all I truly desired."

So he knows how it feels to want something so badly and not be able to have it. I don't know why I take comfort from that.

"Your father returned from duty in 1983. I ended my affair with Catherine. The consequences would have been drastic if our secret was discovered. Your mother would have been an outcast. Suffice to say, she hated me for it, and in a moment of weakness on my part,

I gave in to her pleas for comfort. And we were caught. The letters she sent to me were found. Edward was born in 1985, and your father knew the new baby was not his blood. But, you see, he did not want to rock the boat. He would never risk his position as heir. He needed a wife, children, a stable family unit. Your grandfather was a stickler for tradition. So he kept quiet, and he kept me close. You, Your Majesty, were the icing on the cake of his vengeance."

I balk at him, astounded. "Are you saying I was a pawn to taunt you with?" *That he never actually wanted me?*

"The moment your grandfather passed away and your father became King, he didn't fire me, and he wouldn't allow me to resign. I would receive no pension. It would be made certain I would not receive employment elsewhere. Your father was a ruthless, cruel man, Adeline."

"You mustn't speak ill of the dead," I snap, more out of duty than anything else. I'm shocked, so very shocked by all of this.

"My apologies." Davenport lowers his head, definitely in shame. I feel wronged, and any good things I have been trying to think of my father are suddenly washed away by dirt. I was nothing more than a tool for my father to wield. A *fuck you* to Davenport and a symbol to the rest of the world. A demonstration by your father of unity, that all was fine and dandy. His wife, his children, they were all perfect for the perfect king-to-be. More smoke and mirrors. "How on earth did you and Mother share company every day all these years? If you truly loved each other, how did you stay away and—" I stop abruptly, something slotting into place. "You didn't stay away."

He laughs, and it's tinged with sarcasm. "Adeline, your father had me nailed to his side practically day and night. When he wasn't with me, he was with your mother. He knew where she was every moment of the day. He made sure of it."

Mother is right. My father was a cruel man. He wanted to see them suffer. "And why weren't you in Evernmore with my father when I fled?"

"The shock of Edward's accident. It hit me hard."

I flinch on his behalf. "This is too much." I stand, overwhelmed by the extent of the lies that are the scaffolding of my life. I'm about to leave when I think of something. And though I think I know the answer, I go ahead and ask anyway. "Have you spoken to Edward?"

"I don't believe he would like to speak to me, ma'am."

"You've tried?"

"No. It would be wise for me to put that ball in his court."

"And my mother?"

"I am not in the habit of pestering a grieving woman, Your Majesty. I understand my position. You do not need to warn me."

"I am not warning you, Major." I make my way to the door, Davenport following. "Why would I offer you a job if I wanted to keep you away from my mother?" I look over my shoulder, catching the light dash of surprise on his face before I return my attention forward. "I would like you to reconsider my offer. I believe you still have a lot to offer the Monarchy."

"Very kind, ma'am, but I have other responsibilities now."

I frown at the front door and turn, finding him smiling at his dog. "Oh." Cathy circles my legs a few times before sitting back at her master's feet. "She can come, too."

"Pardon?"

"To work with you, she can come." I don't wait for him to decline. "I'll see you tomorrow at nine prompt." I hit the pavement and head for the open door of my car, leaving behind what I expect is a dumbfounded Davenport.

"How'd it go?" Damon asks as I slide in.

"Enlightening." It's the only word. I've always thought my father was a tyrant, but cruelty wasn't on his long list of misdemeanors. It is now, yet one has to question whether it was justified. Regardless, his bitterness toward my mother's betrayal wasn't a *justified* reason for him to be so hard-handed with me. Or, again, were they the actions of a man who simply wanted the best for his daughter? Or maybe he looked at me each day and was reminded I was born out of spite. That he never wanted me. But the more I ruminate, the more it seems to answer a question I often buried deep within me. If my father had his two heirs, why have another child? But now I know. I wasn't *wanted*. I was a backup plan only. One born to torment a man in cruelty.

I wince, touching my forehead to rub the ache away. I question my ability to do this job, even without the added handicap of daddy issues.

"Back to Kellington, ma'am?" Damon asks, following the cars up front when they pull away from the curb.

Back to Kellington? What will be waiting for me? Sir Don with more official nonsense that'll make my brain burn? Kim with endless press announcements for me to approve? Piles of invitations for me to decline or accept? "I think I'd like you to drive," I tell him, feeling like being trapped in this car is one of the only ways I can escape the ridiculousness of my world. The other way isn't readily available, and that is just cause for more despondency.

Although he's clearly not pleased by my request, Damon speaks into his earpiece to advise the other men of the plan for a little drive, and I smile when he gets short with whoever is on the other end. "Her Majesty would like to drive, so that is what we will do."

So we drive. For an hour, I'm taken on a little jaunt around London, the convoy of cars piquing interest from bystanders and drivers alike, and through my downheartedness, I manage to smile, watching as people stop and stare, obviously curious as to who could need an entourage so large. Possibly only the Queen herself, but she would never simply drive around the city in which she resides. Of course she wouldn't. The idea is ludicrous. A little like the idea that I am, in fact, the Queen.

I'm lost in my melancholy when the car comes to a stop, and I peek out the window to find out why. There's no red light, no traffic stopping us from progressing on our journey to nowhere.

"Why have you stopped, Damon?"

Turning in his seat, he looks back at me. "I think you need a little pick-me-up."

I give him a half-smile on a questioning look. "Is there a champagne fridge waiting for me? Or better still, a bottle of Belvedere?"

"No, there's an American."

I gawk at Damon like he's gone mad. "What?" I all but breathe, my heart bucking. "He's here?" I glance out the window.

"You're not the only one around here who's good at sneaking things in and out of places." He flicks his head in gesture toward the window on the other side of the car.

I gasp and shoot across the back seat, looking at the building outside. The sandstone bricks tell me nothing. We're in a tiny side street. "Where are we?"

"The staff entrance of Café Royal."

My heart kicks. *Josh.* I know I shouldn't be doing this. I shouldn't be extending my time in heaven, therefore heightening the pain when I have to leave. But I can't deny, I could choke on my excitement, my nerves, my anticipation. And I could kiss Damon. I could also dive out of the car and run through the hotel just to get to him sooner. But I must be patient, because getting me in this place unseen is not going to be a holiday. Damon spends a few moments talking into his earpiece, scanning the quiet side street, and all the while my impatience grows. I'm fidgeting in my seat, my breathing erratic. "Just put a bag over my head," I suggest, earning an exasperated shake of Damon's head as the men from one of the cars up front get out and disappear into the entrance. "Where are they going?"

"To strategize." Damon turns in his seat and holds me in place with serious eyes. "Do what I say, no questions."

I nod, more than willing.

"And no sleepovers."

Once again, I nod. I just want to see him, and I will do anything to get that. "Thank you, Damon."

"You'll get me fired."

"I didn't ask you to do this," I point out. "And besides, they've already tried to redistribute you. I wouldn't let them." And this is one of the many reasons why. No one else would dare takes these risks for me. No one else knows me well enough to know what I need. In fact, no one really *cares* enough about my needs, emotionally *or* physically, but Damon. And he knows I really need this. So badly.

"That's reassuring," Damon quips on a wry smile. "Now, the men are clearing the way to Jameson's suite, so hopefully there will be no awkward encounters with any staff or guests."

"And if there is?"

"There won't be." Taking the handle of his door, he lets himself out and fastens his jacket button as he makes his way around the front of the car. Only once he's received the nod from one of his men does he open my door, having a quick scope of the street before doing so. "Walk straight ahead," he says, taking his usual position directly behind me, his hand on my lower back. "The men are positioned at various points along the route. If I remove my hand from your back, I want you to stop. When I put it back, we can continue."

"Okay." I'm hustled through the corridor and we pass through the first door, but no sooner has it shut behind me, Damon removes his hand, and I stop abruptly, looking at him. His hand goes to his ear, his eyes ever watchful.

"We good?" His hand lands on my back again, and I walk on, my stomach performing somersaults. Excitement? Nerves? Fear?

Each member of my security team we pass joins the procession, some moving on ahead as an extra precaution. When we reach the service elevator, I stop and smile at Damon. "How exciting," I murmur, making a few of the other men sniff back a chuckle. Damon, however, ignores me.

"In the elevator," he orders when the doors open, and I quickly put myself in the back corner.

"He's in The Royal Suite," I say, scanning the floors.

"I know." Damon hits a button and puts himself in front of me, shielding me from the doors. "If the doors open before we make it to his floor, remain still and quiet behind me, understand?"

"Understood," I confirm, for the first time checking myself in the mirror. I pull my hair over one shoulder and pat at my flushed cheeks.

"You look fine," Damon says flatly to the doors, his hands linked in front of him. I peek out the corner of my eye at him as I dab my lips with a touch of lipstick.

"Just fine? Yesterday I was the most beautiful queen who'd ever lived."

More suppressed chuckles from his men and another snub from Damon as he stares at the floor counter. "You clearly didn't get much sleep last night," he quips dryly.

I splutter my playful disgust and poke him in the back. "I should have let them redistribute you."

"Behave, Your Majesty. You love our little adventures too much."

"Oh, ha-ha funny." The lift suddenly jolts, and my heart jolts with it. I'm going to see Josh, and despite knowing I'm only worsening my situation, only getting more attached to something I shouldn't get attached to, I can't help the thrill coursing through me. He's the only light in my ever-darkening world. He's the only thing that makes me feel peace.

The doors slide open and two men disembark, checking the corridor before signaling to Damon. When I emerge from the lift, I see men spaced at even intervals. I'm escorted calmly and swiftly, and when we reach Josh's door unscathed and undetected, my heart doesn't ease up with the pounds, but increases. Damon gives the wood a firm rap, and I hear movement from beyond. I hold my breath, bracing myself.

And deflate disappointedly when the door opens and it's not

Josh. To be expected, really, but as I look past his bodyguard, Bates, I still don't see him. "Your Majesty." Bates grins, clearly finding the shift in my status amusing.

"Hello." I smile and move forward with the help of Damon's hand, looking around the palatial suite while Damon and his old friend say their hellos. "Where's Josh?"

"His interview with *Hello* ran over, ma'am." Bates motions to a closed door. "He shouldn't be too much longer."

"Journalists are in there?" I ask, pointing to the door.

"Don't worry, you're safe." Bates flips me a rather inappropriate wink, and I blink at him, just as the handle of the closed door rattles. "Oh fuck." Bates swings wide eyes toward the door, and Damon joins the cursing with a few of his own expletives, diving in front of me. I barely catch the door swinging open, and then I have a wall of men in front of me, blocking my view.

"Safe?" I hiss, resisting poking Bates in the back with my finger.

"Oh, hi," a woman's voice chirps, a little bewildered. "Can you point me in the direction of the toilet?"

Silent, Bates points to the left, and I hear her heels as she goes. "Thanks," she says, definitely wary. The wall of men hiding me starts shuffling around, forcing me to move with them or be revealed.

"Nearly done?" Bates asks the woman.

"Just a few pictures to take, and I might have one more attempt at extracting the identity of this mystery woman from him."

I stiffen, and Bates laughs a laugh that could not be mistaken for anything less than nervous. "Don't bother."

"Come on, you can tell me, can't you?"

Damon's stance visibly alters, from alert to hyper-alert. "No," he answers for Bates.

The woman laughs. "Christ, anyone would think he's dating royalty."

My lips straighten, and every man standing before me shifts a little, awkward, nervous, and then a door closes and I'm being ambushed by them all. "Whoa!" I yelp as I'm hustled through the suite and eventually into a huge bedroom fit for a king. "Don't leave this room." Damon wags a warning finger in my face before shutting me inside.

"And where would I go?" I say to the door, dropping my bag from my shoulder and straightening out my flustered form. Gazing around the space, I can't help the small smile that creeps up on me. The Royal Suite. How very mushy of him. Kicking off my heels, I meander around the room casually, taking in the beautiful décor, the grand furniture, and the elaborate wall dressings. It's palatial.

For me?

I could be in a tent in the middle of a muddy field, but if Josh were with me, it would be heaven. I soon find myself in the bathroom, the sense of opulence carrying through. There's much to admire, but it is the bathtub that keeps my interest. I look over my shoulder to the door, chewing my bottom lip in contemplation. I could have a nice, relaxing bath at my own leisure while I wait for him. What else is there to do? On a crafty smirk, I approach the tub and flip on the tap, and then proceed to pour in a good dose of bubble bath and swish the water. I leave it filling while I head to the bedroom and collect my phone, noticing a pile of magazines stacked neatly on the bedside, as well as a bottle of champagne on ice and two glasses. It's like he's expecting me, and I wonder for the first time if Josh instigated this, or if Damon did. I shrug. I don't care. Detouring, I collect the magazines, the bottle, and a glass, and head back to the bathroom with a smile of satisfaction. I set my finds down within reach and strip down before curling my hair up into a high bun.

Once the bath is full, I slide in on a groan of contentment. And then I lie there in the peaceful quiet, eyes closed, my mind as light as my body.

Complete.

Utter.

Bliss.

"Perfect," I sigh, pouring myself a glass of champagne and taking the first magazine from the top of the pile. Not surprisingly, there's no news in print of my recent promotion to Queen, since it's only recently been made public officially, but there is a whole section dedicated to my family's recent loss, Eddie's renouncement, and the imminent news of the country's new Queen. The picture on the cover is a poignant shot, a close-up of Eddie and me walking behind my father's coffin being pulled by the gun carriage. I swallow and quickly turn the page, finding more photographs from the funeral. And on the next, and the next. My eyes sting, my heart becoming heavier. This isn't what I had in mind. Just for a moment, I want to forget my loss. Forget . . . everything.

I flick through the pages until I reach something non-me related. Actually, that is not strictly true. I smile. Josh *is* me related, not that the world knows it. And to think his face is plastered on the other side of a page that has me all over it. How ironic.

I scan the advertisement. "Eau de Parfum," I muse, tilting my head, happier with my alternative reading material, not that there's much to read. So I simply admire him, all kitted out in a gorgeous, immaculate three-piece suit, with roughed-up hair that totally contradicts his fine threads. It's perfectly Josh. My smile widens. It's perfectly me, too. His smile in the ad is demure, suggestive, a little knowing, the kind of smile where one must wonder what he is smiling about. He could be smiling about our secret. He could be smiling about me. When was this picture taken? All other magazines are forgotten as I sip and admire, sip and admire. I'm quite content, lost in the tub and time, until my phone chiming breaks my utopia.

I reach for it and open the message from Matilda, laughing under my breath when I see an image of a mug she's holding. Her message tells me she just bought me said mug. On the circumference, it reads:

IT'S GOOD TO BE QUEEN.

I call her rather than replying, sinking down into the tub. "Very funny," I muse when she answers.

"What a frightful few weeks," my cousin breathes. "I know you won't appreciate my sympathy, so I wanted to make you laugh instead."

"Thank you, Matilda." Despite her intentions, I still feel an unrelenting wave of despondency. There are so many reasons for me to feel downhearted and sad, yet I'm struggling to identify what misery needs most of my broken heart. It is for those reasons I find it easiest to think about the one thing I have to be happy about right now. Josh. But how long can this craziness last? We have an expiry date. In fact, that expiry date has passed. We're living on borrowed time, if you will. Another sigh. "How are you?"

"Not as highly in demand as you, though *OK!* did print pictures of me out with Santiago."

"*OK!?*" I discard my magazine and riffle through the pile by the bath. "Oh, I have it." Placing my glass down, I flip through until I find Matilda. "Oh my . . ." I breathe, scanning the collection of shots, all of Matilda and the Argentine at various stages of leaving a private function—coming out the door, him holding it open, crossing the pavement with security, and getting into a waiting car. "You look gorgeous," I chirp excitedly. "When was this?"

"Our first date. I was desperate to tell you about it, then, of course, John and . . ." She trails off, and I flinch on Matilda's behalf. "Well, there just hasn't been the right time since."

I feel a little bad for my cousin; I know she would have been desperate to share. Then the world turned upside down. Not only for me, but for everyone. "Did you have a lovely time?" I ask in an attempt to get our conversation away from it all.

"Wonderful." She doesn't sound convincing. "God, Adeline, how could all of this happen? Did you know Eddie was suffering so terribly?"

"No." I grab my glass again and start drowning my sorrows. It was inevitable the conversation would end up here. How could it not? But what I must remember is that, like the rest of the world, Matilda is in the dark about the scandal, the lies, and the secrets. She will swallow the stories being fed to her like everyone else. She'll never know Helen's baby wasn't my brother's. That my mother had an affair with the King's private secretary. That Eddie is illegitimate. That he isn't suffering as a result of his service to our country, but because his world isn't what he thought it was. It's only now I appreciate that Eddie's story will probably be easy to swallow. His behavior now could easily be passed off as a side effect of PTSD. "It is certainly a testing time, cousin. My heart hurts, but I don't feel like I'm being allowed to grieve. To come to terms with what has happened and how I came to be here." I swallow, determined not to expose my emotions. "This past week I've been sent dizzy with protocol. What I must do, how I must do it. All the responsibilities, the expectations. It's nothing I didn't know, but goodness, it's like a mountain on my shoulders. I just want to scream." I don't really need to tell Matilda any of this. She knows. "Part of me wants to run, the other part of me wants to take the bull by the horns, so to speak. To show my father and his minions he was wrong. That I am not an embarrassment to royalty."

"You are not an embarrassment. Stop that. God, Adeline, I wish I could give you a cuddle," Matilda says, probably not knowing what else she can say. It's all very horrific, and that's that. While the world celebrates my succession, I mourn the loss of my life. "Where are you, anyway?"

My glass floats in mid-air before my lips as I gaze around the bathroom of Josh's suite. "Some official nonsense at Claringdon." I purse my lips, hearing how unconvincing I sound. "Did you know I'm patron to over one thousand charities?" I go on, trying to turn it around before I give my crimes away.

"Adeline?" Matilda draws out my name, and I shrink into the hot water. "Where are you?"

I squeeze my eyes closed. "In Josh Jameson's bathtub." I can't lie. There are too many lies. I need someone to talk to about this, and there is no one. No one except Josh and Damon. Josh is bias. Damon will do anything for me. I need someone in Switzerland.

"Oh my gosh," Matilda breathes.

"I know."

"Are you crazy?"

"Yes."

"Adeline!"

"I just needed some space to breathe," I argue meekly. "Somewhere to go, away from the madness my life has become. He's the only one who soothes me, Matilda. He's my only happy place."

"Oh good God, you will be—"

"Sent to Coventry?" I ask. "Dethroned? I'm the Queen, for heaven's sake."

"Exactly," Matilda says, high-pitched and squealy. "And the Queen must marry suitably, not have kinky affairs with Hollywood actors."

"Who says he's not suitable?" I grumble, reaching for my bottle and refilling.

"Thousands of years of royal history, that is who. Or rather, *what*. Every Lord, advisor, and politician in the land. And probably most the population of the bloody world, Adeline. You must marry a carefully selected male and have perfect little princes and princesses."

I snarl to myself. "I thought you wanted to cheer me up."

"You know they won't allow it. You will be forced to marry *suitably*."

"Then I won't marry at all."

She laughs. "Like Elizabeth I?"

"Yes, exactly like her. Strong, independent. She didn't need a man beside her to rule England."

"So you'll be a virgin Queen, too, will you?"

I snort. "We all know Elizabeth I was not a virgin. Like her, I will not be pushed into marriage."

"And like her, you will die childless, and that will be the end of the House of Lockhart. Your family's dynasty will die with you, Adeline."

A nasty bout of pain pinches my gut. "When did you become a champion of the throne?" I mutter moodily. "If you love it that much, you can have it. I'm sure your mother wants it. How is the battle-axe, by the way?"

Matilda laughs. "She's not very impressed with our new Queen."

My eye-roll is dramatic. "Fancy that," I quip. "Will I have to have her banished for treason?"

"Yes, and banish my father, too, will you? I'm sick to death of hearing about your lacking abilities." Matilda's testing parents are probably right. I am lacking, but how dare they say as much? It might be my ego, or maybe my pride, but my father's sister and her husband are two more reasons for me to want to prove everyone wrong. "But, sod the family." She chuckles. "The public is thrilled."

Will they be thrilled if they learn of my love affair with Josh Jameson? Will they still love me? "It is a small comfort during this testing time," I admit.

"Will I have to curtsey when I see you next?"

I smile. "Even if I say no, you will do it to irritate me."

"I will. And since I am your favorite of all relatives, can I put in a few requests?"

"Like?"

"My own driver, for a start."

"You can have the driver who serves The Duke and Duchess of Sussex."

"You can't take away my parents' driver and give him to me." Matilda laughs. "I'll never hear the last of it."

"Oh, very well." I relent, losing the lovely mental image of Victoria's face when she finds out I have *redistributed* her allowances and staff in favor of her daughter. "We will discuss soon." I look up at the door when it opens. The bath water suddenly feels scorching hot. "I have to go," I all but breathe, my lungs empty, my eyes amazed. "We'll talk more tomorrow. Something's come up."

"I bet," she snickers, and I disconnect our call, placing my phone blindly on the edge of the bath. For a second, I catch worry on Josh's face, but then his lips slowly stretch into a lazy, appreciative smile.

"There's a queen in my bathtub." He moves my phone to the vanity unit, and then reaches for his shirt buttons, unfastening them one by one, revealing a chest that stars in many of my best dreams. "And, fuck, does she look good in it." His shirt hits the floor, and he starts on his jeans.

"What took you so long?" Resting my flute on the side of the bath, I lift some bubbles in my palms and send them wafting into the air with a little puff of breath—little because it's all the air I can find in my depleting lungs.

"What took me so long?" he muses to himself, slowly working his fly and pushing his jeans down his thighs. I inhale deeply and exhale slowly. God knows, those thighs are the things of dreams, too, and his hips . . . Lord, his hips. His stomach. Every dip and ravine. The perfectly formed V. And my legs are going to be wrapped oh so very tightly around that waist *very* soon. "Let me tell you what took me so long." He swaggers over, only his boxer shorts left to discard. Placing his palms on the edge of the bath, he braces himself and bends, eyes flashing with sparks of amber amid the blue. "One very nosy journalist who, like the rest of the world, wanted to know who was being hustled into The Dorchester under my hoodie."

"Oh," I whisper, my eyes dropping to his lips. Those lips. Fantastical lips, lips made for kissing *me*. "Are they still chasing that information?"

"They're like wolves."

"Did you feed the wolves?"

Sensing my want, he edges forward and presses his mouth lightly on mine. "You know I would have loved nothing more." Making our kiss only brief, he withdraws and searches out my eyes. "But I love you too much to add to your woes." The sentiment in his voice, in his unbreakable stare, is enough to melt me in the hot water. He loves me. This isn't a whimsical love affair. It's the real deal, and I would be a fool to tell myself anything else. "Do you love me, Your Majesty?"

Yes. I'm madly and stupidly in love with him, too. But I can only nod, that love growing with every second I spend with him. *And every second I do not.* My plight is very real. "Loving you is the easy part," I say softly. "It's everything that comes with loving—" A finger lands on my lips and hushes me.

"No. Not now." He gives me another kiss and rises to his full height, my eyes following him. Then he draws his boxer shorts down his thighs and kicks them off. My eyes drop to where they are inevitably going to drop.

Oh . . .

"Stand up." He extends his hand for me to take and helps me to my feet, the water pouring from my body, suds sliding down my wet skin. "You're a vision."

"As are you."

"Totally inferior." He reaches forward and brushes a light fingertip over the peak of my breast, smiling when my torso naturally concaves and my breaths become heavy. "You think you can escape me?" His hand drifting up my chest, he reaches my neck and flattens his palm on my throat. "Throb . . . throb . . . throb." He takes my hand and rests it on his chest, and the pound of his heartbeat sinks into my palm. I'm worlds away from a life I don't want to be part of. How can I deny myself this feeling? How can I deny Josh? How can I deny *us?* "Turn around so I can see that royal ass I own."

I slowly turn in the water, losing the calming sight of him. But I still have his touch, and it's now sliding down my wet spine, wiping away all anxiety troubling me. My body rolls, my skin flames. He's doing it again, prolonging my agony, taking me to the edge.

Proving everything we both know. "Bend and place your hands on the edge." A firm palm pushes into my back, helping me down until I'm bent and braced, ready for him. And that's where he leaves me for a few more painful seconds, the only sound in the bathroom that of our weighty breathing. I close my eyes and try to dampen my craving, every inch of my skin burning under his gliding hand. Then his traveling palm comes to a stop on my backside. I fall into a trance, anticipating his punishing blow. Willing it on. Begging for it, knowing I'll be tossed further into a mind-spin where Josh is the only thing I see, feel, hear. My skin tingles excitedly. "This won't be the last time I spank your ass." His hand lifts and comes crashing down on my flesh, the film of water only making the connection louder and the sting more brutal. My eyes spring open, and I grunt deep in my throat, tensing the cheeks of my arse.

"I hope it's not," I confess. I wish he could bless me with his punishing hand every day of my godforsaken life.

"Up." He helps me to stand, turns me, and steps into the water. The meeting of our torsos, my wet, slippery boobs sliding across his chest, audibly robs us both of breath. His hand slides into my hair and pulls the hair tie free, and my hair tumbles across my shoulders. I gaze into his stunning eyes, desperation reflecting back at me. "I want you to remember something," he whispers, his eyes jumping across my face. "To the world you are the Queen of England." Cupping both of my cheeks with his big hands, he brings my face close to his, and I hold his wrists tightly, preparing myself for words I know will send my already spiraling mind and heart into further bedlam. "But to me, you are *everything*."

If at any point in my life I've felt hurt, Josh has just put that pain to shame. Because though his words are beautiful, they are more painful, and they momentarily knock me back a few paces, reminding me of who I am and who he is. Because I can be *everything* to him, but nothing at the same time.

"Stop it," he orders, rubbing his cheek on mine, wiping the tears

I hadn't realized were falling. "Right now, it is just you and me, and no status or circumstance can stop that."

"And what about after right now?" My arm slides around his neck and holds him close, as if I am afraid that someone, *anyone*, could storm his suite and tear us apart.

"There will only ever be right now." He reaches to the back of his neck and pries my hand away, holding my forearms and pushing me back a fraction so he has my face again. "You and I will only ever live in the moment, because that's the only choice we have." It's like he knows I need to hear that. Like he's finally concluded it's the only option for us.

And all I can do is nod.

"Good." Pulling me close again, he seals our mouths, and I'm back in the beautiful game we play, kissing the living daylights out of him. "And right now, I'm going to screw you hard. Make you scream." He lowers, pulling me down with him, submerging us in the water. Sitting and resting back, he arranges me on his lap, and I find his mouth again, losing myself in his kiss and lifting myself when he reaches between my thighs. Forgoing his shoulders for the edge of the bath behind him, I grip and whimper as he guides me down onto him. He fills me on one, easy plunge, and I still atop of him, fighting to breathe while maintaining our sealed mouths. Our kiss is serene, flows easily, and the consistent, soft groans from Josh are overflowing with passion. He lets me be for a short while, waiting for me to become accustomed to his thickness within me, before he gently takes my hips and flexes his fingers into the hollows. "Okay?" he asks, nibbling my bottom lip and breaking away.

Okay? I'm so much more than okay. Right now, I'm in a faraway land, away from the status, power, and privilege that has always ruled me. Right now, my status is his, my power is love, and my privilege is having Josh with me. Right now, when my head is heavy with raw emotions, love being the strongest, I wish Josh had told that journalist about me. Right now, I could easily demand he call her back so he can introduce me. It's impossible, but Josh makes the impossible seem possible.

Instead of answering him, I sit up straighter, rolling my hips, taking him deeper.

"Oh, she's sure okay," he rumbles low in his throat, helping me find our rhythm. It takes one grind, two groans, and a million crashes of my heart. As we gaze into each other's eyes, I wedge my hands into his shoulders and flex with him, every plunge achieving unthinkable depths. The pleasure is beyond description. The intensity of our sex is off the charts. Together, we share something that tilts both our worlds, and right now, it's all that counts. Us. Nothing else, just us.

And then a lazy smile crawls across his lips, one loaded with satisfaction and knowing, and mine naturally mirrors Josh's as he strokes his palms across my wet back. I fall forward to kiss him again, but he eases me back. "Stay there," he orders, flipping his hips on a teasing jolt, quickly followed by a lazy grind, extending my exhale. His stare falls to my boobs, his hand cupping one and massaging roughly.

"I want to kiss you," I complain.

"Yeah, well, I want to lie here and know that while the rest of the world is happening, I'm here with the Queen riding me in my bathtub." His head rests back, his smile crooked with pleasure, his eyes firing sparks of burning happiness. "Because I'm pretty damn sure it beats everything."

"Is that so?"

"That is most definitely so. Now, concentrate, woman. You have a man to please." He flips a cheeky wink, the rogue, and what do I do? I lift and slam myself back down, wiping that roguish grin clean from his otherworldly face. Water splashes everywhere, and Josh hisses and curses, reclaiming my hips. "You want to play dirty?" he practically gasps, digging his fingertips into me to the point of pain.

My answer: another lift of my hips and a hard smash down.

"Fuck." Josh's head drops back, and I reach forward and run my wet hand through his hair, dampening the strands. His breaths are sharp, his lips parted, his eyes wild. "Don't challenge me, Your Majesty." There's that drawl again, deep and southern, gravelly and alluring.

I cock my head in interest, seizing his neck and slowly lifting my arse until he is only just breaching my entrance. The head of his cock throbs against me. And he waits. And waits. He waits, shaking, while I dip and withdraw, taking only half of him each time, sending him crazy with my teasing. And when he's got to grips with my new pace and tactic, his body somewhat relaxed, I shock him and smash onto him again. I grit my teeth through the pang of pain, feeling him hit my womb.

"Adeline," he barks, seizing my boobs and squeezing hard. I grab his throat and start rolling and flexing again. He's sweating. "When I'm done with you, your throat will be scratchy from your screams and your body sore." He slips a finger between us, adding to the fullness. "Most of all here."

My smile could be deemed provocative. It is. "Being sore after I've seen you is a given." Whether my arse, my pussy, or my heart. Or all three. "But that pain only reminds me of the time we've had together. So hurry up and make me scream."

I'm on my back a moment later, not quite sure how I got there. He's looming over me, his chest slightly raised with the help of his hand braced over my head on the edge of the tub. There was no splashing in the process of flipping me. "Where is the water?"

"I pulled out the plug a while ago, baby. You miss that?"

All that remains are suds coating the enamel and two very slippery bodies. "I missed that," I admit. Most things escape me when Josh is consuming me.

Like the fact that I am Queen.

He takes my thigh and pulls it up to his hip, keeping hold of the bath. And he re-enters me on a brisk, smooth drive, pushing me up the edge.

"Hold tight," he whispers, sending my hands straight to his shoulders. "And breathe." He doesn't give me a moment to put his second order into action, all air stuck in my throat when he lets loose, slamming into me repeatedly and punishingly. My throat is instantly hoarse from my yelps, and Josh's smile is instant from his satisfaction. His conviction is hampered only a little bit from the slippery bath, his focus too set on achieving maximum depths, maximum indulgence, and maximum noise. His penetrations are dizzying, the emphasis of each pound mind-blowing. I squirm, grapple at his back, try to pull his mouth onto mine to muffle the sounds of my screams. "No," he says, keeping his position so he can watch me unravel beneath him. My thigh held snuggly to his waist, he drives on, his brutality, the sheer strength behind his strikes, completely ruling me. I'm at his mercy, his to control. Just how I want it.

Just how Josh wants it.

My hands go to his hair and grip, my jaw tensing as I climb and climb and climb. "Oh God," I yell, throwing my head back, oblivious to the impact of it hitting the bath. I'm on the cusp of shattering, the vibrations of my body out of control.

"I'm coming, baby," he gasps, raising the bar, starting to shout with every hard hit. As he crashes into me, various limbs crash against the bath, the whole scene crazed and desperate. Blood rushes to my head, and I drop my heavy eyes, finding a sweat-drenched face creased with concentration. Dashes of amber shoot from his eyes, and when he groans and rolls those dangerous hips, coming hard, my world seems to split straight down the middle, and I disappear down the crevice, tumbling, my body weightless.

My climax takes hold, bending my body on another scream, my nails sinking into the flesh of his shoulders, clinging on. And it lasts and lasts and lasts, to the point that I'm struggling to deal with the intensity, shaking like a leaf. "Oh, Jesus Lord above," Josh whispers, losing his grip of the bath and falling on top of me, panting into my neck. My internal muscles are in spasm, constricting wildly around him, probably in shock. I'm out of breath, satisfied, and absolutely beat.

The hard bath beneath me is inconsequential, but Josh still maneuvers us, rolling to his back and breathing out raggedly when I flop my useless body across his chest. Throwing my lifeless arms around him, I settle and let my heavy eyes close, our hearts colliding, fusing on every beat.

I'm his.

Nothing but his.

6

I HEAR HIS voice, distant and rough, but what he is saying I can't tell. I also can't be bothered to ask him to repeat himself, burrowing deeper into the crook of his neck. Then my body is shaking a little, from his laugh, I suspect. I can't be bothered to lift my heavy head to confirm that, either. I'm utterly beat.

"C'mon, lazy bones," Josh says.

"Um-hmm." I'm not certain of what I am being asked to do, but I *am* certain I'm not doing it. "Tired," I grumble groggily.

"Sore throat?"

"Um-hmm."

"Sore between your thighs?"

"Um-hmm."

"Cold?"

"Um-hmm."

Strong arms surround me and squeeze me tightly. "Horny?"

"Um-hmm."

He chuckles and starts moving my dead weight, holding me with one arm while he uses the side of the bath to pull us up. I find my feet and blink my eyes open, and as soon as the light hits my pupils, I plant my face in his chest to hide from the harshness. "You're hard work when you're sleepy."

I ignore him and reattach myself to his front, with my arms and legs wrapped around him like ivy. "That's the best I've slept in weeks. I'd like more." I'm not ready to take on the world again. Hiding in this suite is highly appealing. And highly impossible. There's a job to do, responsibilities to uphold. But the only responsibility I'd like to maintain is my current state of tranquility.

Josh steps out of the bath, sets me on my feet, wraps me in a towel, and then reclaims me and carries me through to the bedroom, laying me on the bed. He sits on the edge while I curl onto my side, bringing my knees to my chest and burying my hands under the pillow beneath my head. "These beds are exceptionally comfortable."

He laughs, his chest swelling as he does. "Only the best for my queen." Brushing some damp hair from my face, he dips and kisses me sweetly. "Are you hungry?"

"No, but I'm thirsty."

"I'll grab some water." He gets up and pulls some jeans on as he heads for the door, and I pout, disappointed I've forced him to partially dress. There are a lot of men somewhere in this suite. Far enough away to miss my shouts of ecstasy? I cringe as Josh reappears with a bottle of water. "What's up?" he asks, motioning for me to make room for him as he pulls off his jeans. I shuffle across the bed, and he rests his back against the headboard, unscrewing the cap off the bottle and handing it to me.

"Where's Damon?" I ask, sitting up and accepting. The cool liquid as it glides down my throat is glorious.

"He got a call."

I hold the water in my mouth for a moment, regarding Josh closely as I swallow. "Oh?"

"I don't want you to panic, but—"

Well, isn't that the worst thing someone could say to me? I sit up, pulling my towel in. "What's happened?"

"Your brother's gone AWOL."

Right now is over. I scramble to the edge of the bed, searching for my clothes as I go.

"Whoa, where do you think you're goin'?" He's before me in a second, stopping me from pulling on my dress.

I don't fight him, stilling in my movements. "I don't know." I look to the door, realizing I'm stuck here until Damon returns, because I'm certain he'll have given Josh firm instructions.

"Come sit." Josh takes my clothes from my hands and drops them to the floor, pulling me back to the bed. My sore backside skims the sheets just as I think of something. "My phone." I'm up again, pacing to the bathroom. I find my mobile on the vanity unit, but there are no calls or messages. Damon didn't want to worry me. He let me stay in my heaven—the saint that he is—while he tended to the increasingly deviant misbehaviors of the Fallen Prince. I go to Josh and strain a smile when he opens his arms for me to join him on the bed. A cuddle. I could do with one of those. What kind of Queen am I, if the task of a delinquent brother sends me into a meltdown? Josh is my haven, but he's not readily available for me to crawl into his warmth each time I'm challenged. But he's here now.

I drop my phone on the bed and crawl up, falling heavily onto Josh's chest with a defeated sigh. "The PR people will be in a right old pickle," I breathe, imagining them running around in circles trying to locate Eddie and implement damage control. "And Felix will vomit all over his Italian loafers."

Josh's slight hitch of his chest is the only evidence of his amusement. "The man's been dealt a heavy blow, baby. You've got to cut him some slack."

"You don't get any slack to cut when you are a Royal, Josh. You simply have to put up and shut up."

With my cheek squished against his pec, his hands work soothing circles across my back as I stare blankly at the wall, taking a little comfort from the sound of his heartbeats in my ear. "That is a very different tone from when I knew you as the Princess of England. You were all guns blazing, so determined *not* to put up and shut up. What's changed?"

"You mean apart from the tiny detail that the crown has jumped two heirs and landed on my head?" I ask, getting a little pinch on my back for my sarcasm. "So much, Josh. So much has changed. I never expected this to happen, so I never contemplated failing. I don't want to fail. All I can hear is my father's words, everyone's words, telling me I'm a disgrace. An embarrassment to the Monarchy. Standing in that office in front of the Accession Council put all other feelings of suffocation I've felt to shame. But I also felt something else. Do you know what?"

"What, darlin'?"

"Determined. The weight of their quiet disapproval only made me more determined. The way they looked at me, judged me. I had the strong desire to run, but I also wanted to order them all to bow to me. How silly is that?" I look at him, searching for an answer. Does Josh think I'm silly? I can't see evidence of it in his soft smile as he combs through my hair with his fingers. "One feels like she is cutting off her nose to spite her face."

"One is too cute when she calls herself *one*."

"Oh, stop." I roll my eyes in exasperation, though I'm truly grateful for his teasing, and settle my cheek back on his chest. I've known Josh such a short time, and I'm surprised—given I'm so fiercely independent—by my inexplicable desperation for him. His input. His smiles. His ear. His impertinence. Everything seemed more bearable with him in my life. I was lighter, happier. I was determined to keep him, no matter the cost. "I want to be lighter and happier again," I whisper to myself, hating the unstoppable sting in my eyes. "I knew my family were nothing more than fraudsters. But this? The lies, the deceit. My mother, Davenport, my father's cruelty?"

"Smoke and mirrors," Josh says quietly, encouraging my face up to his so he can see me. "You've always known it. Maybe now you get to change it. Maybe now you show the world that the Royals are real people, just like them."

I smile at his naiveté. "You think that because I am the Queen of England I get to dictate how the Royal future progresses? That I choose *anything?*"

"Hell, yeah," he replies simply.

Oh, how deluded he is. "I feel the need to hire a private tutor to teach you a little about the British Monarchy."

He nudges me playfully, dipping and biting the end of my nose. "Don't make me spank that royal ass. I've done nothing *but* research the British fuckin' Monarchy all week."

My eyebrows jump up. "Really?"

"Really. And let me tell you, I think it's scandalous that, as Queen, you don't need a passport. What the fuck?"

I laugh, thoroughly amused. "I can't issue a document in my own name to myself."

"And did you know you own every dolphin in British waters?"

"I know that."

"And you have to sign every law passed in your country, so make a law up that says you can be with me. And anyway, isn't it the Sovereign's power to approve?"

I shake my head. It feels terribly heavy. "The Privy Council would never allow it. My army of advisors would never allow it. That's why there are laws. Ancient laws to protect the bloodline, but still laws."

"So, for the avoidance of doubt, a lowly Catholic American actor doesn't stand a chance with the Queen of England?"

I balk. "You're Catholic?"

He balks right back. "You're the Queen?"

I smack his shoulder. "You never mentioned you were Catholic."

"Yes. It's one more reason why we can't be together, because

God forbid the head of The Church of England falls in love with a Catholic." He's truly exasperated, and despite it all being rather awful, I smile.

"Just invent a new law," he says. "There's got to be some perks to being the Queen of England, for fuck's sake."

"I might sign off laws, but I certainly do not create them. Besides, signing them off is a mere formality. Laws are passed in parliament before getting the seal of approval from the palace. It's called royal assent, by the way. The only proposed laws I can veto are those that have a direct impact on the Monarchy."

"The Queen's consent," Josh mutters grumpily. "I know."

"Well done, you." I grin when he snarls. "So that's today's history lesson over. Tomorrow we discuss my ministers."

"Oh, you mean the dudes who wield all your prerogative powers? Awesome. Can't wait."

"Oh, stop moaning and kiss me." I grab his cheeks, yank his face to mine, and land him with a deep kiss that has us both immediately moaning. And all obstacles are forgotten. All heartache masked.

I'm home. Pulling back, Josh is quiet for a few moments, his eyes roaming my face. Every inch of it. What's he thinking now? I bite my lip and wait. And he eventually breathes in and speaks. "My life is in your hands, Your Majesty." His murmured words hit me hard. "I love you. You love me. In today's world, it should be as simple as that."

It should be. But we both know it is not. "The controversy would end the royal family."

"Be the controversial queen, baby."

I smile and cup his cheek, willing him to understand. "All the secrets will be spilled, everyone I love ruined. I can't do that to them, Josh." I'm surprised when he balks, almost offended.

"But they can chain you down to a job you don't wanna do?" I know he's angry because his accent is sharp.

"It's not that simple." I push myself up and move away a little, if only because his irate vibes are burning me.

"Bullshit. Fuckin' bullshit, Adeline. It should be that simple. So you and I, we're going to do this forever, are we? Sneak around when I happen to be in Ole Blighty?"

"What else can we do?"

His eyes widen. "Oh my fuckin' God." And then he laughs. "You really think this is good enough for me?"

I keep my mouth shut with a lack of the right words to say. *What can I say?* He's the one who has pursued us, even when I told him there was nothing we could do. And now he blames me? Confirms that I will never be enough?

"You do," he murmurs. "You expect me to live in the shadows of your life."

"What happened to right now?" I reply pitifully.

"Fuck right now. I want forever, and I want it out there in the big, wide, terrifying world." He's off the bed, yanking his jeans on. "I want to go out there with you and tell the world I'm with you." He throws his arm toward the door before going back to fastening his jeans. "That I love you. That *you* are fuckin' *mine*."

"It's a very romantic notion, Josh."

His hands pause on the fly as he keeps me in place with his cold stare. "I can't sneak around forever, Adeline. And it's fucked-up that you would expect me to."

"Will you stop swearing?" I yell. "So what would you have me do?"

"I'd have you walk away from the one thing that makes you miserable and be with the one thing that makes you happy."

I recoil, taken aback by his bluntness. "You cannot ask me to do that."

"Yes, I can. In fact, I'm not asking, I'm telling you. We both know you don't want it. So give it up, for fuck's sake. Give it up for me."

I'm completely gobsmacked. "You selfish pig." I stand, shaking with rage. "Give up acting."

"Oh, shut up, Adeline. I love acting. It's my calling. Wearing a crown is not your calling unless I'm fuckin' you from behind with one on your head."

My mouth falls open in complete shock. *Not my calling?* Is he saying I can't do it? Doubting me like everyone else? "I should slap your face."

He sneers, daring me, and it's a mockery to chivalrous men everywhere. "Be my guest, darlin'." He steps forward and juts his chin out, goading me.

I can't believe I'm thinking what I'm thinking—it's shameful—but what I actually want to do is head-butt the chauvinistic bastard. "I'm leaving." I pivot and sweep up my dress from the floor, wrestling to get it on.

"Wrong. You're not going anywhere until Damon gets back." He waltzes off into the bathroom, cocky as can be, and slams the door behind him. Then I hear a roar, followed by a bang. His fist meeting the wood of the door.

"We'll see about that," I spit, collecting my things and making my getaway. I open the door, and with my feet moving so fast, I nearly crash face-first into a suited back. "Goodness!"

One of Josh's men looks over his shoulder, a little alarmed. "Okay there, Your Majesty?"

I don't get the chance to reply, as I'm pulled back into the room with a forceful yank. "May I remind you of who you are manhandling?" I yell, shrugging Josh off me.

"No, you *may* not." He holds his palm against the door, blocking my escape, his face twisted in disdain. I huff, matching his threatening stance. His glare is deadly. "And don't turn on your ultra-posh shit with me, just because you're mad."

"I'm not mad. Why would I possibly be mad?"

"Because I'm right."

"Utter nonsense." I flinch as soon as I spit the words, hearing them, and Josh laughs, his head tossed back. "Oh, fuck off," I spit, shoving him away.

"That's more like it. My filthy-mouthed queen."

My despair has rage tearing through me. "I'm leaving." His hand lands back on the door.

"Don't be stupid, Adeline. You'll make it one pace through the hotel and all hell will break loose. You're staying until Damon returns, and that's it."

At that very second, there's a knock at the door, and we both look at the wood. "Your Majesty?" Damon's voice sinks into the room, and I scramble for the handle.

"Damon, I want to leave. Thumbs down!"

"What the fuck?" Josh holds the door as Damon tries to enter, pulling my grip from the shiny knob and flipping the lock. "You and your fuckin' thumbs." I'm lifted from my feet and carried away, kicking and screaming like a naughty toddler. He drops me to my feet, all rather roughly, and points a poker-straight finger in my face, bristling like a grizzly bear, his chest pulsing from his angry breaths. He's trying to think about what to say, his mouth opening and closing like a goldfish. He can say nothing. He's said enough.

"Damon is here now, so I can leave."

"Ma'am?" Damon calls. "I have a very intoxicated prince in the car."

I gasp and shoot my stare to the door. He has Eddie with him? I dash forward urgently, being jarred to a stop when Josh grabs me, yanking on my shoulder painfully. I yelp and hiss, reaching for my upper arm.

"Oh shit," Josh curses. "Adeline, I'm sor—"

"I'm leaving." I swing around violently, rolling away the sharp pain. "You will do what everyone else in the world is supposed to do and respect me."

He recoils, hurt, and slowly shakes his head. I've never seen disappointment on Josh. Until now. And I don't like it. Of all the people I could wish to disappoint, Josh is at the bottom of my list.

Goodness, he isn't even on the list.

"Well, like one of your loyal, devoted subjects, I will do just that." Backing away, he bows his head and sweeps his arm out dramatically toward the door. "Your Majesty."

I've always loved Josh addressing me in the correct manner. Not because I thrived on my status—I didn't; I hated my status—but because with his voice, it never sounded like a burden. It sounded light and carefree. Now, it's weighted down with too much resentment, which is entirely ironic, because that's how I always felt about it. Add the derision splashed over his face, I don't think I've ever felt so inadequate. So small.

I stare at him as he stares at me. There's fire in his eyes. "Don't ever throw your ultimatums at me ever again." I seethe.

"And don't you throw your orders at me. I will *never* bow to you."

"I never asked you to."

"You just did, Adeline." His jaw pulses steadily, and he draws too much breath for my liking, preparing to say something I'm certain I'll hate. "You can be your country's Queen, baby," he whispers, his eyes glassy, "or you can be *my* queen." He steps back. "You can't be both."

Everything inside me dies.

He's right.

It's like a cavern has opened in my chest, and my heart has been sucked into it. *I don't have a choice. Not anymore.* But he will live his life, find his happily ever after. I will live my life shrouded by responsibility. Cloaked in loneliness.

Because he's done. And he's proven himself to be no different to every other person in my life. Shallow. Blinkered by selfish reason. He doesn't think I'm capable of this.

I slowly turn and unlock the door, pulling it open. On the other side, Damon looks grave. "I'm ready," I say simply. Without a word or a look past me to what I have left in the room, Damon positions his hand on my back and then reaches for his earpiece, speaking clear instructions as I'm guided to the door. I keep my sights set resolutely forward, not prepared to remind myself of what I'm leaving behind, as I am steered through the corridors, into an elevator, and out onto the road. It's only now, amid this impossible nightmare, that I consider what I will be walking away from when I've threatened it all these years. My history. My heritage. Or, more to the point, what I'll be walking away for. A relationship with a man who forced me to give up everything I am. A man who laid down an ultimatum. It doesn't matter that I was prepared to leave only weeks ago, because I made that decision. Not anyone else. It was me. But the stakes are now higher, the consequences more severe. And Josh only seems to be thinking of himself. How very fortunate of him to have that luxury. I, however, do not. I have to live my life on a knife-edge of guilt, responsibility, and an unreasonable sense of pride that I want rid of. I have too many depending on me.

"Ma'am?" Damon asks, looking at me carefully. I blink at him and realize we're standing on the pavement in broad daylight, men shielding my body, the door to the car open for me. "You should get in."

I shake myself out of my reverie and step forward, sliding into the car.

"Addie!" Eddie falls across the back seat and crashes into me.

I look at him, alarmed, my nose wrinkling from the rancid stench of him. "Goodness, you smell like a brewery."

"How would you know what a brewery smells like?" He grins, and it's boyish, familiar, but it doesn't make me feel any better.

"You're drunk." I shake my head in disapproval, looking to Damon when he gets in the car. "Where has he been?"

"His Royal Highness has developed a bit of a fondness for Club 62." He starts the car and waits for the convoy up front to pull away before following.

"Ah!" Eddie flops forward, gripping the back of the passenger seat to get close to Damon. "You can't call me that anymore, Damon.

I'm not Royal. Eddie will do."

I disregard my silly brother, my frown deep. "Club 62? I've never heard of such a place. What is it?"

"Shhhh," Eddie slurs, falling into the door when Damon takes a turn. "Don't tell her, it's a secret."

"A gentleman's club, ma'am. One that is highly unsuitable for ladies like yourself. Any ladies, in fact." His eyes meet mine in the mirror. "Unless you work there, of course."

My mouth drops open. "A strip club?"

"Arhhh, Damon," Eddie whines. "You've broken the blood oath."

"I'm not a member, Your Highness, therefore I can't break the blood oath."

My head swings back and forth between the two men, astounded by what is transpiring. "Eddie, you cannot be frequenting such places." The scandal will be outrageous.

"I can do whatever the hell I like, thank you very much. And since I'm apparently unfit for royal duty, I believe I will make the most of it." He suddenly takes on a faint shade of green, swallowing repeatedly. "Oh no."

"What?" I ask, scanning him up and down.

"Oh, shit." Damon says from up front, just as Eddie catapults toward me, retching.

And throws up in my lap.

"Oh my God," I breathe, my hands coming up, the stench immediately filling the car.

"Oopsy daisy." Dragging himself up, Eddie flops back, his brow shiny with a sheen of sweat. And then he laughs. "I just threw up all over the Queen of England." He chuckles, wiping his mouth with his cuff. "Fuck, I've really made it."

"You are despicable," I say indignantly, whimpering at the mess in my lap. "Damon, pull over." I can feel it seeping through the material of my dress, warming my thighs.

"Afraid not, ma'am." He motions to the windscreen, and I look out, seeing nothing but bumper-to-bumper traffic.

"Marvelous," I grunt. "Am I supposed to sit here for the entire journey home with Eddie's vomit all over me?"

My answer is a shrug from Damon and a giggle from Eddie. So I sit deathly still, for fear of spreading the mess, all the way to Kellington, smelling to high heaven.

But at least this particular misery of mine can be fixed with a long shower.

Everything else that reeks of misery in my life is out of my control.

7

I STAND UNDER the spray for the longest time, staring at the tiles before me. After my long soak in the bath and being in the shower for an age washing away Eddie's vomit, my skin has become crinkled. I look at my hands and sigh. The tips of my fingers are lined and opaque. They look old.

Reaching forward, I shut off the shower and take a towel, patting down my body before wrapping my hair in a bun. I slip into my robe and go to the sink, grabbing my toothbrush. As I scrub my teeth, I stare into my glassy eyes, and each time I blink, I see him. How did such a wonderful moment turn into something so horrid? I spit, rinse, and wedge my hands against the edge of the sink, dropping my chin, breathing deeply. If today has taught me anything, it's that Josh and I are more than worlds apart. We're a whole universe apart—a big, black hole of resentment separating us. He doesn't understand, and I was so depending on him to do so. I was a fool for even momentarily believing I could have the best of both worlds. I want the satisfaction of proving so many naysayers wrong, and I want the injection of life that only Josh can give me. But in my world, there is only my world. I have to let one go, and

I don't have a choice of which world it should be. Josh is right. I can only be one queen.

Not my calling? His doubt hurts more than anyone else's.

Feeling drained of energy and grit, I wander into my suite, ready to collapse into my bed and sleep for as long as my mind will allow. Perhaps tomorrow I will relocate my fortitude and reason. Perhaps this ache in my heart will have faded to something closer to bearable. I pull the blankets up to my chin protectively, rolling onto my side.

No sooner have I closed my eyes, the door knocks and opens, Kim appearing. She's armed with her phone, a grey suit today's armor. "What is it, Kim?" I ask, not even lifting my head from the pillow.

"Are you ill?" She takes in my reclined form, clearly very shocked to find me in bed. It's not even teatime. "Shall I call Dr. Goodridge?"

"No. I'm just tired."

"Well, duty calls, I'm afraid." She scans the room, noting my discarded clothes on the floor. A quick raise of her hand has a maid appearing, who scampers around my room collecting my things.

"I'm done with duty for today," I tell her with lacking strength. "I would like to be left in peace." Whatever else could there be to tend to? I'm very certain I've been over every royal protocol and issue in existence this past week, and today has been particularly testing. I'm done for the day.

Kim disappears into my dressing room and reappears a moment later with one of my dresses—a blue formal piece, with black piping on the seams and hem. "I'm afraid there is no peace for you in the foreseeable future." A small tilt of her head and a mild wave of sympathy across her face is an acknowledgment of the challenging times ahead for me. "Her Royal Highness Princess Helen has requested an audience."

Kim's news has me slowly pulling myself up into a sitting position. "Why?" I ask, despite knowing that Kim will not have that information. I've barely been able to look at Helen on the few occasions I've shared company with her, and I know she's been unable to look at me.

Her lips straight, Kim lays my blue dress across the back of a chair. "She said it's of great importance."

I'm sure it is. It's a rather large coincidence that I was officially sworn in only a week ago, the world told I am their Queen, and my sister-in-law, who is carrying my dead brother's illegitimate child, shows up, *demanding* to see me. Maybe I should be surprised it's taken her this long. No one gets an audience with the Queen on demand. I should refuse her. Send her away. But, annoyingly, I'm curious to hear what she has to say for herself.

"Very well." I drag myself out of bed. "Is Jenny here?"

Kim dips her head and backs away. "I'll send her up."

"Thank you, Kim." I'm not above getting myself ready, but, truth be told, I'm lacking the energy to do even that. Besides, I have a feeling I need to conserve what strength I have left to take on Helen.

❧

AS I TAKE the stairs to the foyer, Kim by my side advising me of many things that I need to be advised of, I watch as staff crisscross the foyer of Kellington. The bustle seems busier today, and I definitely spot a few additional faces. "What is Sid doing here?" I ask, seeing the Master of the Household from Claringdon directing footmen here and there.

"A little restructure, I believe." Kim goes back to her phone, scrolling down the screen. "Where was I? Oh, yes. The official visit to Spain has been postponed for the interim, and I've put an itinerary for the next month in your office at Claringdon."

"Why wouldn't you just put it in my office here at Kellington?"

"Because your official office is now at Claringdon."

"That's my father's office." I'll never see that office as anything but my father's.

"As Sovereign, and like many before you, it is now *your* office, ma'am. But until the logistics of your working space is established, I have also put a copy on your office desk here at Kellington."

Then why didn't she just say that? "My office here will remain my office." I come to a stop at the bottom of the stairs and take in the chaotic scene in dismay. This is one of the very reasons I refused to move my residence to Claringdon. It's like a circus there, not a home, and now with the restructure, it is like a circus here, too. "Like headless chickens," I mumble, watching Felix scurry across the tiles with his phone to his ear, two new faces in tow, undoubtedly part of the restructure. I don't need to ask Kim what's got Kellington's head of communications all in a fluster. When we arrived with an unconscious Eddie, Damon was pulled into Felix's office to give every tiny detail of his rescue mission, probably including who was in a five-mile radius of this gentleman's club my brother has become quite fond of. "Where's Helen?"

"In the lounge, ma'am. I'll escort her to your office in a few moments."

"Right then." I cut through the madness, determined to get through this next testing encounter quickly.

When I arrive at the door of my office, I brush my hair over my shoulder and my dress down, pushing my way into the room. "Oh, for crying out loud," I snap, immediately spotting the monstrosity I ordered out of my father's office at Claringdon. I didn't mean for it to be relocated. I meant for it to be thrown on a fire. Is Sir Don purposely trying to rile me? "Felix," I shout, spotting him hurrying past the door toward his office.

He stops and reverses, poking his head around the door. "Yes, ma'am?"

"I realize it's not in your job description, but please find someone to get rid of this thing." I throw my arm up toward the giant portrait without looking at the hideousness.

Felix can't hide his horror, either. Good. I'm thrilled he also thinks it is awful. "Burn it?" he asks.

"You read my mind." I take myself around my desk and lower to the chair. "How is damage control coming along?"

"His Royal Highness Prince Edward's new favorite playground is impenetrable. If anyone talks, they get thrown out. So no one is talking."

"That has to be a good thing, surely?"

"Oh, it is most definitely a good thing, Your Majesty. It's only because of Damon's connections we found out about it. I never knew it existed, and I would like to think there are not many things I do not know about in this world."

"Quite," I agree, eyeing Felix curiously. Is he making a point? Telling me something without telling me? I never got to officially declare my relationship with Josh prior to my father's death, but the mere fact that my American lover was with me when I returned to Claringdon after the royal helicopter crash spoke volumes, even if it has been unspoken of since by the few of my father's advisors who witnessed my homecoming. At least, unspoken with me. Kind of like a silent mutual understanding, yet I know behind the scenes, action was taken to limit *that* particular scandal. And I know because Josh told me of the warning he received. Too bad for them he didn't heed it. Or is it too bad for me? Does Felix know? Is he telling me without telling me he knows? Does he know where I was earlier today? My brain spasms at that thought, my mind back in the suite at Hotel Café Royal with Josh. The bliss. And then the horrible row.

"Ma'am?" Felix prompts, and I snap my wandering mind back to the here and now. "Is that all?"

"That is all." I drop my eyes to my desk and come face to face with a pile of cards emblazoned with the Royal Coat of Arms, a pen set to the side. And to the left, a few drafted press announcements for my approval.

Signing them with a heavy hand, I toss the lies into my tray, ready for Kim to collect. More smoke. More mirrors. I pick up the sheet of paper that details my schedule for the next month, a list of endless royal engagements and appearances. I feel a headache coming on just reading it. "And when does one get to recuperate?" I ask myself, scanning the list of dates. It's non-stop, starting with a state dinner at the White House next week, of which I am the guest of honor. I'm there for twenty-four hours before I return to England to have my first official meeting with the Prime Minister. I yawn without thought. And then the next week, I must travel to Portsmouth to christen a new warship that has been named in my honor. My eyes fall down the never-ending list, my heart falling with it. This is my life now. In order to show my father what I'm made of and protect the wretched secrets of this family, I must fulfil these duties and a whole lot more. For the rest of my days. Because if I do not, there will be anarchy. Lives ruined. I drop the paper and slump back in my chair, feeling overwhelmed and so completely helpless. It is not the best frame of mind to be in when I'm about to face my formidable sister-in-law.

My eyes fall to the door when I hear the knock, though I stall welcoming Kim into the room until I've straightened up in the chair and pulled my mask back into place. How many times? How many times will I do that from this day forward? Suck in a deep breath, brace myself to face my foe. "Come in," I call, joining my hands and resting them on the desk before me.

Kim enters, standing by the open door. "Her Royal Highness Princess Helen, Your Majesty."

The fact that this woman has a royal title is even more laughable than me having one. Her crime, trying to cheat the line of succession in her own favor, is beyond my comprehension. Here I am, conflicted between fighting my royal status and embracing it, often thinking of ways out of this hell, and there is Helen, who so desperately wanted to take on this madness, who got pregnant by another man to secure her position.

She appears, as pristine and well-turned-out as always, every hair on her pretty head perfectly in place. She's in black, a demon-stration of her continued state of mourning. The bow of her head is minimal and forced, no graciousness in sight. And she doesn't address me, not by title nor by name. Impudent woman. Although she does wait to be invited to sit.

"Please," I say, waving a hand to the chair opposite me, which she takes, quietly and calmly. I'm attempting to understand her intention but failing terribly. "You asked to see me."

"Yes, I wanted to clarify my position within the family." Her chin lifts in an act of confidence, which I determine rather quickly is fake.

I sit up straight, never taking my eyes from hers. It's a bit of a staring deadlock, something I would never usually engage in, but with Helen, I cannot resist. Every word this woman has ever spoken to me has been drenched in disdain. Now is no different. "I believe the Queen Mother already clarified your position."

"She told me nothing more than my secret was safe. You were there, if I recall." She's stoic, deadpan, completely emotionless.

"You recall correctly." I collect the glass of ready-poured water to the side of my desk and drink half, moistening my parched mouth. "So am I to assume you are here now to establish what privileges you will retain?" I should strip her of everything, yet the message that might give won't be welcomed by anyone.

"For my silence, yes."

"Your silence?" I all but cough. "You mean the matter of you betraying the Heir Apparent?"

"I did what was necessary to keep the Monarchy stable. The King made it clear I was to produce an heir."

And once again I am reminded of the pressure my father ruth-lessly inflicted in the name of his throne. "I think he meant with his son, Helen."

Her jaw pulses steadily. "Don't you think we tried? For years I've waited each month in the hopes it would be the news I wanted. It never was. I was desperate. What would you have done?"

"We are not talking about me."

"Oh, probably sensible. We could be here quite a while if we were to go over every detail of *your* crimes. And now you're Queen? It's a mockery to the throne." She snorts her disgust, waving a deranged hand in the air. The cool, calm woman who walked into my office has long gone, and I fear I'm heading toward unhinged as well. "And Eddie's deeply affected by his military service? Since when? There's something more to it, there has to be, and Lord knows it must be something serious if they're prepared to let Eddie step aside and hand *you* the crown."

I'm not quite sure what happens, but I'm up from my chair quickly, leaning across the desk. "Enough," I grate, outraged, but not in the least bit surprised Helen would hit below the belt. "Matters of this family are no longer any of your concern. Edward is struggling with readjusting on homeland, and *we* support him." My words are spoken for the sake of it. Helen will know a lie has been fabricated to mask a monster scandal. Of course she'll know, but it is not her concern. My fierce need to protect Eddie overwhelms me, not only from Helen, but from the world. "You may have taken great pleasure in bringing me down over the years, may have gotten away with it, but you will not get away with it any longer. I am your Queen, and you will treat me as such." I don't think I've ever taken greater pleasure in saying those words, and I seem to be saying them an awful lot.

Helen retreats in her chair, her surprise obvious.

"Who is the father?" I question, turning her surprise into squirming.

"That is not your concern now, is it?"

Not my concern? "Am I to be prepared for any unexpected stories from unexpected men to hit the media?"

"Let's just say he has a lot more to lose than I have."

I cock my head, but she remains silent. She won't tell me. Do I care? No. Whoever was stupid enough to fall victim to Helen's

scheming, probably some high-profile businessman, deserves to
sweat. If he even knows the child she's carrying is his "I'll ask you
kindly that if there is a risk of anyone crawling out of the woodwork
with some surprise news, you advise me immediately. And for this
silence you speak of, for your cooperation," I continue, "you may
retain your title as Duchess of Oxfordshire, but your love child will
not have one. You will be given an allowance justified by what I, as
Queen, deem appropriate based on the advice of my closest aides.
You will be given accommodation, the Gatehouse in the grounds of
the Holmestead Estate, and when you remarry, you will be required
to vacate the premises. All of those *gifts* will be withdrawn should
you decide to share your secret, but be warned, *Your Highness*, it
will be you who will be scorned should that eventuality arise. You
betrayed my brother's trust. You are lucky you are getting a thing
from me."

Her eyes scream shock, though she's doing a better job of masking it from her face now. She didn't think I had it in me. Honestly,
neither did I. But now I have truly grasped the gravity of the lies
that have shaped my life.

"When did family become so important to *you?*" Helen practically hisses.

"When it became clear they were depending on me to protect
their name and dignity." My answer comes too naturally, like an
instinct I never knew I had. "Do you have anything further to say?"

Her long inhale tells me she has plenty more to say, yet I know
Helen, and she knows what is good for her. Challenging me wouldn't
be good for her. I'll make sure of it, take her title and her privileges,
because I know how much she values them. Helen is not the kind of
person to cut off her nose to spite her face. She wants security and
recognition. So backing down, she clears her throat. "No, ma'am."

"Then we are done." I push my hands onto the desk and stand
up straight, my furious eyes nailed to my sister-in-law. "Goodbye,"
I add, reinforcing the end of our conversation.

Helen slowly stands, looking a little shell-shocked. She turns to leave, and I just can't help delivering one last jab to her stinking attitude. "You will address me appropriately from this moment on, Helen. And as is required, you will bid me farewell and thank me for my time. *Now*."

She swallows, possibly ingesting her pride with it. "Thank you for your time, Your Majesty."

"You may leave."

She's probably wondering what has happened to me. Lies, that's what. Mountains of them that she and the rest of the world will never know about. But those lies will rule me for eternity.

When the door closes, I take a seat for a few moments and breathe through my own shock. I didn't know I had it in me either, but I keep demonstrating small signs of strength and power. The question is, are these bursts of authority my instinctive nature to do what I am supposed to do as a Royal, or are they acts of revenge on the people who buried me alive for so many years? Am I being dictated by bitterness and resentment? I drop my head back and close my tired eyes for a moment, contemplating just that. "Who are you, Adeline?" I ask myself, because I really do not know.

Mine. Josh's voice tumbles through my tangled mind. *You are mine.*

Yet there is no voice claiming that I should be the Queen.

8

THE SCENERY IS different as I'm driven from Ronald Reagan International Airport in Washington, but my thoughts are the same, my mind spinning around the endless questions, as it has done this entire past week. My life hasn't been absent of busyness, but there is one absence I have felt the most.

Josh.

The man who claims to love me fiercely. I have not heard from him. That lack of distraction hasn't helped balance my thoughts. My conflict is as confusing now as it has been since I learned of my succession, my reason swaying on an hourly basis.

I can do this. I can't do this. I can live without Josh. I can't live without Josh. I am supposed to be Queen. I am not supposed to be Queen.

My mind has constantly wandered to Josh, but each time, as if by magic, or maybe because God knows I am distracted, I have been presented with something to do, someone to see, some place to be. And each time I have fulfilled my obligations, I have felt drained and disheartened. No one who carries the crown should begrudge their duties, and I begrudge mine somewhat terribly. And then I have those waves of defiance creep up on me when I am feeling low, hearing my father's curt words.

You are an aberration, Adeline. A disgrace to the Monarchy.

That may be so, but without question, the public has embraced me. Endless reports in the newspapers, the monarchists singing my praises, and even the republicans backing down. At least, that is what I'm told by the PR team and communications. Apparently, reading the tabloids isn't on my priority list. On that note, I take my eyes to my lap and the magazine Kim got for me for the journey to Washington, the one I am yet to turn the first page of. And as soon as I do, I wish I hadn't. "Good grief, why can't he just go away?"

"Pardon, ma'am?" Kim looks at me in alarm, and I slam the cover shut on the exquisite shot of Josh on a red carpet in a tuxedo.

"Pesky fly," I mutter, swatting the window with the magazine. "It's been buzzing in my face since we left the airport."

"It has?" Kim scans the window while I smack my magazine all over it, mentally shaking my head at myself. I'm surprised my brain was so quick to think, since it has been thumping for weeks. When was that picture of Josh taken? Where in the world is he right now? *Stop!*

"I got it," I say, catching Damon's smiling eyes in the rearview mirror. He can stop with that mockery right this minute. I'm holding him entirely responsible for my heartache. Had he not plotted with Josh to get me to his hotel, I would not be feeling so despondent. Of course, I'm passing the blame, but I will only admit that secretly. Nothing could prevent this hopelessness other than the disappearance of all my woes, and that is not likely to happen. Ever.

"The St. Regis, ma'am," Damon announces as we pull up to the hotel. I admire the frontage for a few moments while Damon gets out and calls on his men, and Jenny starts faffing with my hair and makeup, ensuring I don't look like I feel. A wreck. When Damon opens the door, he looks at me with a fond smile. "Ready?"

"No," I admit wryly, taking a deep breath and sliding out. Men move in from every direction, shielding me from the cameras. My visit to the States has been wildly anticipated, the news endless. This scene outside the hotel is not a surprise to me. There are railings in place, police guarding them. I pull my smile from nowhere and keep my chin high. "Thank you," I say, making it into the lobby unscathed.

"This way, ma'am." Kim motions to the elevators, and I'm soon safely inside being whisked to the heavens.

Sir Don and Dr. Goodridge remain quiet, just as they have for most of the journey here. If I'd had my way, I would have left them in London. But it is unheard of for the Monarch to travel without their private doctor and closest aide. I did, however, get away with leaving David Sampson behind, thank God. I'm still feeling disheartened that Davenport didn't report for duty the morning after I paid him a visit. But did I really expect him to accept my offer? Or, more to the point, heed my demand? Deep down, I didn't. But I certainly hoped.

"The itinerary for this evening," Kim says, flashing me her phone. "We are due to arrive at the White House at seven. We must leave by six thirty to ensure our prompt arrival."

"Six fifteen," Sir Don says to the elevator doors, not gracing Kim with his attention. "If we are to arrive promptly, we must leave at six fifteen."

Kim's nostrils flare, her eyes narrowed on Sir Don's back. "Six fifteen," she confirms, giving me her attention again. "Jenny and Olive will be with you by three to help you get ready."

"Three?" I question. Jenny's gotten me ready in an hour before. Why such a long haul?

A small shrug from Kim. "It's America, ma'am. Your dress for the state dinner this evening is highly anticipated. I don't want to disappoint your fans."

"Oh, you funny thing," I say, letting Damon lead when the doors open and Sir Don and Dr. Goodridge have opened the path for me. "So what you are saying is, I have to knock them dead?" I ask over my shoulder. I catch Sir Don's tired eyes, and I take the greatest pleasure from it.

"Your face will be on every magazine, newspaper, and television tomorrow." Kim grins. "So, yes, let's knock them dead. The world is watching, ma'am. It's your first state dinner *and* with the most powerful country in the world."

"Quite," I muse. No one ever told me twice to pull out all the stops when it comes to my attire. "Then we will do just that," I say, breezing into the suite, feeling a little . . . powerful. And it isn't because the whole of America is watching me. It's because I know Josh will be. Being Queen of England is not my calling? We'll see about that.

I take one of the bags from Olive. "Make sure this is sparkling brightly for this evening," I say, handing the case to Kim.

"What is it?" She rests the bag on a nearby table and flips the catch. I don't answer and instead let her discover for herself. As soon as she's seen what is in the case, she darts her eyes to mine. But she doesn't get to voice her concern.

Sir Don steps in. "Ma'am, you must wear the Sovereign's crown. That tiara is a Spanish Royal Family heirloom."

"I'm wearing my grandmother's tiara." I dismiss his concern and head for the bedroom, not prepared to be told what to do. Not today. Not by him. I'm in control.

9

I STAND IN front of the mirror while Jenny perfects my tousled waves, telling myself off when I realize I'm nibbling my bottom lip. I'm nervous, and I'm a little mad with myself for being so. This is my first official engagement. This is the first time I'm officially representing my country as Queen. "Good grief," I murmur, circling my swishing tummy with a clammy palm.

"Everything okay?" Jenny asks, and Kim looks up from her phone where she's sitting on the couch in the window. Olive, bless her, remains quiet, waiting for another order from Jenny. She's taking her new role very seriously.

"Yes, fine." I brush them off with a little wave of my hand. "Do I look okay?" I ask, making all three women frown. Never before have I asked that question, and it is a huge giveaway to my internal doubt.

Kim shakes her head mildly, going back to her phone, and I can't help but smile. She's wearing a dress. She never wears a dress. "You look particularly lovely this evening," I say as Jenny smooths down the back of my floor-length, strapless, black satin gown.

A tired eye peeks up at me from her phone. "And?"

"And you look lovely," I repeat on a miniscule shrug.

Jenny rearranges the diamond choker that's circling my neck and adds dangling diamond-encrusted earrings to my lobes. "Can you walk okay?" she asks, nodding to where my dress fits tightly until it splays mid-thigh and pools on the floor.

"Well, I made it from the bathroom to here without stumbling. Goodness, could you imagine that? Me taking a tumble in front of all those people?" My nerves escalate, and Jenny dabs my cheeks, probably blotting away the nervous sheen of sweat that's just sprung up on my face. My heels have held me up all my adult life. They won't fail me now.

"This is very unlike you." She goes to her makeup case and pulls out a tray. "What's happened?"

"What's happened?" I laugh. "Do you really need to ask that question, Jenny? A few weeks ago, I was Princess Adeline of England. Defiant, reckless, and lightyears away from the throne. Today, I'm standing in the suite of the St. Regis preparing to attend my first official state dinner at the White House as Queen of bloody England, with millions of people watching."

She doesn't say a word, just holds up two lipsticks. One red, my signature color, and the other a subtle nude. My eyes jump from one to the other, torn. It wouldn't usually cause me such a headache to pick a color for my lips. Red. Always red. But today for some unknown reason, I'm gravitating towards the pretty, non-scandalous nude. Why? "Nude. No, red." I nod, and Jenny pops the lid and twists the color up. "No, nude," I blurt. "God, whatever is wrong with me?" I pace to the bed and perch on the end, feeling at the heavy choker decorating my neck. "No, red." I stand again. "I'm not changing my lip color to appease the stuffy institution. This dress needs red, therefore it shall have red." I put myself back in front of the mirror. "Red," I affirm.

"Red it is." Jenny gets to work painting my lips, and once she's done, she steps back and assesses them. "Lady Danger. Perfect."

"Pardon?"

She holds up the MAC lipstick. "It's called Lady Danger, ma'am."

"How ironic," I muse, rolling my lips and pouting them slightly, deciding that Jenny is right. The red is perfect. And there's no question I am a lady of danger.

"And now this." Jenny approaches, holding my grandmother's elegant tiara, a small smile on her face. "You really are going against the grain, aren't you?"

"They'd have me in a horrendous suit in a heartbeat if I allow it. Could you imagine?" I bet Sir Don is out there right now, waiting to see if I meet his approval. I laugh on the inside. I'm glad I chose red lips.

Jenny laughs and slips the tiara on my head, fixing the hair framing my face once she's done. On a small nod of approval, she steps back and opens the way to my reflection. "It's really very stunning," she muses.

I get the full length of me, top to toe. "Indeed," I murmur, reaching up to feel it, the weight bordering uncomfortable already. The last time I had this tiara on my head, Josh was . . .

I close my eyes and let the memory take hold. It's too powerful to fight off. His palm on my backside. The sting. The sense of abandon. The sound of his voice. His presence that brings me peace. And then his final words.

You can be your country's queen, or you can be my queen. You can't be both.

My heart squeezes painfully. Anger rises from my toes. His doubt. His lack of faith in me to do this job and do it well. He's no better than the other bastards who've made my life miserable. Who question me.

Except Josh can hurt me more.

I can't let him. I open my eyes and drink in my form once more. I look formidable. And I must believe I am.

"I'm ready."

"I think the world will be dazzled." Damon's voice pulls my eyes to the door, where my beloved bodyguard is standing regarding me fondly. "You look beyond beautiful, ma'am."

"Oh, stop," I scoff softly. "You'll make me blush."

"Can I have a quiet word?"

"Oh?" I cock my head, and Damon motions to a private room outside my bedroom. I lead on, intrigued, catching Sir Don on the other side of the room as I pass through, his eyes following Damon and me. He's wondering where we're going. Wondering what Damon has to tell me. I relish the knowledge of his curiosity. Lifting my chin, I enter the room and wait for Damon to shut the door behind us. "What is it, Damon?" I ask quietly.

"Princess Helen, ma'am."

I straighten, a little worry coming over me. "What about her?"

"I hope you don't mind, but I took it upon myself to have a little dig around."

Oh. Interesting. As if I would mind. "And what did your dig turn up?"

"Gerry Rush, ma'am."

My eyes could pop out of my head. "What?"

He nods at my evident shock. "I believe they had an indiscretion a few months ago at a charity gala in honor of war heroes. Mr. Rush donated generously to the foundation."

I don't believe this. "And then donated generously to Princess Helen."

"It would appear so, ma'am."

"Well, isn't that interesting," I muse, starting to pace, unsure whether I should laugh or be disgusted. "The man just can't keep it in his pants, can he?"

"Apparently not. I expect that is why he was trying to contact you. To advise you before you found out from someone else." I frown, prompting Damon to go on. "He was bewitched by you, I believe."

I laugh. "Indeed. So he wanted to explain himself, did he?

Thought I would fall into his arms and declare my undying love for the rogue once he'd explained it meant nothing?"

Damon smiles mildly. "Should I limit damage control?"

"Was he with his wife at the time?"

"She was at the event with him, ma'am."

I laugh. "How cozy." He really is a Lothario. A love rat of the worst kind. Whatever was I thinking, falling for his charm that evening at the Opera House? God, he had my sister-in-law before me? My stomach rolls in revulsion.

I reach up to my forehead and breathe in deeply. "Thank you, Damon." I head for the door. "I'm sure Rush will be more than compliant if he's asked nicely to keep his mouth shut." The man was terrified he'd lose his shining reputation when I was stupid enough to get myself caught up in his web. I doubt very much he'll drop any surprise announcements, but a quiet word in his ear won't hurt to ensure his silence. "And if he's a little uncooperative, perhaps remind him of the photographs we have of him and a certain hooker." Listen to me. I sound like . . . my father.

Another deep breath.

Opening the door, I roll my shoulders and swallow down my apprehension as Olive comes forward with the final touch to my outfit. I take in the sash decorated with the Royal Family Order of my father. "It doesn't really match what I'm wearing, does it?" I quip, letting her place it over my head and under my arm.

"It's a necessity," Sir Don says what I know, as Kim joins me by the mirror and hands me my purse. "Now, tonight. If you find yourself wanting to move along, be rid of someone, or need the restroom, what is the signal?"

"I'll fiddle with the earring in my right ear if I need the ladies'. My left ear if I'm bored out of my mind."

I flick my eyes to my reflection and find Sir Don with straight lips. I would love to leave him here with Dr. Goodridge. Alas, I grudgingly accept that *that* will never happen, not on such an important visit. "Did you catch that, Sir Don? The signal?"

"I did, ma'am."

I smile brightly. "Very good."

Looking at her watch and then to Damon, Kim takes a huge breath. "Ready?" Bless her heart. I know this evening is just as big a deal for her, too. Her first outing as private secretary to the Queen. She is probably as bewildered by the sharp turn of my life as I am. And having Sir Don judging her every move won't help her nerves.

"Ready." Damon nods and waits for me to approach before taking his customary hold. Really, his action is highly inappropriate, was when I was a princess, and even more so now I am Queen. But his gesture has always calmed me somewhat. And I know he knows that.

"Stop being nervous," he whispers, keeping his focus forward. "It doesn't suit you."

"I can't help it." Suddenly, everything about tonight is a little overwhelming.

"I assure you, they will be more nervous than you. Just be yourself."

I laugh. "Really, Damon? That's exactly what I shouldn't be. Sir Don is probably mentally praying I don't screw up." The man didn't shut up on the flight, detailing everything I should know about this evening. I can't deny, though, I didn't take much in. I was too lost in other thoughts.

"Says who?" Damon flips me a cheeky wink as we step onto the elevator, and the familiar, comforting sight lessens my nerves a smidgen. He'll be with me all night, and *that* alone takes the edge off my nerves. Dipping, he looks left to Kim before whispering in my ear. "If you need a cigarette, just give me the nod and I'll make it happen. I have mints, anti-bacterial hand gel, and a miniature of your favorite perfume. We're all set."

"My, my." I chuckle. "You are wasted as my head of protection."

He sniffs and straightens to his full, tall height. "*One* must keep the boss lady happy."

I nudge him in the arm with my shoulder, and he grins at the door. "Very funny."

"I know. When the elevators open, walk straight ahead, not too quickly, and remember to smile."

I nod and take a breath.

I'm ready for you, world.

❦

I STILL HAVE black dots in my vision when we arrive at the entrance of the White House, blinking over and over again to try and clear them. Outside the hotel was bedlam, the flashes and shouts on an entirely new level to anything I have experienced in England.

Beyond the grounds of the White House, it was chaotic, endless police cars deployed to contain the crowds. And here inside the grounds, it's bursting with press, but far more civilized. "Oh gosh," I breathe, not for the first time wondering why on earth I'm feeling so jittery. I've done this all before, not as Queen, granted, but the protocol is pretty much the same. I'm just more important now than I was back then. It's pressure. Pressure not to give the doubters more reason to doubt me. And then I have to ask myself . . .

If deep down I don't want to do this, then why do I truly care?

The red carpet spilling down the steps of the North Portico of the White House is crisp, not a crease in sight. Members of the US Military flank the doors, all armed, one at the bottom of the steps saluting my car as it slows to a stop. Flashes burst from the press gallery, and the President of the United States stands at the top of the steps, pristine in a black dinner suit, the First Lady to his side. She could be mistaken for a model, her willowy frame encased in a white gown. She's twenty years younger than the President, who is approaching fifty.

"Am I attending a state dinner or a wedding?" I ask quietly, noting a train on her dress that would put to shame the twenty-foot-long train my mother dragged down the aisle on her wedding day. The First Lady is also wearing a tiara, white satin gloves to her elbows, and diamonds dripping from every possible place they could drip.

"Melitza Paston had her wedding taken care of the second Ed Twaine was tipped to win the election a year ago," Kim muses. "The country is divided on her. Power-hungry gold-digger, I believe was the latest headline."

"But they love him," I say, watching as the First Lady fidgets on the stairs. I haven't had the pleasure of meeting either of them yet. The last time I was in America, the President was a podgy, balding, cheery man who clearly drank too much if the rose of his cheeks was anything to go by. Ed Twaine, on the other hand, is a rather dashing man, with grey hair and a certain friendly twinkle in his blue eyes.

The soldiers all shift their guns and a few drill commands are shouted before the reverberations of their boots stamping the ground reach me in the car. Damon exits swiftly, pulling in his suit jacket as he rounds the car, standing back while the saluting soldier opens the door for me. A quick look to the heavens, a deep breath, and I find my smile. I gather the bottom of my dress and step out of the car.

"When you're ready, ma'am," Kim says, motioning to the waiting President and First Lady.

I take the steps like a pro, gracefully, elegantly, and surprisingly steadily. "Your Majesty," the President says softly, tilting his head so very slightly. "How wonderful it is to have you here." I offer my hand, which he takes graciously, his smile making his happy eyes twinkle more.

"Mr. President, thank you for your kind invitation."

"Not at all. Please, this is the First Lady, Melitza." He sweeps an arm out to his wife.

Camera flashes go wild behind us as the First Lady offers her hand to me. I feel the President tense, and I think I hear Sir Don

sigh. The First Lady obviously realizes her error and quickly retracts her hand. Then she curtseys, and I can do nothing more than
watch in stunned disbelief. It's not just a normal one-foot behind
the other and a slight bend at the waist. No. The First Lady gives
me a full-on bow, her hands grasping her dress and pulling it out
at the sides as she does.

Oh . . . dear.

Feeling tremendously awkward, I flick a look to Sir Don, who is
clearly as stunned as I am. Straining a smile, I take Melitza's elbow
and encourage her up, aware the cameras are going bonkers behind
me, and without doubt, her faux pas will be splashed all over the
papers tomorrow. She looks at me, a little startled. "No need to
curtsey," I say, having her dart a confused gaze to the President.

I can see his despair, though he is trying to conceal it, and his
wife mouths a *sorry* at him.

I widen my smile, trying to ease the obvious onslaught of embarrassment. "Happens all the time," I assure her, moving between
them when the President motions me there. The flashes are soon in
my face from every angle, though it's all rather calm and controlled
as we pose for the waiting press.

"I hope your journey was pleasant, ma'am," the President says,
motioning us along the red carpet toward the doors.

"Very good, thank you. Although I'm left wondering what one
has to do to get her very own Air Force One."

The President laughs, as does his wife, though her delayed
chuckles are a sign that she's not as quick to catch on. "I think the
royal tradition of flying British Airways is very charming," he says
as we walk.

"You fly on a regular plane?" Malitza looks at me like the world
has gone mad.

"I don't think the royal helicopter would get me here," I tell her,
and for a moment I fear she's wondering why. "Too far, you see."

"Of course." She smiles, taking her beauty up a few notches, her eyes taking in my gown as we wander through the doors. "Your dress is just stunning."

"Thank you." I look over my shoulder to see Damon, Sir Don, and Kim not far behind, the other members of my entourage having dispersed, except for Olive, who is super vigilant, her eyes watching for anything I may need. I find myself winking at her as she comes to a stop behind me, her eyes just about ready to pop out of her stunned head. She's gazing around the space like a mesmerized child.

The President motions for the First Lady to continue through the large double doors as he slows his pace to meet mine. "My deepest condolences on the tragic loss of His Majesty King Alfred and His Royal Highness Prince John."

I smile, if a little tightly, yet I am profoundly grateful he took the initiative to include my brother when extending his sympathy. I feel increasingly maddened by the lack of reference to John while the country mourns their King. "Thank you." We enter a huge room, which I recognize from photographs of my father's state visit five years ago. The East Room. "One could never even begin to fathom the mysterious workings of God," I say quietly. Because he put me in the White House this evening with the President of the United States and all these people looking at me like I could walk on water.

All attention pointing my way, I come to a stop with the President and the First Lady. There must be a hundred people, all dressed to the nines, though none of them upstage the First Lady. Not even me.

After a man, the curator, I believe, has a few words with the President, I'm invited to meet the line of people to my right, all smiling brightly at me. It's daunting, and I only realize when I spot an official photographer at the end of the line that my face must tell them all so. I quickly correct my slip-up and glance across to Damon. Eyes on mine, he lifts his chin subtly, prompting mine to lift with it. I smile my thanks and move to the first person in the line.

The President introduces her, though she needs no introduction. "The Vice President, ma'am."

She waits for me to offer my hand and takes it lightly, no over-the-top curtsey, obviously having received the memo on etiquette when greeting a Royal. The one the First Lady missed. "Your Majesty."

Over the next half hour, Kim keeps close company as I work my way down the line of congressmen, diplomats, and governors. One thing I have learned in my years of royal engagements is not to try and remember everyone's name. That isn't going to change now. It would be impossible. So, if I encounter any of these lovely people again this evening, I will depend on them to reintroduce themselves, which they usually do.

"And this, ma'am," the President says, taking me to the very last person in the line, "is Senator Jameson, though I believe you have already had the pleasure."

My mouth goes somewhat lax when presented to him, and I lose all brain functionality, forgetting myself for a split second. *Hand. Offer him my hand.* I know what I should be doing, but my arm simply won't lift. The Senator must see my struggle, and he must deem it appropriate to break protocol to help me out. I'm grateful.

Taking my hand from my side, he lifts it to his mouth and rests his lips on the back for just a second before laying his other palm across the top. "I could not be more honored to greet you as Queen. Your father would be so proud." He affectionately rubs the back of my hand, the sincerity of his words disarming me further. My throat seems to swell, my mind telling me not to blink and encourage the tears currently pinching the back of my eyes to fall.

Adding to my stupor, every snapshot of my time with Josh stampedes through my mind destructively. I swallow, I clear my throat, I will the tears back. But I can't talk, can't possibly get any words past the lump blocking my throat. It's too much. The Senator's words, who he is, and not only because he was good friends with my father. And like he knows I'm thinking all of this, he simply nods and passes me to Kim.

"Ma'am?" Kim's concerned form crowds me. "What is—?" She

recoils, the penny obviously dropping. "Oh."

I close my eyes, wishing Kim wasn't aware of my affair with Josh. She's also privy to the welts he left on my skin after that fateful night partying at Kellington, even if I didn't confirm the source of my injuries. "All is well."

"Let's hope his son didn't get an . . ." Her whisper fades off, and though I'm not looking in the same direction, I know what I'll see when I do.

"Please say it isn't so," I beg.

"It's so."

Panic eats me on the spot, locking down every muscle I have. Why didn't I anticipate this? Why, oh why, did I not see this coming? His father is a senator and good friends with my father. Every country that has a state visit traditionally invites guests that share a connection to the visiting country, so it would be obvious to have Senator Jameson here.

Don't look. It is what I am telling myself over and over as I fight to find the will to move when gestured by the President. Any hope I had of finding the strength and poise I need to get through this evening like a real queen is slipping further from my grasp. A week has passed with no contact. For a week, I've fought back my thoughts and feelings. For a week, my mind has wandered unstoppably to Josh—where he is, what he is doing. I assumed he was in America, but in Washington? At the White House? Here, now?

"You need to move along, ma'am," Kim says quietly. "Sir Don is watching carefully."

"Right, yes."

"And smile."

I realize with Kim's prompt that my face is lax, all shock, and it is a horrendously huge effort to rectify that. "Of course." I breathe in and force my lips into something as close to a smile as I can manage.

"And stop shaking." Kim looks at me out the corner of her eye, her mouth a line of worry.

I'm trembling from head to toe, adrenaline and fear making it impossible to stop. "I believe I need the bathroom." It's no good. A timeout is imperative, a few moments away from the staring faces so I can pull myself together.

"I think that's a very good idea." Kim has a quick word with the nearby curator, who is keen to show us personally to the restrooms.

"Please, excuse me," I say to the President. "All that water I drank on the flight to keep hydrated is catching up with me."

He chuckles. "Take your time, ma'am."

I nod my thank you and follow Kim, my ladies-in-waiting close on my heels to help with anything I may need help with. Can they locate my composure? Set my mask back in place? The crowds part for me as we make our way through, nods and smiles pointing my way. I try my hardest to return them, but with my drastically depleting equanimity, there is an increased urgency to hide myself until I can be sure I have got myself together.

"In here, ma'am." Kim opens a door for me and runs a quick check of the stalls. Once she's satisfied there are no other guests occupying the space, she lets me in. As soon as I pass the threshold, I turn and take the door, halting Olive's intention to follow me in. She jolts to a stop and looks at me in confusion. "I just need a moment," I tell her, ignoring Kim's disapproving look as I shut the door in Olive's perplexed face.

"Oh my goodness, oh my goodness, oh my goodness." I rest my palms on the door and let my forehead meet the wood. I've been here for little over an hour. I have the whole evening to get through, all the while smiling and concentrating on my conversation and duty. I can't possibly think of anything else other than him at the best of times, but when he's lurking in the background? He could have declined his invite this evening. He didn't have to be here. The whole wretched world knows I'm at the White House tonight, so I can't even conclude that perhaps he was unaware. He knew. He knew I'd be here, but despite each conclusion I am reaching, I need to perhaps spend a little time on wondering *why* he is here. Our last encounter was perfection followed by horror. He said things that were both unreasonable and incomprehensible. Whether he realizes it or not, he threw an ultimatum at me, and despite part of his speech being somewhat accurate, his selfishness struck me hard. How self-centered he sounded, how unthoughtful and inconsiderate. How he doubts my ability, too. He was thinking only of himself, not of what I would be faced with. Not the backlash my family would be forced to endure because of me. And tonight, coming here knowing I'd see him, shows his selfishness again. It's as though he's taunting me for the lack of choice I have, throwing it in my face. I hadn't thought him capable of such a thing. And I feel so very disappointed. What the hell am I going to do? I can't face him. Can't look at the man I thought I knew so well.

I pull my forehead sharply from the door when a knock vibrates through the wood and sinks into my head. "Yes?"

"Need any assistance?" Kim calls.

I don't know. Do I? Pacing to the mirrors, I take one look at myself and conclude that yes, I do need assistance. Perhaps an escape vehicle to get me away from here. Oh, how I would love to get away from here, and if I were anyone else in the world, I would. But I'm not anyone else in the world, and as I'm continuously reminded, the world is watching. Like hawks. "Come in," I call.

I'm quickly joined by Kim, Olive, and Jenny, and while Jenny tops up my makeup, Olive ensures my tiara is straight. And Kim? She's silent. Worried. Disapproving. I bet she is ready to put the PR people on standby. And I bet they're all waiting in the wings for me to put one foot wrong. I bet my father is looking down and shaking his kingly head at his poor excuse of a daughter. That thought alone has me straightening my shoulders and standing tall. "I'm ready," I declare, taking myself in. I expect Josh saw my barely hidden meltdown. I expect he relished the thought of being the cause.

Chin high, a smile in place, I break away from the hands still working on fixing me and leave the restroom. When I open the door, there is a line of people waiting to get in. "My apologies," I say graciously, heading back to the East Room. "What's next?" I ask Kim as she keeps up with my determined strides.

"Reception drinks, a speech from the President, and then from you. Do you need a refresh, or is it all saved?"

"I read that speech one hundred times on the flight. I could say it in my sleep."

"Good. Put emphasize on the finale, passion in your voice. We reserved British need to let go a little when we're with the Americans."

I wince a little. "So since I'm here celebrating our diplomatic ties, I should sound pleased about it? Is that what you mean?"

"It would help," Kim replies dryly. Well, I *was* pleased to be here. Until I noticed a certain guest. Now, I'm not pleased at all. Just worried. And hot. "Then after the speeches, dinner and conversation."

"Where is Sir Don?" I ask, knowing he's never far, lurking, waiting for me to trip.

"He's chatting with the mayor of New York. I believe they know each other from their military days. They're being given a tour of the Oval Office."

I breathe out, relieved. "Okay." As we enter the East Room, I don't look for Josh, but focus on the President when he moves in, having been waiting for my return. "I think it may be time to get you a drink."

Yes, a drink. "A man after my own heart," I say, linking arms with him when he offers. I like Ed. Unlike the previous president, he seems a little more real, therefore likable. Mature, distinguished, and charming. "Tell me," I muse as he leads me through the crowds, "how are you finding the demands of leadership?"

"Well." He smiles, nodding to people as we pass through, all of them following our path to the far side of the expansive room. We stop and a waiter steps forward. The President takes a flute of champagne and places it in my hand. "It is demanding, as you would expect. Fulfilling yet draining. But since I signed up for it, I can hardly complain about it." He chinks his glass with mine. "And you? The life is no different, I expect, but the duties more demanding."

"And I didn't sign up for it," I say without thought, ridiculing myself the moment I utter the stupid words. "What I mean is, it was a little unexpected, of course, and one must take the time one needs to adapt."

"If my opinion is of any value, I would say you are doing a fine job so far."

I laugh lightly. "That is very kind of you, if a little untrue."

"How so?"

Blimey, what am I doing showing my weaknesses so freely? Yet Ed has an aura of friendliness so rarely found in my world. "If I'm honest, Ed," I say cheekily, moving in a little so I'm not heard, "all this queen business is a little out of my depth."

"I don't believe you." His smile only enhances his genuine persona. "The world loves you."

"Maybe so, but that does not mean I have the first idea what I am doing. So you must be nice to me." I grin a little, and he laughs.

"It's easy to be nice to people who are genuinely nice themselves."

My smile now is broad, and for the first time in my reign, I feel like I've found a friend. Someone who understands me. "So does that mean I can continue to class you as an ally to my country?"

"I think it does."

"Splendid. The Prime Minister will be pleased when I debrief him on my trip. He's mighty hard to please."

"Oh, Your Majesty, you are really something else." The President takes some champagne, smiling over the rim.

"Why, thank you. I quite like you, too."

We chuckle together, and I gaze around the huge room, spotting Damon on the far side, his presence large but subtle. His discreet thumbs up is returned by myself, and then I give the charming president my attention once again.

And die on the spot the second I see him. "Your Majesty, allow me to introduce you to Josh Jameson."

The vision before me is enough to put me on my knees. The most handsome man alive, as proven in polls the world over, is staring at me intensely. Dressed in an exquisite black suit, the base of a tumbler sits in his palm. His hair is a little tamer today, roughed up carefully with some wax. His skin is tan, sun-kissed perfectly. Has he been somewhere hot? On holiday?

My brain mush, I offer him my hand. He stares at me for a long time, not accepting, and I glance to the President to see if he's noticed the delay. The First Lady has moved in and is talking to him, so, thankfully, no. My hand is still hanging between us when I force my eyes back to Josh, and like it takes every morsel of his strength, he accepts, defying protocol and dropping his mouth to the back of my hand. I don't know what comes over me—a misplaced power, perhaps, or a need to keep control—but I push my hand to his mouth firmly. "How ironic," I murmur quietly, "that it is now *you* who is bowing to *me*."

His lips stretch across the back of my hand as he tightens his hold, slowly lifting his eyes as he straightens. The sparks colliding between us could set the White House alight.

"You may have a crown upon your head, Your Majesty," he whispers, his thumb now moving in slow circles across the back of my hand, "but remember who your king is."

My chest expands, and I quickly snatch my hand away, remembering where I am and who is here. "It is very lovely to see you again," I say calmly.

"Oh, you've met?" the President asks as he joins us again, seeming pleased by this.

"Yes, I've had the pleasure before," Josh muses, the increasing blaze of his stare threatening to reduce me to dust at any moment.

"I attended Her Majesty's birthday garden party with my father."

"Of course. Terrific." The President looks past me when a man approaches, advising him that it's time for the speeches. "Ah, yes. Shall we?"

I smile and rip my eyes away from Josh, ready to be escorted away, but the curator is now talking with the President, and my escape is delayed. It also means Josh gets his opportunity to move in, which he does swiftly, crowding me. "You wore that tiara on purpose."

"I have no idea what you are talking about," I sniff, refusing to look at him.

"Oh, I think you do."

I'm not fooling him, I realize that, but I would never admit what he already knows. I expected him to see it in a picture tomorrow, or perhaps on television. I certainly didn't expect to be facing him.

Braving confronting him, I smile, that simple gesture saying it all. All smugness falls from his face, his chest expanding beneath his suit on a deep, controlled breath. "You have an uncanny ability to render me stupid, Your Majesty."

My head cocks naturally. "I do?"

"You do."

A lazy, provocative smile creeps across my lips, and it's not something I have the desire to stop, no matter how suggestive it may seem. I've never relished rendering a man stupid as much as I relish rendering Josh stupid. Knowing he's as thunderstruck as I am by our blazing chemistry somehow fills the void inside me with confidence. With power. With smugness. "How very inconvenient."

"I think we need to talk."

"I think you said everything perfectly clearly the last time we spoke."

"And I think you're being stubborn." His jaw takes on an edge of tightness. Angry looks good on him. Sexy. Thrilling. Because it is me who is making him angry. Good. Perhaps now he knows how

I was feeling when I left his suite over a week ago.

"I'm not being stubborn, Josh," I state quietly. "I am being strong, and one *has* to be when in my world."

"Are you saying I make you weak?"

"Yes."

"Bullshit. I make you who you really are, Adeline."

My composure falters. His words sting terribly, reminding me that, of all the people in this world, Josh is the only one who really knows me. Yet if he really knew me, wouldn't he realize that simply being here on such an important moment in my new reign would destabilize me? Of course he knows he would make me wobble. Maybe that's his plan, to prove something. Whatever that might be. Unlucky for Josh, I have a bigger point to prove, and it seems I have to prove it to him now, too.

I flit my eyes left and right, catching Kim's apprehension and Damon's caution. Both are ready to move in. "I believe it would be a good idea to avoid each other for the rest of the evening."

"And what about after that?"

"There is no after that," I say calmly, breezing past him when the President gestures the way. How I got myself through that confrontation is a mystery. The ache building inside me is borderline unbearable, and every reason why I love Josh Jameson is quickly monopolizing my head. His passion, his drive, his unapologetic approach to life. And the fact that when it comes to me, he just doesn't give a shit about my status. Although right now, that lack of deference has made me terribly uncomfortable, and I don't like it at all.

10

I SAID THE words I remembered from my speech, but I fear I was robotic rather than passionate. I'm now sandwiched between the President and the First Lady at the head table, and my wine is being kept to a minimum. Honestly, I could grab the bottle from the server and drink the entire thing in a few glorious seconds.

Thankfully, Josh has been seated at the far end of the room, so catching his eye during dinner hasn't happened. That is, until he stands and watches me as he pushes his chair under and fastens the button of his jacket. I look away.

"You know," the First Lady says from beside me, pulling my attention to her. "That Josh Jameson is sinfully handsome but an utter rogue."

"I beg your pardon?" I splutter, startled.

She stills in her chair and looks at me with worried eyes. "Oh God, Your Majesty, please, forgive me. My mouth sometimes runs away with me. It's just, you're so young, and you seem so relatable. I should remember you're the Queen."

My startle wasn't because what she was saying was highly inappropriate, not in the least. I was surprised because she sounds like she knows Josh on a personal level. "There's no need to apologize," I assure her. "Please, go on."

Melitza looks at me, unsure as to whether she should indulge me in such taboo dinner conversation. She shouldn't, no doubt, but my curiosity is raging. So I do a truly despicable thing and use my position of power to get the information I want. "I might be the Queen of England, but I'm still a woman." I take my half-full wine glass and have a tiny sip. "And women talk." I give her a friendly smile. "Just because we take on a job of this magnitude doesn't change the fact that we are women." Am I hearing myself right? "So, you dated him?"

"Yes."

I nod, trying to appear nonchalant. "For long?"

She laughs mildly. "Not at all. I ended it rather swiftly."

She ended it? Damn it. Why does that annoy me? Goodness, is he here for her or me? Are women in high-powered positions his thing? Is it a sick game to him, to nail the most famous woman he can? Well, he's hit the jackpot with me. Reason after reason spirals until my head hurts. "Why?" I ask.

She smiles and looks past me to her husband, and it all becomes clear. Or does it? Ed Twaine is a handsome man, but he has nothing on Josh Jameson. "Josh wouldn't commit. Avoided exclusivity at all costs. Ed gave me what I wanted. Was a safer option."

Safer. Oh, I bet. And if my memory serves me correctly, Melitza got her claws into Ed Twaine very soon after he was tipped to become President. Did Josh spank her? Tie her up? Oh goodness, I can't even ask those questions, and I despise myself for wanting to. I feel like my heart is being scratched.

"Although I have to say," she goes on, "Josh Jameson is an animal in the bedroom."

The woman has no filter. None at all, and I'm not taking responsibility for encouraging her, because I definitely didn't encourage *that* much information out of her. Not out loud, at least. Realizing

I truly didn't want to know, I smile tightly, probably confusing the poor woman, and turn away from her, catching sight of Josh once again. His eyes. There is determination in his stare, and it's making me feel uneasy. Because he is the one and only person in this world who will not respect my position.

"Did you enjoy your dessert, ma'am?" the President asks, forcing me to drag my gaze away from Josh.

"Delicious," I answer, fighting back the pangs of anxiety attacking me. I need distraction. Anything to divert my mind from . . . *him*. We've talked politics and all things official. Maybe some light chit-chat. Something easy. "So how is married life?" I ask, holding my hand up to stop the server pouring more wine into my glass. Sir Don has been watching my wine glass more closely than he has been watching me.

The President's nod is sharp and short. "A whirlwind romance, I believe the press deemed it."

"Oh, take no notice of the press. They don't know high from low."

"Very true," he says softly, and I smile, prompting him to go on. "I know what they say. My age, her age. That she married me for status and power. But what they don't know is that Melitza is a very wealthy woman in her own right."

"Oh?"

"Her father was a private oil tycoon. Billionaire. He passed away when Melitza was a little girl, only two years after she lost her mother."

"Oh, how terribly sad."

"Very. She can be a little ditzy now and then, but she's a very smart woman. Beauty and brains, an absolute whizz on the stock market."

"Then why does the press have such an incorrect misconception of her?"

"Because I'm knocking on fifty and she is twenty-nine. Because she is beautiful. Because despite being intelligent and driven, she doesn't have the time for politics." He smiles across at her fondly, and I can't help but mirror it. Twenty-nine. One year younger than me. Melitza also has a huge responsibility on her shoulders. "I knew marrying her might hamper my chances in the election campaigns, but I wasn't about to let the American public choose who I should be with. I wasn't going to marry someone out of pressure and obligation."

I inwardly flinch. "Why does she not set the record straight? It must hurt to have the press judge her so very wrongly." I can't help the twinge of guilt I have, because I did the same. I judged her.

"She would rather let them get on with things than have them prying into her fortunes and past family tragedies. In her words, she and I know the deal, so what does it matter? I do my job well. The public is happy with the progress we're making during my time in office. Melitza is here to love me and support me, not to win the public's approval.

I don't know whether I'm in awe of Ed, or if I'm jealous. We have more in common than I ever dreamed, but whereas he is brave and doesn't fold under the pressure, I do. "I know what that pressure feels like."

"Oh, I bet you do. I expect they have someone lined up for you to marry without delay."

"There has been someone lined up for quite some time now."

"Haydon Sampson." The President confirms what the world knows. "Can I speak frankly, ma'am?"

"Of course."

"The woman before me is spirited, funny, and beautiful. Don't let them ruin you. Don't let expectation monopolize on your happiness. The world is a fickle place. Traditions are only traditions if we keep them."

I stare at him, unsure if I want to kiss him or cry. "It's a lovely thought, isn't it, Mr. President? To do what one pleases."

"It doesn't have to be a thought. And please, call me Ed."

"Then you must call me Adeline, Ed."

He laughs, a full-on bout of amusement. "I'm afraid I would be ridiculed if I were to do that, ma'am."

I hum my agreement, though on the inside, while I'm grateful for his valor, I'm feeling disheartened by our conversation. It's a shame that breaking tradition will also break my family. "Well, we're talking frankly, after all."

"I'm sorry." He laughs a little in disbelief. "How inappropriate of me."

"We're still human," I remind him. "And who says it is inappropriate?"

"The world, I expect."

"Why, because you are the President and I am the Queen?"

"Well, yes."

"But we are also friends," I point out, and he smiles. "And friends talk about personal things, do they not?"

"I guess they do." Toasting my glass with his, he regards me fondly. "You truly are incredible, Your Majesty."

His compliment makes me smile, though it's ironic. Because everything the President seems to admire about me is everything the British Monarchy dislikes. "Thank you," I murmur.

He extends the bizarre nature of our first meeting by winking at me. "Welcome."

The President of the United States winked at the Queen of England.

And I like him even more because of it.

11

I'VE TALKED TO endless people. From diplomats to well-known movie directors, though our conversations haven't been nearly as enjoyable as my dinner chitchat with the President. I've not once thought about using my secret signals to call in the reinforcements to save me from a conversation. Until now. I reach for my left ear and start fondling with my chandelier earring as a member of congress bores me to tears over a recent bill that's been passed about gun laws in the South and what it might mean for arms dealers. Basically, he's disgusted that it's being proposed to crank down on gun laws. I have plenty to say on the matter, though I realize it will be nothing this idiot wants to hear.

I spot Kim approaching the table, but the President swoops in beside me, extending his hand in the most gentlemanly fashion. "Would Your Majesty do me the honor?"

I look up at him, a little struck. "Dance?" I question, just in case I've misinterpreted his request.

"I promise not to step on your toes."

On a little laugh, I look to my right where Melitza is seated. It's not expected for me to ask, but I'm courteous and respectful. She nods on a smile of gratitude that I would seek her approval before entertaining her husband's request.

"I would love to," I say, rising to my feet. As I walk the length of the table, I'm increasingly aware of the fading of chatter, all guests slowly comprehending what is about to transpire. Sir Don catches my eye, breaking away from a crowd of men—politicians, I expect—and eyes me on my journey toward the dance floor. His face straight, he takes a sip of his water, and I look away from his quiet disapproval. I'm going to dance with the President. So what?

When I reach the dance floor, I take Ed's offered hand. The big band quietens with our arrival, and I curtsey before Ed as he bows to me. "Just one thing," I say as he takes me in his hold. "There isn't much wriggle room in this blessed dress, so please don't fling me too far."

On a deep laugh, he nods to the band and they kick things off with a dramatic drum-roll that has the crowd laughing, as well as me. "Oh my," I chuckle as Benny Goodman's *Sing, Sing, Sing* fills the room. "Did they purposely choose the most energetic song in their repertoire?"

"Well, it is a happy occasion." On a cheeky smile, the President swings me out of his hold until our arms are extended to full length. "Are you ready, Your Majesty?"

"I don't know, am I?" I ask on a wry smile as the room erupts into applause.

"Something tells me you're ready for anything."

I'm pulled back into a light but rather professional hold, and we're off around the floor, twirling and stepping, laughing and throwing in a few dramatics as we go—the odd forced gasp when I'm twirled out and in again, a few claps of the President's hands when they are free. The flashes of cameras come as quickly as the beats of music and our steps, our spectators loving every moment of our show. I am too, my smile fixed and genuine, and by the twinkle in Ed's eyes, he's also having a wonderful time. There isn't an inch of floor space we don't cover. I can't say I'm a good dancer, and I don't think I have ever danced like this, with so much energy and enthusiasm. But the President has moves, and I can only hope he's making me appear to be as good as he is.

As the music builds toward the end, I brace myself for what I expect will be a spectacular finish. I'm not wrong. I laugh as I'm theatrically tipped back over Ed's arm and held there until the music stops completely. And then the cheers start, delight drenching the room. He helps me up to standing and bows. "Your energy knows no bounds." I chuckle, going against the grain and taking his biceps, resting my cheek against his briefly. "Thank you, that was so much fun."

"My pleasure." Taking my hands, he squeezes and smiles, as the band lowers the tone and starts a less vigorous song. "Oh, Fats Waller." He waggles his eyebrows.

"Ain't misbehavin'."

The First Lady makes her way onto the floor where many couples have already taken up hold and are twirling around us. "Would you mind?" she asks, eyes shining with nothing but love as she looks at her husband.

"Not at all." I lean in and kiss the First Lady on each cheek. "Thank you for loaning him to me."

She laughs, light and carefree. "It's the least I could do for insulting every royal protocol in existence."

"Oh, bugger to protocol," I quip, leaving them to have their dance. It's easy to smile now, even through my slightly depleted breaths, as I make my way through the crowds of people who are smiling fondly at me as I pass. When I catch Damon and Kim matching the smiles of other guests, something comes over me. I'm never one for feeling embarrassed, but a sudden wave of it attacks me, and I dip my head as I walk, my smile now shy and directed at my feet. I'm only a few paces from the edge of the dance floor—nearly away from all of the attention—when familiar male dress shoes block my path.

I barely stop in time to avoid colliding with his frame, and my smile drops, as if it has suddenly become too heavy for me to hold. It really has. What is he doing?

"This song was made for us, Adeline," Josh whispers quietly, slowly raising his hand in offer.

I conceal my hard swallow and look up at him, seeing too much pleading in his eyes. I'm aware of the attention on us, of the anticipation of what might happen next. But I would be foolish to give cause for suspicion, because, as I've told myself a million times before, the world is watching. Sir Don is watching. For Josh, this is a *fuck you* to my closest advisor, one of the men behind the attempts to keep Josh away from me. Has Josh no regard for his reputation? They'll ruin him. "Thank you, but—"

"Please," he begs so very softly. "Don't make tomorrow's news be the Queen declining a dance with Josh Jameson."

But by avoiding bruising his ego, tomorrow's news will be the Queen *actually* dancing with Josh Jameson. I peek left and right, confirming my fears. All attention is on us. "Why are you doing this?" I murmur, and he moves in, taking me in a light hold, one hand on the small of my back, the other claiming my hand. I can't stop him, not without causing a scene that'll be more newsworthy than us dancing together.

"Because desperate men do desperate things." Our chests compress lightly as Josh starts to lead the way slowly around the floor, and my spare hand has no choice but to rest on his shoulder or dangle in thin air and make me look even more awkward.

"And desperate women do stupid things."

"Are you desperate, Adeline?"

"Yes, I'm desperate for you to leave me alone." *Just leave me alone so I have a fighting chance of maintaining my calm façade.*

A subtle press of the flat of his palm in my back is a warning. "Stop with the dramatics, Your Majesty. The acting doesn't wash with me like it does with the rest of the world. Remember who you're talking to. Who you're trying to fool." He pulls me in a fraction, pressing our chests together more. "Your heartbeats say it all."

With my mouth only a few inches from his shoulder, I stare at the material of his suit jacket, feeling the surges of my heart. "And you said it all in your suite. Not my calling."

"When you love someone, you say stupid things."

"You need to stop this."

"I'll never stop." It's a promise. "And quit looking so terrified."

"I *am* terrified," I admit, turning my face a fraction to my left, seeing the dance floor is now full of couples dancing. I force a small smile, anything to fool the spectators that I'm enjoying myself rather than having an epic internal meltdown. My flesh is buzzing, my heart at risk of punching itself free and landing on the dance floor.

"Why?" He looks at me, his face straight, and all I can think is that he's looking at me like I am his day and night, and everyone must be concluding the same. So I look away, only just managing to follow his steps.

"Because I want everything." The words come naturally, just the simplicity of us touching bringing on my honesty. "I want to protect my family. I want to prove so many people wrong." I close my eyes briefly and tell Josh what I'm sure he already knows. "And I want you."

"I'm yours, Adeline. I was the moment you flashed that sultry smile my way."

I didn't think my heart could beat any faster, yet it proves me wrong. "But you don't understand me."

"I do. And that's what frightens me most. I know you can do this." He smoothly turns us when we reach the edge of the floor, flexing his hand on my back. "I shouldn't have flown off the handle like that. I'm sorry. I've been in hell this week, and I'm not going back, so we need to figure this out pretty fuckin' speedily before I lose my fuckin' mind."

My tummy flips, and the smile I was struggling so hard to find slowly creeps up on me. "Your language is blue."

I feel him smile into my hair. "Is that an agreement?"

"The world is watching, Josh."

"But they're not listening." He swirls us around, and I catch the President's eye, but quickly look away when I see he's a little too curious of my interaction with Josh. "Say yes."

"And how do you think we will proceed?"

"We'll start in your suite."

"Josh, I'm being serious."

"So am I. For now, I need reacquainting with what's mine. Tomorrow, we talk."

Words catch in my throat as I try to get them into order. "I can't have another night with you unless both of us know what is happening between us."

"What's happening between us?" he parrots, sounding a little perplexed. "Isn't it obvious, Adeline? And it's already happened. We're in love. And when two people are in love, they do what it takes to be together."

I deflate in his arms a little. Are we back here again? "Josh, what you know about my family and its secrets is the tip of the iceberg. To choose us over them would make me the instigator of my family's downfall. I can't do that." I wish he could understand this. I'm not being difficult. As it stands, it's hopeless.

"I know that." He turns his head slightly so our faces are precariously close. "But I can't be without you. I've tried this week and gone mad. There is no color in my life without you. There is no anticipation or warmth. I'm a man on the edge, Adeline, and my hope that I can fix this is the only thing stopping me from falling."

I swallow, closing my eyes and inhaling through my nose, getting a hit of the scent that is perfectly Josh. "What does this mean, Josh?"

"It means I love you, woman. It means without you, there is no me." He laughs under his breath when I discreetly nudge him.

He knows I didn't mean that. "It means for now we'll have to be careful. But we can't do that on our own."

He's right. There's no way of ever seeing each other without *anyone* knowing. "I trust my staff," I tell him, knowing this is what he is looking for.

"Explicitly?"

"Most of them, yes."

"Most?"

"Well, my closest. There are the ones who mustn't know. Sir Don, for example. David Sampson. In fact, most of my father's close aides who I inherited. They're waiting for me to put a step wrong, and frankly, you are more of a dive-off-a-cliff kind of wrong. They'll eliminate you within the blink of their beady eyes." I shrug a little when he raises his eyebrows. "I speak nothing but the truth. And the fact I'm currently being whirled around the dance floor by you won't be helping."

"I believe it." Josh breaks away as the music comes to an end, dazzling me with a smile that isn't only for my benefit. Sir Don is still watching. I can feel his slitty eyes on my back. "I'll see you back at your hotel."

"How?" I ask quietly as he bows and people start clapping the band.

"Smile, Adeline," Josh orders softly, and I peek left and right to see I am once again the center of everyone's attention. So I smile, curtseying a little in thanks to Josh, trying to look as cool and unaffected as I possibly can.

Our opportunity to talk anymore is gone. All I can do now is think. And I think I might turn to dust when I spot Kim giving me a very disapproving look from across the room. Sir Don looks plain suspicious. My mind is already conjuring up what I will say to him.

It was just a dance.

Yet to me, it was everything. He believes in me.

12

GOOD GRIEF, YOU could cut the atmosphere in the car with a knife. I'm just glad Sir Don is following in a car behind, my body safe from his daggers for now. Even poor Olive and Jenny are tense, and they have no idea what they should be tense about. Damon is quiet, and Kim just stares at me from time to time, as if she might be trying to fathom whether I appear insane, or if I actually *am* insane. Then she'll go back to her phone and continue typing something out, probably an email to herself drafting her resignation.

"Well," I say, my hands on my bag in my lap. "I think that went rather well." I get completely stonewalled by Kim, and Damon simply flicks his eyes to the rearview mirror briefly, his look telling me I'm wasting my breath. Maybe so, but I cannot stand this awful silence for a moment longer. "The President and the First Lady were such lovely people. So down-to-earth and friendly."

"And the man can dance," Jenny pipes in. "That dance will go down in history."

I smile, betting the Internet is already exploding with news of our jaunt around the dance floor at the White House. "I hope I didn't look like a complete amateur."

"Oh, Your Majesty," Olive swoons, still looking as star-struck as she did when we entered the mansion. "And you danced with Josh Jameson, too." God bless her, she has no idea she's just inflated the already gigantic pink elephant in the car. With all the chaos in my mind, I forgot Olive is an avid fan of Josh Jameson.

"So I did." I play it down, flicking cautious eyes at Kim and smiling awkwardly when she gives me the death stare. Oh, for pity's sake. Is this the silent treatment? Am I being sent to the naughty corner when I arrive at my suite? "I think we'll have a meeting in the morning," I say to Kim. "Bright and early over breakfast."

"I think that would be very prudent," she retorts, going back to her phone.

Part of me wants to ask her who in heaven's name she thinks she's talking to. The other part of me knows she is perfectly wise to be worried.

"We still have a crowd," Damon says as we roll up to the hotel, prompting me to crane my neck to see.

"Oh, really? Haven't they seen enough?"

"Maybe the paps are hoping for a dance," Kim flips dryly, turning her phone so I can see the screen. She's taken the initiative to zoom in on the picture, making it so I don't have to lean forward to see. How very kind of her. It's me with the President, midway through a swirl, my head tossed back on a laugh. I'm not close enough to see what is written with the picture, but I expect it is something lovely, since it is a lovely picture. Then Kim swipes left and a picture of me appears again, but this time with Josh. Without thought, I inch forward in my seat. My face. Oh goodness, my face. It's a picture of uncertainty. My eyes are low, my body visibly tense, and I'm completely crowded by Josh Jameson. The words with *this* picture, I really need to see, but Damon opens my door and Kim retracts her arm, taking her phone away before I have a chance to see or even ask. My muscles tense. Shit, this is a catastrophe, and I *know* Sir Don will have been scouring the Internet like Kim. Fabulous. I need to get to my suite and hide myself from all this disapproval.

As I exit the car and Damon guides me into the hotel, I hardly notice the throngs of people or the cameras flashing, my mind too occupied with what the article said. "Okay?" Damon asks as we board the elevator, everyone else following close behind.

I look at him, in a bit of a mind spin. "I think so," I answer, looking at my purse when I feel my mobile phone vibrate from within. I know better than to find it. That can wait until I have some privacy.

"You looked like a true queen on that dance floor, ma'am," Damon says quietly, as if he could be worried Kim or Sir Don may hear him. "Majestic."

"You are getting soppy in your old age," I tease, but I'm once again thanking the heavens for my Damon. Whatever would I do without him to pick me up when I'm down? To encourage me onward and truly look out for me. Not because he is paid to, but because he really actually cares. He smirks, his attention on the backs of the heads before us, as we are carried to my floor. "How's Mandy?" I ask.

"Wonderful," He glances at his watch. "I'll be able to call her in a few hours. She misses me."

It must be such a strain to be apart. I know firsthand, because being away from Josh hurt like nothing else, and I haven't known him for a fraction of the time that Damon has known his wife.

Josh.

My urgency increases somewhat with the thought of him, and I will everyone to hurry and get off the elevator once the doors are open. I'm hustled down the corridor and as soon as the doors to my suite are open, I head straight for my bedroom, leaving everyone behind to do whatever it is they're going to do. Disperse to their own rooms, probably. Except for Damon and his men. They'll do shifts throughout the night. But no one will relax until I'm tucked in safe and tight. And I plan for that to be very quickly. Or, at least, I plan for them to *think* I am tucked in safe and tight.

I reach the door and turn to close it, meeting Kim nose to nose. She is clearly on a mission. "Breakfast," I remind her sweetly, making her lips twist, annoyed. "Eight."

"Should I arrange for that to be a private affair?"

"I think that will be wise," I say with utter finality, just in case she tries to instigate the conversation I do not want to have, not now *nor* in the morning. But by morning I will have at least prepared some words of assurance. But now? My brain is mush. I couldn't possibly muster the strength clearly essential to appease Kim. Yet I know I need to say something. "And if Sir Don happens to press you before we speak in the morning, I'm sure you'll assure him that there is nothing between Mr. Jameson and me. Because, of course, there isn't."

Her mouth now straight, she takes one step back. "Of course, ma'am."

"Very good. Good night."

"You need help undressing, ma'am?"

I see Olive and Jenny approaching behind Kim, ready to help me out of my dress and get this tiara off my head. "I'll manage just fine on my own." I smile to them both. "You've been a marvelous help all day. You should get some rest." I close the door between us quickly and turn to face my empty room.

Empty.

Blissful.

Away from the disdain.

I sigh and lean against the wood, relishing the sound of silence. Until my phone breaks it. And I remember . . .

Hurrying to my bed, I perch on the side and pull my mobile from my purse, finding a message from Josh. There's only a link, and I know what it'll lead me to before I click it and a webpage opens. The picture Kim showed me in the car, the one of Josh and me, is the first thing I see. Goodness, seeing it this closely, it's obvious how uneasy I felt. I look like a rabbit caught in the headlights. Fitting, since that is how I felt. Below is another picture, this one at a slightly different angle, showing the profiles of our faces, our noses close to one another's. This must be later on in the dance, when I had relaxed a little. My fingertips meet my lips when I read the headline.

We think they make the most gorgeous couple! What do you think?

"Oh my gosh." I keep scrolling through the reams of pictures, all Josh and me. There's not one of the President and me, not on this media page, anyway. When I finally reach the end of the album dedicated to us, I go on to read the short passage detailing the state dinner at the White House, how I danced with the President before Josh Jameson swooped me off my feet. My eyes bug when the journalist mentions how precariously close Josh's hand was to my backside. And then my mouth drops open when they mention that Josh's new mystery woman might not be all too pleased with the story these pictures tell. I can't decide whether that's a good or terribly bad thing. It doesn't take me long to conclude that it's the latter. Regardless of the fact that they're still intrigued by the mystery woman that Josh was pictured hiding under a hoodie outside The Dorchester weeks ago, they're also intrigued by these pictures.

In complete exasperation, I drop my phone and flop back on the bed. "A disaster," I say to the ceiling. I should have politely declined Josh and made a sharp exit from the floor. Well, I did try, at least. I can't be held accountable for this media circus. But I know I will be. Sir Don, David Sampson, and everyone else here to supposedly support my reign have been waiting for me to put a step wrong. I didn't simply put one step wrong. I put a million wrong, all around the dance floor of the East Room at the White House.

Dragging myself up off the bed, I go to the mirror and give my reflection a thorough telling off as I remove my earrings. I will be sure to reprimand Josh, too. He must have known this would happen. I reach up to my head to remove my heavy tiara, but my fingers pause as they come to rest on the diamonds. Josh told me he'd see me here. Do I undress? Change into something more comfortable? Or stay as I am? And how in the name of God will he sneak in here when I have Damon and his army guarding the door? I also expect Kim will be on the prowl. Not to mention Sir Don.

So what do I do? Picking up the bottom of my dress, I hurry back to the bed and find my phone. I don't call him for fear of listening ears, so I text him to ask whether I should change or not. His answer is quick and to the point.

Stay in that stunning dress. AND the tiara.

"Oh," I say to myself, frowning at the screen. "But it's so heavy." Reaching up, I flex my neck a little. Now that I'm not distracted, the weight of it is becoming a burden.

And how long must I wait here?

As I go to click send, there's a light rap on the door. "Ma'am?" Damon calls softly. "May I come in?"

"Of course," I say, his head popping around the wood soon after. "What is it?"

He pushes his way into the room. "You have been summoned, ma'am."

"By whom?" I ask indignantly. Oh God, is Sir Don waiting to grill me? What will I say? My mind races with excuses. Maybe I argue that Josh is seeing someone else. That article I just read mentioned Josh's mystery woman. Will Sir Don buy it? I should laugh at myself. Of course he won't buy it. He knows the woman that was hustled into the hotel under Josh's hoodie was me. He was in Evernmore on that fateful day I let my emotions get the better of me and blurted about my relationship with Josh. God, what have I done?

On a cock of his head, Damon lets a small smile curve the edges of his mouth. "I don't believe there is anyone with the power to summon you, Your Majesty," he says, reminding me of who I am. Of course. What was I thinking? It is me who does the summoning now. "Except one person, of course," Damon finishes.

I recoil a tiny bit, unsure, excited . . . breathless.

Josh.

"Where?"

"I believe that part is a surprise."

"That's ridiculous." I laugh. "I'm a hostage in this hotel unless I want the world to see me leaving."

"Do you need your bag?" Damon asks, ignoring my uncertainty and moving into my room to collect if off the bed.

"You tell me," I reply. "Since you are clearly privy to what is unfolding."

"Maybe you'd like to reapply some lipstick?"

"Jenny has my lipstick." I scold myself for not thinking to seize the makeup I've worn tonight from Jenny. "Wait." I make a mad dash for the bathroom. "I think I have a similar shade in here somewhere." Like a frantic woman, I scrounge through the various bags in my bathroom. "Aha!" I hold up the lipstick victoriously. "I have it."

"Very good, ma'am," Damon calls dryly. "Now, not to rush you, but we're on a bit of a time constraint."

"We are?" I put myself in the mirror and assess what is before me. Damon is right. My lips have no color. That must have been the anxious chewing on them. Pulling off the lid of my lipstick, I lean into the mirror to repaint my lips, going straight out of the line the moment the color touches them. "Drat," I curse, snatching some tissue paper to wipe up my mess. "Won't be long," I call, my second attempt no better. I'm shaking. It could be nerves; it could be excitement. What has he got planned for us?

I do my very best to get my lipstick even, but I don't spend too much time ensuring it is. The clock is ticking. "Ready," I declare, emerging from the bathroom. "Now what?"

"Now you come with me." Collecting me, Damon walks us to the door and looks out cautiously.

"Where is Kim? And Sir Don?"

"In their rooms." Encouraging me out, we tiptoe through the suite, and Damon takes the door handle lightly, tense and cringing as he turns it. I'm skittish, constantly glancing over my shoulder for anyone who may rumble our escape mission.

"Where are all of your men?" I whisper.

"I think the less people who know, the better, don't you?"

"Yes, indeed," I agree quickly.

We sneak out of the door, and Damon closes it quietly behind us. And then he breathes out a relieved breath that has me suppressing a chuckle. And in the process of suppressing it, I snort. "Oh my." I quickly cover my mouth, surprised by the very unladylike sound.

"Did you just snort?" Damon asks, clearly shocked, too.

"You know, I believe I did."

There's a few seconds silence, while Damon stares at me, stunned. Then he falls apart before my very eyes, doing a terrible job of retaining his laughter. The sight is really something to behold. I've never seen him so tickled pink, and it's got my own laughs coming harder. "Quick," he splutters, hurrying me down the corridor as we laugh like crazy people, both doing terrible jobs of keeping quiet. He takes us past the elevator and into a stairwell, and only then do I find the will to pull myself together.

"Oh, I've never laughed so much," I admit, drinking down air as Damon works to get himself back in check, constantly letting out little bursts of chuckles as he does.

Once we've both settled, he indicates the way down the stairs. "There's a fair few flights, but it's the safest route."

"Why are you doing this, Damon?" He's going above and beyond.

His smile is soft and fond. "Because, Your Majesty, I think you need to experience both worlds that are on offer to you. To their fullest. Both highs and lows, everything there could be. Only then can you truly decide which one to choose."

I stare blankly at him, taken aback, the signs of a lump forming in my throat. I have no idea what to say. So I say nothing and walk into his chest, giving him a hug I hope tells him how grateful I am. He knows which world I truly want. I think he's telling me in his own little way that I can't have both. I know he's right, but in this moment, I can't think past the fact that the man I love is waiting for me somewhere, and Damon is going to get me to him safely. "You are a very special man, Damon." I smile into his suit when I feel his big arms wrap around me. "Your wife is a very lucky lady."

"I know. I tell her all the time."

I sniffle on a chuckle and break away from him, knowing he's not all too comfortable no matter how much he humors me. "I can't be with Josh without hurting everyone I love." I tell him what he already knows, and he just smiles in that way he does, telling me he understands.

"Would you rather I didn't encourage situations like this?"

I don't answer that. I don't need to. I can't tell him to deprive me of the one thing that keeps me functioning, no more than I seem to be able to deprive myself. "How many floors did you say?" I ask, changing the subject. There's no point continuing, since we won't reach a resolution.

"A few. Want a piggyback?" He's joking, though he might not be laughing when I take him up on his offer. "I think I'll manage," I reply, starting down the stairs.

Five minutes later, I'm struggling. "My toes are pinching," I complain as we take the final few steps.

"After all that dancing you did tonight, you're going to complain about a few stairs?"

"Ha ha." I give Damon an epic eye-roll before he looks out the door. "Okay, nice and quick."

We scamper into the lobby, Damon's eyes ever watchful, though there is not a soul in sight. Not one person. I realize it is very late, but it is a hotel, after all. Most of the guests may be tucked up in their beds, but you can always expect the odd one or two floating around. Not to mention the night staff. "Where is everyone?"

"Lost for two more minutes with the help of management."

Just as he utters the words, I spy someone. "Oh no," I breathe as Damon yanks me behind a pillar. "What is Dr. Goodridge doing up at this time?" I hiss.

"Your guess is as good as mine." He looks around the corner vigilantly. "He's on a call."

"Whoever to?" The old man has never married, has no family. His life, like most royal servants from his era, has been dedicated to the Monarch.

"I don't know, Your Majesty. I can't hear." Damon ushers me along quickly. "In." He wraps his arm around my back as he holds a door open and applies pressure to encourage me through.

I gaze around the empty space, a little lost. "The bar?" A fire is dancing on the other side of the room, the flames framed with a rich, glossy wooden fireplace. I hear the doors close behind me. "What am I doing here, Damon?" I ask, but he doesn't answer, and I turn to see him through the glass panels of the huge wooden doors. On a slightly raised brow, he pulls across some sheer curtains, hiding me. I frown as I slowly pivot to face the room once more. I'm alone, nothing but me and the sounds of the fire crackling. Elaborate, heavy claret curtains frame each window, perfectly set in a swags-and-tails style, never to be drawn. More sheer material hangs within them, blocking out the world beyond. Rich, wooden chairs upholstered in cream for the seats and claret for the backs are set perfectly around each table, and the barstools lining the prominent arched bar match. I've stayed at the St. Regis many times, but never have I been in the hotel bar. It's warm and cozy, despite being very large. And at gone midnight, it is empty aside from me. Even I know that at this time, there is always someone in the bar of a hotel having a nightcap. So where is everyone?

I pout, wondering what I'm supposed to do. Just as I decide to call Josh, I hear movement, just a muffled shift of something—feet, perhaps—and I take a few more steps into the room, searching the far corners. My ability to breathe is stolen from me when I see Josh sitting in one of the chairs, a glass of Scotch in his hand. He's watching me, has been all this time while I've been taking in my surroundings. Goosebumps tickle my skin, erupting into constant prickles of anticipation. He's still in his dress suit, looking obscenely handsome, but a little something has been added to his attire. Something I recognize. I latch onto my bottom lip as I lift my eyes from the little pink hanky stuffed into his breast pocket, finding his wild eyes again. I would go to him if my legs were not listless and useless. I would talk if I could find my tongue.

Keeping me in place with his fierce gaze, he finishes the last of his Scotch and sets the tumbler lightly on the table before rising from the chair. His hands slip into his pockets and he takes slow, measured steps toward me, doing what Josh Jameson does best. He makes me impatient and desperate. His smile glows, growing the closer he gets until we are body to body. Taking me in his hold, just the same as at the White House, he remains still for a few seconds, and then the voice of Fats Waller joins us.

"You think you can relax now the world isn't watching?" he asks quietly.

I'm so happy, I could cry. "I think so." I make a point of holding him firmly, something I could not do only a few hours ago.

"Good. And I get to hold the royal ass I adore." His hand falls to my bottom, cupping it over the smooth black satin of my dress. He gives it a little squeeze, and I give him a mock disapproving expression that he completely ignores. "I also get to do this." He kisses me deeply, lifting me to my tippy-toes as *Ain't Misbehavin'* plays softly around us. Our reunion isn't as frantic as I would have expected, given how much I've missed him. But it is as intense as always, our tongues softly dancing and exploring each other's mouths, his palm slipping to my nape and holding me as close as he can get me. And we kiss forever, catching up on lost time. It's times like these the weight on my shoulders lifts, and I'm free as a bird, content and untroubled. I'm not who I really am, but a woman allowed to be in love with a man who is besotted with her. Is there a way? Can I truly have everything? Can I be with Josh and maintain the Monarchy's carefully constructed façade?

I don't mean for my lips to falter on his. I don't mean to flinch. But it's inevitable when I silently admit the answer to my questions is a solid no. My compliant position on the throne is the only thing keeping all of the nasty secrets locked away.

"Stop it," he whispers, withdrawing a little so we're no longer kissing, but our mouths are still touching. "I didn't go to all this trouble so you could sulk."

I snap myself out of it and tell myself I need to live in the moment, as I always have where Josh is concerned. There should be no thoughts of tomorrow; it's all about *right now*. And right now is perfect. "We're alone," I say, forsaking the comforting sight of Josh to take in the sumptuous bar once more. "How did you manage this?"

Josh also takes a little peek around the room. "A very rich anonymous person paid an obscene amount of money to privately hire it for a few hours."

Anonymous. How clever of him. "So we won't be disturbed?"

"The staff will be curious, of course. But Damon is on watch and the manager knows there's a healthy bonus in his back pocket if he ensures our privacy."

"But he doesn't know who is in his hotel bar?"

Josh shakes his head and drops a light kiss on my cheek, as we continue to slowly sway in each other's arms, and Fats Waller continues to bless us with his words. "Money is power. Mind you, so is being the Queen."

I inwardly laugh. "I have no power." If I did, life would be wonderful. "Thank you for the link you sent me." Another disapproving look, and Josh once again ignores it.

"Is she?" he asks.

I frown up at him. "Is she *what*, and who is *she?*"

"Is the mystery woman in my life jealous of the story those pictures tell?"

On a light laugh, I rest my cheek on his shoulder, and he starts to turn us, so very lazily. Like we have all the time in the world. "We shouldn't feed their curiosity, Josh. You put on a show. It was very dangerous."

"Adeline, I don't put anything on when I am with you. Everything that happens between us is naturally explosive. I can't help that our chemistry is so obvious."

"Then you should have kept your distance."

"That's about as impossible as asking me to control my desire for you."

I sigh into him, staring over his shoulder to the sheer drapes hiding us from the outside world. I'm falling into that despondent mood I so hate, when the impossibility of us hits home. "You stole the President's thunder," I muse.

"Ed won't mind. He's never been a man who thrives on attention."

"And you are?"

"Only if that attention comes from you." Constricting his hold on my neck, he pulls me from my cozy resting place. "And since I've gone to all this trouble so we can see each other, I want every bit of your attention on me."

"So demanding," I quip. "And what would you have me do?"

His gorgeous lips pout in silent contemplation, and he gazes to the ceiling for a few moments. "Let me think about that. First, I should get my queen a drink." He frees me from his embrace and takes my hand, leading me to the bar and lifting me to a stool.

"But there's no barman," I point out as Josh rounds the bar and puts himself behind it. Grabbing a coaster, he places it in front of me. "Welcome to the St. Regis, darlin'. What can I get you?"

I laugh as I get comfortable. "You're my barman?"

"I'll be whatever you want me to be."

Not a secret, my head yells, diverting me off my course of contentment for a split second. I soon pull myself around and scan the drinks menu that Josh hands me. I can't allow myself to tarnish this time we have. "Let me see."

"Nothing from the cocktail menu," he tells me, and I look up. "I haven't got a fuckin' clue how to make a cocktail, and I'm not wasting our time together trying to figure it out."

I can't argue with him. I don't want to waste time either. I flip past the cocktails and run my eye down the spirits. Then I snap the book closed. "I think perhaps I'll stick with champagne." No cocktail making, no mixing, and no wasting time.

"Very good choice." Josh goes straight to the champagne, as if he predicted my choice and sought it out in preparation. He's quick to remove the foil and pop the cork, and then he is on the stool next to me pouring. "So how was your evening?"

Odd question, since I know Josh is aware it was a strain of epic proportions. "Lovely," I opt for instead. "Although listening to the First Lady tell me that you used to date was rather unpleasant."

He falters in his pouring, glancing at me. "We dated briefly. It was nothing. She told the Queen about her previous relationships?"

"I was equally surprised," I admit, avoiding the fact that I encouraged her. "And I think she was serious about you."

He shrugs. "I've never led a woman on, Adeline. Never given false hope." He hands me my flute. "I've never been into a woman. Not before you, anyway."

My smile can't be contained. "Into?"

His smirk is devilish. "In *love* with. Better?"

"Much."

"Good. Now, how was your flight?"

I frown as I sip, and Josh settles back on his stool, comfortable and waiting for my answer. *How was your evening? How was your flight?* "Fine. Why are you asking me these questions?"

"I want to know what it would feel like for us to be normal."

"But we are not." I indicate around the bar with my glass. "As proven by this hotel bar you have paid to clear so we can see each other."

His scowl is playful. "Nice tiara."

Just like that, my senses heighten. "Nice hanky."

His lips pout as he glances down at the pink material hanging out of his breast pocket. "You know, I planned on wining and dining—"

"I've heard those words before." I laugh lightly, making him smirk devilishly.

He gets up off his stool and removes my drink from my hand before tugging me down. "Dancing," he goes on, "kissing, and feeling you." Both his hands move to my backside and squeeze, at the same time pushing my waist into his. He's rock-hard. Throbbing. *Boom.* My veins run hot. "I was going to feed you your favorite champagne and dirty cheeseburger." He circles his groin, his smirk becoming dirtier. "But now—"

"What?" I breathe. What now?

"Now . . ." His lips meet my jawline, and he licks his way up to the hollow below my ear. Holy good God, I'm falling to pieces in his arms. "I only want your beautiful mouth around my dick." He bites down on my lobe and tugs playfully. The moan that escapes me is feral and rough. I feel feral, too, could happily rip his suit from his body and devour him. "And then I'll slip inside that sweet, royal pussy of yours"—a jolt of his hips knocks a whimper from me—"work up slowly and carefully"—another jolt, and another cry—"until I'm pounding, and you, Your Majesty, are screaming."

"Oh God." I grab his trousers in search of the fly, but I'm quickly and abruptly stopped. Outraged, I look into liquid amber eyes, my jaw ticking. His face is impassive now. Expressionless. But his eyes dance in satisfaction. No one will stop me from having what I want in this moment, not even Josh. I try to tug my hands out of his. And get absolutely nowhere. "Let me go."

"No." He pushes my hands away and steps back, out of touching distance. What is he doing? I step forward, and Josh steps back again. He's making a point. I'm beginning to feel like I need him to breathe, and Josh is proving that. But what about how he feels? Isn't he as desperate, as hungry and in need? I step forward once again, and once again Josh removes himself from my space, enough to be out of reach. My eyes fall into irritated slits, but Josh's face doesn't change at all. Still deadpan. Although his eyes give him away. They tell me he's struggling. I need to turn this around, and in a moment of impulse, I fall to my knees before him, my gaze heavy and provocative.

"Fuck," he whispers, his composure slipping, his body shaking with the strength he needs to remain at a distance. But he will. I know my American boy. His mind games, his deep need to prove that I need him as much as I want him, won't allow him to break. So I find the words I know will shatter his resistance.

"I bow to no one," I whisper, blinking slowly, feeling intoxicated and dizzy from the sparks colliding between us. "Except you."

His big chest expands on a deep breath, his hands trembling. And he drops to his knees, too. "Want to get into trouble with me?" he asks quietly. His question catapults me back to the day of my thirtieth birthday and makes me realize how far we have come. And I know that is his intention.

"Until the day I die," I confirm, speaking nothing but the truth. It is so easy to love him. But everything else is so hard. It shouldn't be. Loving someone and being loved should mean everything else you have to contend with in life is easy. Because you have each other. You're supported. You're taking the world on together, side by side. Except that world isn't *our* world. No one else has our problems.

"Adeline?"

I blink and refocus my attention to right now. "I'm sorry, I—"

"Get here." Falling to one palm, he leans forward and gives me his other. I take it and walk on my knees to him, and he drops his arse to his heels and sits me to the side on his lap, brushing my masses of waves over one shoulder. I curl in close to his chest and immediately feel the heat of his breath spreading across my scalp. "Not much of a temptress now, huh?" He sighs.

"Sometimes one just needs a cuddle."

"And sometimes *one* needs to stop thinking things that distracts *one*." He cuddles me harder, a lame kind of punishment. "Especially when *one's* boyfriend is about to get his dick sucked."

I laugh into him, pushing myself out of his chest. "Sorry, darlin'," I quip, my attempt at a southern American accent downright diabolical. "Bloody hell, that was awful."

Josh falls apart against me, the sound of his laughter the best kind of medicine. "You're so fucking cute."

I nudge him, but immediately follow it up with a wince.

"What's up?"

Reaching up to my tiara, I grimace. "I've been wearing this thing for hours. My head is about to fall off." I'm suddenly not on Josh's lap anymore, but on my back on the floor. My tiara tumbles, he crowds me with his body, cupping my face, and kisses me hard on the lips.

"Not before I fuck your mouth."

I gasp. Josh gasps.

And then it is all very serious again as we stare at each other, the tension building up, back to where it was before I let the horrible things dampen it. "On your knees." He moves off me and stands, helping me up until my eyes are level with his groin. Bending, he blindly reaches for my tiara and carefully slips it back on my head, spending a few moments arranging my waves around the precious metal and stones. This time, he starts to unfasten his trousers himself, and my hands twitch by my sides, desperate to help. He reaches into his boxers. He pauses, watching as my tongue sweeps across my lips. And then . . .

I hold my breath as I take in every inch of him, marveling at his taut flesh and thick shaft. My mouth waters. My body rolls in waves with my breathing. I peek up through my lashes and see his head low, his eyes hooded and dark. With one fist wrapped around himself, he takes my nape with his other and pushes me forward until the tip of his cock meets the corner of my mouth. And he glides it from side to side across the seam of my lips. I close my eyes and wrap one hand around his, my tongue darting out and catching him. He hisses. And before he gathers himself, I open my mouth and take him as far as our hands around his base allows. He growls, his fingers digging into my neck. He's velvet. I am wanton. He jerks and flexes his hand for me to let go, so then I take my hand to his arse, and he holds the sides of my head with both hands. And then it is just my mouth around him. I hum and close my eyes, advancing forward slowly, taking as much as him as I can handle. A lot, but by no means all. Retreating, I graze my teeth lightly to the very tip and quickly sink back down again. He is trembling, every part of his body vibrating around me. Once I've teased him enough with my slow, lazy pace, I take up my rhythm and start pumping steadily and meticulously, each drive of my mouth being met with a ragged groan. His hips start to move, his hands holding my head tighter. His veins pulse against my tongue, blood surging. I open my eyes and gaze up, finding his face is pointed toward the ceiling, his throat tight, his jaw ready to snap. Every sign I see and feel tells me he is about to reach his limit. His head drops. He straightens my tiara. I smile around my mouthful of his flesh, and he smiles back.

Then I slowly suck my way to his tip and start kissing my way down his shaft. Mumbled words start to spill from his mouth, none of them coherent.

"Do you want to come, Josh?" I ask as I lick firmly up the length of a ballooned, throbbing vein. His head is heavy and limp, his eyes barely able to remain open. His parted lips allow air to pass in short, fast gasps. He's sweating. I've never seen anything so enthralling.

Without a word, he dips and hauls me to my feet, spinning me and bending me over a stool. I whimper as my palms sink into the

gold material. Leaning over and reaching around me, he takes my
hands and sets them on the backrest of the stool. "Hold tight, Your
Majesty," he whispers into my hair. His voice is so close to my ear,
it sinks in and swirls my thoughts further. He gathers up my masses
of hair into a fist and pulls, tugging my head back as he bends to
find the hem of my dress. It's drawn slowly up until my waist is a
mass of black satin. My knickers aren't removed, just pulled aside.

I stare ahead to the doors where Damon is just beyond, as well
as the rest of the world. The thought doesn't panic me. There's
nothing to be considered in this moment except how much pleasure
I'm about to experience. As Josh places a fingertip on my shoulder,
I close my eyes and breathe through his light touch. The heat is
bordering unbearable.

Like his fingertip is charged with electricity, I shake as he drags it
down my back. I can see with my eyes closed. Every tiny movement
he makes, every touch he gives me, I can see it all so clearly. Like
an out-of-body experience, like I could be standing in the shadows
watching two people get lost in each other.

He reaches between my thighs and strokes me softly. We inhale
at the same time. We jerk in sync. We both release air on moans.

"If I were to ever beg you to do something for me, Adeline, it
would be to remember this." He sinks his finger into me and sweeps
far and wide, pushing me onto my tiptoes in my heels. "Whenever
you're feeling uncertain, remember how it feels to be with me."
His finger is gone and a second later, my eyes spring open, and I'm
full to the brim with his cock.

"Josh," I yell, and one of his hands covers my mouth for my
trouble.

"Quiet," he hisses, pounding forward mercilessly. I moan into
his palm, clenching my eyes closed and searching for the willpower
to sustain this without telling the entire hotel what is happening
in the bar. "Here." Josh dangles his pink hanky in front of me, and
my mouth drops open automatically for him to stuff it inside.

Once he's ensured my silence, both hands fall onto my hips. And I breathe in through my nose, filling my lungs with air Josh lets go, and I am instantly thrust over the edge of all control, my fingers clawing into the material of the stool. Slam after slam, he gives me no space between his brutal drives, his mind lost, his body a slave to pleasure. I can hear the gratification in every one of his grunts. Can feel it every time his groin slaps my arse. Can see his unrestrained desire in my mind's eye. I can taste it on my tongue, his essence still there. And I can smell it in the potent sex-drenched air. Josh is overloading all my senses, to the point I could collapse from the intensity. The muscles in my arms solidify, bracing me against the stool. My legs lock. My torso hardens. My climax is powering forward, and there is nothing I can do to stop it. I spit the hanky out on a muffled cry, my head jerking when Josh yanks on my hair. I feel the very epicenter of me swell with heat and blood, the pinnacle of my pleasure just on the horizon.

"Sweet Jesus," Josh gasps, his body folding over mine, his last few thrusts a little haphazard and uncontrolled. Stars burst into my hazy vision and my orgasm rips through me ruthlessly, holding me hostage in its clutches. On one last shove, he hits me deep, and I feel his essence pour from his body and fill me as he curses his way through it. Breathless and unable to hold myself up any longer, my torso collapses to the seat of the stool, Josh's body coming with me. Dazed, I stare across the bar into the dancing flames of the fire and zone out, utterly replete. Josh's arm curls under my stomach and clings, his face buried in my hair at my nape. I can't move. I can't talk. I can't even think. I'm useless. So I let the fire hypnotize me as my mind replays every perfect second of the brutal fucking I was just victim to. I'm in heaven. Back where I belong.

13

AFTER A WHILE of listening to our loud breathing, I finally find some strength to utter a few words. "Are you alive?"

"Yeah," he replies, turning his face onto my back and kissing me. "That was a pretty fuckin' awesome nightcap, darlin'."

"I don't think I can walk."

"Me either."

"And my tiara is really hurting now," I add, wincing as I tilt my head and it digs in behind my ears. I'm going to have a headache for a week.

Josh lifts himself off me, and I grimace when our clothes peel apart, damp with sweat. He snatches a few napkins from the bar and wipes up the inside of my thighs. "Come here." Helping me to turn, he smiles, rearranging my hair, which I'm certain must look frightful.

"How bad do I look?" I ask as I help him out and refasten his trousers.

"You couldn't look bad if you tried." Reaching for my tiara, he removes it, unraveling a few locks of hair that are caught up in the platinum and diamond weaves.

"Oh, that feels so good." I flex my neck, my relief instant. "I've never worn it for so long before."

Placing it on the seat of the stool, Josh turns me and lays his hands on my shoulders. Oh my, he's going to rub some life back into me. I relax under his working hands melding into my flesh where my neck meets my shoulders, humming my appreciation.

"Anyone would think you had my dick inside you again."

I smile into my darkness, rocking on my heels. "I think this is better." His hands wrap around my neck and lightly squeeze, and I reach up on a laugh to stop him from strangling me. "Rub me," I plead, needing more of his magic hands.

He goes back to massaging, and I go back to humming. "Was it worth the wait, mystery woman?"

"It was." Although I know our sex will be as explosive even without the longest times in between. Even when we're not catching up. It's just how it is with us. Electric. Consuming. It's everything. Yet there will always be horrible lengths of time when we're apart. There will always be more desperation on top of the already unbearable desperation. There will never be a time when I can just jump him and let him take us away, not without planning or meticulous risk management. I hate that there might be more weeks like the one I've just had, feeling heartsick over his silence. Or when his life gets crazy and he's on the other side of the world. Or when he loses hope in us again. Or the lack of a consistent us. I'm not free to see him when I please. I can't take a day off work when I wish and clear my diary to see him.

Sad once again, I swallow when he moves in and circles his arms around my shoulders, squeezing his face to mine. "If I could have anything in the world right now," he murmurs, "I would have you in bed with me. You'd be naked. I'd be naked. We'd cuddle and talk about nothing and everything. I'd make you breakfast in bed, and we'd shower together. I'd make love to you whenever I damn well please, and I'd savor every second."

I refuse to let how amazing that sounds tear me up inside. I mustn't dwell on the fact that his idea is a luxury we may never have. Instead, in a moment of spontaneity, I decide we *can* have that. "Let's do it." I wriggle free from his grip and whirl around to face him.

The uncertainty on his face is really quite adorable. "In the words of the woman I love," he says, holding the tops of my arms and hunkering down a bit to get us at eye level, "how do you suppose we do that?"

My upper body sags under his hold. He wouldn't usually let the trivial issue of dozens of royal staff and security stand in his way. He laughs in the face of challenges. It's one of the many reasons I adore him. "And where is the man *I* love?"

With only a second to consider my question, he looks to the doors hiding us from the rest of the hotel. "I'm right here, baby." Sliding one of his hands down my arm, he threads our fingers and starts pulling me toward the exit. "How many people are in your suite?"

"Damon and his men do shifts throughout the night."

"And the rest of your army?"

"They have their own rooms on the same floor."

"And what time are you woken up?"

"I have a breakfast meeting with Kim at eight, so I expect Olive will be whipping my curtains open at around six thirty."

He opens the door a tiny bit and peeks outside, whistling to get Damon's attention. Within a few seconds, Damon is with us in the room. His eyes jump from me to Josh, and I come over all self-conscious, reaching up to my untamed mane and patting it down.

"Don't waste your time on your hair, ma'am," he says wryly. "But maybe wipe the smears of red lipstick off your cheeks." Turning his attention to Josh, Damon nods his head sharply while I rub my palm across my hot face. "You, too."

I look at Josh with a clear mind for the first time since he bent me over the bar stool. His face is a mess of red smudges. "Oopsy-daisy."

I press my lips together to suppress my chuckle.

"Can you get us to Adeline's suite?" Josh asks, as he swipes his bristly cheek with the back of his hand.

"No." Damon's answer is short and final as he turns to leave again.

"Please, Damon," I beg. "I promise no one will find out."

He stops and turns. "How? You've got everyone sleeping in nearby rooms and your ladies-in-waiting will be up at the crack of dawn to get *you* up at the crack of dawn."

"We'll get Josh out before," I assure him. "Everyone will be none the wiser."

"Except me."

I pout and flutter my lashes. "I won't ask you to stick your neck out for me ever again." It's a fib, and Damon knows it.

"Yes, you will," he sighs, looking to Josh. "Six o'clock, you're out. I'll be waiting to escort you before Her Majesty's ladies arrive to wake her."

Josh salutes. "Yes, boss."

"Fuck's sake," Damon grumbles, taking himself to the door. He checks outside and calls us forward. "We go separately. Josh in the elevator, Her Majesty and I will take the stairs."

"Anything you say," I agree without hesitation. "Wait, where's your security?" I look at Josh for my answer. He'll be ambushed if he's seen. Not to mention the fuel it will add to the fire already burning its way through the online media platforms. First, they dance. Then it's discovered that they're in the same hotel a few hours later?

"Bates," Damon calls softly across the lobby, and two seconds later, there are four of us.

"Oh, how prompt." I smile brightly at Josh's bodyguard. "How are you, Bates?"

"Very good, ma'am." He doesn't look all too pleased to see me, but I don't take it to heart. Josh and I must be the biggest headaches

Damon and Bates have ever had.

"The Presidential Suite," Damon tells his old friend. "Stay in the elevator until we make it up the stairs."

"Right," he sighs, and then jerks his head to Josh for him to get a move on, returning his attention to Damon. "Blackjack and a whisky?"

"Blackjack, yes. Whisky, no."

"Oh you must, Damon," I jump in, adamant. "I insist." It'll make me feel a whole lot better about making him endure yet another stakeout.

Damon doesn't acknowledge my demand and instead watches as Bates leads Josh away. Only once they're in the elevator does he quickly run another check of all corners before ushering me toward the stairs. "Nice and quick."

"I'm going as fast as I can," I assure him, every muscle I have now awake again and beginning to ache. As soon as we're in the stairwell, I groan at the first set of stairs. Coming down is one thing. Going up is another. "I'm going to be too exhausted to even talk once I've climbed all these," I moan, lifting my dress and starting my ascent. "And how come Josh got to take the elevator? That doesn't seem at all fair. Can we not wa . . . oh!" There's suddenly no ground beneath my feet, my body draped over Damon's shoulder. "Damon! What in heaven's name are you doing?"

"I believe I am carrying the Queen of England up the stairs so she can conserve her energy for her secret American lover, ma'am."

Whatever do I say to that? "A piggyback would have sufficed," I tell him as I brush endless locks out of my face. "This is a little outrageous, don't you think?"

"I think more outrageous things may have happened in the hotel bar, Adeline," he quips tiredly, and I burst into embarrassed flames.

"I have no idea what you are talking about," I retort indignantly, cringing like I have never cringed before. "We drank champagne and talked."

"Of course you did, ma'am. All rather civilized, I expect."

"Indeed," I reply, shutting down the awfully awkward conversation. Goodness me, it's times like this I'm not so fond of the fact that Damon knows me so well. No other knows how to get my cheeks tinged with embarrassment like he does.

Considering Damon is no spring chicken, he carries me up the stairs like I'm just another layer of his clothing. We leave the stairwell as Josh and Bates appear out of the elevator, both looking at me bobbing up and down on Damon's shoulder as we pace down the corridor quietly.

"Was she gonna hightail it?" Josh asks quietly as he trails us.

I look up and grin at him. "My feet are aching. It's been a long day, what with endless men twirling me around a dance floor."

Josh rolls his eyes dramatically. "I don't know how I feel about another man carrying you over his shoulder."

"Damon doesn't count."

"Will you two shut up?" Damon hisses, and I quickly snap my mouth shut, drawing an imaginary zip across, making Josh grin and Bates chuckle. "The men are in the lounge area." He puts me on my feet. "I'll move them into the dining room to clear the way and once you're in your room I'll clear them out." He looks to Bates. "So it'll be just you and me tonight."

"Good with me."

"Wait here." Damon disappears into the room and only a minute later, he's back. "Go."

I'm about to break into a sprint when, once again, the ground disappears from under my feet. "Josh," I yelp, earning a filthy glare from Damon. I slap my hand over my mouth as Josh runs through the suite with me over his shoulder bobbing up and down erratically.

The door closes, and finally it is us again. "Dress off," he demands, dropping me to my feet and pulling at his tie. "Everything off." His body is stripped of clothes so fast, I haven't even found the zip of my dress by the time he's naked.

"That was impressive," I say in utter amazement, distracted from finding my illusive zip when my eyes dance across his flesh. "And so is that."

"Why are you still dressed?"

"I can't find the stupid zip." I wriggle and worm around with my arms up my back. "Olive is usually available to help me."

"You'll have to make do with me." I'm turned away from him.

"Such a hardship." My words are but a sigh as Josh finds the zipper with ease and virtually yanks it down, yanking me back a few paces in the process. "Easy, tiger," I quip. "Oh." I'm grabbed around the waist from behind and hauled up his body. "Josh!"

My shock is ignored, and I'm carried to the bed, more or less tossed on the mattress, and then he's making quick work with those talented fingers, getting my bra and knickers off. And then I'm naked. His eyes burn holes all over me as they jump across my flesh.

"Oh, today is a good day." His face falls between my boobs, and he inhales deeply. I can only laugh as he mauls me, feeling, sucking, and licking his way from one boob to another on constant hums of happiness. My hands find his hair, my fingers threading through the dark waves, and I relax into the soft bedding, so utterly content. "Don't you fall asleep on me," he warns, walking on his fists up the bed either side of my body until his face is hovering over mine. "Did I tire you out?"

"No, I'm just very relaxed." *So happy and at peace.*

His smile is gorgeous. Simple and gorgeous. "Me, too." He lowers slowly, his gaze flitting from my lips to my eyes constantly. And just when I breathe in and prepare for our kiss, he lifts a little, resuming his painstaking studying of my face. I'm a little slighted, but watching him watching me with so much concentration is truly pleasurable, too. No one has ever looked at me the way Josh looks at me. Not with this much fire in their eyes. No one has taken so much time to really see me. Not like they want to devour me and box me up all at the same time. And no one has ever gone to such great lengths and taken such risks just to be with me.

As Josh's mouth lowers, I put pressure on the back of his head, in case he thinks to retreat again, but this time, he does not, and I'm quickly absorbed by the power of his kiss. Deep but soft. Intense but quiet. My arms encase his shoulders and hug him to me, and we roll on the bed, putting Josh under me, the angle of our mouths changing. And we roll again, back to the center of the bed. This simple thing of being in a bed, being able to kiss and be naked, and simply be . . . together. It's everything to me and more. Doesn't every couple in love deserve the right to have this? By law of human nature, you should be able to express your love for someone. Not hide it.

For ages, we just kiss and feel. My hands wander, his hands wander, but most of all we simply kiss. My lips are swollen and sore, but nothing will stop me from having this time. To not have to rush and worry. It's been such a wonderful evening, and I'm not ready for it to end just yet. As soon as I fall asleep, it will be morning before I know it. And Josh will go his way, and I will go mine.

It's Josh who decides to end our marathon make-out session, breaking away from me and giving me a small smile before rolling to his back and tugging me into his side. I settle, my leg tossed over his thigh, and sigh a really contented sigh. I watch my finger draw lines across his chest as he plays with my hair. "Does your father know you are here?" I ask quietly.

"What do you think?"

"I don't know," I admit. "The way he looked at me this evening, I couldn't tell if it was disapproval, sympathy, or both."

"Both." His answer is so assertive, and it gets my mind spinning with what Josh has told his father about us. He must sense my curiosity because he goes on before I have the chance to ask. "He knows we had a thing."

"A thing?" I don't know why that bothers me. "Is that what this is? A thing?"

He nudges me, and it is definitely in warning. "It was a thing when Dad saw us at the royal stables that time."

With Josh's reminder of that lovely day, I lose all indignation. I think that may have been the day when I truly grasped the gravity of the trouble I was in. Not trouble in the sense of anyone finding out, but trouble in the sense I was already falling for the scandalously sexy American. "And now?"

"Now you are *my* thing." I hear the smile in his voice.

"I am, am I?" I quite like being Josh's thing.

"You know it."

I peek at him on a satisfied smile and get a tap on the end of my nose, making it wrinkle. "And what does your dad think we are now?"

"A dangerous combination."

I pout, injured, and even though I know it to be true, I still ask, "How so?" I want Senator Jameson's perspective.

"My father knows of the repercussions. He's worried about me, and what lengths your people will go to in order to keep me away. In his words, it'll portray you in the best light possible, and me in the worst."

Biting my lip, I resettle my cheek on Josh's chest and resume my absentminded tracing of his skin. "Didn't I already tell you that?" I mumble, my mood taking an unwelcome nosedive. "It is one of the endless reasons why no one can know about you. And that is why your stunt at the White House this evening was so reckless. Why did you do that?"

I feel him stiffen beneath me, and I know if I were to look up into his eyes, there would be the angry flashes of amber. "I did it because I wanted to dance with the woman I love."

"Nevertheless, you have piqued media interest when we should be doing everything to avoid *any* attention at all."

"So fuckin' kill me," he sighs, and my finger halts in its delicate trailing. "And there is nothing your people can do to keep me away."

He's fighting to keep his temper in check. I decide it wise not to correct him on that. There is plenty they can and *will* do.

"I don't want to argue," I whisper as I look up at him, feeling my emotions getting the better of me. "Especially since you will leave tomorrow, and I don't know when I might see you again."

"Fuck," Josh breathes, his hand going to his hair and raking through. He closes his eyes for a moment, calming, and then starts moving, sitting himself against the headboard. He negotiates my limbs until I'm straddling him, his knees bent behind me so I can lean back. He gives me imploring eyes, his hands holding mine. "I'm a jerk. It's just so fuckin' frustrating, Adeline."

"I know." It's all I can say. But he knew this. When he cornered me at the White House, he knew all of this. "Do you still want to be here?" My question isn't a trick one. I wouldn't blame him if he didn't, if he suddenly comprehended the impossibilities, but what could I do? Nothing is the answer. Absolutely nothing, which makes me even more powerless in this misconceived powerful role.

His face is plain disgusted. "Did you really ask me that? Yes, Adeline, I do. I'm staying and hoping we can find a solution. There *has* to be a solution."

I hope and pray for that solution, too. "You know I can't make any promises, Josh. I'm at the mercy of my family's history. Of the lies."

"No promises, no, but tell me we can at least discuss it. Don't write off our future just yet." Taking his hand to my nape, he pulls me forward until there's no space between the end of our noses. "After we argued in my hotel last week, I thought really hard about us. Whether I can be the world's biggest secret. Whether I could be happy having you without being able to share my love with the world. And bottom line, I can. I can do that, because my life without you in it isn't really a life anymore. It's a sentence. But, believe me when I say, Adeline, if there is a way for us to be together, I will find it."

If. Such a little word with such a big meaning. After a week of feeling so horrible, believing he'd given up, knowing he's so determined to pursue us brings some peace to my weary and battered soul. I can work with *if.* "I believe you," I tell him, because that is what he needs to hear. "And I will never stop searching for a solution, too." I drop into his chest and take comfort from both his resolve and strong arms holding me.

We could talk in circles forever and things will never be any different. Goodness knows, I've talked myself in circles for weeks. Not only desperately searching for answers to my exhausting problems, but also constantly questioning my integrity. I'm asking Josh to be happy being my secret. I'm asking him to accept what are really quite unreasonable terms to a relationship. If there is no solution to our plight, can I let Josh exist in the shadows of my life? Can I keep him for my own selfish reasons, even if I know it will slowly kill him? I swallow, not wanting to answer my silent questions. And I grip him tighter. I question if I should let him go, because keeping him really is selfish. But I can't help myself.

"Hey, what's up?" he asks, feeling my constricting hold.

I shake my head into him, willing the tears of despair not to come. "I love you so much."

He sighs, kicking his legs off the side of the bed. He finds his feet and stands with me curled around him, obviously concluding I'm not ready to let him go. "How about that shower?" he suggests, and I'm grateful. Distraction.

Carrying me to the bathroom, I'm encouraged to my feet, the shower is flipped on, and the room swathed in steam a minute later. As Josh approaches me, slowly with heavy eyes, I hold my breath and brace myself. "Right now," he says roughly, bringing me back around, "I'm going to make love to you in the shower."

This is better. No more wasting precious time with my melancholy. My lips part to release the stored air in my lungs, and Josh uses it as his opportunity to slip his tongue inside my mouth. My hands don't have a chance to find his shoulders, the sound of buzz-ing coming from the bedroom disturbing us. I grumble around his lips, quickly throwing my arms around him, my way of telling him he's not going anywhere.

"God damn it, my cell." Josh pries himself away and reverses his steps, giving me sorry eyes when he sees the expression on my face. Unhappy. "I have to get that. It'll be my publicist, and she'll freak out if I don't answer. Don't move."

The mention of Tammy sets my nerves off again. "Wait, does she know where you are?"

"What do you think?"

I know Josh's publicist wasn't pleased about our involvement. That was as plain as daylight each time I encountered her. "So, I'm *your* secret, too?" This makes me feel so much better. We are each other's secrets.

"No, I just haven't had the chance to tell her we're back together."

"Oh." There goes my theory and sense of mild comfort. I cannot even imagine what Tammy will say to Josh. That's not true at all. Of course I can imagine. It will be heavily based around a warning, maybe even a threat to quit as his publicist. Because there is no denying I'm the worst possible problem she could deal with. The ripple effect of our involvement seems to keep spreading.

A mild wave of dread crosses his face. "I should have called her before the Internet exploded. Get in the shower," Josh tells me, turning at the door. "I'll be two secs." He leaves, and I begrudgingly do as I'm told, soaking my hair under the hot spray and washing my face.

It's bliss, the hot water welcome on my body, but it's also very lonely. I kill the time removing my makeup, and once I'm done and can't possibly clean anymore without washing myself away, I wipe the condensation from the screen to find the door. "Josh?" I call, but I get no answer. I shut off the shower and wrap myself in a towel, venturing into the bedroom to find him. He's sitting on the end of the bed, his phone in his hand, staring at the screen. The stiffness of his body sets alarm bells ringing, and although I cannot see his face, I can sense his sharp jawline is cut further with anger. Not to mention the fact that the familiar burning amber in his eyes is pretty much reflecting off the screen of his phone as he studies it.

"Is everything okay?" I ask, keeping myself at the doorway, afraid to get too close for fear of being burned by the rage flaming his skin. What is wrong with him?

His head slowly lifts, and my fears are confirmed. He looks positively homicidal, and now I'm more fearful of what has provoked him. I cannot bring myself to ask him again, my body fidgeting nervously where I stand. "No, Adeline, everything is not okay." He stands, and with just those few words, it's clear the source of his anger involves me. His nostrils flaring, as if he's forcing calm breathing through his nose, he brings his naked body across the room toward me, and I start pulling my towel in protectively. "This," he breathes, holding his phone up, "is not fuckin' okay."

My wide eyes fall to the open webpage on his screen. And the picture dominating it is me. And . . ."Haydon?" I say, my mind quickly placing the picture of us. We're in the palace grounds, and he's handing me something. "Oh my goodness," I breathe, taking the phone from Josh's hand. The ring he bought me. It's in the little box he's passing to me. I swipe my finger up the screen to scroll, looking for whatever words may be with the pictures. I find no words, just another picture. This one of him putting the ring on my finger. I close my eyes and count to ten, at the same time wondering why Josh is so angry. Is it simply because my gift from Haydon has been leaked to the press adding more fuel to the speculation of our supposed relationship? "You know he gave me that ring," I say, looking up at Josh's bristling form. "I cannot help that the information was leaked." Although I plan on finding out by who.

Josh doesn't relax, but tenses further. When he speaks, it is through a jaw ready to snap. "I don't give a fuck about his piece-of-shit ring. He's not even putting it on the right finger. Read the article."

I dare not, so I simply stare at Josh. He needs to calm down.

"Oh, don't you want to read it?" he asks, snatching the phone from my grasp, making me recoil a little. Not that he notices past the fury dominating him. He is absolutely blinded by it, and I am getting increasingly frustrated. And annoyed. Why on earth is he so worried about something like this being released when he knows the history behind it? I ran away to Scotland for him when my father tried *again* to make me marry Haydon.

"No, I don't want to read it," I grate. "It'll be a pile of rubbish, and likely send my temper into orbit."

"I don't blame you. It's pretty fuckin' nauseating, even if it's a pile of trash. Here"—he laughs sardonically at the screen—"a dinner planned between Haydon Sampson's family and the Queen's family and closest aides."

"What?" I blurt, confused.

"Oh, yes. Apparently, the arrangements are in place to seal the deal between you two." Ever the alpha male, he probably hates feeling his life is out of his control. I'm conditioned, I expect it, but Josh is going to pop. "The Queen herself accepted Haydon Sampson's dinner invitation to thrash out the details of their union with both families." He scrolls again, shaking. "An anonymous source confirmed the Queen's satisfaction that things are moving forward nicely with the man she's been tipped to marry for years."

I'm so shocked I cannot even find any words, leaving Josh to rage on, his mobile phone sure to crumble in his fierce grip at any moment.

"A coronation and a wedding. But which will come first?" Josh mimics the question with so much sarcasm.

My head begins to ache. How did this happen? Who wrote these lies?

Josh's phone hits the floor with force, bouncing on the carpet at our bare feet. "I fuckin' hate this. I should go out there, find the bastard that spilled these lies, and ram my fist down his fuckin' throat."

Jesus, he looks perfectly capable. "I have never accepted a dinner invit . . ." I fade off when something horrible comes to me, my eyes widening, my feet taking me a step back. "Oh God, no," I say, more to myself than to Josh.

"Yes, I know. Irritating as fuck, huh?"

I stare at him in silence, but my mind is screaming.

He pulls up. "Wait, there's no truth in this . . . is there?"

I bite my lip, nervous.

His mouth falls open. "Adeline, tell me they are lies."

"I agreed to have dinner with the Sampsons. Plural." I swallow, hating the sight of Josh's face distorting in disgust. "Sabina recently lost her husband, and David his father, and then one of his closest friends. It was just to appease—"

"What the fuck?" His lip curls with the mention of Haydon's father. I can't blame him. The man is a cling-on; his desperation to have some kind of status and importance is sickening. This is part of his doing. Sir Don, David, and the rest of the rotten, obsolete bastards who want what is *best* for the Monarchy and not what is best for their Queen. I bet Sir Don went straight to his hotel room and called David. I bet they plotted and schemed, anticipating the pictures of Josh and me. This is their retaliation. Their way of getting back the control and deflecting the attention from where they don't want it. It's their way of trying to force my arm, to make me do something I refuse to do. "Why the fuck would you do that?" he bellows, incensed.

He's not the only one. I'm suddenly so very angry, my temper brewing dangerously. Had Josh not paraded me around that dance floor for the world to see, this would not be happening. This is just as much his fault, and he has the nerve to stand here and be mad with me? I can see the tight muscles in his face loosen somewhat as he regards me, his thoughts clearly curious. He's wondering what I'm thinking, wondering why I also look like I might murder someone. Well, I'll happily enlighten him.

"Why the hell are you so bloody mad?" I ask through gritted teeth.

"*Why?*" Josh looks incredulous. "The press is telling the fuckin' world that an announcement about the engagement of my fuckin' girlfriend is imminent." He throws his arms up in the air heavily. "And it isn't to me."

"Deal with it," I spit, shouldering my way past him, with not the first idea of where I plan on going. It's not like I have the luxury of freedom to escape his unreasonable arse. "Since you instigated it."

"Me?" he asks from behind me, sounding truly startled by my accusation. "How the fuck is this my fault?"

I swing around, holding my towel in place with hands that are vibrating angrily. "Because had you not been so bold and trapped me on the dance floor, Sir Don wouldn't have seen us together, there would be no bloody pictures for the press to speculate over, and the damn bastards who believe they still rule my life wouldn't have retaliated by feeding the press other pictures anonymously. That's how."

"Bullshit," he spits, almost laughing, as if my claim is absurd. It isn't. That's what we're dealing with now. These are the bloody lengths. "You still agreed to have dinner with the prick," Josh rants.

"No, I didn't. I said yes to Sabina, to David and—"

"You're mine, Adeline. If I want to fuckin' dance with you, then I fuckin' will."

Oh my goodness, how many times has he dropped the F-word in the past few hours? My ears could bleed. "So you admit it?"

"Admit what?" he sneers.

"Tonight was all just about your stupid, manly ego. You should have just pissed up my fucking leg, you possessive arsehole." I will not apologize for my bad language. I'm too bloody mad.

"You think *that* was possessive?" He prowls forward, and I walk

back, clinging to my towel. "No, darlin', that wasn't possessive."
He grabs me and thrusts me lightly but firmly into the wall. "Let
me show you possessive." His mouth collides with mine, so hard,
my head hits the wall behind me. "This is possessive," he growls,
taking me violently, his tongue whipping through my mouth. There
is a stubborn, reasonable part of me that tells me to fight him off
and slap his face for his behavior. There is a side of me that loses
all reason and willfulness where Josh Jameson is concerned. And
then there is another side of me, the unruly side, that loves the fuel
he adds to my flames.

Dominated by my anger, the source of which I have momentarily
forgotten, I release my towel and fist his hair viciously, returning
his brutal kiss stroke for stroke, force for force.

"Oh, she's angry, too, huh?" he pants biting my bottom lip so
hard I'm sure he must have drawn blood. Pushing his forehead to
mine, he glares at me, and I glare right back. He might be pissed
off, but so am I.

Very boldly, I push into him with equal determination, if not
with equal force. My forehead is becoming numb, the term locking
horns never being more appropriate than now.

"Yes, I'm fucking angry," I pant, my breathing already diminished. Whether that is by desire or fury, I couldn't tell you.

"You turn me on so much when you cuss." His smile is wicked.
"Ready for some angry sex?"

"Yes."

My thigh is grabbed and yanked up to his waist. "Good, because
I need to expel some of this rage before I do something I regret."

"Like what?"

"Ruin everything." He lifts me from my feet and smashes our
mouths back together, our kiss ferocious as he walks us to the bed.
We fall onto the mattress in a messy tatter, and Josh finds his place
between my thighs too quickly for me to prepare for his invasion.
He slams into me as hard as carnally possible and yells, his face tight,

his anger still potent. I choke on my held scream, not prepared to give him the satisfaction of hearing it. He's looking at me like he hates me. Good, at this moment in time, I hate him, too. I hate him for being careless. I hate him for being reckless. I hate him for being so unreasonably sexy when he's mad. And I hate him for being the center of my universe.

I match the fire in his eyes with equal heat, taking my fingernails to his back and dragging them down his flesh. He stiffens, arching his back a little on a suppressed hiss. But he doesn't try to stop me. On the contrary, I'm sure I see goading in his stare, and not one to disappoint, I pry my claws from the base of his back and scratch him from his shoulders to his arse once more. And in retaliation, he withdraws quickly and pounds back into me on a grunt. "Again," he demands, willing on the pain I'm inflicting. "Pain is the only thing that's going to penetrate the anger, Adeline. So do it again."

My nails sink back into his shoulders and drag slowly down his flesh. His head tossed back on a throaty growl, he crashes into me again, jolting me up the bed on a cry. "Again." Braced on one arm, he reaches for my wet hair and fists it, provoking me. "Fuckin' do it."

I yell and do as I'm ordered, scratching at his back, each stroke of my nails instigating a pound of his hips. Sweat coats both of our bodies, our fiery passion taking the sex into harmful territory. I'm sore, every strike hitting me unfathomably deep, my scalp tender from him pulling my hair. I'm hurting everywhere, but the pain is more bearable than the anger. The pain is less damaging than the rage. I space out, my glazed eyes centered on Josh above me as he slams home over and over, his jaw no longer tight with anger, but tight with pleasure and pain. I know he's preparing for his climax when he releases my hair and supports his torso with two arms again. I relieve his back of my vicious nails, sure it must be a roadmap of red, swollen lashes, and slap my palms into his chest. His biceps are bulging where they are braced either side of me, the sounds of our bodies slapping echoing around the room. My veins burn, my stomach muscles ache, pressure building between my thighs. I seize it and hold myself on the edge, waiting for the sign I need that he's about to shatter. The sign is Josh holding his breath until his face goes red, and when his hips start to shake on every strike, I let go, forcing my eyes to remain open. My vision distorts, Josh bucks on a yell, and I'm suddenly freefalling in darkness, the pressure releasing and swirling through me like an antidote for everything poisoning me. Anger, frustration, pain. It's all gone in this moment, and there is only Josh. Only us. Only *right now*.

I reach for his neck and pull him down, my lips finding his with ease. His moans into my mouth are ragged and broken as we kiss each other through our highs. And it goes on and on and on.

Until we both eventually sigh.

Falling limply onto me, he twitches, holding himself deeply, his eyes clenching shut from the sensitivity being too much. Our tongues become clumsy and random, his drenched body slipping across mine like it could be ice.

Kissing his way aimlessly across my cheek to my ear, he doesn't find the strength to kiss his way back, burying his face there. Our breathing is loud, our hearts sprinting. I can hear my pulse in my ears, can feel Josh's neck veins throbbing. I'm drained of all energy. And I am drained of all anger.

Giving into my heavy lids, I close my eyes and curl all my limbs around him. "They're going to force you to marry him." Josh only just gets his words out over his labored breathing. "And there is nothing I can do to stop them without hurting you."

I stare at the ceiling, hating the helplessness in his usually sure voice. "You don't need to stop them." I squeeze him tightly in the hopes that it adds to my reassuring words. "Because I will."

They no longer have power over me.

I am the fucking Queen of England.

No one will make me bow.

14

WITH JUST A slight shift of my body, every muscle I have, and many I *didn't* realize I have, pull painfully. "Oh, ouch," I mumble sleepily into the pillow, my face screwing up. I still and try to relax, sprawled on my front, and wince as my mind takes me on a little journey, refreshing my sleepy memory of why I'm hurting so much.

Angry sex, he said.

He wasn't wrong.

Willing my head to lift, I manage to turn it on the pillow until I'm looking the other way. My lips, something else that's hurting, smile when I find Josh mirroring my pose, splattered on his front, his gorgeous head sunken into the pillow. He's unconscious, his mouth open a little, his dark hair a mussed-up mess. My hurting body quickly forgotten, I peel my front from the sheets and wriggle across the bed. He doesn't stir, his lids not even flickering. He's dead to the world. And adorable.

On my side, my head now sharing his pillow, I reach forward with a fingertip and tickle the end of his nose, making him wrinkle it in his sleep. I keep my amused chuckle at bay and lightly brush at it again.

He twitches, one eye opening narrowly. "What are you doing?"

"Nothing." I take the sheets and pull them down his back, ready to lie on him, and come face to face with the aftermath of our angry sex. *Oh God.*

"How much damage did you do?" he asks sleepily as I stare at his mutilated back.

Shame washes over me. "I think we should avoid angry sex in the future."

"That bad, huh?"

He looks like he's been thrashed, the lines spotted with dried blood. "Josh, I'm so sorry." I hope he hasn't got any filming in the near future that requires him shirtless. And if he has, the makeup artist will have her work cut out.

"I asked for it." He rolls his shoulder blades. "Come give me a hug." He makes no attempt to move, so I take his hint and climb on his back, spreading myself gingerly all over him. He hums, his arms coming up above his head on the pillow. "Your boobs feel good squished into my back." He sighs. "You okay?"

I lay my arms over his, my cheek squashed into his skin. "Very well. You?"

"Fuckin' sore."

"You asked for it."

He ignores me, but lifts his arse a little, jolting me. "When are you flying home?"

I pout to myself with the reminder that our time is coming to an end. "Today."

"That sucks." His voice is quiet and rough, through sleep *and* disappointment. "I have to leave for LA tomorrow. I was hoping that by some miracle, we might've got to spend the day together."

LA. Once again we will be a world apart. "A new film?"

"Yeah."

"How long are you there?"

"Indefinitely."

My heart sinks, though I cannot possibly be surprised. It's where he lives, after all. "One thinks that you should only accept roles for projects in the UK."

He chuckles lightly, craning his neck awkwardly to look at me. "Would I be able to see you more if I were in London?" he asks, and I scowl. "There. Whether I'm thousands of miles away, or just one mile away, the distance is the same. We're still a world apart." Settling back on his pillow, he goes quiet, thinking, and I hate that his thoughts are likely as depressing as mine.

"So when will I see you?" I ask, rather unfairly, though I'm finding it difficult to see past my need for something to cling to. It'll be the only thing to get me through his absence.

"You tell me, Adeline. I already told you, I'm at your mercy."

Is he punishing me? Making a point? And has he forgotten I am at the mercy of so much more? Regardless, I don't want to spend our last moments together arguing. So I relax and savor the feel of our skin touching in all the places it could touch. "I love you," I tell him quietly, the words coming instinctively. "Please remember that. *Always* remember that."

There's a short silence before he whispers, "I love you, too," though there is pain in his words. Is it because he really doesn't want to love me? Because that would be the easiest thing here. To not love. To not need. To have the ability to walk away without feeling like a part of you has been ripped from your body. There are moments like this when it is all so very hopeless. And then moments like last night when hopelessness is forgotten. But our time together will always have an end point. There will always be a storm after the sun has shone.

The mood now flat, I find strength to turn it around. "Tell me about your new role."

He juts his bum up again and starts to turn over. I lift to allow him the space, giving him sorry eyes when he hisses as he comes to rest on his back. Settling, he smiles when I wedge my elbows into his pecs and rest my chin on my hands, attentive and ready to listen.

"I'm a psychopathic professor of psychology."

My head retreats on my neck. "Sounds ideal. Was last night research?" I ask, thinking that Josh looked very much like a psychopath while we argued.

"Being psychotic isn't about being angry. It's a personality disorder."

I raise my eyebrows cheekily. "Oh?" The way Josh can go from calm to lunatic in the blink of an eye surely qualifies him. He rolls his eyes, catching my line of thought, though he refrains from scolding me.

"I have an affair with another member of the faculty and become the subject of her studies. It's being pitched as *Basic Instinct* meets *A Beautiful Mind*." His palms land on my bottom and stroke wide circles.

I withdraw a little. *Basic Instinct*? I don't claim to be a film buff, but I'm sure I have heard it's a bit raunchy. And Josh said *her*. He becomes the subject of *her* studies. "*Basic Instinct*?" I parrot, trying my very hardest to sound interested rather than disturbed. He nods, a slow smile forming, though he doesn't say a word, but rather lets my mind spiral further. He knows what I'm thinking, and now I know I heard right. It *is* raunchy. There will be sex scenes. "Who's playing *her*?"

"Tia Piper."

I balk at him. "Tia Piper?"

"You got trouble hearing this morning?" He's taking the greatest pleasure out of my uneasiness. Where Josh Jameson was voted Hollywood's hottest man, Tia Piper was voted alongside him as Hollywood's sexiest woman. Tall, leggy, Amazonian-like looks. And, worst of all, she's recently left her rock-star husband. I remember reading about it with Matilda over champagne.

I flatten my forearms on his chest and lay my head on them, hiding my discomfort from Josh. "She's pretty." What a stupid thing to say. She is more than pretty. She's a goddess. And Josh is going to be getting naked with her. I grimace.

"Is the Queen feeling threatened?"

"I have no idea what you are talking about," I retort, my indignation bringing the utter snob out in me, making Josh laugh. I scowl, an unreasonable thought coming to me. I hope she sees the state of his back and wonders who inflicted the injuries.

"Hey." Josh shifts, and I roll off him to my back. His smiling face is soon hovering over my twisted one. "If it was deemed appropriate for the Queen to feature on The World's Sexiest Women List, you would have left the competition standing."

"Does that mean you are more attracted to me than her?" Where has this needy, jealous streak come from? I don't like it in the least.

"Adeline, to me you are beyond the scale of beauty." He drops a pacifying kiss on my lips. "By a million miles."

He's sweet, but he hasn't denied my fears. "She'll see you naked. You'll have to kiss her, and she'll have to touch you in places only I should touch."

"It's my job. At least no one is trying to force me to marry her."

"No one will force me t—" I'm silenced by his mouth before we fall into the realms of a potential argument once again. I'm grateful to be distracted, realigning my focus on the now.

"In my world, there is only you, woman," he mumbles across my lips between the strokes of his tongue. "She's not my type. Not at all. *You* are my type. Only you."

"You mean a Queen?"

"No, I mean *my* Adeline."

I could burst with appreciation. "Will you call me every day?"

"I won't get through a day without that, so yes." He works his lips onto my cheek. "I quite like this jealous streak."

"Oh, behave." I laugh as he mauls me. He may do, but I most certainly do not. It's only just occurred to me that I'll be helpless to stop the women throwing themselves at his feet. There will be nothing I can do while I'm locked in my palace being Queen.

"You trust me, don't you?" he asks, as if reading my mind. "And your answer dictates whether I slap that ass of yours stupid."

I smile. "I trust you." But I'm wondering whether I should say I don't, if it means his palm on my skin.

"Good. What's the time?" Josh blindly reaches for his mobile on the nightstand as I look across to the drawn curtains.

Reluctantly, I say what I've been dreading all night. "We'd better get you out before everyone wakes up."

Josh huffs his displeasure and glances at his phone. "Fuck."

"What?"

"It's 7:45."

"Oh, stop it." I roll my eyes and relax back. "It can't be. Olive would have been in here ages ago to—"

The door swings open, and both our eyes dart toward it.

There's not a moment to consider the fact that we are both as naked as can be, not a chance to hide our dignity with the sheets. Olive is standing in the doorway, her hand on the knob, her mouth hanging open. She's a statue, as are we, us staring at Olive, Olive staring at us. For bloody ages. My brain has completely malfunctioned on me.

I see the second she comes back to life, because she physically shakes herself to do it. Backing out of the room, she bows her head. "Pardon me, ma'am." The door closes, though Josh and I don't stop staring at it, not for a very long time.

"Bloody hell," I finally breathe, bringing my hands to my face and covering it. "Bloody, *bloody* hell."

"Yeah," Josh confirms simply, pushing himself up to his knees. "What now?"

"God damn it, where in heaven's name is Damon?" I ask myself, shuffling to the edge of the bed. I scurry across the bedroom and wrap myself in my robe. "Wait here."

"What are you doin'?"

"I need to talk to her," I say as I head for the door.

"Will she say anything?"

"Olive? God, no. She's a sweetheart, but she tends to get herself in a fluster." I open the door and find Olive on the other side, looking no less startled than when she fled my room. Her body is static, frozen in shock. I offer her a small smile as I pull the door closed behind me.

"I'm so sorry," she whispers, looking on the verge of breaking down. "I didn't realize you had company, Your Majesty." She's ripping herself to shreds, and it saddens me that she clearly thinks I am about to rip her apart, too.

"Olive." I reach for her shaky arms and hold her in place, stemming her trembles. "You weren't to know." For goodness sake, what is Damon playing at? "Where's Damon?"

Her limp arm lifts and points across the room, and on a heavy frown, I move forward a few paces until the couch comes into view. Damon is sprawled across one end, catching flies, and Bates across the other end, snoring. A large empty bottle of Scotch is set on the table before them, playing cards scattered across the wood. I shake my head in dismay and turn back toward Olive. "Have you seen Sir Don this morning?"

"I haven't, ma'am."

"Kim?"

"She's waiting in the dining room for you, ma'am. I didn't wake you earlier because it was a late night. I thought you would like a lay-in. But then Kim arrived and reminded me that you had a breakfast meeting and I thought I would get into trouble because I should have woken you earlier and now I wish I hadn't because I believe I shouldn't have seen what I just saw and it's all gone horribly wrong." She reaches for her pumping chest, and I fear she may fall into a full-blown panic attack.

"Calm down." I go to her and take her hands. "Now, I need you to do something for me."

"Anything, ma'am."

"Can you keep Kim in the dining room? And if Sir Don comes to my room, tell him I will be ready soon. Don't let him in." She starts to nod obediently, and I smile fondly at her. "You do that, and I'll take care of the rest." I turn her by her shoulders and send her on her way. "And Olive?" I call quietly.

She looks over her shoulder as she hurries away to fulfill her brief. "Don't worry, Your Majesty." She gives me an over-the-top wink, her mouth opening as she does. "Your secret is safe with me."

I can't help but laugh a little as she goes, not in the least bit doubt-ful that it is. "Thank you, Olive." She disappears, and I return my attention to my wayward bodyguard. "Now, then," I say to myself, marching over. As I bend to poke him, I get a waft of stale Scotch. I wrinkle my nose in disgust and stab at his shoulder with my rigid finger. "Damon," I whisper, getting nothing. "Damon, wake up." My finger pokes turn into light smacks of his cheek when I get no response. "Hey, you drunken fool." I inject a little more power into my hand and slap his head.

"Hey!" He scrambles up into a straight sitting position and darts wide, foggy eyes around the room. "What's going on?"

"You drank yourself unconscious," I inform him as Bates starts to stir at the other end.

Damon takes a few moments, blinking and gathering his bearings before finding me. He looks me up and down, frowning. "What are you doing up?"

"It's nearly eight." I wait as the penny slowly drops. And when it's landed and settled, he shoots up from the couch.

And immediately wobbles, forcing me to catch his arms before he topples. "Fucking hell." He rocks back on his heels, his face screwing up. "I had a drink."

"You don't say," I tease, only releasing him when I'm sure he's steady. My gesture is silly. If he were to fall, my little female frame would never stop him.

Coughing his throat clear, he straightens out his disheveled form. "Well, you did say I could."

I can't argue with that. I did, but it looks and smells like Damon and Bates had more than a drink. The rather large empty bottle confirms it. So does his lack of a wake-up call.

"Where's Jameson?" Bates croaks, wedging his palm into the arm of the couch and pushing himself up. He also staggers, his body half bent for a few seconds before he deems it safe to straighten to his full height.

"He is still in my bed." I fold my arms over my chest, trying to look all disapproving when actually I'm rather amused. "And now I will leave you two the challenge of getting him out without every member of my staff seeing."

"Got any rope?" Damon asks Bates.

"Nah. We could tie some sheets together and lower him down."

Damon chuckles, as does Bates, while I watch on, certain they must still be drunk. "Or we could just grab a maid and stuff him in her washing cart," I suggest on an exasperated eye-roll.

They both stop laughing and look at each other.

"Do not even think about it," I warn, seeing their intentions. "Kim's in the dining room. One of you will have to make sure everyone else is busy and out of the way while the other gets Josh out of my suite." I head back to the bedroom, hearing the two men laughing together like a pair of kids. "I hope you are calling for someone else to drive," I say to Bates. There's no question he'll be over the limit. I look back as I take the door handle, waiting for his confirmation.

He snaps himself out of his giggling fit and straightens. "Of course, Your Majesty."

"Very good." I enter the bedroom and find Josh dressed. "Our security men have hangovers."

Josh seems delighted by this, his smile huge. "You're shittin' me?"

"No, I am not *shittin'* you." I put myself in his chest, my arms linked around his waist, and look at him. "I have a meeting with Kim in a few minutes. You'll have to sneak out."

"Story of our lives, huh?"

"It seems to be," I sigh. "I'll keep Kim busy, Damon and Bates will do the rest." Our lips touch, and the goodbye kiss is here. Naturally, my arms lock around him tighter, forcing him to reach back and pry them away. I'd protest, but I know Josh is doing what I should be doing. Not prolonging the inevitable. Making it as easy as possible. "Don't go," I plead unreasonably.

But he just smiles and breaks away, landing one more chaste kiss on my lips. "I'll call you." He ushers me away from him, and I take backward steps so I get to see him for as long as possible before I reach the door. He looks lonely all by himself in the middle of the room. His lips quirk at the corners as I force my body to turn. "Adeline?" he calls, stalling me.

"Yes?"

"Don't marry anyone while I'm gone, 'kay?"

My nose wrinkles and I leave, hoping that isn't a true worry for him. Because it shouldn't be.

15

I MAKE IT to the dining room table at eight on the dot, though my promptness isn't noted. My undressed, un-showered form, however, is. It is far from being the good start I hoped for. As gracefully as my sore body allows, I lower to the chair and smile my thanks when a coffee is poured for me. After spending a purposely extended amount of time studying my unpresentable form, Kim goes back to her phone, making sporadic notes.

"Oversleep?" she asks without looking at me. Her attitude isn't really acceptable, but I refrain from pulling her up on it.

"Apparently so." Reaching for a pastry, I pick at it while I wait for Kim to finish whatever it is she is doing. I've nearly eaten the whole thing by the time she kindly gives me her attention. "Come on, then," I say, speeding things along.

Without a word, she starts pulling sheets of paper from a file on the table, sliding each one toward me leisurely. I stare at the pictures, all of Josh and me on various parts of the dance floor at the White House.

"It's speculation." I push them all away and take another pastry. I'm giving her nothing. "Besides, I'm sure my supposedly imminent engagement to Haydon Sampson is diverting any media attention from those pictures." I eye her as I take a nibble of my new pastry and sit back in my chair. "Did you know about it?"

"Of course not." Kim seems highly offended, and I believe her offence to be genuine. "And with all due respect, ma'am, I don't think even the end of the world would detract the attention from these pictures."

"Anyone would think it *is* the end of the world," I grumble. "I danced with Josh Jameson. What of it?"

"What of it?" Kim leans forward in her chair. "Adeline, can you see the looks on both of your faces?" She pushes one of the photographs toward me, and my eyes drop. "If you try to tell me that there isn't something going on between the two people in this picture, then I'll eat my hat."

She's one hundred percent right. You can see the chemistry coming off the page. I breathe out, a little stumped. I'll look like a total fool if I deny it. "I danced with Josh Jameson," I repeat, shoving the picture away and returning to my pastry. "If others choose to make more of it, that is their problem, not mine." I'm a fool.

Kim falls back in her chair in total exasperation, clearly concluding the same. "I know . . ." She drifts off and leans forward over the table, dropping her voice to a mere whisper. "I know what happened that night at Kellington."

"No, you made assumptions." I never confirmed a damn thing.

"And were my assumptions wrong?"

"Yes," I sniff. "There has not been, and never will be, anything between Josh Jameson and me." Picking up my coffee, I look to Kim as I take a sip, my front never wavering. That is, until I catch sight of something behind her. I cough on a swallow, battling to keep my eyes from widening.

"Adeline, this is me. I've known you for years," Kim goes on, and I nod, absentminded as I watch Damon tiptoe across the other side of the room, Josh close behind. I get a small wave from Damon and a forced worried expression from Josh. I drop my coffee cup to the saucer a little heavy-handed, turning my startled stare onto Kim. "I'm sorry, what?"

She frowns. "I said, this is me. I've known you for years, so I know you're not being truthful."

She basically just called the Queen a liar, and she would be right. But one thing I have learned in my journey to today is that the Monarchy hasn't survived on truths. "I've known you for years also, Kim, and I'm sorry to say you seem to have a stick shoved up your arse since your change in role."

Her face drops. "I'm trying to do my job. To advise you."

"Your job is also to support me. I have enough people *advising* me." I glance up to see Damon and Josh have almost made it to freedom. Thank goodness. "Kim," I return my attention to her, "your job may be somewhat different, but I am not. I expect I will run into many brick walls during my reign, be told exactly what I must do. Some things, I won't have a choice. Others, I will stand my ground as long as it's not detrimental to anyone going forward. Whether you agree with me or not, I need you in my corner. I need a friend, and you have always been a friend to me."

I watch as she softens in her chair, and her lip definitely quivers. "I just want to do the best job. I want to impress, show I'm capable."

For years, Kim has been by my side. I have never seen her falter or look vulnerable. But seeing her concern reminds me that it's not only me affected by my new position. Damon has handled my role change seamlessly, as I would expect. Yet clearly, Kim is feeling more pressure than I understood. Until now. She is capable but needs to be bolstered and trained. Davenport needs to return. God, I so wish he would return. I silently accept that *that* isn't going to happen. I haven't heard from him, which I guess is his answer without formally answering me. So I need Kim to understand she is my confidant, and I need her to rise to the level required. "Who do you want to impress, Kim? Who do you want to do the best job for?" I ask. "Them, or me? And since your future is in my hands, I suggest you consider your answer wisely."

Her elbows hit the table, her hands holding up her heavy head. "Of course, you." There is nothing but sincerity in her tone, and maybe a little regret.

I reach across the table and take her hand, giving it a thankful squeeze, and I am just drawing breath to voice my thanks, when a huge clatter sounds.

I look up and find Damon on the floor and Josh standing over him, an array of various luggage items caught up in his legs. "Shit," Damon curses as Kim swings around. "Missed those."

Josh snorts, Damon shrugs sheepishly, and Kim slowly turns back toward me, her head tilted in question.

Oh shit. What fools.

"Oh look." I smile sweetly and pop another small pastry into my mouth. "Josh Jameson is staying in the same hotel as me."

"And the plot thickens," Kim sighs.

16

"WHAT DUMB ARSE put all these bags here?" Damon grumbles as Josh helps him up from the floor. "Hasn't anyone heard of risk management?"

"I have," Kim quips. "Apparently it's not necessary around these parts."

I shoot her a tired look and get up from the table, holding up the coffee pot. "Caffeine?"

"God, yeah." Josh moves in quickly and seizes the goods from my hand, surprising me with a hard, chaste kiss on the lips before pouring and downing his coffee.

I press my lips together and flick Kim a cheesy, nervous grin. "It seems someone is thirsty."

"And me." Damon moves in and gets his fix, too. "Jesus, my head is banging."

"What's going on?" Bates appears, taking in the scene. "I thought this was a stealth mission? No one mentioned coffee breaks." He paces over to the table and takes the pot from Damon. "Give me that."

Kim's head hits the table. "Oh my God."

"Oh, calm down," I breathe, pouring them all more coffee, which they drink down ravenously. "It isn't the end of the world."

"Yeah." Josh backs me up and stuffs a pastry in his mouth. "No laws have been broken," he waffles on, his mouth full.

I can't help my grin.

Kim shakes her head. "I can't even appreciate the fact that I'm so close to Josh Jameson. And, for the record, royal laws carry serious penalties."

Her words sting, though, begrudgingly, I cannot deny that she is right. The consequences of my actions could not only ruin my own life, but that of the people closest to me. "You are such a pessimist," I mumble, lowering back to the chair. "I fell in love. So bloody hang me."

The room falls silent, and everyone stills. Staring at me. For a second, I wonder why. Then I rewind though the past few seconds and realize why I'm being gawked at like I could have risen from hell. My lips twist awkwardly as I drop my gaze to the table. I can't take that back.

"Yeah," Josh says quietly, discarding his half-eaten pastry and rounding the table to me. On a grin so large it could possibly split his handsome face, he braces his hands on the table and gets up close to me. "Say it again."

My eyes narrow on him, causing his stupid grin to widen. "I will not."

"Oh, you will." He grasps my cheeks and squeezes. "Louder. So there's no misunderstanding."

The egotistical pig. "I love you." I relent to his demand, and rather than worry about the fact that Kim may have just passed out across the table, I let Josh kiss me. And it isn't just a peck. It's a full-on tongues and moans thing.

My surroundings are so easy to forget in times like these, and I scramble to grab my equilibrium once he's relieved me of his mouth. The satisfaction shining at me isn't something I can ignore.

He's thrilled. So pleased with himself, and, apparently, with me.

"How bad did it hurt?" he asks cheekily. "You proclaiming your love for me?"

"You're stupid."

"You make me that way." Turning to Kim, Josh helps himself to another pastry and tosses it into the air, catching it perfectly before ripping off the edge with his teeth. "Breathe, Kim. You look like you're gonna pass out."

He's right. She's white as a sheet. "Kim, this isn't as bad as you think." I'm lying, of course. For her, it is terrible.

"And how did you fathom that?"

"We're careful," I tell her. "And I trust my closest aides."

"Ma'am?" Olive's unsure voice drifts into the room and Kim closes her eyes to gather patience.

"It's fine," I tell Kim. "Olive knows."

"Great. Am I the last?"

"No, Sir Don doesn't, and he can't."

"Give me a break," Kim mutters. "You think the picture of you and Haydon splashed in every online news publication this morning was a coincidence?"

I flick a wary look to Josh. He's stopped chewing. He looks savage again. "Regardless of what he suspects, I will work tirelessly to never confirm." I have to if I'm going to keep Josh safe from their retaliation. I look across to Olive, who's patiently waiting for my attention. "Everything okay, Olive?"

"I was just packing your things, ma'am, and I can't seem to find your Spanish tiara."

"Oh, it's on the—" I freeze in my seat and dart my eyes to Josh, who has resumed munching his way through his breakfast. "My tiara."

"Oh." He points to the bedroom with his pastry. "It's on the—" His arm drops. "Oh fuck."

My eyes widen as I pray he isn't about to say what I think he may be about to say. "No," I plead.

"I left it in the bar."

"No." I drop my head to the table.

"You're careful." Kim mimics my words and gets up from her chair. "I'm going to hunt down a priceless Spanish tiara." She turns to Damon, who is definitely still drunk, rocking back on his heels looking rather vacant. I smile to myself as Kim throws an arm in Josh's direction. "You get him out of here before anyone else sees him." She stomps off, exasperated, and slams the door behind her.

"Come on." Bates grabs Josh and starts to manhandle him out of the suite. "We've way outstayed our welcome."

Josh breaks free and rushes over to me, landing me with a forceful peck. "I love you, too." He bites my nose and lets Bates reclaim him and wrestle him away, leaving my lips pressed tightly to stop my smile. He doesn't take his eyes off me until he's out the door, stumbling clumsily as Bates tugs him along.

I glance around me, to the chaos I have caused.

This is my life now.

My face could split with my epic grin.

17

WHEN WE PULL up at Kellington the next day after hours of travel, I'm utterly exhausted. I've held off from confronting Sir Don on his underhanded move, wanting to wait until I've restocked on energy and grit. Josh has wiped me out, albeit in the best possible way. I slept for most of the flight, though I don't feel any better for it.

Kim was only mildly appeased when she tracked down my tiara. Thank heavens, a cleaner found it early in the morning and handed it straight to her superior. No explanation for it being in the bar in the first place was given, and I'm pretty sure Kim's face told the member of staff not to ask. She ranted for a little while about the potential backlash, but I don't see the risk that Kim does. The manager knows that an anonymous person paid obscene amounts of money to hire the bar privately. Why couldn't that anonymous person be me? Maybe I just wanted a peaceful drink in a regular bar. I went to argue my case, but Sir Don had turned up at my suite, shutting us both up about my disappearing priceless family heirloom.

Damon opens my door and I slide out, straightening and moving my bag to the crook of my arm. He still looks terrible. One of his other men had to drive, and I could tell once Damon had sobered up, he was embarrassed. "Feeling okay?" I ask.

"Very good, ma'am." His face is deadpan, and mine is anything but.

"You're funny when you are intoxicated," I say, taking the steps to the doors, my amusement dropping when I spy David in the foyer. Oh God, what is he doing here? I should rip strips off him for his part in the latest news, but again, I'm too tired to take them on right now.

"Welcome home, ma'am." He smiles a most sincere smile as I pass him, pulling off my gloves.

"Thank you." I hand my bag and gloves to a waiting maid. "I do believe it was a very successful trip."

Sir Don's smile tightens as he joins us. He doesn't agree, of course.

My bags all pass me, various footmen carrying them. "No unpacking just yet," I tell Olive as she follows them all. "I'd like to have a few moments alone in my suite." I promised Josh I would call him the moment I arrived home, and I'm desperate to talk to him.

She nods and continues as I wriggle out of my coat for Jenny. "Anything else, ma'am?" she asks.

"You get home." I start taking the stairs, my feet set to burst out of my shoes. Taking them off during the flight was a dreadful mistake. When it came to prepping me for landing and the media who would be waiting, I could barely get them back on, my ankles a little puffy. Dehydration, Kim had claimed. And lack of sleep the night before. I had silently grinned as Olive stuffed my feet into my heels, remembering my time with Josh second by second.

"When may I expect you to be ready for your debrief?" Sir Don calls as I reach the top of the stairs. "There is much to discuss, ma'am."

I stop and stare forward, my eyes narrowing somewhat. Yes, there is much to discuss, and first on my priority list is the report on Haydon and me. Which, come to think of it, I must speak to Haydon about, too. I don't want to believe that he was privy to the devious stunt my aides pulled. Yet now I wonder why he hasn't called to assure me if that is the case, since it must have been news to him, too. "When I have rested, Sir Don." I leave him with only that.

When I enter my suite, I sigh and wait for my bags to be set down and everyone to leave me in peace. Then I collapse on the bed and call Josh. He answers after just one ring, and I relax at the sound of his rough voice. "Tell me you found the tiara."

"We found the tiara," I confirm, and he breathes out. "I know. It could have been a disaster."

"You're telling me. It's my favorite sex toy." He is so serious, and I snigger down the line, though talk of the tiara reminds me that behind my ears are still sore from wearing it for so long. "Hang up," Josh says.

"What?"

"I want to see you." He cuts our call, and the next second his face is on my screen.

"Oh, FaceTime," I muse, accepting. I don't prime myself ready for him to see me, don't check my hair or face. Josh has seen me in all states, and now he is about to see me jetlagged. When the connection is made, his face appears, his gorgeous, rough handsomeness dominating my screen. "I look a fright," I warn him quickly.

"Shut up." He's outside, the blue sky dotted with fluffy clouds in the background.

"Where are you?"

"Just leaving the hotel to head to the airport." He turns, looking to someone and nodding his thanks. "It's a bit chaotic." Turning his camera, he pans it onto the street a few yards away from the hotel where masses of people are crowding the pavements, photographers as well. "See?"

"All for you?" I tease, hearing fanatical women screaming his name.

"Well, the Queen of England left yesterday so they needed someone else to hound. I'm the next best thing."

"Wait." I sit up, suddenly comprehending that if I can see all of those people, perhaps they can see me. On Josh Jameson's phone. "Josh!" I grab a pillow and hide behind it, as well as turning my phone down onto my bed. "Turn your phone around."

"Oh, shit." When I peek at the screen, I can see him again. He gives me a sorry smile. "I dropped that ball, huh?" He looks away for a second, then lowers into the back of his car. I just catch a glimpse of Bates. He still looks rough. "They're too far away. Don't panic."

"You need to be careful."

"Yeah, yeah, so I'm told. Although your bodyguard dropped the ball first." He laughs, pulling the door shut, and his eyes shine. "You do realize he owes us." Hitching an eyebrow, he slips some shades on, depriving me of the sight of his swirling blue eyes.

"Owes us how?"

"Well, it's his fault a few more of your people now know about your dirty little secret, therefore he is obliged to assist in future secret meetings."

"I hadn't thought of that."

"Well, do think of that because I've changed my schedule."

He has my undivided attention all of a sudden, and the mild grin of his face tells me he's enjoying the sight of me getting excited. "You said you were in LA indefinitely."

"There's a week's hole in the schedule. Something to do with the permit we need for a few locations."

"And?" I question, willing him to get to the point, my excitement building.

"And I thought I might pay my girlfriend's country a little visit." My smile could split my face. "When?"

"Next week. We're spending this week filming on set at a local college. Then I have a clear week. I'll let you know when I'm flying in, so get that pretty queenly head thinking about how the fuck I'm going to be able to spend that whole week with you and your tiara."

Good heavens, I would have to disappear off the face of the earth in order for that to happen. My excitement is dampened by a nasty dose of reality. But then something comes to me. Maybe I would like a timeout at the Evernmore estate. A slow, cunning grin forms, stretching my cheeks.

"I don't know what you're thinking," Josh says as he watches me mentally plotting, "but I like the look of it."

"I think I have an idea."

"Good. Now get some rest, *my* Queen. I have a call with Tammy."

I grimace. "Good luck with that."

"I love you."

"I love you, too."

Josh hangs up and I spread myself across the cool sheets, content and happy. One week. I can get through one week until I can be with him again.

18

"YOUR MAJESTY." THE call of my name sounds distant, carrying across miles of space until it is just a whisper in my ear. "Your Majesty." I try to ignore the irritating, albeit quiet sound, and find my dreams again. "Your Majesty." If I hear my title one more time, there is a possibility I'll start screaming. "Your Majesty."

"What?" I snap, my eyes springing open. I find Olive looking a tad startled, standing at the side of my bed. I blink a few times, registering the daylight pouring in from the windows. Confused, I push myself up against the headboard. I'm still dressed. Olive is here looking all bright and breezy. And there's a tray with morning coffee set on the table in the window. "Did I miss a day?" I ask, rubbing at my sleepy eyes.

"Kim wouldn't let them wake you last night, ma'am," Olive says as she starts pouring my coffee. The thought of Kim holding Sir Don and whoever else back from disturbing me makes me both appreciative and amused. "But it does mean you may be super busy today."

"I bet," I sigh, pulling the covers back and wandering across to her, taking the coffee on a thankful smile. "Are they all here already?"

"Yes, ma'am."

"Right." I sit myself in the chair by the window and gaze out across the grounds. "Call my mother, Olive," I say, thoughtful. I need to check in on her. Make sure she's okay. "Ask her to join me for breakfast." Sir Don and David Sampson can wait. If I'm going to be challenged all day, I need some energy first. As well as a pep talk from my mother.

"And Sir Don?"

I cast my eyes to Olive. "You can tell Kim to advise him I will be available from ten o'clock." I would love to see his face. "And tell Eddie I'd like to see him for breakfast, too."

Olive falters for a split second, and my head naturally tilts in question, a little worry creeping up on me. "I don't think Prince Edward returned to Kellington last night, ma'am."

"Then where on earth is he?"

"I'm afraid I don't know. I overheard Damon telling some of your protection officers to visit a place. The name escapes me."

I sigh. She doesn't need to tell me the name. Oh, Eddie. "Thank you, Olive."

As Olive leaves to fulfil my requests, I sink into the chair, trying my hardest not to let myself drown in the water slowly rising. Eddie, Sir Don, David Sampson, all pushing problems my way. Problems I don't want. I have spiders in my head, all scurrying around spinning tangled webs. I need to straighten out those tangled thoughts and find my poise before I let Sir Don and David find me.

❧

MY FEET STILL ache, but I make a point of wearing the highest heels Jenny can find, matching them with a cream Victoria Beckham piece that sits just below my knee with cap sleeves. No cardigan. No tights. No pearls around my neck. "Earrings?" I ask as she spritzes my heavy waves with shine spray.

"I have just the thing," Kim says as she enters my suite. She takes me in, her expression reading my mood by my outfit. Formidable. "You look lovely. Seems a shame to waste it on those who won't appreciate it." She hands me a small box.

"What is this?"

"Something someone gave me to give to you." Her eyes flick to Jenny, cautious.

"What?"

"They're very lovely." She turns and heads back out. "I'll see the men to your office once you've had breakfast with Her Royal Highness the Queen Mother."

"Thank you," I say, looking at the box.

"Go on, then." Jenny presses. "Open it."

I look up at her, thinking, fiddling with the small box in my hands. "Do you mind?" I ask gently, feeling like I perhaps need to be alone. As silly as it may seem, I sense Josh all over this box.

Jenny doesn't question my request, of course, backing out of the room, albeit with a definite quizzical look on her face. She wasn't present when Josh was inconveniently discovered in my hotel suite. I trust Jenny, probably more than Kim, yet caution and fear is warning me to keep those in the know as low as possible.

Jenny stops at the door, her hand on the doorknob. "I know," she blurts on a hissed whisper.

I solidify. "Know what?"

She quickly checks behind her before shutting the door and scampering over to me. "Forgive me for being so forward, ma'am, but I know about you and Josh Jameson." She bites her lip and watches my startled face as I try to comprehend what she's telling me.

"How?" I breathe, not even thinking to deny it.

Her whole body deflates, like it is a weight off her shoulders. "After we returned from the White House, I couldn't sleep. Jetlag, I think. I didn't want to disturb Olive with my tossing and turning, as we were sharing a room and she was sound asleep, so I went for a wander. I saw Damon carrying you to your room. And Josh

Jameson was following." Her lips quickly form a straight line, as if she's stopping herself from saying anymore.

"Oh, I see." I clear my throat, imagining Jenny's reaction to her discovery. I need to have a word with Damon. His stealth skills are slipping and now, more than ever, he needs to be top of his game.

"I'm sorry, I couldn't keep it in anymore. I won't tell a soul, I swear, ma'am."

"I think that goes without saying, yes?"

"Of course." Her eyes drop to the box in my hands, and then return to mine. I know what she is thinking before she speaks. "Is it serious?"

Serious in the sense of our relationship, or serious in the sense of the consequences? Yes would be the answer to both, though I know Jenny's angle is the former. Dropping my backside to the edge of the bed, I breathe out heavily. I've known Jenny for years, and she has become a great friend during that time. I know I can trust her. "Well, would you consider being in love with someone serious?"

I see an excited squeal building, but the wretched worry I feel myself is holding her back. It's very sad it is deemed a worry for a woman to be in love with a man. Especially when she is single, and so is he. Sad and frustrating.

"You don't have to tell me what you are thinking," I say, though she doesn't know half the reasons why my future with Josh is impossible. Jenny must see me shrinking, because she comes to sit beside me and nudges my arm.

"Open it."

I smile and pull the pretty pink bow loose, and the paper wrapping the box falls away, revealing a little black case. "I'm a little nervous," I admit, staring at it.

"As nervous as you were when Haydon Sampson gave you your birthday gift?"

I laugh. "Goodness, no." Flipping the small gold catch, I pull open the box as I pull in some air. My inhale catches. "Oh my," I whisper, blinking away the shards of light that escape from the darkness. A gorgeous pair of diamond earrings are nestled in the velvet cushion. I realize the sentiment the second I decipher that the design of each pretty earring is an M and a Q, the two letters entwined together. "Aren't they stunning?" I say to Jenny, pulling one out and studying it closely. Truly stunning, and not because they are perfectly cut diamonds. It's the meaning that is stunning to me.

"Yes, but what do the letters mean? An M and a Q?"

"My Queen," I breathe over the lump in my throat. "They mean, My Queen."

"Oh my God." Jenny's palm meets her chest, and I look at her, my eyes welling with tears. "Why are you crying?" she asks, looking completely thrown.

"Because he makes me so happy, and I can't tell a soul." I roughly wipe at my face, so furious with myself for letting his gift unearth such a reaction from me. "I'm sorry."

"Don't be." Jenny smiles softly as she takes the earrings from my shaky hands before I drop them. "Here, let me." She sweeps my hair over my shoulder and puts them in for me, standing back when she's done. "Beautiful."

I nod, feeling at them in my lobes. I'll never take them off. Not ever. "How is my face?"

"Blotchy." Jenny sets to work refreshing my makeup, putting extra on. I feel like I'm being painted for battle, which is ironic, really. Because I know a battle is on the horizon. I'm just not quite sure what it is I'm defending. "You're good."

Brushing down my cream dress, I square my shoulders and head to meet Mother in the dining room. As I'm wandering down the center of the gallery landing, staff stooping and greeting me as I go, I have a compulsion I can't fight off. Pulling my camera up on my phone, I stop and lean on the banister, holding my hair away from my face on one side and puckering my lips in a kiss. I snap the picture and send it to Josh.

I love them. And you. Your Queen x

As I look up from my mobile, I notice unmistakable surprise on some of the footmen's faces. "Yes, the Queen just took a selfie," I say, laughing a little when they nod their approval. "Have a good day."

I find Kim faffing with the cutlery on the table when I enter the dining room, checking everything is where it should be. "Mother isn't here?" As I ask my question, Kim nods past me, and I turn to find her in the doorway behind me. "Mother." I go to her, quietly noting how sallow she looks. I don't kiss her formally on the cheek, and instead take her in an uncustomary hug. Although surprised, she embraces me. She's lost weight; I can feel it.

"My darling, you are glowing."

I can't return her gesture. I'm a little alarmed by the loss of meat on her bones. Pulling away, I give her a small smile that she returns fondly, reaching for my cheek. Her eyes fall to my ears when her hand shifts my hair. I will my body not to stiffen enough for her to notice, watching her as she brushes across my earring with the dainty tip of her finger. "Pretty," she says, as simple as that, returning her attention to me. "Shall we eat?" Leaving me a little struck dumb, she glides across to the table and takes a seat. Josh was in the maze when I learned of her affair with Davenport. Of course, I know where the earrings come from as well as the significance of their design. My mother would not. In fact, I doubt anyone but Jenny would know. Although I am somewhat curious why Mother hasn't mentioned Josh to me since that day.

While I try to fathom whether she truly believes Josh and I are no longer seeing each other, I watch Mother as she helps herself to a slice of toast and meticulously spreads a thin layer of jam on it. I take a seat as one of the footmen pours our coffees before standing back, waiting for his next job. I give him a subtle nod, telling him to leave, which he does hastily, shutting the door behind him. It's silent for a time, except for the quiet, ladylike chews of Mother working her way through one corner of her toast. I cast my eyes down the long table and the endless empty chairs lining it, then around the detailed cornicing of the ceiling. This huge, beautiful space is just one of dozens of rooms at Kellington. All beautiful rooms within a beautiful palace. A beautiful building containing everything ugly.

"Your trip was successful?" Mother asks, pulling me back to the table. She places her half-eaten slice of toast down and brushes the crumbs off her hands.

"Yes." I'm not in the least bit hungry, but I take a slice for myself and start buttering it, just for something to do with my hands. "The President is a truly delightful man."

"And you danced with him."

Doesn't she approve? Straining my own smile, I place the toast I buttered on my plate untouched. "I think it went down rather well."

"Indeed. He wasn't the only man you danced with either, I'm told." She laughs lightly as she picks up her china coffee cup delicately. "You were quite on form, I hear."

On form, *she hears*. From whom? "I believe you must be speaking of Josh Jameson."

"Are you seeing him again?"

I still in my chair, cautious. Isn't it an awful world when one cannot trust her own mother with her secrets? Lord knows, I am keeping enough of hers. I should be sure of her confidence, yet I am not. She's grief-stricken, hurt, and desperate to keep us safe from ridicule. And for my sins, I feel the same where she and Eddie are concerned. "I am not seeing him, Mother."

Whether she believes me or not, she returns to her toast and resumes picking at the corners.

"How is Edward?" I ask.

"Very good." She's quick to answer, and I frown, stunned. Not as I understand it. Has she checked up on him at all? I don't get the opportunity to ask. "I trust you have reconsidered your living arrangements."

I slowly lower my cup to the saucer. "Pardon?"

"Claringdon. It is where you must reside."

"I've had this discussion with Sir Don already, Mother."

"And I don't think Sir Don reiterated how important it is for you to be at Claringdon. There's more staff, more space."

"I am but a little Queen," I say with too much sarcasm. "How much space can one need?"

"More than Kellington has to offer. I won't enforce much on you, Adeline, but as the Queen of England, you must reside at the official royal residence. You are breaking an age-old tradition if you do not."

I breathe in deep and hold it. Tradition? *Or rules?* I've broken more traditions and rules during my short reign than I expect all previous monarchs have combined. "Have it your way." I relent, far easier than I should. At least Claringdon is vastly larger than Kellington. There are more quiet places, more space to hide. "But I am taking my staff with me."

"It is not *my* way, Adeline," she says softly. "It is the way of history." Placing her napkin on the table, she stands. "Now, if you will excuse me, I have a day at the stables arranged."

"You're leaving already?" I ask.

"Afraid so, my darling." She breezes out of the dining room without another word, and I reach the solid conclusion that Mother only came here when I requested our breakfast together to have me agree to living at Claringdon. And probably because she was asked to talk some sense into me. Will they see her as the voice of reason where I am concerned? Will they constantly use her as a weapon against me?

I gently tap my teaspoon on the tablecloth, resting back in my chair. Is my mother now one of them? *Now?* What am I thinking? When have I ever felt my mother's support of me? Her position has always been about status, as she confirmed herself, so why would I expect her to simply wish to dine with me? I know she loves me, but her devotion to the throne still comes first. To the Monarchy.

Always the Monarchy. Never for me.

I look at my phone when it chimes, and I smile mildly. My American boy. My secret. Is he now the worst-kept secret?

> *Happy you love them. Even happier you love me. I had them commissioned after I spanked your ass in the woods. Would have loved to give them to you myself. It's after midnight here. Will call you later, baby x*

"That was a quick breakfast." Kim enters the dining room, carrying a few newspapers, and I can't deny my skin turns a little cold. Setting them on the table, she looks at me questioningly as I set my phone down.

"Looks like I'll be living at Claringdon."

"Ah, yes, I do believe that was on today's agenda," she says so very casually, making me tilt my head. "It was agreed your desire to remain at Kellington would be seen as *detrimental* to the Monarchy."

I inwardly snort. "Of all the things they could label detrimental, they choose the living arrangements?"

"Earrings look lovely, by the way."

Kim's statement takes my fingers to my earlobes, and I play with the diamonds thoughtfully. "Mother thought so, too. I think she's suspicious."

"Suspicion is to be expected. He was with you on the day we lost the King, Adeline. You'd be naïve to think you can fool them into believing you and Josh are no more, especially since your little rumba around the White House."

I laugh, pouring Kim a coffee. "It was not a rumba, Kim."

"No, but it was as sexually charged."

My hand falters as I set the coffee pot down, my eyes flicking to hers. Her lips are straight. Damn Josh and his lack of control. "In any case, I must do everything I can to convince them otherwise." Josh will be Public Enemy No. 1, and I dread to think what they might do to tarnish his reputation. I can't let that happen because of me. "I feel like my mother is working in cahoots with them." Something horrid comes to me. Could they be threatening her? Using her past sins as a tool to get what they want? The fact that they don't want me on the throne is beside the point. On that little detail they are powerless. The way things are going, I will be dancing like a puppet very soon. Lord, I already agreed to Claringdon. Whatever next? Determination begins to heat my veins.

Kim stands from the table. "Ready?"

"Do I look ready?"

"Well, ma'am, your choice of dress screams ready, but the body in it looks a little flat. I suggest you find the Adeline sass pronto before we make it to your office or they will eat you alive. Come on."

She's right. The spiders are creeping back into my head, and I need to be rid of them. I stand on a deep breath and expel it calmly. "It's going to be a long day, isn't it?" I'm doomed. Just the thought of taking on one single day is exhausting. I have a whole life of this.

Kim just smiles, and we walk together toward my office, my mind racing with various scenarios to various matters that will be sprung on me. Control. I must take the control. "Oh, thank goodness they got rid of it," I say on entering my office, noticing the monstrosity of a portrait has been removed. "I hope they took an axe to it."

Kim laughs as I take my chair, my eyes widening at the piles of correspondence covering the surface of my desk. "Don't worry," she assures me, pulling more chairs around my desk. "I checked it all this morning. Nothing pressing."

"Thank you, Kim." I open my top drawer and swipe my desk with my forearm, clearing the space.

"That's one way to deal with it," Kim quips dryly, taking her seat. Her hands go to her lap. "Shit, I'm nervous."

I frown at her stiff form. "Why?"

She startles. "I didn't mean to say that out loud. And I just said *shit* in front of the Queen."

I chuckle, the cobwebs in my mind being burned away by replays of Josh's vulgar mouth. I would tell Kim not to worry, since my ears have been made to bleed regularly recently by a certain American, but the door knocks and opens, and all of the cobwebs are suddenly back.

"Your Majesty." Sir Don puts himself at the end of my desk, David Sampson following closely behind.

"Sir Don. David." I nod and motion to the chairs.

"Your Majesty." David smiles a smile that could be mistaken as fond, if I didn't know him better. "How lovely you look today."

I notice Kim shift as I study him lowering to the chair, my face straight, showing no appreciation for his compliment. He's on the charm offensive. It won't wash.

I wait for Felix to find his seat, looking as uncomfortable as Kim. "I trust you are all well." I lay my forearms on my desk, sitting forward in my chair, alert. I get a nod or sound of acknowledgment from everyone, before Sir Don clears his throat, ready to launch into his list of things to cover, all of which I'm sure will test me. "I have some questions from The Minister of Works, ma'am."

Of course, my coronation will be the first item on his agenda. But what flowers and decorations I will have is not top of *my* agenda. The Minister of Works will have to wait for the information he needs to create the spectacle the world is waiting for.

"He has asked me to—"

"I believe that *I* would like to lead today's meeting, Sir Don," I say, silencing the room and thickening the atmosphere. He lowers his files onto his lap and rests back in his chair, subtly nodding. I stand, maybe to be taller than everyone in the room, or maybe so they can all see how unqueenly my dress is. Maybe it's both. I need to gain control and maintain it. Walking to the window, I gaze out, thoughtful for a few moments, leaving them waiting for what I may lead with. I know exactly what, and I know Sir Don must be anticipating some kind of backlash from me. I'm simply making them wait for it.

Slowly turning, I brace my hands on the back of my chair. Sir Don has had years of being controlled by my father. Does he think he can overpower me because I'm female? "I understand there was a certain report in the newspapers regarding my relationship with Haydon Sampson."

Silence.

No one owns up to it. Of course, they wouldn't. "It was both misleading and inaccurate, and the world would do well to know that." I look to Kim. "Draft a statement to that effect."

Her eyes widen, and David practically twitches in his chair, as well as Sir Don. Kim and Felix, however, look plain stunned.

Clearing his throat and his surprise, Sir Don sits forward in his chair. "Forgive me, ma'am, but—"

"Forgive *me*, Sir Don, but I am your Queen and you *will* back down." I give him a look that dares him to challenge me, watching in silent satisfaction as he shrinks into his chair. Good. He needs to know that if he wants to throw fire at me, I will fight with fire. Fire hotter and wilder than his. I'm not above correcting the public's misconceptions. He will soon learn that any morsels he feeds the press will be dowsed down with fact from me. "Now that is settled," I go on, "let us please discuss how we plan on handling His Royal Highness Prince Edward."

"I'm afraid he has gone AWOL again, ma'am," Felix says, not telling me anything I didn't already know.

"He needs help," I declare, not prepared to let them constantly trail Eddie so they are there to clear up his messes and hide his misdemeanors from the media. Because they *will* trail him. Not to protect Eddie, but to protect the Monarchy.

"Help?" David asks, clearly interested.

"Rehabilitation. I would have thought that was obvious."

"Out of the question." Sir Don snorts, and David laughs. "They claim discretion, but there is always someone ready to leak the identity of patients. I don't know how, but we can't risk it."

"Oh, Sir Don," I purr, a half-smile on my lips. "You do yourself an injustice. You are so very well versed with knowledge on how things are leaked to the public, are you not?"

Silence. Good.

"So you propose we leave him to self-destruct, do you?" I ask. They would rather lock him in the tower than truly help him. "I won't hear of it." I look to Kim again. "I want Edward to have some help."

"I'll look into it, ma'am." Kim scribbles down more notes.

And the last thing on my agenda. "I will be taking a holiday in Evernmore."

"Out of the question," Sir Don argues, with no hesitation whatsoever. In fact, he almost laughs at the mere suggestion.

I fix my dropping shoulders. "How so?"

He slides a sheet of paper across my desk, before sitting back, hands resting on the arms of his chair. "Your schedule for the next few weeks, ma'am. Two of the engagements are annual events that have never been missed by the Monarch since their founding."

My eyes drop, as does my stomach. "Royal Ascot," I breathe. "Of course."

"I'm sure Your Majesty is keen to see your royal colors paraded for the first time," David intervenes.

"Not to mention your annual visit to the Royal Opera House for the opening night of the Royal Ballet," Sir Don adds. "I believe the performance this year is highly anticipated in the ballet world."

"And you have a meeting with the Archbishop of Canterbury at Westminster," David goes on. "The order of service needs to be finalized."

My righted shoulders soon start dropping again, as I slowly realize I'm going nowhere in the next few weeks, and, by all accounts, I will not have any room in my schedule to sneak some time in for

Josh. "Order of service for my coronation, I assume."

"Indeed." David looks so bloody excited I could vomit. "A date has been set."

It has? "For?"

"August."

"That's less than two months away," I blurt, slowly sinking. "Was it not deemed appropriate to consult me on such a decision?" I am truly deluded. I do not get a say in such decisions. A date is agreed by these twits and the government, and whether or not I may be available isn't a concern. Of course I am available. What else do I have to do except wear a crown and look important?

"The world is waiting, ma'am." David smiles brightly. "It will be a wonderful celebration."

"Right." I slowly lower to my chair, all control I strived to seize lost. My stride has been well and truly charged down by these jobsworths.

"Which brings us to the next item on the agenda." Sir Don stands, and I'm even more weary.

"And what is that?"

"We believe, as your advisors and champions, that Your Majesty would do well to find a husband."

"Here, here," David chants, and I look at him with a death stare, panic setting in, all of my waning strength quickly dowsed in fear.

My champions? Rubbish. No matter how they play this matter, I refuse to bend. I've given up too much already. I've relented on certain things. Not this. Never.

Getting up from my chair, my patience fraying, I place my palms on my desk and lean forward. "Firstly, we have already discussed this issue. But in case it's already slipped your mind, I will remind you that I asked Kim, not a moment ago, to draft a statement correcting the misleading information that the public have been fed regarding the status of Haydon Sampson in my life. So talk of finding me a husband is off the table. Secondly, I buried my father *the King* and my brother only weeks ago. It would be disrespectful toward them both and my mother to give this matter a moment more thought. One would believe you'd understand the insensitivity to my family and the country's time of mourning to suggest—" I'm cut short when Olive enters without knocking, earning disapproving glares from Sir Don and David. "What is it, Olive?" I ask.

Her eyes seem to speak to me before her words do. "There's someone to see you, ma'am."

I frown, releasing my desk and straightening. She looks nervous, and it certainly isn't her job to advise me of visitors, though I think better than to ask who it is.

"Really?" David throws his hands into the air in exasperation. "Hasn't anyone told this nitwit not to disturb the Queen when she has an audience?"

Poor Olive flinches, and it is all I can do not to pick up my crystal paperweight, a gift from the King of Norway, and throw it at David's ignorant head. Ignoring him is a task, but one I force myself to do, if only to maintain my feigned stability. Rounding my desk, I take Olive's elbow. "Excuse me," I tell the room, and Kim makes to stand, ready to come with me. I give her a subtle shake of my head, making her lower to her seat, her mind catching up. I need ears in here while I'm gone, and I also need someone to watch David and Sir Don in case they decide to come and snoop.

Closing the door behind me, I just about jump out of my skin when Olive shrieks, "I'm sorry, ma'am. It's just Major Davenport was here and he was refused at the gates and sent away, and I thought you should know."

I look past her, down the corridor. "Well done, Olive." I give her arm a little reassuring rub and pass her, heading for the nearest telephone, the nearest except for my office. I find one on the half-moon occasional table at the end of the corridor. I dial the only internal number I know. The main switchboard. And as soon as someone answers, I throw my request down the line. "Put me through to the main gates, please."

There's a slight pause, the operative wondering if he is speaking with who he thinks he is speaking with.

"Quick as you can," I add.

"Yes, Your Majesty. Certainly, ma'am. Straight away, ma'am."

"Main gate," a low, gruff voice says only a few seconds later.

"Hello there," I greet calmly, looking up when Olive finally catches up with me. "I have been informed that I have a visitor."

"Your Majesty?"

"Yes. Now, about this visitor. It is someone whom I would very much like to see, so it would be most unwise for him to be turned away. Am I making myself clear?"

"Yes, ma'am."

"Very good. Show him in." I hang up and turn to Olive. "Please ensure Major Davenport makes it to me with no further obstructions," I tell her, looking over my shoulder to my office. "I will be waiting in Felix's office."

"Yes, ma'am." Olive dashes off, and I quickly hurry back to my office to stall Sir Don and David Sampson further, because even though Kim is there, they will still come in search of me should I be gone too long.

I pop my head around the door. "Terribly sorry." I smile. "Lady Matilda has arrived early. Now I need the ladies'. Won't be a tick." I pull the door closed on them and scamper to Felix's office, walking circles around the desk. I'm nervous. It's been over a week since I went to see him. I assumed it was a no. Could he be here to accept?

When a knock sounds on the door, I spin toward it, my voice high-pitched when I call, "Come in."

"Major Davenport, ma'am." Olive opens the path for him, and I never thought I'd see the day when I'd be pleased to receive him. He is back in his fine threads, his back is poker straight once again, and his moustache and hair as perfect as it always has been.

He stops, hands joined and held behind his back. "Your Majesty," he says softly. "Thank you for seeing me without notice."

"Not at all." I work to calm myself down. "But why didn't you call to speak with me, Major?"

"I did," he says dryly. "Unfortunately, you have been unavailable each time."

"Oh, really?" I reply, anger brewing. The bastards. Who the hell is in charge around here? I motion to one of the soft chairs in the corner. "Would you like to sit down?"

"Thank you." He makes his way over, and I follow, lowering to the chair opposite. We settle and silence falls, him offering me a small smile, me returning it.

"What can I do for you, Major?"

"Ah, yes, of course." He clears his throat and lifts his chin. "In hindsight, ma'am, I do believe I was rather hasty in declining your offer."

There is a flash of light in my darkening world. "Does that mean you accept the job, Major?" I try not to sound excited.

"If Your Majesty will still have me, then yes."

My grin is too hard to contain. "And you will advise me in *my* best interest?"

"First and foremost. I believe you have other aides who will advise in the Monarchy's best interest."

"Oh, I do." I regard the Major quietly for a few seconds, thoughtful. "May I ask what changed your mind, Major?"

"Boredom," he says matter-of-factly. I can believe it. Major Davenport has been like a piece of furniture around these parts for as long as I can remember. He must have been going stir-crazy. "But most of all," he goes on, "it will be a novelty and an honor to actually serve." He looks away when I swallow hard, regretting every moment I cursed him.

I wonder if my mother has anything to do with his change of heart. After years of loving her from afar, has he struggled while he hasn't seen her? I decide quickly that those are considerations for another day. Right now, there are more pressing matters waiting for me in my office. "I'm glad that is sorted." I stand and brush my dress down. And in this moment, some of my earlier strength and fire returns. I believe I've found another ally. I never thought I'd see this day, and even though I'm surprised, I feel more confident. More like . . . me. "Can you start serving now?" I smile when he looks at me in question. "Sir Don and David Sampson are waiting for me in my office." And I cannot wait to see their faces when I return with Major Davenport. "Shall we?"

"I believe we shall." He stands, and I watch as he visibly draws air. "After you, ma'am."

I give him an impish grin and lead the way back to my office, walking in confidently and assertively. "Gentlemen," I declare as they all turn toward me. "And lady," I add, smiling at Kim. "I'm thrilled to share the news of Major Davenport's return to royal duty."

"Good morning." The Major gives polite nods to all the mouths hanging open.

"Please, join us," I say, taking my place back at my desk, suddenly supercharged with grit. "Now, where were we?" I look to David and Sir Don. Both men are looking at Davenport in utter shock as he quietly lowers to a chair. I cough to get their attention, tilting my head in prompt for them to continue.

Sir Don drops his stare to his files, brushing through his silver hair with a limp hand. "Marriage," he says. "You must marry."

"I am not getting married."

"It's unheard of," David jumps in. "Not since the seventeenth century has a Queen been without a husband."

"Oh, you know what they say, David," I muse, sitting back in my chair. "Be fashionably different."

His face. Oh, if I could take a picture and frame it, then I would.

"You will not be taken seriously until you have formed a stable family unit." Sir Don is getting increasingly angry.

"By you, or the public?" I ask.

"By everyone."

I could laugh at him, the preposterous fool. He thinks me being wed will make me a better queen? It actually might, but not being wed to the type of man he has in mind. There's only one type of man for me. American. Hot. Actor. Josh injects me with more passion, more determination. More fire. "Next on the agenda," I say, rather dismissively.

"Your Majesty, with all due respect, I—"

"Now, you see, Sir Don"—I level him with a serious, formidable stare—"I keep hearing those words. *With all due respect.*" Rising from my chair, I pull a drawer open, taking out my secret stash of cigarettes and boldly lighting one. "One can only assume you don't think much respect is due, since I'm not receiving any from you." I take a draw and expel it slowly, watching his face contort in disgust. Oh, he can bugger off. After being surrounded by my father's putrid cigars for decades, what's a bit of cigarette smoke?

"Your Majesty," Sir Don sighs, his patience wearing thin.

"I believe Her Majesty is finished," Davenport intervenes, earning an almighty sneer from Sir Don.

"She serves our country."

"And *I* serve the Queen." Davenport's face is expressionless, so very serious. The most serious I have ever seen it, yet this time it makes me smile rather than grimace. And I can't help but wonder if Davenport is also here for a bit of revenge. David Sampson and Sir Don have watched him be trodden down by my father for years. Sir Don knew of the Major's affair with my mother, and even though David didn't until recently, because Sabina kept it from him, I know he treated Major Davenport with the same disregard as my father and Sir Don. Because he is a plain arsehole.

Sir Don does not appreciate the Major's intervention. "I am merely—"

"Telling me what to do," I finish for him. "Sir Don, I think it is high time we deal with this matter once and for all, then maybe you and I will get along a lot better. I appreciate your knowledge. I appreciate your wisdom, and I am not ignorant to the fact that I will need your council on many things." He is a descendent of one of the most credible Lord Chamberlains who has ever served, after all. Of course he wants to maintain their status and value to the Royals. But enough is enough. I look to David briefly, just so he knows that all this also applies to him. "But I will never appreciate your advice when it comes to who I can marry and when I should marry them."

"Who you should marry is part of the package, ma'am," Sir Don says.

"Well, as Queen, I am changing the package deal, and that is that." The room falls silent, and I maintain my fixed expression, leaving no scope for them to come back at me. "Now, if you don't mind, it would seem I am moving house this week." I smile sweetly. "One must pack."

Everyone leaves promptly, including Kim, who is grinning from ear to ear. "Girl power," she mouths, and I laugh, stubbing out my cigarette. "Major." I call as he goes to leave, too. "Two minutes?"

He sees everyone out and closes the door. "Yes, ma'am?"

"Thank you," I say sincerely. "For backing me up."

"You handled yourself rather well without me."

That's not true. I was drowning before he showed up, and my confidence was only found because of his presence. "Nevertheless . . ."

"You know they won't let this go, don't you?" His look is both sympathetic and warning. I'm not sure which is strongest, though both are worrying.

"Yes," I sigh, picking up a solid silver Parker pen and rolling it between my fingers. "They'll have my mother pleading to my more reasonable nature tomorrow, no doubt." It's ridiculous that me refusing to marry a man who I do not love is deemed unreasonable. But that is my world, more so now than ever.

At the mention of my mother, Davenport noticeably tenses.

And speaking of my mother . . ."Where's Cathy?" I ask.

"Doggy daycare. Anything else, ma'am?"

I shake my head and watch as he goes, knowing more certainly than I did before that one of the reasons Davenport is here is because of my mother.

He misses her. I am not the only one who's being kept from my one true love.

19

"WELCOME HOME," KIM quips as we slowly roam the rooms of Claringdon. I can only sigh, taking in each vast room as we pass through, my eyes being reacquainted with the ultimate of all royal residences. Except it is now *my* residence.

Aside from my trip to Portsmouth, I've not seen outside my father's office or my new suite in the two days I've been here. Watching my parents' possessions being shipped out in such a military fashion was painful. It was all very impersonal, as if the routine of waving goodbye to one Sovereign and welcoming another is just par for the course. Which, I guess, it is. Except the previous Sovereign was my father. The wretched guilt I hope one day I will get used to clamps down on my heart.

"How are you getting along with Major Davenport?" I ask Kim, diverting my mind. I should have perhaps given her the heads-up on his return, but as far as I was concerned, Davenport had declined my offer and, though disappointed, I didn't expect him to reconsider.

"Well, that stick isn't completely up his arse anymore," she says dryly. "Now I'd say it's more partially wedged."

I laugh. "Good to hear."

"He knows what he's talking about, I guess." Kim shrugs. "And he's surprisingly patient with my lacking areas of expertise."

"Very good." I knew they'd work well together, each covering the other's blind spots.

"And it was surprisingly nice to have someone to be smug with when the statement went out setting the record straight about you and Haydon."

I laugh under my breath. "David and Sir Don still look like they've been slapped in the face."

"I like that look on them."

"Me, too. Did you get hold of Edward?" I ask, running a fingertip over a solid oak console table as we pass. Of course, there is not one speck of dust on the wood.

"I'm told he is still in bed."

"With a gigantic hangover," I muse.

"Or he's avoiding you," Kim adds, and she is probably right. Kim found a private clinic, one that would be perfect for Eddie, but he didn't take too kindly to the suggestion when I proposed it over dinner on the last night of my residence at Kellington. Apparently, he hasn't developed a drinking problem. Apparently, he is perfectly stable. Apparently, he is simply making up for lost time and fun.

"He hates me." I fold at the thought. He doesn't see me as trying to help him, but more telling him what to do. Taking my new role and running with it, I think he said.

"He doesn't hate you. He is just a little lost right now. The first step to fixing a problem is admitting you have one, and as far as His Royal Highness is concerned, he doesn't have a problem."

"Very true."

"I don't know of many war heroes who party like Prince Edward," Kim muses, all too casually. "I mean, I thought PTSD was more like depression."

I flick my eyes to her as we round the corner, seeing she looks all too casual, too. Of course, no one knows of the true reason behind the throne skipping Eddie, only those who already knew about his illegitimacy prior to my father's death. But Kim isn't stupid. Neither is the world, but my right-hand woman obviously feels like she has known me for long enough to subtly pry. She knows it is just thicker smoke and more distorted mirrors.

Checking we are alone, I pull Kim to a stop and close the space between us. "Kim, you and I both know Eddie isn't suffering from Post-Traumatic Stress Disorder."

"Of course I know." She rolls her eyes. "But I've been in royal service long enough to know not to ask."

My lips straighten, a *really?* look passing across my face.

She shrugs. "It doesn't stop me from wondering, though."

"Wondering out loud?"

"Sorry."

"Don't be. But trust me, don't waste your energy wondering. It is past even my comprehension, and I have been unfortunate enough to deal with this family all my life."

"As long as you are okay."

We start wandering again, and I smile. Okay? I have been back from Washington for three days, and I've been drowning in duty. Am I okay? No. I'm not, and with each day that passes, I am being worn down more and more. How long until I'm nothing?

I look up on a deep breath, trying to refuel on strength, and come to a grinding halt in my heels. "Is this some kind of cruel joke?" I blurt, marching over to the wall.

"What?" Kim, sounding perplexed, joins me.

"This." I throw an arm up at the portrait. "I told them to burn the damn thing." It's haunting me, for crying out loud. They must be doing it on purpose. I grimace as I remind myself of my dire state of dress and lack of life in my eyes. This is how they want me to be. All traditional and proper. Dead on the inside. "Urghhhh." I grab the frame and start yanking at the huge painting, trying to physically rip it from the wall. I'll burn it myself if I have to, just to be sure it is not going to spring up somewhere else and send me off the deep end. "I want this hideous thing out of the palace," I shout, wrestling with the frame that refuses to budge.

"Adeline," Kim hisses, trying to pull me away. "I'll get someone to remove it."

"I've already asked. Twice! Doesn't my authority around here stand for anything? No one listens. No one respects me." I've finally lost it, my equilibrium tossed to the wind and scattering far and wide, never to be pulled back together. "It's a damn joke." I yank hard, and something dislodges, sending me flying back with half the gold frame in my hand.

"Your Majesty," Kim yells, shocked, catching my arm to stop me from tumbling to my backside.

I stabilize myself and drop the piece of wood, brushing my hair out of my face, a little out of breath. I look to my left. Then I look to my right. Over a dozen members of royal staff have come to a standstill, some carrying trays, some carrying files, some carrying nothing. But one thing they are *all* carrying is a shocked expression. I straighten my shoulders and find my poise, a joke considering they've all just witnessed the Queen having an epic meltdown. "Please have this painting removed and burned," I say calmly, and they all scatter like ants, going about their duties once more. My chin drops to my chest, hopeless. "I can't even have a meltdown in my own home without being watched and judged."

"Maybe hold it in until you get to your private quarters in future," Kim says, kicking aside the wood I ripped from the wall.

"I think I'll go there now." I leave Kim to fix my mess and take the shortest route I know to my private quarters. A secret passage, one I haven't used since I was a child. It's the only quiet, dark, and truly private place around here.

I pull back the corniced panel at the end of the Picture Gallery and enter the dimly lit passageway. It smells dank, just as I remember, as I walk the cobbled ground to the end where it forks. I smile, a fond memory of my childhood creeping up on me. They're rare, so I seize it and relish in the reminder of the days when Eddie and I used to play hide and seek in the many secret passages hidden within the walls of the palace.

I reach a junction where five passages meet, creating a star-like shape. I remember all of the routes, know where each of these passages lead to. Except one. The forbidden passage, the one we never dared venture down as children for fear of our father's wrath. Nibbling my lip, I pull my phone from my pocket and turn on the torch, shining it down the path. It veers off to the left around fifty meters down, preventing me from seeing more. Before I have made a conscious decision, my feet are walking down the cobbles, following the path. It goes on forever, far longer than I remember the other passages being. Where will this one lead to? Each one of the others lead to various corners of the palace—one to the library, one to the Throne Room, one to the kitchens, and one to what is now my private apartment. But this one? I can't even get a sense of the direction I'm heading in, the twists and turns too many.

I finally reach a brick wall, and I feel around the cold stone, look-ing for any kind of latch or lever. Nothing. So I resort to shining my torch. "Ah." I spot something at the top right-hand corner and reach up, taking a firm hold. It takes a lot of elbow grease—one can only assume it hasn't been used for many years—but I eventually feel the decades of dust and dirt giving way, and on one last yank, the secret door opens. I cough and splutter as my nose is hit with the particles of dust that have been dislodged, and I sneeze, not once, but three times. "Bless me," I splutter, rubbing the end of my nose.

I step forward and crane my neck around the opening. "Oh my," I breathe, taking in what I have found. Suited men scurry everywhere, though they aren't in royal uniform. These men aren't my staff. A slow grin forms as I slowly understand where I am. It's part of the open palace, an area of the colossal mansion closed off during the summer months for tourists. This right here is the Blue

Room, a huge, iconic space that used to serve as a ballroom before my grandfather, the then King, had it transformed into a gallery for his many paintings, most of which have been restored and re-hung for tourists to admire. I quickly put myself back in the damp passageway and secure the door. I can't help the smile on my face, and as if he has heard my mind going into overdrive, he calls me. I connect the call excitedly. I haven't spoken to him for two days, his filming schedule and the time difference getting in our way. "Hello."

"Hey, darlin'." God, his voice is the cure for everything. It also makes me miss him all the more. "How . . . ou . . ."

"Josh?" I say, looking at my phone. Damn it. My service is spotty. I rush down the passageway. "Josh? Can you hear me?"

"There you are," he says, and I come to an abrupt stop, hoping I don't lose him again.

"Sorry, I have a bad connection."

"How you doin'?"

"Terrible. I miss you, I hate my job, and I just had a meltdown in front of endless staff."

"Oh?"

"It's just another day in the life of a queen," I flip casually, keen to move on to less depressing things. "Where are you?"

"Eating breakfast. You?"

"I'm in a secret passageway at Claringdon."

"Oh, sounds . . . secret. How are you settling in?"

"I hate it."

"Okay, let's change the subject before you fry yourself with your spitting rage. Tell me what your wonderful mind has been conjuring up for when I land back in the UK."

"My original plan isn't going to work."

He's silent for a few moments. "Not good enough. Why?"

"I had intended on escaping to Evernmore, but my schedule won't allow it."

"Stupid schedule."

"But I think I have another plan," I tell him, grinning like a mad woman. "Are you listening?"

"Hit me with it, baby."

I smile. God, I'm a bloody genius.

20

I CAN'T SAY the days pass quickly because they don't. They drag painfully, despite being kept busy with various outings and meetings. By Friday, after being bombarded with the plans of my coronation, I decide I *more* than need a timeout. More specifically, a whole week in Evernmore with nothing but Josh, me, and absolute privacy. Though I begrudgingly accept I have already waved goodbye to that idea. So I settle for the next best thing. It's risky, it's reckless, many would probably call it crazy and undoable. But where Josh is concerned, the risk is worth it, and the recklessness is par for the course for me. I'll make sure it is doable. I'm about to come out of my skin if I don't see him soon. To talk to him and be challenged, simply because he likes to spar with me, not because he wants to contest me. To learn more about him and what his hopes are for the future. To laugh, so uninhibited. To just be . . . me.

Making a hasty exit from my office, leaving Sir Don, David, Davenport, and Kim all watching in surprise at my speedy exit, I dash down the hallway.

"Your Majesty," David calls, coming after me. "Wait."

My face screws up as I pull to a gradual stop, allowing him to catch up with me. "Am I keeping you?" he asks as he rounds me.

Yes! "Not at all, David." I smile, and it is a strain. Being cornered alone with either Sir Don or David, without the support of my newest confidant Davenport, is always a worry. I always expect they will again attempt to browbeat me into submission where my relationship status is concerned. "What can I do for you?"

On a slap-worthy smile, he slips his hands halfway into his waist-coat pockets. I can't help but think he looks like a begging dog. "Dinner this evening, I am very much looking forward to it."

I'm sure I growl under my breath. "Dinner?" I believed I'd effectively cancelled my *dinner* with the Sampsons when I sent out the statement putting the public straight about Haydon and me.

"Yes, as arranged."

"By whom?"

He laughs a little. "Well, you, ma'am. Just yesterday after we returned from the opening of parliament. Since we lost His Majesty and Prince John, the family hasn't dined together. We should come together. Support each other."

The family? Oh, the man infuriates me. I think hard back to yesterday, yet I cannot locate the conversation David is speaking of. It shouldn't be a surprise. My brain was completely numb after listening to politicians outline their plans for the parliamentary year. Highly unprofessional, I realize, but I was distracted by thoughts of Josh and the fact that I get to see him today. And I should be shown a little forgiveness, since every single day I have been full steam ahead with a job I despise. Yes, I won't allow myself to feel guilty for thinking of my secret, hot, god of an American lover while the head of the Conservative Party was talking about the National Health Service. About it being stretched to snapping point and what their plans are to rectify that. I plan on being stretched soon, by Josh, and I know there will be a snapping point. "Dinner this evening," I muse, frantically searching for a reason to wriggle my way out of it.

"Everyone is so looking forward to it."

I smile tightly. "Indeed."

"Everything okay, ma'am?" Davenport appears from my office, eyeing David with the wariness he deserves.

"Yes, David was reminding me of the dinner arrangements this evening."

"Oh?" Davenport says, for the first time making me wonder if I'm being tricked. Maybe I didn't agree. Maybe David went right on ahead and arranged this evening's get together without my agreement, and now he is using my absentmindedness against me. "I don't recall any dinner arrangements."

The look David fires at Davenport only further confirms my fear. "I don't believe you were present *or* invited."

"Would you like to join us, Major?" I ask, if only to irritate David. I have no intention of going myself. I just haven't figured out how I'm going to get out of it.

"That would be lovely, ma'am."

"Wonderful." I smile.

"I'm sure Her Royal Highness the Queen Mother will be thrilled to see you," David says through gritted teeth, aware that with Davenport around the table, too, his scope to resume his mission to try and convince me to wed his son will be limited, if not diminished completely. I would tell him there will be no chance to convince me, anyway, because there will be no dinner this evening—I plan on finding Kim as soon as is reasonably possible and have her cancel it—but I'm rather enjoying David's testiness. His nerve to mention such a sore, private matter in pure, obvious spite has me stepping forward and leveling him with a deadly glare, one I am sure would turn him to dust if he were not such a hard-hearted arsehole. "That is all," I say simply, dismissing him in the most abrupt manner.

As he slinks away, I peek out the corner of my eye to Davenport, and I hate seeing the pain in his eyes—pain he is trying so hard to conceal with contempt. I know he hasn't so much as seen Mother since he returned as my private secretary, and I know that because he has been stuck to my side. He's taking his new role very seriously, seems to have something to prove.

"Major, I'm feeling a tad queasy," I say, rubbing my stomach, hoping I look as convincing as I sound.

"A side effect of your run-in with David Sampson, I expect," he quips dryly, refusing to look at me. Maybe because he knows what I'll see in his eyes. It's too late. I have already seen.

"Would you inform everyone I don't wish to be disturbed?" My plan is coming together piece by piece.

Now, he looks me over with a little concern. "Should I call Dr. Goodridge?"

"No, no." I falsely strain a smile, making it look like it takes too much energy. "I'm sure some rest will work wonders."

"Very well."

"Why don't you go and see Dolly?" I suggest, a little conniving. Mother has spent endless hours sitting with Dolly while my cook has pottered around the kitchen. I think she likes the company, her other chef far less friendly, and Dolly would never dream of turning my mother away from the kitchen. Only yesterday I found her helping stir a cake mixture. She looked like she was in her element, and it was a pleasure to see. Hopefully Dolly is making cakes again today.

Davenport can't hide his knowing smile. He knows my game. "I must say, now that I think about it, I am rather hungry."

"Good," I chirp, a little too happily for someone who is supposedly unwell. I drop my smile and turn on my heels. "Please, excuse me." I hold on to my tummy all the way to the other end of the room, before quickly checking over my shoulder. Davenport has gone. I drop my hand from my stomach and pick up my pace, darting toward the secret door. As soon as I am safely inside, I call Josh.

"You'd better get your ass in gear, Adeline. I'm starting to be recognized." He sounds a little panicked, but I did warn him the risk would be worth the reward.

I pick up my pace. "My service might drop. I'll call you back if it does. Where are you?"

"By the disgusting yellow couch thing you said to be at five minutes ago. The tour is moving on, and I'm lingering like I want to do bad things to the yellow couch."

I chuckle. "I'm nearly there."

"Nearly where? Here?" He sounds so shocked, and it makes me smile. "When you told me to be in this spot, I thought Damon was going to be here."

"Damon doesn't know you are here. Nobody knows." It's the safest way. Plus, no one can stop me if Josh is already in the palace.

"Then how . . . ?"

"Just wait. Is it very busy?"

"Yeah, these people love all your royal shit. One Chinese dude even claimed to be marrying you."

Snorting down the line, I take a sharp right and follow the passageway. "How badly did you want to tell him that I belonged to you?" I grin like a fool, following my feet as quickly as I can.

"Badly. You know, this yellow couch looks like someone spewed all over it."

"It's Elizabethan and belonged to the only other unmarried queen in English history." I reach the brick wall and feel up to the right-hand corner.

"Does that mean you'll get a puke couch? Because if so, I ain't fuckin' you on it."

"Behave." I laugh as I gently ease the door open, just a fraction, and peek through the gap. I spot him and Bates immediately. Josh's head is covered in a cap, and his body sporting a leather jacket with the collar flipped up. His jeans are ripped. He has spectacles on. If he's trying to disguise himself, he's failing. He looks every inch the Hollywood star he is. "Hey," I whisper down the line, watching as Josh glances around him.

"Where the fuck are you?"

"Here."

"Shit, are you in the walls?" He turns on the spot, looking everywhere except to the huge tapestry covering the secret door that I'm hiding behind.

"Josh."

Bates starts craning his neck too, both of them completely confused, their foreheads weighed down with lines. "Fucked if I know," Bates grunts.

"Stop frowning." I laugh.

"Okay, now you're scaring me."

"The tapestry."

He swings around, removing his glasses as he does, and in a second, he spots me. "Fuck . . . me." He hangs up, gives Bates a slap on his shoulder without looking, and makes his way over hurriedly. And as soon as he's within touching distance, I grab him and yank him in, my mind lost, attacking him with a kiss.

"Jesus fuckin' Christ," he growls. "I've missed you." I'm up against the cold bricks being mauled to death, and it is absolutely wonderful, his tongue, my tongue, our lips reunited.

"The door," I mumble around his mouth, blindly feeling for it to push it closed. I feel nothing and grudgingly release him to find it. We've somehow staggered a few meters into the passage in our lustful spin, so I shoot forward to close it, but as I'm about to shut out the world, I catch someone staring right at me.

I freeze, taking in the mouth hanging open, the wide blue gaze, the utter astonishment on her face. There's a lollipop halfway to her mouth. She must be six, maybe seven. But she knows exactly who she is looking at.

I give her a smile, a wink, and then rest my finger on my lip. "Shh," I whisper, closing the door.

Josh grabs me from behind and swirls me around. "You are fuckin' brilliant. But tell me I haven't got to spend all my time with you in these dungeons."

"They're not dungeons. They're secret passages."

"For what?"

"To escape the enemy. To take shortcuts. To sneak one's boyfriend into the palace undetected."

"I fuckin' love secret passages, especially when they lead to you." He's on me again, pushing me up the cold wall with the force of his kiss. My arms naturally curl around his shoulders and my pace naturally meets his. I hum, over and over, peace that is only obtainable when I'm with Josh engulfing me. "I just paid thirty bucks to see my girlfriend." He bites my lip and pulls away, giving the end of my nose a little rub with his. "I better get a refund on my ticket."

"Bucks?"

"Pounds. Whatever."

"Are you quibbling over a few quid?"

"I don't know what the fuck quibbling is."

"Splitting hairs."

"Yes, I am." He drops me back to my feet and makes a big fuss of me, brushing my hair over my shoulders and drawing across my cheek, as if he's reminding himself of every detail of my face. "And do you know what's really fucked up?"

How about everything? "What's *fucked up*, Josh?"

He grins at my dirty mouth. "Your face on the bills, that's what's fucked up. I can't pay for a damn thing here without having to see you."

Wow. The Royal Mint sure didn't waste time replacing my father's face with mine. "Doesn't that make you smile? That you get to see me whenever you like."

"I want to *see* you, Adeline. Not just see you." He pulls me into his chest and squeezes the life out of me, and I am absolutely fine with it. "What's the grand plan, then?"

I take one last hit of his manly scent and look up at him. "It's so easy, it's brilliant."

He gives me an interested look. "Is that why no one knows?

Because you didn't need any assistance?"

"Exactly." I point into the dimly lit space. "This is one of five passageways. One leads to the Throne Room, one leads to the kitchens, one leads to the Picture Gallery, one leads to the library and the last one leads to—"

"Your cunt?"

I choke on nothing, locking and loading my palm and swinging it at his bicep. "You animal."

He catches my wrist, his face straight. "That's a yes, isn't it?"

I narrow playful eyes on him, not quite believing I'm entertaining such vulgarity. "Well," I say. "It leads to my private quarters, which in turn, I guess, would lead to—"

"Your cunt." He hauls me up onto his shoulder on a little squeal and starts marching down the passageway. "There is a god after all."

"Josh." I laugh, my stomach muscles tight as I bob up and down.

"So no one will come into your private quarters?" he asks, not slowing his steps.

"I'm ill."

"You better not be. We have lost time to catch up on."

"No," I breathe, spotting something poking out of his back pocket. "I told Davenport I'm unwell and I don't want to be disturbed." I reach down and pull out the paper.

"How is he settling in?"

"Very well. What's this?" I ask, flashing it over my shoulder for him to see.

"Lines. I need to practice. You can help me later after I've fucked you so hard your screams will reach every corner of the palace."

"Josh is home," I sing, laughing as I get a sharp spank across my backside.

"Which way?"

"Two o'clock."

"Jesus, it's creepy down here."

"Are you scared, Josh?"

"Only of you, baby," he counters softly, this time giving my bottom a rub rather than a slap. "Only of you." He slows to a stop and lowers my dreamy form to my feet. "We can't go any farther."

"Which means we have reached our destination," I declare, reaching up on my tiptoes and pushing my lips into his spikey, familiar cheek. "You have to be quiet. This opens up just down the corridor from my apartment door, so we have a few feet of open space to pass without being seen."

He shakes his head in dismay. "I've wrangled wild horses easier than this. I just want to spend some time with my girlfriend, for fuck's sake."

I recoil, a little injured. "And I'm trying my hardest to make that happen," I retort shortly. "But if it's too much trouble, then feel free to—"

I'm silenced by his mouth on my lips, his body crowding mine. "Shut the fuck up," he warns me. "I'm thinking out loud. I'm sorry."

It strikes me in this moment that Josh must always be thinking those thoughts. Resentful thoughts. Living on the edge of irritation and stress. Not dissimilar to me. "I'm not your average girlfriend, Josh," I whisper, damning the dejection that's creeping up on me. "You've known that from day one."

He groans, resting his forehead on mine and rolling it slowly. His eyes have dulled, and I damn that, too. This whole situation is making us feel things we shouldn't be feeling when we're so consumed by each other. Nothing should be powerful enough to penetrate our bubble. But the British Monarchy is.

"I didn't expect to fall in love with you back then," he whispers. "And neither you nor I expected you to fall onto the throne with a fuckin' noose around your neck."

"I'm sorry," I mumble pitifully. His analogy is rather accurate and equally agonizing. I do feel like I'm waiting to be hanged, and at the same time watching my mother and brother on the next platform helplessly. Their fates in my hands. Rope around their necks. My choices dictating whether the block is kicked out from beneath their feet.

"Fuckin' hell." Josh blows out a gust of stressed air and pulls me in for a cuddle. "I'm a jerk."

"And I'm a weak queen."

"No," he states adamantly. "Don't talk trash. What you're going through, what you're doing, probably makes you the strongest queen that's ever lived." He squeezes my chin between his thumb and finger. "We'll find a way."

Will we? "The only way would be for me to fire Sir Don, David Sampson, and every other member of my Privy Council, which in itself is impossible. I don't have that power. And even if I could, I would be left all alone with not the first idea of how to approach endless tasks expected of me. And then my kingdom would crumble, the smoke and mirrors would crumble with it, and that'd be that. The same tragic ending."

Josh slides his hand down to mine and clenches firmly. "I can't let myself believe this is it for us. Sneaky meetings, a secret affair. No." He shakes his head as if to reinforce it, reaching up to remove his cap and mussing his flat hair. "Now, are we going to stand in the dark forever feeling depressed, or are you taking me back to your place?"

And there he is. Making me forget. Smiling, I turn toward the door and release the latch, pushing it open a little. "It's clear," I whisper, edging out with Josh trailing, holding my hand. "Run," I blurt, making a mad dash across the carpet, dragging Josh along with me, laughing. We make it to the door and fall inside my apartment, slamming the door behind us. No sooner have I caught my breath, I'm pinned to the back, my dress yanked up to my waist. I don't think to stop him, my hands taking on a mind of their own and shoving his leather jacket from his shoulders until he's forced to release me and wrestle it off. It hits the floor with a thud, and I grab the hem of his white T-shirt, pulling it up and off in one swift tug. His jeans are next, unbuttoned fast and shoved down a little, and though we're both working quickly, it doesn't feel fast enough. My stomach turns and between my thighs is weighted down with heat and desperation. His erection springs free, taut and dripping.

I suck in air.

He reaches for my knickers and wrenches them from my body on a loud rip.

More air.

He regards me quietly, staring between my thighs as he takes hold of himself. He strokes once, and I pant in answer.

His eyes are low.

His mouth is open.

His chest is pulsing.

Stepping forward, he circles my lower back and pulls me close, purposely brushing the tip of his arousal across my swollen clit. I miss a few too many breaths, dizziness setting in as I let him pull my thighs around his waist. I lock him in tightly, hooking my ankles together as he nudges at my entrance. Bringing my palms to his shoulders, I maintain our eye contact as he slowly sinks into me.

The only sign of his struggle is his tight jaw. "Oh, fuckin' hell," he growls, his face twisting, almost evilly, as he bucks his hips and sends me up the wall on a cry. "Jesus, Adeline," he breathes, sinking his face into my damp neck, retreating and jerking forward uncontrolled. I drop my head back, close my eyes, and let my senses take over, escaping everything other than right now. "What would the world say"—he strains to talk as he consistently thrusts me up the wall, slam after slam, stabbing me deliciously—"if they could see their Queen being fucked against a door?"

"I don't care." My voice is scratchy and raw, my hands wild and frenzied, grabbing at his back. I can feel his muscles undulating with his every advance, waves of sweaty flesh rolling under my touch.

"What would they say if they knew how dirty their Queen is?"

"I don't care," I yell, pushing back the building heat, knowing it's taking me too close to letting go. I'm not ready yet.

"If they knew she loved it hard." With that, he pounds into me unforgivingly.

I drop my head and find his eyes. "I don't fucking care," I grate, threading my fingers into his hair and fisting. I care about nothing in moments like these. But the second I'm down from the highs Josh takes me to, when my mind is stable and I'm not blindsided, it is a very different story. Not a passionate story, not one bursting with love and uninhibited lust, but one tormented by hopelessness and lies. A calm summer's day chased away by black clouds and destructive storms. That is us. We're cursed, in a sense. "I don't care," I whisper, forcing back my glum thoughts.

Josh could challenge my words, but he knows what I am thinking, and he will not challenge that. Instead, he brings our mouths together and ups the tempo of his claim, grunting into my mouth with each merciless thrust. My tongue stabs at his, rushed and clumsy. I have no room to focus on our kiss when every sense is making my head spin. The friction of his shaft entering me pushes me that little bit closer each time, until my hands start to smack at his shoulders, my only way of telling him I'm on my way and there is no going back.

"Yeah?" he asks, biting my lip hard. The pain mingles with the pleasure between my thighs, his claiming brutal but consuming. "I can feel it." He bites up to my ear, never faltering in his rhythm. I yell and smack my head against the door, his hot breath in my ear accelerating my build. He slams one hand into the wood, squeezes my backside with his other. And then he whispers in my ear, "Come," and it is game over. My body goes rigid, a natural attempt to control the power of the orgasm ripping through me, squeezing Josh's hips to the point I'm hurting. "Fuck," he chokes, nudging my cheek with his. My heavy head lifts with too much effort, but once I get a glimpse of his blue eyes rimmed with the familiar amber, it's very easy to keep my attention on him. "I'm still coming," he pants, swaying into me a little more calmly, allowing me to feel every pulse and surge as he spills everything he has.

"Me too." My stomach muscles are rock-hard as I cling onto him, both of us struggling through the pleasure, the power of it taking its toll on our bodies. We're charged, electricity rushing through us, making both of us shake violently.

"Christ." Josh falls forward and traps me against the door, his body the only thing keeping me up as my muscles slowly unravel and loosen. "Okay?"

"I think so." I let my head fall limply back and wait for my heart to thump its way back down to an even rhythm.

"The hospitality around here is second to none," he says, still utterly out of breath, the words strained. I can't find the strength to laugh, but I smile into my darkness. "You lost your tongue?" He dips his chin to his chest, looking out the corner of his eye. I just about manage a slight bob of my head. I've also lost all feeling in my legs, so he had better not let go of me just yet. A cheeky smile ghosts his lips. "You look good freshly fucked." I hitch a brow. "By me," he adds, pouting as he scans my face. "Sweaty, flushed." On a tilt of his hips, he pushes deeply into me. "Warm and wet." I hum, and he chuckles. "C'mon, let's get you—"

Knock, knock.

"Your Majesty?" Olive calls. My eyes go all round. "Are you in there?"

"Oh fuck," Josh whispers, and out of nowhere, I find some energy to slap my hand over his mouth.

"Pardon?" Olive says.

I land Josh with a warning look, my heart rate, that was just reaching resting pace, fast-tracking to a loud sprint. "I'm fine, Olive." I see Josh grin into my palm, obviously finding my high-pitched voice amusing. "I'm just feeling a little—" Josh bucks his hips, his semi-erect dick punching me deeply. "Sick!" I cough, and he chuckles.

"Oh dear." Olive sounds genuinely worried, and Josh and I both jerk forward when she tries to open the door. He pushes his weight into mine and slams it shut again, and Olive yelps in surprise.

"Fine, Olive," I yell, failing miserably to strip the panic in my tone. Josh's amusement grows, as does my aggravation. "Really fine."

"Should I call Dr. Goodridge?"

Josh reaches for my hand and pulls it away from his mouth, winning easily when I try to stop him. "No to the doc, but yes to some Advil. My dick's sore." He takes my hand and places it back over his mouth, smirking again at my incredulous face. He's a child, thoroughly relishing in my panic.

"Fine, Olive," I grate. He can suffer a sore dick. "Please do leave me in peace." Only a fraction of me has room to feel terrible for Olive. She's just worried, bless her, just trying to do her job.

"Very well, ma'am." Her voice grows distant. "Call down if you need anything."

"I will." I wait only a few seconds before I give Josh a few light smacks around his head. "Are you trying to get me in trouble?" I ask, releasing my legs from around his waist.

He puts them straight back to where he wants them and replaces my arms around his shoulders. "Remember when we first met?"

My eyes want to roll, but instead narrow. "Yes. You were uncouth and inappropriate." And I loved every second of my meeting with him, from the public garden party, to the very private spanking in the maze.

By the glimmer of mischief in his gaze, he knows where my thoughts are. "I asked you if you wanted to get into trouble with me." He secures my nape and holds me firmly. "I never imagined this."

"You're a rogue."

"Me?" His smile is all too loveable.

"Yes, you."

And it stretches as he moves in and shows me how loveable he is with a soft, swirling kiss. "So your master plan is to hide me in your room?"

"Yes. But *room* is lacking somewhat."

"For how long?"

"You are my prisoner, Josh Jameson. Held at Her Majesty's pleasure, quite literally." I place my lips on his forehead, smiling into his skin. "I will keep you for as long as I please."

"I can think of worse things." Tilting his head back, he finds my throat and licks his way up to my chin, biting lightly before easing me to my feet. "Steady?"

"Just." I pull my dress down as he refastens his button fly. "Want a tour?"

"Of your room?"

"Like I said, *room* is a little lacking." I motion around the space we're standing in, and for the first time Josh takes in his surroundings. "This is the lobby."

"Your room has a lobby?"

"My private quarters has a lobby." I walk around the circular oak table in the middle, with bright fresh flowers bursting from the glass vase upon it. "And this is the sitting room." I take the handles of the double doors and push my way into the large, airy space, where soft blue couches have been placed on the center rug and gold drapes frame the huge windows.

"Fuckin' hell." Josh stands at the door, taking in the vast space. "And it's just you?"

"Well, unusually, this queen doesn't have a husband, and children are not imminent, so, yes, it is just me."

"And no one will disturb us?"

"No one enters when I've explicitly told them not to."

"How many bedrooms does this place have?"

"Four."

Josh wanders in, his young, shirtless, American, muscly torso looking good surrounded by all this old British history. "Four," he repeats, gazing to the high, decorative ceiling. "Hiding me isn't going to be as hard as I thought." His head drops. "This place is bigger than my condo in New York."

I shrug, the grandeur of the palace of no consequence to me. It's only a reminder of who I am. "The bedrooms are through there." I point to the double doors at the other end of the room, and he raises an eyebrow, heading there.

Stopping on the threshold, he peeks through, but doesn't venture inside. He's thinking, and I'm curious to know what. Whatever it is, it's stopping him from entering my bedroom and that in itself is a worry. What's on his mind? Turning toward me, he regards me quietly. My curiosity goes through the roof. But he shakes his head and starts wandering around again, picking up this, then that, looking high, then low. His moves are slow and measured, his concentration deep. I go to speak more than once, but each time I draw breath, he picks up something else and examines it, stopping me. A framed photograph of my grandfather on his coronation. A small trinket pot that holds a golden nugget given to my grandfather by the Grasberg mine in Indonesia. A solid silver crucifix given to my father by the Pope. Each time, Josh sighs, placing the items down carefully and continuing with his thorough examination of my private quarters. He does this for a good ten minutes, leaving me with nothing to do but watch, part fascinated, part worried.

He eventually circles the entire place until he makes it back to me. "What?" I ask, lowering to one of the couches, getting the feeling I might need to sit for this.

"I don't know." Josh casts his eyes around the room again. "I feel weird."

I can't keep my frown at bay. "Weird?" That has to be a new one. "I'm not sure I know what you mean."

"This?" He motions round him, to the opulent decor, I expect, and I find myself taking it in, too, despite it being very familiar.

"Your *home*." He looks a little lost all of a sudden, his big body swamped by the even bigger room. "I don't know why it's just hit me, but it has. Like a fuckin' baseball bat. You're the Queen of fuckin' England."

Should I be worried? I don't know, but fear is creeping through me unstoppably. "You are a bit slow," I murmur, nothing else coming to me. "That's old news."

"But today it seems like new news. The guided public tour of your palace, the detailed rundowns on every priceless piece of furniture we passed. The collection of paintings, every one of your ancestors dating back centuries. Kings, queens, princes, and princesses. This." He throws his arms up into the air, gesturing to the space I hate. "I'm not good enough for you."

I pull in air so fast, I'm sure I've stripped every scrap of oxygen from the room. Who is this man? I don't recognize him. This isn't my American boy, but a man who has had his confidence knocked out of him, and I positively hate the sight *and* sound. "You *are* good enough for me," I murmur pitifully.

"Says who?"

"Me."

"But what you say counts for nothing, remember?" He smiles. It's not one of his usual dashing smiles. It doesn't knock me sideways, make me dizzy. Because it is sad, and it is also laced in pity. Pity for me, because I am deluded. Pity for him, because he is not.

"What are you telling me?" I don't want to know. Whatever it is, I can't fix it.

On a massive, strained sigh, he walks to me and takes a seat beside me on the couch, then holds my hands. My fear rockets as I stare at him. "I'm saying—"

"Are you breaking up with me?"

His lips straighten, not helping with my current state of mind, and that sadness painting his face becomes more vivid. "No." He shakes his head as he says it, and I fold with relief. "The British army couldn't chase me away, Adeline. And that's what's even more fucked up. Although I know my relationship with you is restricted, I'm prepared to take what I can get, because you have become a vital part of me. And trying to make it through a day knowing I will never set my eyes on you again will be the end of me, so if sharing you with the world is what I need to do, then it's a sacrifice I'm willing to make. Because my love for you is far stronger than my love for me." He reaches for my cheek and wipes away a tear that I hadn't realized had fallen. "You are more important and being here has made me realize that. I don't need to share my love for you with the world. I thought I did, but I don't. That was my ego talking. I only need you to know how much you're loved. By me."

I snivel and blink, more tears breaking free and rolling. "You know if there was a way, I would take it in a heartbeat. I would give up all of this for you if it wouldn't ruin my family."

"I know that now. I get it." He grabs me and hauls me onto his lap, falling back against the couch, cuddling me close. "I was an asshole for ever suggesting you choose. Your loyalty is one of the things I admire most about you."

We settle, bunched together, close and warm. And that's where we remain in a silence that is peaceful, no screaming thoughts or unspoken words. Because right now, we both accept that this is us. We are fire and passion and assertive and violent. But we are also love, with its many facets and complexities.

And right now, that love is bringing us peace.

Rest from the storm.

Quiet within the chaos.

21

JOSH LOOKS GOOD in my massive shower with solid gold fixings. He looks good in my carved, solid wood four-poster bed, the luxury sheets tangled around his legs. He looks good sprawled on the antique King Louis XIV couch in his boxers, his arms thrown so casually above his head. He looks good roaming my private quarters, his bare feet sinking into the plush carpet, his lovely hips wrapped in a small towel. Basically, Josh Jameson is the most beautiful thing in this entire palace that's stuffed full to the rafters with beautiful things.

And now he looks good propped up against my headboard, his legs bent, the papers I pulled from his back pocket earlier in his hand. He's practicing his lines, his concentration intense. It's a sight to behold, something I will store away in my mind and call upon whenever I need to picture him.

As I stand in the doorway to my bathroom, toweling my hair dry, I take the greatest pleasure in watching him. Just admiring him. How handsome he is. How serene and comfortable he looks, which is a relief beyond measure after our heart-to-heart earlier. How much I love him, and how quickly that love is growing. Will there come a point when leaving him is too much to bear? Reluctantly, I admit I'm already there. He's here now, with me, but he will have to leave again, and that taints our time together whenever we are lucky enough to steal it.

Tightening the tie of my robe on a sigh, I pad over to him. His eyes don't leave the script he's holding, but a blind hand reaches for me and helps me onto the bed. He spreads his thighs, and I take his silent order, sitting between them and resting back on his chest, his script lifting to give me space before lowering again so we can both see it.

His chin rests on top of my head. "What's this?" he asks, pulling at the silk of my robe.

"A robe."

"No." He puts the paper in my hand and unravels the tie, encouraging me forward so he can pull it free from under me. "It's something else between us," he says matter-of-factly, though softly, tossing it aside and letting me settle again, reclaiming his lines. I bet he wishes he could rid us of everything between us so easily. Like I do.

I keep quiet as Josh resumes his concentration, his spare hand drawing circles on my thigh. With the words of his latest project so close, it is practically impossible not to read a few. I've never seen a screenplay before. It's fascinating.

And then it's quickly sobering. Muscles tense without me telling them to, and I immediately scold myself for it. "What's up?" Josh asks, laying a palm on my forehead and pulling back until I'm forced to look at him.

"Nothing." I sound as unconvincing as I must look, and Josh catches it. "Nothing," I repeat.

I don't like the knowing smile slowly forming before my eyes. It means he knows exactly what's up.

God damn me. "Do you really have to slide your hand up her thigh?"

He returns his attention to the script and scans the lines. "Apparently so."

I flinch and drop my head, avoiding his measured eyes. "Oh." I read on, a glutton for punishment, clearly. I start mentally kicking myself. But I continue, the torture quite addictive. He touches her breast. She moans. He circles her nipple with a fingertip. *What?* I frantically reverse my reading, trying to find where it states she is wearing something on her top half. *She* being the beauty starring alongside Josh in this film. I nearly throw up when I find the part that tells me Josh removes her blouse just before he has his hand on her inside thigh.

"I don't like this." It comes from nowhere, startling me, and Josh, too, judging by his little jump beneath me. I screw my face up in disgust, not only because of my abrupt words and how needy I must sound, but because I can't stop picturing Josh with his hands all over another woman's body.

He brings the script closer to my face, like some kind of cruel, inhumane bastard, and my traitorous eyes feast on the horror some more. He kisses her chest. He holds her by her throat. He takes her with anger and passion. "Josh," I yell, swiping my arm out and sending the papers scattering to the bedroom carpet. It's all I can do not to gather them up and toss them on the fire in the sitting room. Yuck.

A few moments later, he's motionless beneath me, unmoving, quiet, and I'm still scowling at the strewn papers on the floor. I can't see him, but I can sense his laughter building, rumbling in his tummy under my back. And then it bursts out of him above me. My lip curls of its own volition, my arms folding over my chest moodily. I don't see what's so funny. To me, everything on that page is all rather *un*funny. I shudder, my stomach twisting. I have no space in my mind to consider how I'm behaving. All I can see is Josh. And her. Boobs out, Josh's lips kissing every part of her naked torso. I grab a pillow and sink my face into it, trying to crush the images while Josh laughs on, thoroughly amused. Bastard.

"Hey." The pillow is snatched and flung across the room, and I'm pinned under his body a split second later, his grinning face pushed close to my sulky one. "You know, in all the time I've known you, you've never behaved like a spoiled princess. Until today."

Oh, the cheek. "I'm Queen, actually," I sniff huffily, only increasing his laughter. "And I have never been spoilt. This is not being spoilt. This is being . . ." I fade off, just stopping myself in the nick of time from confessing how jealous I am. I'm really quite a joke. My behavior is screaming jealousy. It isn't as if Josh needs my confession to confirm it.

"What?" he pushes, clearly wanting it anyhow.

"I'm—"

"Jealous?"

"God, no." I'm the biggest fool to ever live. "I'm merely thinking that . . ." My words die once again, and Josh's grin cracks his face. On an epic roll of my eyes, I relent to what we all know. "I'm jealous."

"Praise the fuckin' Lord," Josh sings, rolling us so I'm above him. He's utterly thrilled by the notion. Good for him. I am not. "It's just a job, baby. Just like yours is."

"I don't have other men feeling me up."

"No, only wanting to marry you."

"Yes, and as I have explained so many times before, I won't allow it." I don't like his doubtful look, so I reinforce my promise. "I"—I inch up his body a little more until my mouth is on his chin—"won't"—my lips kiss up his cheek to his ear—"allow it," I breathe, smiling against his skin when I feel a pulse kick in against my thigh. "Like I won't allow you to touch another woman."

"Be reasonable, Adeline," he moans, shifting beneath me. "It's not going to be how you're imagining it."

I clamp down on his ear and drag his flesh through my bite. "You kiss her. You touch her. That's enough."

I'm quickly wrestled away, set on my backside halfway up the bed, a good meter between us. I would think he's lost his patience with me, but then I catch the fire in his eyes. He gets to his knees, and I follow his lead, mirroring him. He could melt me with his stare, turning my blood to lava without so much as a touch. I wait with bated breath for his next move. What will it be?

Slowly reaching forward, painfully slowly, he rests the tip of his finger on my hard nipple, and up in flames I go. White-hot heat tears through me ruthlessly. "It won't be like this," he says quietly, circling my nub slowly, each lap stripping away my breath until I'm barely breathing at all. His erection is growing rapidly, jutting proudly from his groin. "I won't have this reaction." He flicks his head down, eyes still on mine. "And when I do this . . ." He walks his fingers down my stomach to the apex of my thighs, coming forward on his knees as he does and forcing my backside from my heels, lifting me, giving his hand more space. I close my eyes and swallow. "I won't find this." His finger plunges into me, the wetness letting it pass with ease. His mouth hits my neck, and I grab his hair, holding him there, moaning. "There won't be these gorgeous, low, desperate sounds." Rearing back, he slowly drives forward again. My fingers claw at his scalp. "And I will hate every second of my touch being wasted on someone other than you." His hand is gone, leaving me high and dry, and he takes himself back to the headboard. "I love you. Stop being dramatic."

I stare at him incredulously. Well, that told me. But despite my slight and a lack of being taken to the end, I can't help the twerk of my lips.

He cocks his brow. "Get that royal ass back here now before I tan it. And bring my script with you."

"Are you telling me what to do?"

"Yes. Do it."

I'm gathering up his script far quicker than my pride should allow. "One day, I'm going to come to one of your sets and watch you work." I hand over the screenplay and crawl back onto the bed, curling into his side so he can continue to learn his lines with no risk of me having a mini meltdown.

"Let's arrange that for a day when there are no naked women, yeah? I had you marked as many things, but possessive wasn't one of them."

I stop myself from challenging him, since it is very much true. I have an unrelenting desire to keep him all for myself. "I might keep you locked up here for all eternity." I roll onto my back, looking up at him. "A sex slave, as such."

"I'm a slave to you every day of the week, darlin'." He goes back to his lines. "No need to lock me up. Leave the restraining to me." His hand feels for my hair and starts playing with the strands as concentration invades his face once again. Playtime is over; he needs to work, but apparently the newfound playfulness in me isn't ready for it to be over just yet. I roll back onto my side and reach for his thigh, drawing circles across his skin with the tip of my finger, each one moving up a fraction until I'm mere inches from his manhood. I peek up at him; his eyes are still on the script. Pouting, I walk my fingers inward and stop just shy of his groin. His dick twitches, and I secretly smile, victorious.

Then he seizes my wrist and looks down at me disapprovingly. "You're like a puppy vying for attention."

"I just want to make the most of our time."

"Speaking of which, when am I free to leave?"

"Why, do you want to?" I ask, pouting.

"No." He stretches the word out, flattening my palm and holding it on his thick thigh. "I just wondered how you planned on getting me out."

"Easy," I declare, proud of myself. "The passageway, of course. But it'll have to be when the palace is open to tourists again."

"Again?"

"Yes, it's gone six o'clock." I watch in quiet amusement as he grasps what this means.

"I'm not leaving tonight, am I?"

I slowly shake my head. Not tomorrow either, if I have my way. And I plan to. This is perfect. Privacy, peace. Being together, relaxing, the big wide world at a safe distance beyond the palace walls. No one will dare enter my private space if I have explicitly told them not to, and I have explicitly told them not to. We're safe, and that is a wonderful feeling to have when I'm with Josh.

His lips pull into a straight line. "I don't know if I should spank your ass or congratulate you."

"Spank me," I retort cheekily, flipping myself over and raising my arse. It serves as a red flag, his work soon forgotten and cast aside in favor of my bottom. He growls as he kneels over me, stroking over the peak of my bum, and I sink into the pillow on a happy sigh.

Bang!

My head shoots up, and Josh's stare darts to the doorway of my bedroom. "That wasn't your palm meeting my arse, was it?" I ask, scrambling up to my feet.

"Nope." He's under the covers fast, and I'm running across to the doors. I make it to them just in time to see Kim entering the sitting room. "Oh gosh," I whisper, slamming my bedroom doors shut.

"Your Majesty?"

I turn and splatter my back against them, my wide eyes on Josh. His lips are pursed, a sort of *you-asked-for-this* look in his eyes. "No one enters when you've explicitly told them not to?" he says, sarcasm in his tone.

I scowl at him. They usually don't. Seems everyone around here is getting a little bit *too* relaxed. "I've said I don't want to be disturbed," I call.

"How are you feeling?" She's right behind the door.

"A little better," I reply. "More sleep will help. By morning I'll be back to normal."

"But your guests have arrived, ma'am. They're waiting."

I toss a frown at Josh. I haven't the foggiest idea what Kim is talking about. Guests? Waiting?

"Who?" Josh mouths, and I shrug.

"Who? I'm not expecting any guests."

There's a slight pause, Kim possibly looking at the wood between us with an almighty frown, and then . . .

"Oh bloody hell." It comes to me. The dinner plans that David insisted I approved, and I know for certain I did not. I forgot to tell Kim to cancel. And now they're here. "Oh, bloody, bloody hell."

"What?" Josh hisses across the room, impatient.

"I assume it's come back to you, ma'am," Kim says sardonically. "And I thought you would be pleased to hear that His Royal Highness Prince Edward has arrived."

"He has?"

"Yes, and Jenny is on her way up to help you get ready."

"No!" I yell without thinking. "I mean . . ." God, *bloody* hell. There's simply no possible way I can refuse Jenny's help this evening, not for such a dinner, and not without raising all kinds of suspicions. "I'm just taking a shower."

"Just?"

"I was asleep," I spit back in defense, sagging against the door. I can't believe this. "Tell her to wait for me in the sitting room."

"As you wish," Kim sighs, and soon after I hear her low court heels hit the wooden floor in the foyer of my apartment.

"Oh God." I sprint across the bedroom to my bathroom and land in front of the mirror, hearing Josh calling me as I go. My hair is damp, my skin makeup free, and I haven't even applied any moisturizer. I'm a blank canvas, yes, but it takes time to make a blank canvas something other than blank.

"Will you tell me what the hell is going on?" Josh appears in the reflection of the mirror at the bathroom door.

"I have guests for dinner tonight," I explain. "I didn't arrange it, David bloody Sampson did, and I forgot to tell Kim to cancel it this afternoon." I glare at him in the reflection. "Because I was distracted."

"Hold up." Josh looks apprehensive, and he has every right to. "Sampson? That tally-ho motherfucker arranged this? But you told me you dealt with this supposed dinner."

"I did. Apparently another was arranged." My lips twist. I know what's coming next.

"Will *he* be there?"

I keep quiet, not needing to answer. Of course Haydon will be there. Worryingly, and infuriatingly, I suspect David has not yet given up on his quest.

"Fuckin' great." Josh turns and marches away. "So you expect me to sit up here while you're down there with that cocksucker licking your fuckin' ass."

I follow him on light feet. "You could practice your script."

I get the death stare thrown my way as he lands heavily on my bed. It's completely warranted, since I just gave Josh such a tough time over a sexy scene in a movie. "If he so much as touches you, I'll know."

I can't help my chuckle. "Baby, no one can touch me," I say, avoiding mentioning the fact that Haydon hasn't seemed to pay much regard for that protocol since my succession. But he will when I correct him. And I *will* correct him.

Josh's eyebrow hitches slightly, and I watch as it slowly dawns on him. "No one can touch you because you're the Queen," he murmurs.

"Because I am the Queen," I confirm, making it trickier for him to hide his grin.

"I can touch you." He relaxes a bit, his stress leaving his strung body. "I can do what the hell I like to you."

"I can see this pleases you."

"Oh, it does." He grabs his phone and dials someone, holding it to his ear. "But just in case."

"Who are you calling?"

He dismisses me by looking away. "Damon, it's Josh."

What? I shoot across the room and dive on the bed, trying to seize his phone. I get held at arm's length with ease.

"She's having dinner. A lovely family affair. Watch her. Or more importantly, watch Haydon Sampson."

I bat and smack Josh's hands away, dying to yell at him, but knowing I'll give myself away if I do. Damon will wring my neck if he knows I'm hiding Josh in my private quarters.

"What?" Josh turns his eyes back to mine. "It's your night off," he mimics.

"Oh, I forgot," I chirp without thought, realizing my error the moment it's tumbled from my stupid mouth. I slap my palm over my lips. *Oh no.*

"Yes, I'm with her." Josh gives Damon what he wants with no fight. "No, I'm at the palace." He starts shaking his head as I drop my head in despair. "She doesn't look like she's in the talking mood."

I start shaking my head, too, agreeing with him. I'm a dead woman.

"Will do." Josh hangs up and drops his phone. "You're in deep shit, Your Majesty."

"Why did you call him?" I ask, annoyed, diverting the blame to Josh, since, metaphorically speaking, it is entirely his fault. "Damn it, Josh, he will have my guts for garters."

"No idea what that means." He laughs, snatching his script up and burying his face in it. "What's the problem, anyway? He was in Washington. He knows about us, that we're sneaking around seeing each other. He's set most of our sneaky meetings up, for fuck's sake."

"Josh, look around you." I stomp my way to the bathroom and start haphazardly, and very angrily, slapping makeup on my face. "You are in Claringdon Palace. I put you in here, and that is a step past reckless that Damon will skin me alive for. The reason he wants to know everything, why he helps, is so he can ensure my protection."

"You're in the palace," he shouts from the bed. "What the hell can happen to you in here?"

As I rub foundation onto my cheeks, I take myself to the door so he can see me. So he can see how serious I am. "There's more danger to me within these walls than there is outside of them, Josh." I pull my hands away and regard him closely as my words sink in. Remorse soon replaces his sightedness. He understands. I didn't tell Damon because he would never have allowed it. In the outside world, he's protecting me from the media, which in turn protects me from *them*. In here, he's protecting me from them and them alone, and I am dancing dangerously close to the fire right now.

Without another word and leaving Josh on the bed with his realization, I back into the bathroom and resume getting ready. By the time I've mindlessly finished my eye makeup, Josh has found the will and courage to come find me. He looks full to the brim with remorse. I brace my hands on the edge of the sink, staring at him in the reflection as he stares at me.

"Adeline, can you even comprehend how it feels to know there is something I can't protect the woman I love from? Not because I physically can't, but because she won't let me?"

I feel for him, his despondency decorating him like a badge for the world to see. "I don't need protecting, Josh." My swallow is lumpy. "I just need loving."

His shoulders drop, and he comes to me, turning me away from the mirror and pulling me in for a hug. "That bit comes naturally, Adeline. Everything else doesn't."

"I can handle myself," I say, squeezing him with equal force. I don't confess the very reason I can handle myself is because he gives me the strength. "You know that."

"Oh, I know that." I'm released, and I know it kills him. Dropping

a kiss on my forehead, he sighs through it. "You'd better get your
ass moving."

He turns and leaves me to finish getting ready, his feet dragging, his shoulders low. I hate this look on him. And my horrible
circumstances put it there.

22

THE MOMENT I make my entrance into the huge dining room, I realize what I have walked into. A trap would describe it best. This is the cozy family dinner that was reported in the press, between Haydon's family and mine. The one I vetoed. This is the dinner that is, apparently, the first steppingstone to our engagement. I stare down the length of table lined with my family, including Aunt Victoria, her husband, Phillip, and my cousin Matilda. And on the other side, Uncle Stephan, his wife, Sarah, David Sampson, Haydon, and Sabina. Oh, and Dr. Goodridge, too. Despite my request, I know someone has called him because he's immediately assessing me, looking for what may be wrong. There's nothing the old man can give me to cure what I have. Irritation. Fury.

Everyone stands when my arrival is announced, surprisingly Eddie, too, who looks gaunt, his skin sallow. The sight of him, my habitually bright and breezy brother looking lost and angry, breaks my heart. He could have refused this dinner, yet he hasn't, and deep down in my heart of hearts, I know it is because he loves me. He wants to be here for me when he's probably suspicious that attempts are going to be made to twist my arm into marriage. Again. He's always liked Haydon, but he has equally always accepted he is not the man for me. My brother is the only reason I don't turn and walk out. Knowing he is here, and Josh is waiting for me in my private quarters, replaces some of my irritation with fortitude.

I give Eddie a small smile as I make my way to the table, hoping he reads my gratitude. Victoria and Phillip's poorly hidden looks of disgrace follow my path the entire way, though I don't acknowledge their disdain. I truly cannot be bothered. A footman pulls my chair out at the top of the table, the center of the show, and I lower, thanking him quietly.

Then everyone else sits, too. Sabina, ever tranquil and lovely, shoots me a soft smile, while David looks like the cat that got the cream. Haydon has been conveniently placed to my right, as close as one could be.

"Stunning as always, Your Majesty," he says, loud enough for everyone to hear.

"Thank you." I smile tightly, catching Matilda's knowing gaze. She's right at the other end of the table, way out of talking distance. Undoubtedly a good thing. What I have to say to her is not appropriate chitchat over dinner. And I'm not sure I'll vent quietly enough.

"We hear Spearmint is doing well," David chirps, kicking off the conversation with something nice and easy.

"Very well." I nod when I'm offered wine, barely holding back from snatching it up before the server finishes pouring. "I'm very much looking forward to seeing him and his jockey decorated when he's ready to race."

Sabina raises her glass. "To Spearmint."

I smile and toast, too. "To Spearmint," everyone chants as our starters are placed before us. I look at the scallops, usually one of my favorites, but my appetite is nowhere to be found. I can only assume that no one else is hungry either, as no one has begun eating. I take a sip of wine, feeling uncomfortable. Everyone is looking at me. I glance at each of them, and it is only when my eyes fall to

Uncle Stephan and he lifts his fork that I realize.

They're waiting for me, of course. "Please, begin," I say, taking my drink to my lips again. A liquid dinner it is for me.

Chatter is all very bland throughout first course and second, my interaction consisting mainly of smiles and one-word answers. I have no appetite for food, and I have no appetite for conversation. Eddie hardly speaks a word, and Mother looks at me constantly in question, as if trying to encourage me to engage with my guests. But they're not my guests. They're David's.

I feel my mobile phone vibrate in my lap and look to see a text. From Josh. Aware of the outrage it will cause if I were to use my phone during dinner, I discreetly open the message and read it.

I found your tiara. It looks good on me.

A little snort of laughter escapes when a picture follows his message, of Josh looking all adorable and smug with my tiara resting on his head to the side. But while I'm amused, I'm also annoyed with the reminder that one of the only people in this world who I actually want to spend time with is upstairs in my suite, waiting for me while I have dinner with many people who I really don't want to spend time with.

"Adeline?" Haydon says, winning my attention. His neck is craning, as if he is trying to see what is in my lap.

"I apologize." I drop my phone and force myself to eat a spoonful of the chocolate tart I hadn't noticed has been put before me.

"Nothing important, I hope." He slips a big helping of the tart into his mouth around a huge smile.

Yes. Something *very* important. Something more important than Haydon, and those here who do not deserve my time. Enduring these dinners has always been testing, even when I could sit in silence, happy to be ignored by all. Now, as center stage, and with every look given to me, every word spoken, the water is rising, drowning me. "Nothing important," I murmur, setting down my spoon.

I turn my attention to my mother on my left. I have thought a few times throughout dinner that she seems a little vacant. As if she is here in body, but far from here in spirit. "Mother?"

She snaps from her daydream and finds me, painting a smile on her face. "A lovely dinner," she says out of habit, just for something to say.

"It was." I look up when Davenport enters the room, his eyes falling straight to my mother. She goes to her wine and loses herself in the glass, her stiffness visible.

"Would you please excuse me?" she asks, getting up from the table before I have answered. I watch her briskly leave the room, and it isn't until she has gone that Davenport makes his approach. It's only now I remember I invited him to eat with us. Why isn't he? I look to David. Silly question. Or is it? My eyes turn to the door where my mother just scurried out.

As everyone watches on, Davenport lowers, turning slightly so his back is to the rest of the table. "Damon has just arrived, ma'am," he whispers. "He is asking to speak with you as a matter of urgency."

Shit. I clear my throat and glance to the doors that lead to the foyer, imaging my disgruntled head of security pacing the marble floor. "Would you please inform him that I am currently entertaining guests." Being at this table is suddenly appealing. "I'll see him in the morning."

"He's being rather insistent."

"So am I," I retort, leveling him with a look that dares him to argue. "Thank you." The finality in my tone does the trick if my warning expression hasn't, and though obviously raging with curiosity, Davenport nods in acceptance and backs away. "Dinner was delicious, I'm sure you will all agree," I say, forcing my eyes back to the table.

"You hardly touched it," Victoria says, waving a footman over to pour her more wine.

Keeping my glower at bay, I take my napkin from my lap and rest it on the table. "One has been feeling rather off today."

"Anything I can help with?" Dr. Goodridge asks, once again assessing me.

"I'm sure it's nothing," I assure him, turning my attention to Uncle Stephan and his wife. "How are you, Uncle?"

His grin would be wicked if he would reveal it. "Marvelous, dear niece."

"Very good. And I hear things are going very well with Santiago, Matilda." There is no denying the light in her eyes at the mention of the Argentine's name. "Maybe next time he could join us."

Matilda's smile is bold and knowing. "I would love that, thank you."

"I'm seeing someone." Eddie pipes up, surprising everyone around the table. It's the first words he's spoken since we have been seated, and they are quite some words.

"And who is the lucky lady?" I ask in jest, a wry smile on my lips. A lovely woman. Perhaps that's what he needs to pull him off the slippery slope to utter disgrace and ruin.

"I believe you may know her," Eddie tells me casually, finishing off his last inch of wine before holding it up for a refill. "Hallie Green."

"The name is familiar," I muse, wracking my brain as Stephan chokes on something and a footman dashes to help, on standby in case he needs the Heimlich maneuver.

"I'm fine," Stephan coughs, holding his napkin to his mouth as he gives me round eyes. I frown, and he shakes his head, taking off his spectacles and rubbing at his watery eyes.

"Hallie Green?" Phillip looks at Eddie in utter disgust. "The model?"

On a smirk, Eddie toasts thin air. "Yes, you know of her?" His head tilts in interest, and Phillip retreats, looking around the table, uncomfortable.

Stephan is choking again, and this time his wife smacks his back. What's going on? I'm bemused, as well as confused. "Hallie Green," I say again, and something in the way that Victoria looks at her fidgeting husband nudges my brain. "The glamour model?" I recoil, my glass hitting the table. The busty blonde is a regular in newspapers, usually either with her boobs out or with a scandalous Kiss and Tell to share. Matilda and I have often rolled our eyes at the latest from the brash woman who is a leech when it comes to high-profile men, her curves and sex-appeal sending them stupid.

"She's really rather misunderstood." Eddie ignores my shock and works his way through his fresh glass of wine. "Maybe next time we all have a lovely family dinner, she can join us, too."

Victoria snorts. "Preposterous. Such a harlot would never be welcome to dine with the Royals."

"Shut up, Victoria," Eddie says tiredly, making her recoil as if she could have been slapped. "I know you have always secretly believed you could do a better job than any of us, but you're not and never will be Queen, therefore it isn't your call to decide who is or isn't welcome around the table."

Victoria's mouth drops open, and she elbows Phillip, snapping him into dutiful action. "You will not speak to my wife in such a way."

Eddie snorts. "You can shut up, too, you uptight old fool. You're only here for status and money, you parasite." He chuckles to himself, while I can do no more than watch on, flummoxed. "You familiar with Hallie, are you, Unc?" Eddie asks Phillip, his smile cocky.

"I refute your insinuation," he barks, but I saw the way Victoria looked at him when Hallie's name was mentioned. It had death in it. "I don't know of her."

"Yes, you do." Uncle Stephan, now over his coughing fit, jumps into the conversation. Or argument. "She's a regular at that private gentleman's club you and your yuppie friends like to hang out at."

My jaw hits the table, and Eddie starts laughing hard in his chair. It's bloody anarchy—Victoria hissing and spitting, Phillip blushing various shades of crimson, Stephan and Eddie looking like they're having the time of their lives. I realize I should be calling a halt to this circus, but, frankly, it's rather entertaining, if not enlightening. I look to Haydon. His face is both amused and exasperated, and then to David who is shaking his head in dismay. Sabina, however, just gives me that soft smile she always does, never judging.

"So," Eddie says, looking back to me, "can she?"

"Can who what?" I ask, lost for a moment.

"Hallie. Can she join us for dinner?"

He's got me held to ransom, and I am far from appreciative. He's simply rebelling, putting my past efforts to defy my status to shame. He has purposely found the most outrageous woman he can to prove a point, whatever that is. He must be crazy. That woman will be splashed all over the papers in a few short weeks telling wicked tales about Prince Eddie. And worst still, I bet they will all be true.

Glancing to David, I detect his intention to put a call in to the PR and communications people, and I nod subtly to him, telling him he should do it sooner rather than later. What I'm doing now isn't a queen's duty. It's a sister's duty. Eddie isn't thinking straight, so I have to think straight for him.

"I think that's a very good idea," I say, if only to appease my brother. I'll get this nonsense sorted out before it comes to dinner. Appeasing Eddie, however, means provoking most of the other people at the table. Many of them remain silently disapproving.

Except Victoria. "How ridiculous." She shoves her napkin on the table. "The day I eat with such a commoner will be the day I lose all faith in the Monarchy."

"Enough," I order, low and threatening, my eyes on her and her alone. She shrinks in her chair, and this time she doesn't prod her husband for backup. Will this woman ever learn her place? When it's appropriate to talk and when it's appropriate to shut the hell up? I want to ram those plums she has in her mouth down her throat until she chokes. I feel unreasonably furious. Victoria swipes up her glass, looking away from my glare before I singe her skin with it. *Yes, know your place,* I think, looking away when someone enters.

Mother glides across the room, taking in the scene as she lowers to her chair. "Apologies, I hope I didn't miss anything important."

She really didn't, though I choose not to tell her so, instead reaching forward and tucking a loose strand of hair behind her ear. She looks flustered, and I once again wonder if inviting Davenport back into royal employment was wise. She looks at me, her smile strained, and my hand pauses as I withdraw from fixing her hair. She's usually so perfect—her hair, her makeup, but I've just pushed an out-of-place strand away, and I'm certain I am looking at lips that have had the lipstick recently rubbed off, remnants of it staining outside the line of her lips.

Oh my . . .

I pull back my hand, studying her closely. She gives me nothing, returning to her drink. Is she . . . ?

"Adeline." David pulls me from my silent contemplations, his palm on his son's shoulder. "Haydon has a surprise for you."

Everyone falls silent and all attention falls on me. Oh no. "I'm not all too fond of surprises." I swallow, trying to make my words firm rather than worried. "Haydon knows that."

"Every woman loves surprises." David laughs. "Even if they claim not to."

I can assure him, I hate surprises. "Really . . ." A box lands on the table before me, and I lean back in my chair, as if I can escape the tiny harmless thing. The problem is, though, it is not harmless. Nothing about what could be in this box is harmless. I gulp, my eyes glued to the leather, my hands refusing to pick it up. Fear mixed with a growing anger starts to dominate me. I knew this dinner was a fix, but I never anticipated Haydon would be so bold to do this. Not in front of everyone. Not because his father told him to. Is he that thick-skinned? Can't he read my body language?

Tearing my eyes from the box, I look to my mother. I hate her peaceful gaze. I look to David and want to slap him. He has me cornered. I look to Sabina and find her lips straight, as are Dr. Goodridge's. Matilda looks sorry for me, as does Stephan and his wife, while Victoria and Phillip look entirely indifferent. Eddie sinks his teeth into his bottom lip, regarding me quietly. And Haydon? He looks so very nervous, his face carrying a sheen of sweat. How could they do this to him? They are immoral—his father, Sir Don, and the rest of the corrupt fools.

He clears his throat as I stare at him blankly, reaching for the box and dropping to one knee. *Oh God, no.* He pulls it open, but I can't bring myself to look at the ring and further confirm what is happening. "Adeline, I have been more than patient. I have loved you since we were children, and now is the perfect time for us to take the next step."

I am struck utterly dumb, as well as frozen in my chair. Which, of course, hinders the possibility of me stopping this runaway train from crashing spectacularly. "I promise to stand by your side, support you in your reign, be there for you in every way I can. You need a husband. I love you, Adeline Catherine Luisa Lock—"

"Haydon, stop." I reach for his hand, his mouth snapping shut. I *need* a husband? Well, of course, because a little, feeble female could never possibly hold down such a high-profile job without a man by her side to support her. I inwardly laugh. This is a step too far, boldness to the worst degree. I flash David a dark look, knowing he is one of the main culprits. Enough is enough. Tomorrow, I will lay down the law, and if my warnings are not heeded, I won't think twice about stripping titles. "I'm never going to marry you, Haydon." I hate the hurt in his eyes. I hate it so much. "You have to stop this. Move on. Find a woman who deserves you and needs you, because I'm afraid I do not." I stand from the table. "Please excuse me." I walk away on stable legs, though my heart is pumping wildly. I'm full to the brim with tenacity. I've had a bellyful of this ridiculous matter, and now it can finally be put to rest. I've said my piece, and those who do not listen will regret it.

Damon is in the entrance hall waiting for me. I can see he is ready to let loose, his friendly face cut with annoyance, but the second he catches my expression, he backs down, remaining silent.

I hold my hand out, prompting him to go to his inside pocket without delay or question. He hands over the goods, and I head for the drawing room that leads to my escape. I'm lighting a cigarette before I make it outside, polluting the historical room. I don't care.

Letting myself out of the glass doors, I pace toward the botanical garden and stop, staring into the clouds of green. I hear Damon's footsteps, and then I don't.

"You needn't have come," I tell him, pulling on my cigarette like I need it to breathe.

"You've smuggled your secret boyfriend into the palace, Adeline. I very much needed to come."

"And I'll smuggle him out."

"I'm not going to ask how you managed it, but however you did, it's stupid."

"The secret passages," I tell him, exhaling into the night-time air. "One leads to the Blue Room."

"It's not gated?" His alarm is warranted, though I hadn't given it much thought myself. Until now. The Blue Room was added to the palace tour only last year.

"You can only open it from the inside." There will be a metal gate on the entrance to that particular passageway in no time at all, and I expect some heads will roll, too. I have one last puff of my cigarette before I flick the end into the shrubs and turn toward Damon. "I won't apologize."

"I didn't ask you to."

"But you don't approve."

"Of course I don't approve. You've always walked a fine line between recklessness and stupidity, but this is a step too far." His jaw is tight. "Your Majesty," he adds, for two reasons, I expect. He's just given me a royal dressing down, so to speak, and at the same time reminded me of who I am.

"Haydon just proposed to me." There is not one little bit of emotion in my voice. I feel nothing. "I said no."

Damon only nods, and I can't help but think that he appears to be bracing himself for something unpleasant on the horizon. "Right," he breathes.

"That's it? *Right?*"

"What do you want me to say? You must have known it was coming."

I drop my eyes to my feet, staring at my pretty black heels. "I never expected to be put on the spot like that." Humiliating Haydon doesn't sit well with me, but if David and anyone else think that I will bow to pressure like that, they can think again. How could Haydon have been so blind while he's waited years being *more than patient?* For what? Does he really not care I'd never marry him for love? That I'll never feel that way toward him? I should have told him to stop embarrassing himself before the entire family, but if he is so blind he needs me to tell him, he's a fool. Just like his father. The sly bastard. "I should get back to my room." I reach up and lay my hand on Damon's shirt. "I'll see you tomorrow." Brushing past him, I make my way back into the palace.

"Adeline," he calls, pulling me to a stop at the door. I don't turn to face him, but I do wait. "Be careful."

I can only smile, but it's an effort. I detour through the kitchens to avoid running into anyone, my presence in the busy space causing a silent stir as I pass. As I take the grand staircase, my mobile rings, and my brow bunches when I see who is calling me. Is he trying to have us smoked out? "I'm on my way," I say as I answer, using the handrail to help pull my drained body up the steps.

"Oh good," Josh says, his voice noticeably high. "Because we have a problem."

"What?"

"One of your ladies just swung by."

I have no energy to panic, though I do hurry my steps. "Who?"

"The one who walked in on us in Washington. She won't talk. She's just staring at me."

"Olive," I conclude, rounding the gallery and picking up my pace, not because I've found my panic, but because I know Olive will be on the verge of heart failure. Especially if Josh is still strutting around in his boxer shorts. I fall into my apartment and scan the space. Empty. I hurry through to the bedroom, finding Olive static by the door, mummified, and Josh standing by the bed looking a little scared. As I feared, he's in his boxers, his impressive chest on full display. Between that and his gorgeous face, it's no wonder Olive is hypnotized.

I approach her calmly and take her arm. "Olive?"

She turns blank eyes onto me but says nothing.

"Come on." I guide her out of the room, looking over my shoulder to Josh as I go. I can tell he's wondering where my meltdown is. "Do you need to sit down?" I ask as we pass the couches.

She seems to come to life now that she's out of close proximity to Josh. "You need to warn me, ma'am." She starts shaking her head, panic rooting and growing like weeds. "Oh my days." Her eyes dart to the door of my bedroom. "Josh Jameson is in the palace."

"Quieten down, Olive," I scold her gently. "You'll be heard."

"My heart can't take such shocks, ma'am."

"I'm sorry, Olive." I feel terrible. The weight of my secrets is becoming too much for her. "I feel terrible for shouldering all of this pressure on you, truly, I do."

"Pressure?" She almost laughs, but it is nervous. "No, ma'am, you're misunderstanding me." Her arm shoots toward the doors again, where Josh is beyond. "Josh Jameson is in your bedroom, and he is wearing boxer shorts."

"Oh."

"I thought I was on the set for one of those high-end perfume ads."

"Olive, you have seen Josh's . . . physique once before," I remind her. "At the St. Regis."

She shakes her head. "I was half asleep. And the light was poor. And he was in bed. Oh my, Your Majesty, how do you maintain your composure?" She is going to burst at any moment. And then, like she could have been stabbed with a pin, she deflates and straightens, looking worried. "Oh my goodness, forgive me, please. How inappropriate of me. My mouth runs away with me sometimes, and I have no control over it. I'm terribly sorry, ma'am. So sorry. It was highly—"

"Olive, stop it." I take her arm and lead her to the doors. "There is nothing to apologize for." Opening them, I indicate that it's time for her to leave. I don't waste any breath telling her to keep my secret. She will. "And if you must know, I *have* never and *will* never be able to maintain my composure in Josh's presence, either."

Her little face bunches with contained delight. "I think you are wonderful, ma'am. I really do."

She's the sweetest. "As are you, Olive. Now go home."

"Yes, ma'am." She scuttles off, and I close the door, dragging myself to the bedroom. Josh has put himself back on the bed, his arms folded over his chest, his face splashed with worry. "Why aren't you panicking?" he asks.

"Honestly, I just can't be bothered." All I want to do is crawl into bed and let Josh keep me warm all night. Kicking off my shoes, I unzip my dress and let it fall to the floor. I don't take my makeup off, and I don't remove my underwear. Josh watches me closely as I pad across the carpet. He gets under the covers and pulls up the sheets in invitation, and I crawl in and splatter myself all over his chest.

"How was dinner?" he asks, a little hesitant, as if he's scared to know.

"David Sampson is still an arsehole, Haydon still a puppet." I don't say any more than that. Josh is likely to fly off the handle if I tell him. "Eddie is dating a glamour model/porn star who has her boobs out at every opportunity, and I'm pretty certain my mother is having a secret affair with Major Davenport."

"Wow," is all Josh says, and I laugh a little under my breath, because yes. Wow. But it is all just more smoke and more mirrors.

I close my eyes and let my mind focus only on Josh's hands caressing my back. He doesn't press me for more information. It's as if he knows I will break if he does.

But I won't break . . . because I'm already broken. And Josh is the only thing currently keeping the cracks together. I refuse to believe he is just a temporary fix, because that would be accepting my world has been blown apart.

And I'm trying so hard not to shatter with it.

23

I FELT NO better come morning. I slept soundly, but my head ached the second I opened my eyes. I had a deep, lingering, nasty feeling swirling in my gut, a sense of foreboding I just couldn't shake. I escaped it for a while when Josh rolled me over and slowly dragged my knickers down, turning me onto my side and curling his body around mine. One shift of his hips put him inside me, and his slow, continuous grinds carried me to a land I wish I had a one-way ticket to. But, alas, I must always return from my place of peace and deal with the rotten world in which I reside, maintaining the façade. I inwardly yelled at myself for letting my woes momentarily ruin my only happiness, reaching back for his hair and bowing my body into his, rolling my backside into his every grind.

We came together.

Quietly.

Calmly.

He whispered, "I love you," and I kissed him in reply. We cuddled, silent, and I was sure Josh sensed the ill feeling, too. Although he didn't say a word, and neither did I.

Now I'm in my casual jeans and a chunky-knit jumper, pulling on my Uggs as Josh waits for me by the door, smiling. "That look reminds me of the night you went AWOL and turned up at my hotel."

I return his smile as I join him. "I've gone AWOL more times than I care to admit since meeting you." Reaching up, I straighten his baseball cap, not that it needs straightening at all. It's just . . . I remove my hands and step back. "Ready?"

"Yeah." He looks at me in question, but I disregard it and pull the door open, walking straight out without so much as checking the coast is clear. We make it into the passageway and I lead on, every step I'm taking toward Josh's freedom feeling like a step toward my downfall. He's quiet, I'm quiet, the tension in the tight, dank space thick. When we reach the end of the line, I turn and give him a meek smile. I try my hardest to force some zest into it. I know I fail.

"I had a lovely time." It is all I can think to say. My diabolical family dinner aside, it was really quite wonderful. Even when I was lost in my tormenting thoughts once I had returned, those tormenting thoughts were so much more bearable with Josh cuddling me until I fell asleep and my tormenting dreams took over.

Josh steps forward, concern like an emblem emblazoned across his face. I hate to see it, and I hate that I am the cause and there is nothing I can do to prevent it. "You walked out of your apartment without a care in the world," he says quietly.

"Sorry?"

"Back then." He thumbs over his shoulder into the darkness. "You didn't check the coast was clear. Why?"

Because I don't care. I don't say that, though. There is much I haven't said, and I shouldn't. The proposal will send Josh straight to crazy town. My frame of mind is dangerous. "I'm just tired." That is true. Tired of . . . everything.

"Adeline, you're scaring me."

I'm scaring myself. Josh reaches for my cheek and brushes gently across it with the pad of his thumb. "Tell me."

Tell him. Tell him I'm just about ready to pop with frustration. Tell him I'm about ready to scream and not care if the world hears. Tell him that I fear for him. For me. For *us*. "I wish you didn't have to leave," I admit, walking into his chest.

"The fact I'm here is a miracle in itself." He embraces my need for contact, holding me tightly. "And when will we be together again?"

"Tomorrow," I tell him. "Where are you staying?"

"The Ritz. In the Prince of Wales Suite. But how?"

"I'll find a way," I promise, because I will. And I will have shaken off this funk I'm in. "Go." I usher him away, his hand holding mine until the last second, as well as his eyes, and the moment the door closes, I do what I have been desperate to do since I walked out of the dining room last night.

Cry.

It pours out of me unstoppably, my sobs suppressed by my tense body and my hand covering my mouth, yet it is loud, the sound being carried by the small, contained space, echoing off the bare brick walls. I have to beg my weak legs not to give way, locking them to stop my back from sliding down the rough stone and crouching on the floor to make myself small. Hopelessness is eating me alive, scratching relentlessly at my soul and spirit. I must stop it before everything I stand for disappears. I must stop all of this madness.

Roughly rubbing at my cheeks, I take long, controlled breaths, fighting against my jerking body. I can beat this belligerent on-slaught of despair. The essence of me, it can't be lost, or that will be the end. Of me. Of Josh and me. I'm not prepared to let it end, no matter what.

I look into the darkness of the passageway, something fierce rising up from my toes. Resilience. Courage. Grit. It crashes through me like violent waves, destroying the loathsome weakness in its path. No more. I will not be held hostage by this godforsaken institution any longer.

I stalk down the passageway, assertive and bursting with resolve, my mind made, my focus set. This ends today. Today, I need to smash through some of the smoke and mirrors.

When I make it out of the fusty bowels of Claringdon, I head straight for my suite to get ready, needing power in my dress as much as in my attitude. As if Jenny has secret knowledge of my frame of mind, she's waiting for me in my suite, the straighteners heating on the heat mat, her box of magic tricks open as she sharpens a red lip pencil. "I'll be in the shower," I say as I pass her. "I think I'll wear my charcoal pencil dress with leather piping."

"Good choice, ma'am."

I disappear into the bathroom and shower quickly, constantly chanting encouraging words in my head. By the time I'm done, Jenny has my dress laid out, as well as my black patent stilettos, and the earrings Josh bought for me are on my dressing table. Nothing else. Just the earrings. I sit and let her work her magic, drying and straightening my long dark hair, which stretches it down to my lower back. My eyes are lined with a perfect flick at each corner, and my lips artfully painted red. I slip out of my robe and step into my dress, then my heels, and let Jenny fasten the back zipper.

Done.

I put on my earrings as I leave, wandering through the palace toward my mother's private quarters. My phone rings as I'm checking myself in the mirror outside her door. When I catch sight of the screen, my fortitude wavers for just a second, my brain ordering me to ignore the call. "No," I tell it, looking up at myself in the mirror as I connect. This is all part of the process. "Haydon," I say in answer, staring at myself and the formidable creation Jenny has made of me.

"Adeline, what happened?"

Closing my eyes to gather patience and strength would be easy, but none of this is going to be easy, so I maintain my staring dead-lock with myself, if only to remind myself of who I am. I can't only let them do this to me anymore. I can't let them do it to Haydon. "I don't love you, Haydon."

"Not now, I know. But you will grow to love me. That's how it works."

I grind my teeth, frustrated. "Not in the real world, Haydon. That is not how it works in the real world. It's how it works in this family. In *our* world. In the real world, you fall in love with someone and marry her because being without her is unthinkable. In the real world there are sparks and chemistry and need."

"We will have all of that, Adeline. You just have to give us a chance."

He's been brainwashed. He can't truly want to be with a woman who does not love him. Why would any man want that? My fortitude slips, and I close my eyes. "I'm in love with someone else, Haydon," I say, a last resort to simply make him see. And, really, Haydon should be the first to know. I take no pleasure from the hurt I know he will feel. But I also take no blame. I have fired my arrows straight for as long as I can remember, made it clear that a romantic union between us will never happen. Every blind and misguided conviction he considers real has been built by his father and my advisors. They have added bricks to his wall of hope, and I am the one who has to bash that wall down.

There's silence, and I open my eyes to face myself once again. "Haydon, did you hear me?"

"It doesn't matter."

I balk at myself in the mirror, and for the first time I wonder if Haydon already knew. Did David tell him about my confession in Evernmore? Surely not. Why would he? For them, the less people that know about my affair with Josh, the better; it makes it easier to hide. Plus, it might change Haydon's feelings toward me. Or, apparently, not. "Of course it matters."

"It doesn't matter, Adeline. Because I can make you fall in love with me. You just have to let me try."

I feel like I am bashing my head against a brick wall, my every word falling on deaf ears. He hasn't even asked me who I'm in love with. But again, did he already know? "It does matter, Haydon. It matters to *me*." I turn toward my mother's suite. "I have to go."

"Adeline—"

I hang up and spend a good few moments relocating my grit, then I rap softly on the door. Mary-Ann answers, her head bowing a fraction. "Your Majesty."

"Can you please tell my mother I would like to see her?"

"She isn't here, ma'am. I believe she may be having breakfast."

"Thank you, Mary-Ann." I leave, my sights set firmly forward, not acknowledging anyone or anything as I pace through the palace. When I make it to the dining room, it's empty, the table completely clear. On a frown, I back up and cross the foyer, my heels clicking evenly. I find Felix halfway down the corridor that leads to the communications and PR offices. "Have you seen my mother?" I ask.

"Not this morning, ma'am."

I turn and head toward the library, asking everyone I pass if they know where she is. Not one person has seen her. "Sid," I call, seeing his back disappear into the library. The Master of the Household reverses his steps and straightens, his hands joined in front of him. "Your Majesty."

"I'm looking for my mother."

"I don't believe I have seen her this morning, ma'am."

My shoulders drop, and I back up, thinking. "Thank you, Sid." Where in heaven's name could she be? My feet pivot, taking me toward the offices. I really don't know why I'm heading this way, yet I seem to be following my nose naturally. Instinct? I pass Kim's office, then Felix's, and note as I slip past the PR suite, the door slightly ajar, that Sir Don and David are in there with various other staff. One should barge right in and demand to know what they are discussing. But I don't, no matter how curious I am. Besides, I'll call a meeting with them very soon, and it will be them who will listen to me.

When I reach the office at the very end of the corridor, I knock once and take the knob, turning and pushing . . . against a locked door. I drop the handle and stare at the wood, listening for movement inside. No movement. No sounds. "Major Davenport?" I call, knocking again. Nothing. I step back, nibbling my lip, my eyes narrowing as I think. I pull up Davenport's number on my phone and dial, stepping closer to the door. It rings from inside before going silent, and I quickly end the call before dialing my mother. Her phone rings from beyond, too, just once, and then there is silence again. I lower my phone slowly, staring at the door.

And I knock once more and wait. It takes them only a few seconds to decide to answer. They have been smoked out, and there is no escaping it. I'm not at all mad. I would never have invited Davenport back into royal employment if this would be an issue for me. In fact, I secretly hoped they would give their love a second chance. There's no question both of them deserve happiness after living in this hell all these years. What I am mad about is, like me, they are sneaking around so they don't rock the Monarchy. It is just one more reason that what I am about to do is the right thing. Never more than now have I wanted so much to destroy the smoke and mirrors.

The door creaks open and Davenport looks beyond me first, checking the corridor, before opening it a little bit more to reveal my mother. I smile on the inside, because today she doesn't look gaunt or drained. Today she has light in her eyes. "Your Majesty," Davenport breathes, his eyes on the floor.

"I would like to speak with my mother alone. I will be in my office." I turn and walk away, stopping at the PR suite on my way. I don't knock, just push the door open, and everyone looks at me in surprise, all the talking halted by my presence. "Please be in my office at ten. I don't want to be disturbed until then." I don't wait around to be questioned by Sir Don or David, closing the door behind me. I pass a footman in the foyer and take the stairs. "Please have tea for two sent to my office."

"Yes, ma'am."

I reach the top of the stairs and cross the carpet to my office, finding Damon and Kim outside. "My mother will be here shortly. Please see her in," I say to Kim as Damon opens the door for me. "And I've ordered some tea."

"Of course." Kim throws Damon a look edged with curiosity and a little worry.

"Thank you, Damon." I give him a soft smile as I go to close the door, but he stops it with his foot, regarding me carefully.

"I don't like this look on you," he says frankly, taking in my dress, my killer heels, and my red lips. He doesn't mean what I'm wearing, but more how I'm wearing it. He's known me for long enough to read the signs of my mood.

"Me either," Kim pipes in, no holding back. "Do we need to be furnished with any information?"

"No, I believe I have everything in hand. Please be here at ten o'clock. Davenport, too." I close the door on their worried faces and take myself to the desk. The red box of doom is square in the middle, Kim having placed it there, but rather than open it and discover what requires my attention or signature today, I push it aside and sit back in my chair, gazing around the room I have feared all my life. The room where I received every warning and demand. The room that signifies impossibility and restraint. The room where I shall now take control.

The knock at my door is light before Kim enters, opening up the path for my mother. "Her Royal Highness the Queen Mother."

"Thank you, Kim." I motion to the chair in front of my desk, and Mother glides across the room toward it. I can tell she's assessing me, trying to gauge me. I don't want to be this stern and together in front of her, but I don't want her to mistake any easiness I display as submission.

As Mother settles in her chair, Kim lets a footman pass with a tray. "Here, please," I tell him, moving the red box farther to the side.

"Would you like me to pour, ma'am?"

"No, thank you." I smile my thanks and wait for them to leave before reaching for the teapot. "Tea?" I ask Mother, holding the lid as I pour.

"Yes, please."

"Very good." I prepare us both a cup and pass Mother's across the desk before collecting my own, holding the saucer with one hand and the teacup handle with the tips of my fingers. As I stare at my mother, I realize my hold of my tea is exactly the same as hers. Queenly. She was a good queen consort. Devoted, dutiful, compliant. Everything I am not.

I place my saucer down and take the cup, wrapping both hands around the hot china. "Am I to assume that last night during dinner, you weren't in the ladies', but in fact in the arms of Major Davenport?"

Her dark eyes fly up, and I hate the fact that her hands are shaking. "You assume correctly."

I could call her a hypocrite. I could scorn her for being deceitful. I would never, but I could. What I am, actually, is happy for her, yet irritated she can't express her happiness to the world. Or even to me. She will not let anyone see the grieving widow smile.

As I sip my tea and Mother sips hers, waiting for what I may say next, I think very hard about what that might be. Where do I start? How will she react to what I have to say?

"I want you to be happy, Mother." That is the perfect place to begin, however alien the very notion may be. No one in this family has ever operated on other people's happiness. No one has ever made moves with that at the forefront of their minds. It's always protocol and tradition first. Happiness is at the bottom of the list of priorities.

"Happiness is something we don't get to choose to have, my darling."

"You are wrong," I counter. "We can choose to have it, but we must settle for it in secret. We must hide it."

Her head tilts, her shaky hands setting her cup and saucer on the desk. She is spilling more than she is drinking. "We must do what is best for this family."

"No, we must do what is best for the Monarchy. If we were doing what was best for this family, then we would all be talking, not to mention smiling. Yet we are not." I, too, set my china down, sitting forward in my chair, wanting her to see my eyes when I say what I am about to say. "I am in love with a man, Mother," I tell her clearly, no falter in my voice whatsoever.

"The American," she replies quietly, and I nod very mildly. Because, who else?

"And because I am Queen of England, it is determined I cannot be with him. Yet I didn't choose to be Queen."

"But you are."

"By default and nothing more. Becoming Sovereign should be dictated by desire, ability, and passion, none of which I possess."

"You will make a good queen, Adeline," Mother says, sitting forward now, too. "Your people love you. Your country loves you. Sacrificing love is a small price to pay."

I shake my head, smiling sadly. "But to me, it is the ultimate price. One I am not willing to pay. We are not in the dark ages anymore. This is the twenty-first century, and the Royal Family needs dragging into it. If my people love me so much, then they will be happy for me."

"Are you suggesting making an American actor the public companion of the Queen of England?"

Companion? There we are, the dark ages. "No, I am saying I wish to make him the public *boyfriend* of the Queen of England."

"Queens do not have boyfriends, Adeline."

"This one does," I retort shortly. "And you may be happy to ig-nore it, to brush it under the carpet and hope age-old intervention will shield it, but I am not. I won't walk away from the throne. I won't throw our entire heritage to the wind. I will prove I can do this, and I *will* be a good queen, but if I am expected to do this job effectively, I can't be expected to give up the one thing that gives me the strength. Josh gives me strength. He makes every day in this office bearable."

"And what about your family?"

I'm not sure if she speaks of the secrets, or them giving me the strength. "Just because my secret is revealed to the world, doesn't mean Eddie's has to be. Or yours." I pause a beat. "Unless you want it to be."

Her dark gaze widens. "You are completely and utterly deluded, Adeline. You are suggesting spilling everything to the world. I've told you before, we will be publicly shamed."

"I don't mean *all* of your secrets." Goodness knows, there are too many, and I maintain I would never want Eddie exposed as illegitimate, or my mother's infidelity bared to the world. "I mean your relationship *now* with Major Davenport."

Her head recoils on her slender neck. "I'll be crucified. Your father is barely cold in his grave."

"We will handle it delicately," I tell her. "I'm not suggesting we release a statement airing every detail of your relationship. I'm suggesting over time, we release small nuggets of information to the press. We build the story, take control. We have the power to do that, Mother. And then there will be no hiding. There will be no sneaking around." I reach across the desk and take her hands. "You can live, Mother. For the first time, you can live happily, just how you want to."

Her bottom lip quivers, and I know she is fighting her hope to believe it could be. Because it *can* be. I'll *make* it be. With all I have,

I will make it so she can be happy and let the world see. "They will never allow it. Davenport and me, you and Mr. Jameson It can't happen."

My hands tighten around hers, evidence of my frustration. "I'm not prepared to be on the throne any longer unless I can be with Josh. I shouldn't have to sacrifice love for responsibility. Besides, *they* will have no choice."

"Why? Are you are going to blackmail them?"

Releasing her hands, I rest back in my chair. "I'm sure an abdication is the last thing they need when the country is slowly returning to normal."

Her gasp is loud. "You can't abdicate." She shoots up from her chair. "Goodness, Adeline. There will be a public outcry. Questions will have to be answered."

"Let them answer them, Mother. The reason we are here now is because every man and woman who advises me comes from a long, proud line of royal protectors. Their very reason to breathe is to protect the British Monarchy. That isn't going to change if I am no longer Queen of England. Neither will it change if I choose to take a man who falls outside the lines of acceptance. Their purpose is to protect the secrets, and they will continue to do exactly that."

Her eyes are wide, her body still. I can tell she's doubtful, but I have thought of little else all night. I'm not exposing anything except my love for a man. I don't know why I didn't see it before. Every threat is worthless. Every pull of my strings has made me fear the worst, but, really, the only way anyone will find out anything is if *they* tell them. And I would put my life on it they will not.

"I think you are making a grave mistake." Mother sits down again, and her fingers twiddle nervously in her lap. "You are underestimating them yet again."

"No, Mother. I think they are underestimating *me*. I'm in love with an American actor. A sex symbol. A southern man who swears like a sailor at times. But he makes me happy. He breathes life into me, and I'm not sacrificing him for anything. Not even the British throne."

She stares at me for a while, caught between shock and . . . what is that? I would like to think it is awe. Maybe pride. But I don't have the chance to conclude. She quickly pulls down her mask and rises from her chair. "Then you must do what you have to do, Your Majesty. Good day." She breezes out without another word, and I more or less flop back in my chair. That's it? The door closes quietly, and I sigh. Mother was the easy part of this equation. Which makes my dread increase tenfold as the minute hand on the clock slowly ticks its way around to ten o'clock.

Two minutes.

One minute.

I jump when my phone rings. I quickly snatch it up. "Josh," I answer, ready to tell him I will call him straight back as soon as I have dealt with Sir Don and David.

"Tell me I'm not looking at what I'm being told I'm looking at." He sounds like a man on the edge, consumed by red-hot rage.

"I have no idea what you are looking at," I say quietly, my eyes darting across the desk. A second later, my phone chimes in my ear, and I pull it away to see Josh has texted me a link. Everything is telling me that this link will lead me to a rage similar to Josh's, and I shouldn't open it. But my finger hits the screen anyway, and I'm soon looking at the source of Josh's fury. My muscles tighten, my body going rigid in my chair. "No," I whisper, staring at the picture of Haydon on his knee, a small box being held out to me. I'm stunned into silence, staring at what I know the rest of the world will be staring at. From the angle, I can tell this picture came from the left side of the table. David's side. How dare he do something so blatant? How dare he disrespect me in my home? I slowly bring my phone back to my ear, a red mist of anger falling across my vision.

"He proposed to you?" Josh asks, his voice tight. "So he can't touch you, but he can ask you to marry him?"

"I said no."

"Of course you said no." He laughs. "You left that dinner and came to bed with me. I made love to you. Cuddled you all fuckin' night. The man is fuckin' deluded, and I swear to God, Adeline, I'm gonna kick his stupid ass if he doesn't back the fuck off. But what I want to know from you is why you didn't fuckin' tell me? I need to know shit like this, Adeline. Prepare for headlines like this."

"It shouldn't be in the damn headlines. And I didn't tell you because of this," I counter. "Because I didn't want last night to be spent with you yelling at me for something I'm not responsible for."

"Fuckin' Christ, Adeline," he breathes, obviously as exhausted by the whole mess as I am. "This is driving me insane."

"I'm fixing it," I assure him, now watching the second-hand creep around. Josh is with me at breaking point. This is one more chink to repair. One more betrayal to get past.

The door knocks.

"I have to go."

"Fix it, Adeline," he scathes. "Or I will be there to fix it myself. I can't sit back and do nothing while this jerk tries to take my woman."

Part of me finds the thought of Josh going on a rampage through the palace appealing. Part of me dreads the damage he could do. I'm sending him over the edge. "I'll call you." I hang up and stand from my chair, my veins burning. "Come in."

Kim pokes her head around the door. "Felix would like to speak with you, ma'am."

Felix. I have no doubt why. He must have found out about the article, too. "No need, Kim. Tell him it's in hand."

She nods. "Everyone is here. Shall I see them all in?"

"Please."

She opens up the path, announcing Sir Don and David Sampson, then Felix and Major Davenport. "Sit," I say curtly. I have no room for graciousness. The moment they are all in their chairs, I turn my phone around and let them see the screen, scanning their faces as I do. Felix shakes his head in disgust, matching Davenport and Kim, but surprisingly, David and Sir Don look disappointed, too. Good actors. "In my home," I seethe. "At my dinner table. How dare you infiltrate my privacy so boldly? How dare you twist the truth to further your goals? Do you think I will stand back and let you do this?"

"Your Majesty, I was just as alarmed when I heard," David splutters.

I scoff, staggered that I am expected to believe him. "Alarmed?"

"Of course," he says, a little high-pitched.

"So you knew nothing about it?"

"I refute what you are insinuating."

"Are you telling me you didn't take this picture?"

"Of course I didn't."

"Then you won't mind if Major Davenport takes a look at your phone, will you?" I grate, nodding for Davenport to do so.

David hands his phone over with no protest. He even unlocks it for the major. How very kind. It's now I realize there is nothing on that phone to be discovered. He's hidden his tracks. When Davenport shakes his head, confirming my conclusions, and hands the phone to David, I'm certain there's an edge of smugness behind his apparent blank expression. God, have I ever hated a man so much?

"Regardless of who and why, the rumors will be put to rest immediately. Felix, prepare a statement for my approval."

"Yes, ma'am." He starts scribbling notes.

"And prepare another, announcing my friendship with Josh Jameson." I stare at Sir Don and David, aware that Felix has stopped writing and is looking at me in complete shock.

"Pardon, ma'am?"

"Adeline," Kim breathes, but Major Davenport remains quiet. As if he expected this, and I know he did. Because my mother told him.

My eyes remain on Sir Don and David as I speak. "I am in a

relationship with Josh Jameson, and I have been for some time. But you know that, don't you?" Of course they know. They were at Evernmore. "We are in love, and I for one am not prepared to let anything stand in our way. Not my advisors, not my country, and not my crown." Oh my goodness, I've never felt so empowered. So strong. David and Sir Don remain speechless opposite me, their expressions frozen in shock. "I think it is high time we all stop ignoring it, don't you agree? And I won't tolerate your underhandedness any longer. We will announce our friendship, initially. Let the world absorb the news, and then we will gently and masterfully break the news of our relationship."

Sir Don looks like he is on the verge of a heart attack. "Your father would turn in his grave."

"Maybe so. But as you have kindly reminded me, my father is dead. Now I must think about my family. And me."

"And what about my son?" David snipes, and I laugh.

"You are a snake in the grass, Sampson. A cling-on. The closest you will ever get to the crown is being one of my advisors. I won't marry Haydon so you can bask in the glory. I will be with a man of my choosing, not yours."

"You need a suitable husband," Sir Don cries.

"I need you to shut the hell up or get the hell out," I yell, reaching my limit. I slam my fist on the desk, making Kim and Felix jump. Davenport remains composed, and Sir Don and David's red faces become redder. "I will release you from your duty, make no mistake. You are not indispensable." Their knowledge and wisdom are great, yes, but I can no longer be scared of tackling my duties without them. For what I lose in experience, I will gain in loyalty.

"Your Majesty." David seems to gather himself, calming somewhat. "I strongly urge you to reconsider."

"My mind is made up." I lower to my chair. "You can either work with me, or you can leave."

"It is our job to advise you," David says calmly. "To protect you and the throne."

"I don't need your protection in this instance."

"I heartily disagree, ma'am." Sir Don reaches into his inside pocket and pulls out something, placing it on the desk before me.

"What is this?" I ask.

"It is something that may change your mind, ma'am. About the American."

It is all I can do not to laugh when I see the picture. Oh my, they really are prepared for me. "We have played this game before, Sir Don. A trashed hotel room, women's undergarments left conveniently on the floor. Is this the best you can do?"

He frowns. "A trashed hotel room?"

God, give me strength before I erupt. I look at Felix, and he looks confused and gobsmacked. *Yes, Felix. I believe Sir Don was responsible for that.*

"This is due to be released in tomorrow's newspaper, ma'am."

I drag my eyes back to the woman who is posing like any expert glamour model, all boobs and pout. I read the words below.

My wild night with Josh Jameson.

"Very good, Sir Don." The red mist is getting thicker. They are paying hookers now? "You fall short on one thing, though." I brush the trashy-looking trashy-talking woman aside. "I know Josh better than anyone, and that woman right there is not his type." Plus, he wouldn't do that to me.

"Your Majesty, this is not fabricated," David says, pointing to the papers. "It is genuine, I assure you."

"No, David. It is merely another attempt on your part to bully me into complying. It will not work."

"So you are happy for this to be released to the world?" Sir Don asks.

"Of course I'm not, and since it displeases me, you will do everything in your power to stop it being released." I turn to Felix, and he sticks his back to the chair, wary. "I trust I can depend on you, too, Felix."

He nods.

"Good."

"I believe the story is already in the hands of the press," Sir Don declares. "Unfortunately, on this occasion, our sources have been somewhat lazy."

"How very convenient. And tarnishing Josh's reputation is more important to you than keeping your job?"

Sir Don stands, pulling in his suit jacket. "I took an oath to protect the crown, like my father and my father's father. My life has been devoted to serving the Royal Family. At the very least, I can leave my employment knowing I maintained my oath to the very end. A queen should not marry out of love, but out of strength. And to be clear, Your Majesty, I did not fabricate that story. It was sent to me by an editor."

"And why did the editor believe *you*, not Felix, would be interested in anything to do with an American actor's behavior?"

He takes a deep breath, no doubt attempting to find an appropriate lie to answer with. "I don't know that."

"So convenient." Raging bloody mad, I throw a hand toward the door. "Get out."

He bows his head, his last display of respect to me, and leaves my office, shutting the door quietly behind him. I look to Davenport, maybe searching for some help. I get nothing from him, just his stoic face and his stiff body.

"Your Majesty," David says, gaining my attention. "I played no part in Sir Don's games, I assure you."

He's an embarrassment. A liar and a backstabber. He can't back-pedal now. "That is all," I say resolutely, and he darts his eyes to the others. What is he doing? Searching for backup? "I said, that is all."

"You're firing me?" he asks, a little laugh behind his unsure words.

"Indeed I am. And mark my words, Sampson, you will rue the day you ever crossed me if you so much as *think* about breaching your oaths to the crown. I will sign your death warrant in blood with no hesitation, do you understand me?"

"Your Majesty," he murmurs pitifully. Unsure and reluctant, David stands, his eyes wide in his head. He's dumbfounded. Good. He wanders out of my office in a daze, and once he's gone, I very nearly crumble to the floor, exhausted and drained.

"Drink, ma'am?" Davenport asks, getting up and wandering over to the globe. He pours me a Scotch without waiting for my answer, brings it over, and sets it on a coaster on the desk.

"Good idea." I take it and sip the burning liquid down, hoping it will burn away some of the rooted anger.

"Do whatever it takes to recall that story," I tell Felix.

"Of course, ma'am."

"May I?" Davenport asks, retaking his chair and putting one leg over the other, back straight.

"Please."

"Our relationship with the press is a fickle thing, ma'am. One that should be handled carefully. Every journalist is looking for the story to make their name, but there is no better story than one shrouding the Royals—good or bad. It supersedes everything."

"What are you saying, Major?"

"I'm saying, given Your Majesty is adamant of her next steps regarding her relationship with a certain American, it may be time for us to forge new relationships. As a rule, we have only ever entertained the more, let's say, noteworthy publications. We have never been in full control of the . . . how must one say it?" He thinks for a second. "More unreliable prints."

"Let us not beat around the bush, Major. I think you mean the gossip papers."

"Indeed. I'm sure they will welcome an invitation to report Royal news that will benefit both parties. As well as maintaining our current relationships, of course."

"And this will benefit us how?"

He stands and wanders to the fireplace, looking at the picture of my father. I wonder if he's thinking that maybe had my father given him the chance, he could have served him better, like he's trying to serve me.

Major Davenport hums to himself before he goes on. "As I see it, a certain editor of a certain publication holds a certain scandalous story on a certain American actor." Is he purposely dragging this out? "Said editor does not know a royal—namely, the Queen—is connected to said American actor."

"Oh, for pity's sake, Major. Will you please just spit it out?"

He turns toward me, smiling a little. "We need to give him something else to report. Something more newsworthy than an unreliable nightwalker shouting her mouth off." His eyebrow hitches, mirroring mine. "An exchange, if you will. No news is more worthy of recognition if it is accurate and, more significantly, about a royal."

I stare at him, trying to unravel my poor tangled mind. "Are you suggesting I announce my relationship with Josh in a newspaper where on the next page there will be a pair of boobs?"

Kim snorts, and Felix gasps, the mere notion outrageous. Even *I* can appreciate that. Davenport chuckles. "No, ma'am. Any exclusive news about the Queen most certainly isn't for a newspaper that prints pictures of *bosoms*. Especially the kind of news detailing a potential suitor."

"Well, that is quite a relief." I laugh.

"I am suggesting that we perhaps tempt them with some other royal news."

"Such as?" I can't think of anything else to tempt them with, at least not what I would be happy to divulge. Then it hits me. I balk at the major. "You want to make something up?" Isn't that the entire reason we are sitting here now debating this?

"Not at all, ma'am. But I do think that the recent departure of two of the longest-serving royal advisors may pique some interest."

"You want to throw Sir Don and David to the wolves?"

"Those wolves are waiting for Mr. Jameson, ma'am."

His statement hits me like a brick in the face, and I snap my mouth shut, my mind suddenly mushy, unable to think clearly. "Isn't that immoral?"

"May I be direct?" he asks, and I nod because that is all I bloody want him to be. "This whole institution has been built on immorality, Your Majesty. Moves being made, games played, all to benefit the Monarchy. You are simply adopting an age-old tradition to get what you want, just like every other king and queen in history. The question I have to ask you, ma'am, is: are you prepared for the potential backlash of exposing your relationship with Mr. Jameson?" His head cocks, waiting for an answer. I'm mute. So he goes on. "There is no denying, more people love you than don't, but could this be a step too far?"

"Do you think it could be?"

"Of course. *Anything* could be a step too far." Davenport comes to me, standing by the side of my desk and looking at me in a way that tells me he cares. His hard face is soft. "You are about to change the face of the Royal Family, Adeline." When he says my name, it is both unfamiliar and comforting. "It is my job as your private secretary to advise you of every eventuality. The good and the bad. I'm not adverse to change. But, be warned, where you gain admirers outside of this institution, you will gain enemies within."

My swallow is hard. Because I know he is right. They're effectively trying to blackmail me. Threatening to ruin Josh's reputation if I don't relent to their demands. "They are already my enemies, Major. I'd rather have Josh around while I tackle my role and deal with those enemies."

He smiles, stepping back, nodding mildly. "Then I believe I have some calls to make. We will discuss Your Majesty's announcement once this has all been cleared up." He walks to the door and stops, looking back. "And one more thing."

"What?"

"I assume you have discussed with Mr. Jameson his role."

"I'm sorry, I don't understand. His role in what?"

Davenport frowns. "Your life, ma'am. You do realize if you want to be together, Mr. Jameson will become a Royal. There is only one job a Royal must have." His eyebrows rise. "Being a Royal."

"Are you telling me he has to give up his career?" I laugh, the thought never crossing my mind. I could never ask him to do that. "We're dating, Davenport. Not marrying."

"So all of this is so you can *date* a man?"

I snap my mouth shut.

"As I thought. I will leave that matter in your capable hands." He looks to Felix. "Onwards and upwards, I think is the term."

Felix dives up from his seat and scuttles after Davenport, and I finish my Scotch in one fell glug. I can't possibly ask Josh to give up his career for me. But would he?

"I see plainly now why you would have him serve you," Kim says, watching the door close. "My mind just doesn't work in that way."

I hum my agreement over the rim of my glass, silently thanking the heavens for Davenport, while also damning him for raising such a sobering point. "Would you mind giving me a moment?" I need to call Josh. To tell him everything that has happened.

Without a word, Kim leaves my office, and I immediately dial him. "I've fired Sir Don and David Sampson," I say the moment he answers, not giving him the chance to say hello.

"What?" He sounds as shocked as one would expect. "What about everything you said? That you need them? That you would crumble without their knowledge and guidance."

"I have other advisors. They can't get away with this. The pictures in the press of Haydon and I were just another way to try and back me into a corner. They had the nerve to deny all knowledge of your trashed hotel suite, too. They must think I'm stupid."

"Wow," he breathes.

"Josh, I've . . ." I fade off, not relishing the thought of sharing the next piece of the puzzle. "I've ordered an announcement to be drafted. About us. I want to share our friendship with the world first, and then slowly progress to our intimate relationship."

Silence.

"Their response was to present me with a news report that's running tomorrow in some trashy newspaper. A prostitute has sold her story."

He sighs. "Tammy just told me."

"Then why didn't you say?"

"You didn't give me the chance. But tell me you don't be—"

"I don't believe it," I assure him. He shouldn't need to ask that now.

"I need a drink," Josh mumbles, and I smile, looking at my empty glass.

"Beat you," I say quietly, rolling it across the desk. "Are you sure you want this, Josh?"

"Are you seriously asking me that question? Don't fuckin' insult me, Adeline. I've been desperate to show you off to the world."

"Show me off?" I question on a wry smile. "I think they are all relatively familiar with who I am."

"Yes, but they're not familiar with the fact that you're mine." He sounds so assertive when he says that, so sure. I don't know why I momentarily questioned it. "This is so fucked up, Adeline."

"I know. But Davenport and Tammy will get it sorted. And we need to have a conversation about your terrible language, Mr. Jameson. One cannot be seen to be dating such vulgarity."

He laughs, and the sound is pure joy. "Does that mean I can't spank your ass in public?"

In my mind's eye, I see MPs, councilors, and royal advisors all fainting. "There will be no public arse spanking."

"Fair enough. I promise to behave in public, but I make no

promises for when we're in private."

"I wouldn't expect you to," I say on a grin, looking up when I hear a knock. "There's someone here to see me."

"No sweat. I'm having drinks with some industry people this afternoon. Just hangin' at the hotel. I'll call you later."

Excitement engulfs me, something happening I never dreamed would happen. "Okay."

"Love you, gorgeous."

"I love you, too." I hang up and breathe out, so much weight gone from my shoulders. "Come in."

Kim enters, her expression wary. God, what now? "Sabina Sampson has requested an audience, ma'am."

All that tension returns, but I fight it back with all my might. This is to be expected, I guess. I ought to get what I know will be a difficult conversation out of the way. "I will see Mrs. Sampson," I declare, my voice sure.

"I believe she is on her way from the royal stables. I'll show her to your office the moment she arrives."

"Thank you, Kim."

The door closes, and I start chewing the corner of my phone, my mind off on a tangent. I cannot believe I have fired two of my father's chief advisors. I look to the ceiling. Is he looking down on me? Shouting at my stupidity? I close my eyes and breathe out. What kind of mad world am I in? On a shake of my bewildered head, I close my eyes, utterly spent.

∽

THE DOOR RAPS, and I jump in my chair, blinking my eyes open. I'm disorientated, my gaze jumping around my surroundings trying to gain my bearings. My father's office. No, *my* office. I turn my phone over to check the time. Lord, I dozed off. Forty minutes have disappeared. "Come in," I call, clearing my throat after.

"Mrs. Sampson," Kim declares when she's opened the door.

"Thank you."

She lets Sabina pass and backs out, closing the door behind her. "Is it all quiet on the western front?" Sabina asks.

Is she here to beg my forgiveness on behalf of her snake of a son? I slide my phone onto the desk, joining my hands. "Sabina, I'm sorry this has—"

Her hand comes up, stopping me. "That's enough of that, now." She motions to a chair. "May I?"

"Of course. Please."

She sits, her eyes on my empty glass. "Bad day?"

I drop my eyes to the glass. Does she know? Or is she referring to last night when I rejected her grandson? "I've had better."

Her head tilts, her smile more than fond. "Tell me about this American."

I pool in my chair, so grateful. This can't be easy for her. Her grandson rejected, her son fired. This woman has always been such a support to me, and now more than ever I am so thankful. Honestly, it is a shame I can't bring myself to feel the same way about Haydon, because Sabina has always been like a grandmother to me.

"He's wonderful," I say, almost shy. "The kind of man who will worship the ground I walk on but not think twice about putting me in my place if I need it. With him, everything is so much more brighter." I shrug, wondering if I should rein myself in. This can't be easy for her to hear. But it feels so good to finally talk about him. "Like the darkest days can be chased away with a cuddle and a few words. I have always doubted my capabilities from the second I landed on the throne, Sabina. It's not a job I wanted, you know that, but I have it now, and I must do what I must do. I thought my need to prove myself was enough. It wasn't. But Josh is. He's what I need, because with him I can do anything. Even this." I throw my arms up, indicating our surroundings and where I am sitting.

"That's a special thing to have," she says quietly, almost reminiscent. "And is he ready for this circus?"

"He has his own circus to contend with daily, Sabina. This will be just another layer of crazy to him."

"And for you, my dear," she adds, smirking. "So when do I get to meet him? Officially, I mean."

"I don't know," I answer truthfully. "Davenport is handling everything. Josh is here in London for the next week; I hope before he leaves. And for official meetings with the family, I have no idea how that will work." I'm nervous just thinking about it.

"I expect he has to fulfil his current commitments first, anyway," she says casually, and I shrink a little, deciding here and now I will never make Josh choose between his career and me. I know how much it means to him, how happy it makes him. Goodness, if the world can accept my relationship, it can accept he will have a job outside of being in a relationship with the Queen.

"Sabina, would you excuse me?" I ask, getting up from my chair.

"Of course, dear." She stands, too, walking out with me. I open the door for her, and as she passes me and I start to follow, we run into Haydon.

I still.

"Grandmother," he says, giving her a kiss on the cheek.

"My darling. What are you doing here?"

"I was hoping Her Majesty would spare me a few moments." He looks at me, and I fold on the inside, feeling so terrible for him. I can't do this. Not now.

"I must speak to Major Davenport." I'm passing them quickly, leaving them to watch me make my hurried escape. "I'm sorry, Haydon," I call. But I have more important matters to deal with right now than Haydon's bruised feelings. Heartless, yes, but he's a victim of his own stupidity, too. Right now, I have another case to plead.

24

MY CONVERSATION WITH Davenport went as well as could be expected. Not very well. But I stood my ground and stated firmly that I was not prepared to change Josh, as that was the damn point of all this in the first place. He is who he is, and changing that would make a mockery of me.

As I sit at my desk, constantly looking up to check the time, I slowly work through the red box while Kim works opposite me. "The New Year's Honors List?" I ask, looking over the candidates. Each one has a detailed reason for appearing on the list, from sports stars and singers to scientists and charity founders. "Graham Miles," I muse, remembering him clearly grilling Josh during that interview I watched with Matilda. "For outstanding contribution to TV."

"He's an institution in himself," Kim says. "And loved by the country."

"*Sir* Graham Miles *CBE*," I declare, circling his name a few times with my Parker, smiling as I do.

"You're a delinquent."

I scoff, dropping my pen and glancing at the clock again. It's gone eight o'clock. Why hasn't Josh called me? Surely he's finished having drinks. "There has to be some perks to the job," I say quietly. "Pass me my phone, will you?" I can't wait any longer. If I interrupt drinks, so be it.

"Where is it?" Kim starts lifting papers across the desk in search of it, and I do, too, moving my red box to the side, frowning when I find no phone. "Whatever have I done with that?"

"When did you last see it?" Kim asks, taking her own phone and raising it to her ear.

I think. And think. "I spoke to Josh earlier." Scanning the desk once more, I then go to the drawers and start pulling them open. "I spoke with Davenport, had lunch, met with the PR team."

"It's switched off," Kim says, now frowning, too. "Did it run out of battery?"

"I never let it run out of battery." I get up and head out, wracking my brain for when I last had it. I find Davenport in his office, the door open. "Major, do you recall me having my phone with me when we spoke earlier?"

"I couldn't say, ma'am. Shall I call it?"

"It's switched off," I tell him, noticing the chair in front of his desk is off skew. It's always set at a perfect forty-five degree angle. He's had company. *Mother.* As if to make a point, I step inside and take the back of the chair, turning it a few inches to the right, putting it back in its rightful place. Davenport watches me, and I smile, just a little, before leaving. I poke my head around the door of the empty PR suite, scanning the empty conference table. "How odd," I say to myself, looking down the corridor when I hear footsteps. Damon paces toward me, and if I am not mistaken, he looks rather ticked off. "Why haven't you gone home yet?"

"I can't find my phone," he mutters, looking past me into the PR suite.

A wave of unease ripples through me. "Have you called it?"

"Yes, it's switched off."

"Mine, too," I reply, my gaze falling to the floor and scanning the carpet, as if both phones might appear there. When I look back to Damon, his forehead is heavy. "I can't find my phone, either."

He recoils, then his head cocks. "When did you last have it?"

"I can't be sure." I admit. "You?"

"In the kitchen. Dolly was making me a sandwich. I went to the toilet, got caught up in talks with my men, and when I got back it was gone."

"There has to be a perfectly reasonable explanation," I say, walking off and meeting Kim in the foyer.

"Have you found it?" she asks, her phone at her ear again.

"No. And Damon's is missing, too."

Kim's phone drops from her ear as Damon moves in and claims it. "Do you have last location set?" he asks, looking at me.

"I don't know." I shrug. "Palace security has always dealt with phone security."

He grumbles under his breath and starts tapping away at Kim's screen. "Offline." Damon stills, thinking.

"My phone?"

"No, mine." He hands Kim her mobile. "Last location is registered as here."

"Then they have to be somewhere." I laugh. "There can't be a phone thief on the loose in the palace. And besides, my phone is of no use to anyone unless they know the million-digit passcode."

Damon hums, his mind whizzing. "The last known location of my phone was the palace. That doesn't mean to say it's still here." He marches off, and I watch his back disappear down the corridor to the offices.

I throw my arms up, exasperated. "Where are you going?"

"To wipe our phones," he calls back, and then it hits me why he is so twitchy. Lord, the text messages and pictures on my mobile!

"Bloody hell," I breathe, running after him. "Can you access a phone without the code?"

"If you know what you're doing." He enters Davenport's office, me hot on his tail. "We have a situation." Damon ushers a perplexed looking Davenport out of his chair and takes the seat, going straight to the desktop.

Davenport looks to me for an explanation, since Damon is now preoccupied, tapping away at the computer. "My phone is missing," I explain, not liking the roundness of Davenport's eyes as a result of my news. "Damon can remotely wipe it."

"And assuming it's been stolen, what might the perpetrator discover should they gain access?"

I shrink on the spot, but my shoulders are high and tense. "A few pictures, maybe," I all but squeak. "And a lot of text messages."

His eyes roll so hard, there's a risk he won't see forward again. "Lord, have mercy," he breathes, going straight to his own mobile and making a call. I can do no more than watch as Davenport barks orders down the line to some poor individual, and Damon talks to palace security from the desk phone, trying to get access to my phone from the computer.

"Oh boy," Kim says from behind me. "You're in big trouble now."

"Oh, be quiet," I snap, my panic growing with every second that passes while I wait for news from either of the two frantic men at the desk before me. Every picture on my phone flashes through my head, except they are not on my phone, but on the front page of a newspaper. One of me in my underwear wearing my Spanish tiara. One of me blowing Josh a kiss, looking all seductive. One of Josh half naked, his hips wrapped in a small towel. The endless text messages between us. *Oh, bloody hell.*

"Done." Damon smacks the desk and drops back in the chair, giving me a glare that could make me disintegrate. I smile, meek and nervously. "They could have gained access before I wiped it, though," he adds.

"Felix," Davenport yells, and a few seconds later, my head of communications skids down the corridor on his loafers, his glasses a little skew-whiff in his haste.

"Sir," he practically pants as Davenport stalks toward him, his phone still at his ear.

"I have the top section covered." The major shoves a piece of paper at Felix. "Call every editor on the bottom section and make sure no incriminating pictures of Her Majesty or Mr. Jameson have turned up on their desks. Be discreet."

Felix looks horrified, and my stomach sinks some more. "How do you suggest I be discreet?"

He's right. Without coming right on out and asking, how can one approach this?

"I don't care," Davenport yells, losing his composure. It's an unfamiliar sight, and, honestly, I'm rather scared. "Use your damn initiative, boy."

"Sir." Felix slinks off, his tail between his legs, and I go back to watching the chaos of Davenport's office—Kim pacing, her phone to her ear, Davenport stomping, barking down the line, and Damon still glaring at me. I don't know why. I hardly put the phone in the thief's hand.

"I'll step outside," I say, backing out of the room, keen to escape the tension. I scuttle to the kitchen and find Dolly clearing up the last of the pans, whistling as she does. "Hello," I say, pulling her round from the cupboard she's stretching to reach.

"Oh, Your Majesty. Whatever are you doing in the kitchens?"

"I need a drink, Dolly."

"Right away." She abandons the pots and hunts down some champagne, quickly popping the cork. "I will have to go find a flute, ma'am. We don't keep glassware here in the kitchens."

"Just give me a mug," I say, motioning to the many cupboards. "A jug, a saucepan, I don't care. Actually, the bottle." I give her grabby hands and take the bottle straight to my lips once she's handed it to me.

"Oh dear."

I swig down a good few inches of the bottle and slam my bottom onto a chair at the large table. I know Dolly knows better than to ask, and I can't very well tell her. "Long day." I sigh, turning the bottle an inch one way, and then the other, back and forth as I stare at the label.

"Apparently so," she muses, going back to her pots and pans, leaving me to drown my sorrows in peace. What a mess. Or is it? Maybe Damon and Davenport are being over cautious. My phone could be anywhere in this sprawling building. But Damon's, too? It is rather a large coincidence.

"Can I get you anything before I leave, ma'am?" Dolly asks, pulling on the apron strings at her back.

I lift the bottle to the light to check how much I have left. "I should be fine, thank you," I say, taking another swing as she hangs her apron on the pantry door hook.

"Very well. If you're feeling peckish, I've just made a batch of my salsa. The crisps are in the pantry. Top shelf to the far right. I've had to reorganize everything. I couldn't find a blasted thing in this new kitchen."

"Thank you, Dolly." I force a smile as she collects her giant bag and leaves me. I have no appetite for food, only for alcohol. Damn it, I can't even ring Josh to tell him about this mess. Glancing at the kitchen clock, I note it's now nearing nine o'clock. He should have called by now. I lift the bottle to my lips and more or less pour the champagne into my mouth.

"Found her," Davenport shouts, making me jump at the table and swing around, the bottle still at my lips. His disapproving look is wasted. I could not be any more disgraced, apparently. Damon appears, too, and they both join me at the table, silent, as I slowly lower the bottle from my mouth. They're assessing. Judging. Oh, for heaven's sake.

"How was I supposed to know my phone would go missing?" I refrain from directly mentioning the pictures *or* detailing them. This is mortifying enough already.

"We've contacted every editor in London. No pictures or messages, so unless any of them are good liars, we should be okay."

"Should be?" I question, not liking the sound of that.

"Do you know how many editors there are in London alone?" Davenport asks, tilting his head, as if waiting for me to actually answer.

Of course I don't know. A lot, I would guess. "So what you are saying is, you have done all you can and now all we can do is wait?"

"Indeed." Davenport nods. "What I would like to find out in the meantime is who would steal your phone, as well as Damon's."

"Are you being a little paranoid?" I ask tentatively. "And besides, who in the palace would want to expose discriminating pictures of me? Everyone is here to protect the damn crown, not shame it." I get two ferocious glares pointed at me. "I think maybe I will be quiet." I submit, sliding down my chair and hiding in my bottle once more. And though it thoroughly hurts my head, I force myself to think about who could have stolen it. Sir Don and David Sampson are out of the question, surely? Like I said, their sole purpose is to protect the Monarchy, not dirty it. But maybe now they don't care about it, since I fired them earlier. I look to Damon and Davenport in turn, pouting. I know they're thinking along the same lines. But would Sir Don and David Sampson so blatantly disregard my order to maintain their oaths?

"We should accelerate the announcement and also add that you're in a relationship Mr. Jameson," Davenport declares, standing up from the table. "Our calls have turned up no results, but I'm not willing to take the risk." His stressed eyes land on me. "Has Kim drafted the statement?"

I lower my bottle to the table carefully. "I don't know." Davenport turns on his heels and marches out of the kitchen, and I'm up from my chair like lightning. "Wait!" I shout, and he turns at the door, impatience rife on his face. "You're going to tell the world we're in a relationship? *Now?*" Oh my goodness, all this time I've wanted nothing more than the world to know, and now my stomach is doing cartwheels at the thought that it finally will.

"When control is showing signs of slipping away from you, you take it back. Your phone is missing, and as it stands, we do not know where it is. There are pictures and messages on that phone, ones that will expose your *intimate* relationship with Mr. Jameson. I assume you do not want your courtship revealed in that way. And we don't know the motives of the thief, if at all there is a thief. So, as I said, we're taking back control." He carries on his way. "I will consult with you in due course."

I stare at the empty doorway, my heart racing in my chest. The world will know. I grab my bottle and guzzle down the remainder of my champagne, anything to wash away the anxiety crawling up my throat. "I need to speak to Josh," I gasp after I've finished my last swallow. He needs to know. His PR team needs to know. "Where's the nearest phone?"

Damon points to the wall on the other side of the kitchen where a phone hangs, it's only purpose, usually, to take incoming orders from around the palace. I dart over and lift the receiver, and stare blankly at the buttons. I have no idea what his number is, and in desperation, I look to Damon. It's a long shot, but . . .

"No clue," he says in answer, standing. "Where's he staying?"

"The Ritz. Prince of Wales Suite."

Without a word, Damon leaves the kitchen and I scramble to replace the receiver before running after him. Back in Davenport's office, he hits the keys of the keyboard and finds what I need, dialing the number into Davenport's desk phone. It rings, and when a member of reception answers with a polite, "Good evening, welcome to The Ritz London. Benjamin speaking, how may I assist you?" I lunge for the phone to talk. I miss it by a fraction, Damon reaching it first and scowling at me as he takes it to his ear. "Josh Jameson's suite, please."

"I'm sorry, we don't have a guest by that name, sir." His words are perfectly clear, and I slump where I stand.

Damon reaches to his forehead and rubs into it. "I don't know what name his reservation is under, but he is staying in the Prince of Wales Suite."

"I'm sorry sir, we don't have a guest by that name with us at this time," the receptionist repeats robotically, reading from a well-rehearsed script.

"This is urgent," Damon grates.

"I'm sorry, we don't—"

"Oh, for heaven's sake," I yell, snatching the phone from Damon and diving from his reach.

"Adeline!"

"I demand to be transferred to Josh Jameson's suite. I am the Que—" The phone disappears from my hand and Damon slams it down, his look pure filth. I scowl back, annoyed. "It was worth a try."

"Sometimes, Your Majesty, I could bloody strangle your reckless neck."

I drag my feet across to a chair and drop down. "What else would you have me do? He needs to know, Damon. That announcement could be out there before I see him. I can't let him find out like that."

"What, that you're in an intimate relationship? Because I'm sure it'll be old news to him," Damon quips, flicking the desk phone aside with a heavy hand and dropping into the chair with equal force to mine.

"Funny ha-ha."

"It wasn't supposed to be."

"So how do I get hold of him, clever clogs?"

"Shut up for a minute," Damon snaps, and I recoil, indignation flooding me, not that Damon would notice because he's not looking at me. No one else would dare speak to me in such a way. If he were anyone else, I would now be tearing into him. But Damon isn't anyone else.

I watch him sulk and think, my eyes drifting across to the clock again. Nine thirty. My fingers start to drum on the arms of the chair. It's the only sound in the room, and it must start to irritate Damon because he gives me another one of those death stares. Goodness, someone is grumpy today. "Sorry." I stop with the drumming, and Damon goes back to thinking. He clearly has a bad feeling about this, but I have to admit, I am still on the fence. The only people who work closely with me would never want to expose such sordid pictures of me *or* reveal my affair so carelessly.

I look at the clock again. Nine forty-five. I'm getting restless. For all I know, Josh could have been trying to call me for hours. He would have tried Damon, and then met a brick wall. He'll be worried. I have to see him. "Damon," I say, dragging his name out.

Slowly, he pulls his eyes up from the desk. I smile sweetly. He immediately starts shaking his head. "No." It's so final, not that I take much notice.

"Yes," I counter, rising from my chair.

"No, Adeline." Damon gets up, too, and starts following me out of Davenport's office when I dismiss him and leave. "All my men have knocked off. I have no phone. No."

"Yes," I repeat snootily, reaching the foyer. "I need to see Josh and tell him of the imminent announcement."

"No way."

"Olive," I call.

"No. No, no, no." Damon watches as Olive appears, ever ready to serve.

"Would you please fetch my coat and purse?"

"Yes, ma'am."

"No," Damon snaps, making the poor thing jump. "I am not taking you anywhere this evening."

"Wrong," I counter, moving closer to him. "You will take me, or I will drive myself." I'm speaking nonsense. I have polished off an entire bottle of Moët. Not to mention I have no idea where the keys for the cars are kept at Claringdon.

As Olive appears with my coat and holds it up for me, I slide my arms in and accept my bag, staring down my rather aggravated head of security. He better not make me remind him of who he serves. Because I will. On this occasion, I most definitely will.

"You are the Queen of England, Adeline. You cannot gallivant across London at a moment's notice without security measures in place. Traveling without a means of communication is out of the question."

I turn to Olive. "Do you have a mobile phone?"

Her wide eyes jump between Damon and me. "Yes, ma'am."

"Would it be terribly cheeky for me to ask if Damon can borrow it?"

"You cannot be serious," Damon mutters.

"Of course, ma'am," she chirps as she darts off, ever happy to help.

I turn my smug gaze onto Damon. "Problem solved."

"I have no men."

"But I trust you explicitly with my wellbeing, Damon," I say, my voice soft and genuine. Because it's the truth.

Olive returns and hands a grumpy Damon her phone. "The code is my birthday."

Jaw tight, he takes Olive's phone. "Which is what?"

"December tenth."

"You're a sweetheart, Olive," I say, smiling brightly before turning my smile onto Damon. "Ready?"

On a growl, he rakes a hand through his hair and turns, stamping his way to the door, making a footman jump when he yanks it open with such force, he might rip it off the hinges. "If you were anyone other than you, I would have quit years ago."

I smile. Because when he says *other than you*, he doesn't mean the Queen, because she's quite important.

He just means me. Because he cares.

25

DAMON IS TWITCHY. He does not murmur a word for the entire journey, and I stop myself from trying to strike up conversation. I know my Damon well, and I know it will be a complete waste of breath. So I keep my words to myself and instead think about where I'm going to start in explaining to Josh how we have fast-tracked from a gentle, carefully mastered approach to the media, to a full-on *Bam!* Queen Adeline of England is in a relationship with Hollywood actor Josh Jameson. In just a few short hours, the media is going to spiral into a meltdown over one of the hottest stories of the decade. Probably the last century, actually. In fact, this news will probably supersede all other breaking news that has come before. Part of me smiles to myself. The other part is trembling in a corner.

When Damon pulls up to the side entrance of the hotel, he sits for a moment, staring at the building. I let him be, let him mentally plan his next move. It's gone ten thirty now, and though it is getting late, the hotel is still bustling. I can see for myself through doors and windows. On a sigh, he looks over his shoulder to me, his eyes traveling the length of me and back up. They stop on the silk cream scarf that's looped around my neck. I start unraveling it before he has the chance to ask, folding it into a triangle before laying it over my head and tying a thick bow under my chin. "I'll have my arm around you," he informs me. "Tuck yourself into my side and keep your face down."

I nod, knowing he won't appreciate the lift at the corner of my mouth. "Like a sweet romantic couple." I can't stop myself, and Damon's eyes blaze with annoyance. I can tell there are a million choice words he would like to throw my way, but he keeps them contained to his mind and gets out. As soon as the door opens, he's blocking it, helping me. His arm goes straight around my shoulder and hugs me close, starting to walk us into the foyer. I do as I have been instructed, keeping my face pointed at my feet. I don't need to look to know the lobby is busy, the sounds telling me of the hustle and bustle.

"Okay?" he asks, moving us quickly but steadily. I nod rather than speak, my head resting between the crook of his arm and his chest. I feel as safe as one could feel, secure and content nestled in Damon's side.

When we reach the elevators, he allows a group on men to board, letting them go without us. He's waiting for an empty lift. When the next dings its arrival, a couple disembark, and Damon hustles us inside. He smacks the button for Josh's floor, still keeping me close.

"Hold the lift," someone shouts. I naturally look up, but quickly correct my mistake, darting my eyes to the ground. I catch sight through the closing doors of a woman running toward us, weighed down with two suitcases. Damon makes no attempt to stop the doors from sliding closed. "Bastards," I hear her yell, and I peek at Damon on a wry smile.

"If only she knew," he muses, keeping his focus on the doors and his eyes firmly forward. He's tense, waiting for the lift to stop at one of the floors, but like an act of God, we sail straight to Josh's floor.

As we walk down the corridor, my tummy does that wonderful

thing it does when I know I'm about to see Josh. It's a mixture between feeling sick with nerves and feeling sick with excitement. Damon raps the door firmly, constantly scoping our surroundings. I listen carefully for movement beyond, but I hear nothing. "Maybe he's not here," I muse to myself, getting closer to the door and pressing my ear against the wood. I'm certain he said they were, in his words, *hangin' at the hotel.* If I've forced Damon across town at this hour and under duress for nothing, he's going to be even more annoyed with me.

I jump out of my skin when Damon's big fist lands next to my head on the wood. "Bloody hell," I yelp, firing a deadly stare his way. "You did that on purpose."

I'm ignored once again, and this time it's Damon who gets up close and personal with the wood, listening.

"He's not here," I say quietly, disappointed. I have no way to reach him. What am I going to do? Davenport will have to stall. I can't let an announcement go out without talking to Josh. "What are you doing?" I ask when Damon pulls something from his inside pocket and bends down to the key card reader. I'm ignored, his attention set on his task. "Are you breaking in?" I dip, too, watching as he slips something into the slot. "Oh, how very James Bond."

Damon pauses in the jiggling of whatever he's jiggling in the slot, casting his eyes to the side. Tired eyes. "Your Majesty, with all due respect, will you please shut your bloody mouth?"

I press my lips together and unbend my body. "I don't like you very much when you're grouchy."

He closes his eyes, a gathering patience tactic, and resumes doing his fancy 007 business. The light blinks green. "Oh my." I slap my hands over my mouth, both surprised by his secret talent, and to keep myself from saying anything else that will push the buttons of my head of protection. Gently, Damon pushes the handle down and leans his shoulder into the door, opening it a fraction. I know the second his shoulders visibly tense that something is not right, and when I reach to touch his arm, I feel his tenseness, too. "Damon, what is it?"

He pushes the door open, revealing the entrance hall of the suite, and my eyes fall on one of Josh's security men slumped on a chair. My hand moves to my heart. For a second, I really panic, thinking he's hurt, but then I hear the sounds of his snoring. "Is he asleep?" I ask, moving inside and approaching him.

"It would seem so." Damon tucks his tool back into his pocket and gives the man a poke in the arm. He stirs, snorts a few times, and resumes his peaceful slumber.

"Well, that's disgraceful," I sniff, outraged, spotting a bottle of Scotch by the leg of his chair. I dip down and pick it up, presenting it to Damon. It's half empty, and Damon looks thoroughly disgusted.

"Bates will rip him limb from limb," he seethes, walking through to the lounge. As I follow, I glance around the space, noticing more empty Scotch bottles. On tables, shelves, sideboards, the floor, the couch.

"Well he did say they were having a drink," I quip, kicking a can of something away from my feet. I'm feeling a little less appalled than Damon, judging by the wicked curl of his lip. I follow his stare and find what's irked him even more. "Oh dear," I murmur, spotting Bates sprawled on a couch, an empty bottle across his chest. And in a chair opposite, another one of his men, again unconscious.

I watch as Damon kicks his way through the discarded bottles to the couch and shakes Bates violently. "Wake up, you dickhead."

Bates jerks and jumps, his eyes springing open in shock. He squints to focus on me. "Oh, hey, ma'ammmmm."

He is utterly inebriated. "Bates," I say flatly. "Where's Josh?"

"I dunno," he slurs. "I must have passed out." He struggles up to a sitting position, holding his head. "Fucking hell, early drinking sessions are never a good idea."

"Drinking on the job is never a good idea period," Damon grunts, catching a bottle as it rolls off the couch.

I step over various pieces of rubbish and glass, making my way through the mess toward a bedroom, frowning at my feet as I go. This was a wasted journey. They're all plastered. Josh is never going to remember me telling him anything come morning. Taking the handle of the door, I push my way inside to darkness, the brightness of the space behind me offering the only light in the room. I look down at the floor when my heel catches in something, and unable to see what, I bend my lower leg, bringing my foot up to my backside. I reach for the small scrap of material and pull it free, holding it up in front of me. My heartbeats slow. My eyes haven't focused enough in the dim light to see exactly what it is dangling from my fingertips, but my body's reaction is telling me. I feel as if my blood's temperature drops a few too many degrees, and my veins are cold. And then my eyes focus, and my slow heart rate picks up and starts booming. I release the slinky lace knickers, letting them drop to the floor. My shaky legs struggle to walk, my eyes watching the floor as I go. I stop and pick up something else and stare at it silently for a few seconds. I drop the bra and swallow, spotting a heap of back material close by. A dress. And next to it, some black boxer shorts. My mouth dries, making swallowing now impossible. I shake like a leaf as I force my forward steps, my heart about to explode, my mind silently praying over and over for a plausible explanation. I tell myself that this has happened before. That Josh has been set up. Or maybe he's not in this bed. Maybe the silhouette of a body I can see isn't Josh. Maybe the woman's clothes littering a path to the bed are . . . whose? Maybe I'm in the wrong room. Maybe those boxer shorts are one of his security men's.

I reach the bed and stare down, willing my eyes to focus in the darkness. They won't, and are not likely to when they are filling with water. "Stupid," I say to myself, feeling for the switch of the lamp by the bed. Of course there's an explanation. I knock over a few things, hear a few sounds, human sounds, sounds of people stirring, and finally find what my shaky hands are looking for. I flick the switch and turn toward the bed.

"Oh my God," I wheeze, my eyes finding his face. I cough, stepping back. I close my eyes and open them again, blinking to try and clear my vision. The blinking releases the tears, and my vision does not change. I drag my blurry eyes down the length of his naked body, coughing when I see a condom covering him. My stomach turns, and I fight back the nausea, my attention now on the slender female hand resting on his stomach. She's on her side, tucked cozily under Josh's arm. I look at her face, a small sob slipping past my wobbly lips. He's holding her close.

I don't want to be here, don't want to stand here and stare at one of the most painful things I've ever seen, but for all the will in the world, I can't look away. It can only be my mind forcing me to endure it, to make sure the sight is embedded in my head forever so I can remember what a bastard he is.

The lengths I went to so we could be together.

The risks I've taken.

All for nothing.

Anger starts rolling with the emotions, swirling through my body dangerously. I hear someone come in the room behind me. Damon. I hear his inhale of shocked breath. I wipe at my eyes violently, straightening my folded form. The woman moans on a little stretch, shuffling in closer to Josh's side. And his bicep flexes, pulling her in. My teeth clench so hard, they could crumble. Reaching up, I take out my earrings one by one and toss them on the bedside table, the small clatter stirring them both once again. But neither of them wake up. They're in a deep sleep. Exhausted.

I turn around and face Damon. His face is cut with shock, disgust, fury. "I would like to leave," I say calmly, walking toward him. When his stare finds me, every emotion disappears and he switches into professional mode, collecting me and leading me out of the suite. I mildly note that Bates is snoozing again. I also note now that there is another couch at the far end of the room, another one of Bates's men splattered on it with a woman draped over him.

I have never felt such a sense of fury. And the hurt just seems to make it worse. I'm a fool. Blinkered by lust and excitement. I could have ruined everything.

But instead I have simply ruined myself.

26

I HAVE NEVER truly felt lost. I had thought I'd felt it, but this past week, I realize that I really never have. Not like this. I have never questioned my worth or doubted myself; I was always rather confident with who I was, even when faced with my father's wrath and disappointment. I wasn't happy, of course, not really, but I was content with who I was. To hell with everyone else.

Now, I'm just a silly woman who made a terrible mistake, and very nearly made an even bigger mistake that would have changed history. Now, I'm a woman who has proven why I am so wrong for this world I am in. Now, I'm a fool. And, worse still, everyone around me knows it. There has been no mention of his name. My mother hasn't acknowledged the absence of the announcement I was adamant of making. She doesn't know why Josh is no longer in my life because she hasn't asked me. When did wanting a cuddle from your mother become such a big hope? Damon has walked on eggshells around me, as have Kim and Jenny, and Olive is faffing more so than usual. Everyone is wary. Everyone is watchful. Except Eddie. He's not even come to see me. Hasn't called or checked in.

And it is only now I realize that, in some ways, I am actually made of royal stuff. I'm cool and composed to the world; my agony undetectable. But when I'm alone, I fall to pieces. I can't get the images out of my head. I can't stop thinking about how stupid I have been. One second I blame myself . . . *of course he would get it elsewhere.* I was hardly readily available to sate him when he so desired. And the next second, I'm throwing something at a wall and pretending it is Josh's head, shouting him to hell and back for betraying me.

I will never trust again. I will never love again. Loving someone is as good as accepting that one day your heart will be broken. It's accepting you are no longer in control of your feelings. To love is to expose one's self. And I never plan on letting that happen again.

My only saving grace during this turmoil is that no photographs have appeared in the papers. And they weren't likely to, since my damn phone was found under the couch in the Claret Lounge a few days later. My phone may have been missing all the contacts, photographs, and messages after Damon had it wiped, but there were endless missed calls from one number. His number. He'd tried to call me the morning after I walked out of his hotel suite and left him in bed with another woman. It stoked the anger. I handed my phone to Damon and told him to have palace security block Josh's number.

Damon, however, never found his mobile. I'm coming around to Matilda's way of thinking. It was a sign. I was supposed to lose my phone. I was supposed to go to the hotel. I was supposed to discover Josh was a lying, cheating bastard before it was too late.

I sit on the end of the bed, my hands in my lap, trying to psyche myself up for this evening. A cocktail reception in honor of . . . me. A kind of pre-coronation occasion, apparently. I didn't contest. On top of the personal lessons I have learned during this wretched time in my life, I have also learned it is far easier to be their puppet. To nod, to listen, and to maybe air an opinion that will be completely ignored. I have had no opinions. Therefore, I haven't yet been ignored. Not even by Sir Don and David Sampson.

I refused David's request for an audience, and that of Sir Don, too. I couldn't face them the day after I discovered Josh . . .

I quickly snap my thoughts back into line. The fact of the matter is, I refused. I knew looking them in the eye knowing they were partly right, even if they went about it the wrong way, was a job I was not up to. I was so raw. I couldn't let them see me like that. They were reinstated. I didn't request it, but I also didn't contest it when Davenport advised me it was the right thing to do. My respect for the major has grown tremendously since I discovered who he was, but that day it grew more. He could have let me leave Sir Don and David unemployed. After all, I know he hates them as much as I do. But instead, he cast aside his own grievance and put my best interests first. And now, my only best interest is being Queen and doing a good job. Sir Don and David Sampson are good for nothing else, but they are good for helping me do that. Not even my pride stopped it. Maybe because I'm not feeling anything anymore. Not shame, not embarrassment. Nothing. And to be fair, they haven't been smug. They know Josh is no longer on the scene, though *why* isn't information I will share. Not that they care. He's gone. That's all that matters to them.

Then Sabina came to see me, and, honestly, she was the only person to sit me down and give me the cuddle I so needed. She let me cry. She let it all pour out, no judging, no scorns or advice. She was just there. My release of emotions on her gave me the strength I needed to finally face Sir Don and David a few days later, though nothing was mentioned about Josh. Nothing was mentioned about much, actually. It was all kind of like it never happened. I should be used to that by now, but nothing could ever make me feel like nothing ever happened. I so wish it could, but that is a luxury out of my reach.

I stand and wander to the mirror. I barely recognize the woman before me. The blush-pink gown is subtle and pretty, my lips a soft shade of pink, and my hair is loosely pinned in pretty curls around a sparkling tiara. Not *that* tiara. I will never wear *that* tiara again.

Olive appears at the doorway, her smile as sorrowful as it has been this past week. Not that she really knows why she is sorry for me. All she knows, like most people, is that Josh is gone, though why will never be revealed. "It's time, ma'am."

It's time. It's time for the mask to play its part, except this mask is a different mask to the one I have always worn. This mask is hiding heartbreak and pain.

I gather up the bottom of my dress and leave my suite. As I'm walking through the palace, I ignore every mirror I pass, though I do pay thought to the way I am gliding, almost effortlessly. It's how I have always observed my mother's glide—a robotic action, perhaps—as though she mastered the art of moving without feeling, her legs carrying her with no need to think. The way she is supposed to glide. It's graceful and elegant, but it is by no means assertive *or* confident. And I finally know how she learned it, how she perfected it. She detached her heart. She wrenched out her broken, splintered heart and threw it away. I was a product of that broken heart, and I suspect every sighting of me reminded her of my father's spite and revenge, and every sighting of Davenport reminded her of what she'd lost. So, she became ethereal. Detached. Frozen.

And now it is my turn. My turn to glide in grief.

I nod to Damon when I arrive at the closed doors, then to Davenport and Kim who are waiting to remind me of who is here. "The Prime Minister, first, ma'am," Kim says, as Jenny dusts my cheeks with something. "And then the Foreign Secretary and Chancellor of the Exchequer. The Archbishop of Canterbury, then the Australian Prime Minister." She continues to reel off the titles of important people as I stare at the wooden doors before me. "Anything else?" she asks. I look at her in question, and she sighs. "Just smile, ma'am." And as if by magic, my blank expression follows her command. I smile.

"Please do make sure I at least have a drink in my hand for the entire evening," I say to anyone who will listen, though it is Olive who voices confirmation. "Okay, then." I swish the skirt of my dress and pull back my shoulders. It's the sign that Davenport needs to open the doors. The sound of a string quartet greets me first, and then a sea of smiling faces as the soft sounds of the music fades.

"Her Majesty Queen Adeline of England." My title rings through the ballroom like a tormenting echo, as I stand on the threshold, my mind blank.

"Ma'am?" Kim whispers from a few paces behind, jolting me into action. I step forward and offer myself to the first person waiting to greet me. The man who runs my country. "Prime Minister," I say, raising my hand.

I hear no words that are spoken to me over the next hour. I see mouths moving, I nod my head, and I smile. It is about all I am capable of. And, really, isn't that all that is expected of me?

≈

TWO GLASSES OF champagne are what get me through that endless line of people. Maybe another two bottles will get me through the rest of the evening. There isn't really much for me to be enjoying, but what I am finding very fascinating is watching my mother and Davenport do their very best not to catch each other's eye. Mother looks beautiful in her navy gown, sapphires dripping from her ears and neck. Her dress is still rather conservative, but something about the way she is wearing it makes all the difference to her presence. For the first time in a week, I manage a real smile, so wishing she would let go a little and embrace the potential happiness before her. But I realize, she will not allow it. Royal behavior and decorum is too heavily ingrained into her.

"You look lovely this evening, Mother," I say as she comes to me, saving my ears from the drone of Victoria's voice. I haven't been paying much attention to what she is saying, but I expect it will be unpleasant toward someone or something.

"You are very kind, dear." We touch cheeks and she acknowledges Victoria with a subtle nod.

"Edward isn't here," I muse, not at all surprised but still a little injured. He's been elusive this past week, but I did hold hope that his absence would come to an end this evening. As ever, I'm disappointed and hurt.

"The boy needs reining in before he shames the family," Victoria mutters into her glass.

"The boy is a man." I earn a little dismissive sniff, but she shuts her wayward mouth. When I think the night couldn't be any more tedious, I spy David Sampson approaching, and it is all I can do not to turn and run. He looks all too happy, has been as chirpy as one could be all week.

"Your Majesty," David gives me an over-the-top greeting. One might call it arse licking.

"Good evening, David." I smile, forced, and give Olive the signal that I am ready for another glass. "I haven't seen Sabina." Just as I say that, I spot her, looking wonderful in a plum taffeta gown. "Oh, here she is." Her face, as soft as usual, brings a natural smile to mine. "You look beautiful, Sabina."

"Oh," she laughs, fussing with the material. "It has been a long time since I dressed for such an occasion."

"Wonderful evening," David sings, his shoulders starting to jump when the string quartet up the tempo of their piece, raising his Scotch to someone. "Excuse me, I have many people to say hello to."

"And I need the ladies'," Mother says, breaking away. *The ladies'.* I'm sure. I scan the room for Davenport, not seeing him.

"Adeline, it may not be my place, but I'm really very grateful that you have reinstated David."

I give Sabina my attention and take her hand, squeezing. "It is nice to see you two are back on track."

"Yes, it is a relief, I must say." Her hand hits her chest. "Family is so very important."

And my family's secrets very nearly ruined her relationship with her son. "Indeed," I agree, feeling a hand on my back. I jump, and Haydon rounds me, a charming smile on his face.

"Grandmother," he says, kissing Sabina before acknowledging me. It is actually frowned upon to greet someone before royalty, but simply because it is Haydon and Sabina, I feel fondness rather than offense. Their relationship has always been one to be envious of. "Your Majesty." Haydon takes my hand before I offer and kisses the back. "I don't think I have ever seen you looking so beautiful."

"And very unlike me," I quip, making them both chuckle. "Thank you for coming, both of you."

"My pleasure." Sabina lifts her skirt and slips away, very conveniently, leaving Haydon and me alone.

"Very subtle," I joke, watching as Haydon takes my fresh glass of champagne from Olive and sets it in my hand.

"You know she adores you." Haydon takes a glass for himself, too, as I look down his body.

"New suit?"

"I was told it was a special occasion." He shrugs. "I'm not sure what's so special."

I laugh, and it's a surprising sound, one that stops me from laughing the moment I start, simply because I'm a little shocked. I laughed. "Me either," I add.

"Adeline." Haydon drops his playfulness and turns serious eyes my way. I withdraw, and he smiles. "I'm really very sorry about everything you have been through."

"Haydon, please don't," I beg, the momentary glimpse of normality gone as quickly as it was found.

"I'm sorry. I just want you to know I'm here for you."

After everything, he really is too sweet. It's more than I deserve for being so stupid. Not that he knows the extent of my stupidity. Josh is gone. That's all anyone knows. "Thank you."

"And you know I will always love you, no matter what."

I breathe in. "I know that," I admit. For his sins, he will never stop, no matter how much I tell him to.

"So that is why I want to try this again." He is suddenly shrinking before me, and I wait for my body to go into shock, for my mind to tell my mouth to scream. But it doesn't happen. I'm a statue. Mute.

He pulls a box from his pocket.

My eyes fall onto it and stick.

The music stops.

Silence falls.

My heart . . . doesn't thump in a panic.

"Adeline Catherine Luisa Lockhart, I will serve you until the day I die. Whether as your husband, or as a mere servant, my loyalty will never waiver." He hesitantly pushes the box toward me. "Will you marry me?"

I don't think. I don't ponder. I don't look around at the hundreds of people staring at me. I don't consider the fact that Haydon knows I'm in love with another man. Or was. "Yes." I watch Haydon, his eyes wide.

"Yes?" He slowly stands, as if he needs to be nearer to my mouth to make sure he did not mistake my answer for a no.

"Yes." It is the only answer. Sadly, I have kissed goodbye to my true happily ever after. I can give Haydon his. Then at least I have some kind of purpose. It's just another one of my strings being pulled, but this time it is me who pulled it. As backward as it may seem, that helps me in my helpless situation. I can't carry on constantly fighting the wolves away. I don't have the strength anymore. My injuries are too deep to recover.

Haydon stares at me, and I shrug. He knows my heart is far from his. I've never been anything less that straight when it has come to my feelings. This is simply a marriage of convenience, just like every other marriage in royal history. I have fallen victim to the institution, and for the first time in my life, I don't care. My happiness was snatched away brutally a week ago. I can't be that kind of happy with Haydon, but I can be comfortable. And who knows, maybe I really will grow to love him like that.

Applause erupts in the room, and it seems to awaken Haydon from his inert state. He scrambles to remove the ring from the box, a huge sapphire circled with diamonds. I offer my hand. He shakes as he slips it on. And for the first time in the thirty years we have known each other, he kisses me. On the lips. Only a peck, though still a kiss. I don't feel it. I don't feel anything. As soon as he releases me, my face muscles work as if programmed, making me smile as he turns me toward the crowds.

I'm his to control.

I'm impervious.

I've learned the art of acquiescence.

I am trapped in a never-ending tunnel of echoed well wishes. I am little more than a robot as I smile at every face before me, letting Haydon lead me around the room, showcasing his trophy. Every so often, he sweeps his arm out toward me, like . . . *just look at her.* In my mind's eye, I see journalists across the world working through the night to get the news to the people. I see pictures of Haydon and me in this very moment, the happily engaged couple. I see me wandering aimlessly down the aisle of Westminster Abbey ready to sign my eternal love over to a man.

The wrong man.

I see me standing beside Josh's bed in his suite, staring at something that changed my life, my spirit, and my faith. Forever. I see betrayal and lies, just more deceit to dictate me.

Pain radiates within me, sweeping through my body mercilessly. And I let it take hold, not bothering to fight it off.

When I finally blink, the haze dissipates, and I find my mother across the ballroom. She's still, quiet, watching as I let myself be paraded in front of my guests. She isn't smiling. She is just watching. As always, silent and detached. Indifferent. Because she lived this.

"The happy couple," David Sampson sings, muscling his way between us, an arm around each of our shoulders. It is little more than madness, every single person in this room falling victim to the deception, getting caught in the huge web like stupid little flies. How can they be so foolish? So ignorant to this circus?

Sabina approaches, her smile soft and searching. She must be as surprised by my answer as I am. "My dear girl." She claims me from her son and grandson and takes me in a hug, her slight frame supporting mine. "Are you okay?" she asks in my ear.

"It is the right thing to do, is it not?"

"Probably." Releasing me, she holds me at arm's length. "Just remember one thing, Adeline. Haydon adores you with every fiber of his being. Every woman deserves that kind of love."

And does the man not deserve that kind of commitment in return? Alas, marriage is just another duty in this job. Something else to be done for the greater good. For everyone else, except for me. Everything that happens from here on doesn't matter. Not to me. I am not merely caged anymore. I am caged, chained, and gagged. Things I swore I would never be.

WHEN MIDNIGHT STRIKES, I am guided from the ballroom by my devoted fiancé, faces smiling at me as I go. I look to Haydon. He is thriving, his face bright and cheery. He's so happy. As my feet blindly lead me with the help of my husband-to-be, I search deeply for the smile I should be showcasing.

No smile.

Damon catches my eye as we pass through the doors, his face as stoic as I have ever seen. Why I would try to fool my beloved bodyguard that I am as thrilled as everyone else is beyond me. But I do, straining to find my smile, forcing it onto my lips with too much effort. His inscrutable face remains expressionless.

Our journey to my suite is silent. I can't even hear my heart beating anymore. But though I am numb, I feel . . . something. It is only when the doors to my private quarters come into view that I realize what that something is.

Tension.

Anticipation.

Oh goodness, is Haydon expecting to come in? Is he expecting to consummate our union? Our first time together? My stomach rolls, nausea taking hold. Throughout this madness, I never paid one thought to what would be expected of me as a wife. Just that of the Queen.

When we reach the door, I notice Haydon's hands are stuffed in his trouser pockets, his eyes downcast, his lips twisting a little. He's thinking. He's thinking the same as me, though where I am dreading it, he is expectant.

"Thank you for walking me back." The words spill out in a rush, my desperation getting the better of me. There is no way I would be able to sleep with Haydon tonight. Maybe ever.

"You are very welcome." We come to a stop at the door, the tension and awkwardness tripling.

"I will see you tomorrow, I expect." I couldn't be any more blunt, and when his shoulders drop somewhat, I feel only a smidgen of guilt. *I expect I will see him?* Of course I will see him tomorrow. I am marrying the man, after all. He'll be taking up residence in my private quarters. He will share my personal space. My bed? "Good night," I say, taking the handle of the door.

"Adeline." He reaches for my arm, and for all the will in the world, I can't stop myself from tensing from my toes to my tiara.

Full of caution I can't hide, I look at him. And he moves in, his lips getting closer and closer to mine. My mind yells at me to move, to pull away, to stop him. But shock keeps me where I am. I close my eyes, as if to hide from what is about to happen, and as soon as I have darkness, I have Josh. His face, his smell, the feel of him. Then a foreign smell, one I don't recognize. Hot air breezes across my lips, and my eyes flip open. I turn my face in the nick of time, and Haydon's lips land on my cheek. "Thank you for a lovely evening," I say, pushing my way into my quarters and shutting the door quickly behind me. My back meets the wood, my knees give, and I sink into a heap of wretchedness. Reaching up, I pull my tiara from my head and set it by my thigh, then gaze at my ring finger. It looks all wrong. It feels so heavy. *Everything* feels heavy. Pulling it from my finger, I place it on the floor and drop my head back, looking to the crystal chandelier. I can't cry. There are no more tears left to fall. I'm a dry, brittle vessel of a woman now. Slowly dying.

One unbearable day down, endless to go.

27

I CAN'T BEAR to look at the magazines and newspapers anymore. It's not the pictures and excitement that irritates me, but the fact that my smile in every picture is so completely fake. I'm not sure how the dread behind it isn't being seen by the world. One week on, my engagement is still headline news. One week on, I have still avoided any intimate contact with my fiancé. One week on, he is still ignoring it. That's irritating, too. So is David Sampson's stupid, grinning face. And the fact that Sir Don is being nice to me. And one more thing that is getting right under my skin is the lack of contact from my brother. His support is needed now more than ever, and I feel he is the only one I can turn to. But he's not answering my calls.

"Damon," I call, setting my coffee down and pushing away today's newspapers that have kindly been set out with my breakfast. "Please find Prince Edward and tell him I wish to see him."

"I believe he is currently sleeping, ma'am."

I study Damon, reading between the lines. My brother has been frequenting that seedy gentleman's club again. "Thank you," I sigh, and he leaves without another word. What am I going to do? Eddie can't avoid me forever.

Kim wanders in, and I raise a curious eyebrow, noticing her usual grey suit has been switched for a black one, making her red hair seem redder.

"Is it a special occasion?" I ask, taking my pastry and slicing through the center.

"I would say shopping for your wedding gown is a special occasion." She motions to a chair and sits when I nod.

Of course, I forgot about that. "Why do you say shopping? Are we leaving the palace and actually visiting shops?" I put a piece of butter on one half of my pastry and spread.

Kim ignores the fact that my question is rhetorical. "No. The dresses have arrived this morning and have been taken to your suite."

"Marvelous." I pop my breakfast in my mouth and chew, cocking my head when Kim sighs. "What?" My mouth is full, making my words muffled. Very unqueenly.

Kim leans over and speaks quietly. "Your lack of enthusiasm is starting to be noticed."

Dropping the other half of my pastry, I wipe the corners of my mouth with my napkin and stand. "Frankly, Kim"—I push my chair under the table, holding the backrest—"I really couldn't give a fuck." I turn and wander away from her stunned face. "Let's try on some dresses," I sing, so completely over the top. I slap on my smile and make my way to my suite, Kim on my tail. My lack of enthusiasm is being noticed? I laugh to myself. So they expect me to dance for joy, do they? Faint with excitement when they told me my wedding is coming *before* my coronation. Because having a husband is apparently going to make me more of a queen. This, of course, means I will be married off in four weeks. The Earl Marshall has spiraled into a tailspin, his Royal event-organizing skills being tested to the limits. I'm sure he hates me, too.

"Have you decided on Haydon's title yet?" Kim asks once we make it into my suite. "Sir Don needs to announce."

"No."

"Well, can you?"

I turn tired eyes onto her. "Prince Haydon of Adeline's Vagina?"

"You are so bitter, it's making you look old," Kim sighs, and I recoil. "And while we're speaking some home truths, I think maybe you are letting yourself go." She points her pen to my wet hair that is scraped into a high bun. "Do you want to go down in history as the bitter, bedraggled queen?"

"Well." I laugh. "Who shit in your coffee this morning?" I frown as soon as I say the words, wondering where on earth they have come from.

"I could ask you who has shit in yours for the past *week*. Come on, Adeline. Just tell me what on earth has happened." I go into my shell and look away, making Kim sigh. She knows I won't speak of it, and she eventually gives up waiting for an answer. "I'll be back shortly."

"Thanks," I mutter, dropping heavily to the couch in the lounge area. I look across to my bedroom. The double doors are open, revealing the end of a huge mobile dress rail. I see white protection bags and lots of pairs of shoes on the bottom rack. Will any of those dresses be black, because I should wear a black dress. I certainly feel like I am in mourning.

An army of people enter, and Kim hands me a huge file. "The collection."

I take the file, which is more like a wedding album, all white leather and silver font, and rest it in my lap. A tall lady approaches, a tape measure draped around her neck. "Your Majesty, can I please say what an absolute honor it is to be awarded the task of helping you choose your wedding gown."

I strain a smile, setting the file on the couch beside me as Kim comes forward and introduces the lady. "Madam Beaumont has dressed high-profile brides for thirty years, ma'am."

"Very good." I get up and wander into my bedroom.

"Since you declined my offer to design your gown, ma'am,

and you had no preference on style, I have taken the liberty of bringing my new collection to showcase. You are the first to see it, ma'am." Madam Beaumont overtakes me and gushes all over the rail, pointing at dresses that I can't see because they're all concealed by protective covers. "I'm sure there is something made for you in here. We can adapt it, of course, if you so wish." She claps her hands and a young girl appears, her hands full. "Set it up just here, Frances. Right in front of this mirror so Her Majesty can see herself in all her glory."

All her glory? I glance across to the mirror to which she is referring, catching sight of my reflection. I frown and reach up to my hair. Kim is right. I look a fright. "Let us get on with it, then," I declare, taking myself to my bathroom.

"Your robe, ma'am." Olive comes after me, followed quickly by Jenny. The second the door closes behind us, I strip down to my underwear and let Olive help me into the robe. Neither she nor Jenny murmurs a word. They don't express any excitement.

"Would you like me to dry your hair?" Jenny asks, a little tentatively. "And do your makeup?"

"I'm trying on dresses." I fasten the tie of my robe. "No need to make it more complicated than it should be."

She backs up, flicking a concerned look to a cautious-looking Olive. They are walking on eggshells around me, two of the few people who are sensitive to my melancholy, along with Damon. Everyone else is pretending I wasn't secretly seeing another man. Why I am not now is something only Damon will ever know. I sigh, dramatically dropping my chin to my chest. "I'm sorry for being so moody these past two weeks."

Of course, Olive rushes to placate me. "Oh, no need—"

"Yes, Olive, there is very much a need." I reach for her arm, as well as Jenny's, holding on to them both. "It is not your fault I'm miserable." Both women are positively dying to know what happened between Josh and me. But they are way too respectful to ask, unlike Kim. Regardless, I give them just a little in the hope they understand my despondency. "I was blinded by possibility and hope. Now I realize I was very stupid. We were from very different worlds, and I see now it would never have worked. I'm just very sad I was so foolish."

"I don't think you're foolish, ma'am," Olive says, ever so sweet and naïve. "And if you were, it was because love made you that way."

"Here, here," Jenny adds, her smile soft. "But does that mean you should marry Haydon Sampson?" The immediate fall of her smile tells me she's mentally retracting that question. Like she shouldn't even ask. She probably shouldn't. But this is Jenny.

"If I were a normal woman, then no. But sadly, I am not a normal woman, am I?" I release them and correct my fallen shoulders. I know better than anyone that I was preyed on in a moment of weakness. Caught off guard, feeling heartbroken and lost, I was cornered by Haydon and the voices in his ear. "And now I am in way over my head." I smile at them both. "So I guess I should get on with things, yes?"

They nod, as do I. I open the door to find Matilda has arrived, her form as contemplative as ever. I give her a nod of assurance that I'm sure doesn't wash. "My mother?" I ask, looking for her. Should she not be here for her daughter's first dress fitting?

Kim goes straight to her phone and dials. "She will be joining us shortly."

"Indeed," I breathe, knowing exactly where she will be. "I believe she had a meeting with Davenport." I step up onto the small podium that has been set up. She has had a lot of meetings with Davenport recently. And seems to have avoided me in the process.

The first dress is carefully taken out of the protective bag, and it is all I can do not to scowl at the gown that is far from my style— all frills and excess material. I will look like a throwback from the eighties.

"This is a particular favorite of mine, and I think it will be perfect on you," Madam Beaumont gushes.

I keep my dubious look at bay as she helps me into the masses of material, keeping my thoughts to myself. I wriggle like a worm, tugging it up more roughly than I should, not that Madam Beaumont pulls me up on it.

"Oh, Your Majesty," she sings, stepping back with her palms covering her delighted mouth. "It is sublime on you."

I turn toward my reflection. The long, puffy sleeves make my arms look like they could be bulging with muscles beneath, the tiered ruffles of the skirt made to conceal all kinds of lumps and bumps. The modest neckline is beaded, the bodice a busy lace design. Frankly, it is awful. I look shocking. Hideous. "That will do," I declare, stepping down from the podium.

I turn for Olive to unfasten me, ignoring the collection of stunned looks being thrown my way. "You're not trying on more?" Kim asks the question that everyone else wants to ask but dares not.

"As Madam Beaumont said, it is sublime." I step out and walk to the bathroom, hearing Kim coming after me.

"Adeline, it is dreadful," she whisper-hisses.

I stop and pivot at the door, finding my private secretary checking over her shoulder to make sure she hasn't been heard. When she returns her attention to me, I don't whisper. "My entire life is dreadful, Kim. So the dress matches, yes? Suffocating, compliant, covering all my sins. I would say it is perfect."

Her eyes close briefly, her years of working for me telling her I am not going to be convinced otherwise. "A reminder about your first official engagement with Mr. Sampson tomorrow evening at the Royal Ballet," she breathes.

"Can't wait," I quip. More fake smiles. More avoiding his attempts to kiss me. And in public, it will be worse. Poor, delusional Haydon will be desperate to give the world a picture of him kissing his bride-to-be.

"Jenny will be here to help you get ready. Did you try on the gown sent by Elie Saab?" My lips twist, and Kim sighs. "I will have a seamstress waiting for any needed alterations."

"Thank you." I close the door and gaze around my bathroom. My eyes fall on the mirror. On my reflection. The reflection of a woman I do not recognize. A hideous woman. And before I know what has happened, I have thrown everything I can lay my hands on at the glass.

Shattered.

Destroyed.

28

NO ALTERATIONS ARE needed. The long, silver gown fits as if it has been made for me. My headdress is embellished with aquamarine stones, my chandelier earrings a perfect match. I look more like myself on the outside, but on the inside, I am dead.

Haydon is waiting at the bottom of the steps as I descend, smiling a smile so full of happiness it makes my insides twist with guilt. "Wow," is all he says, his head lifting and lowering constantly as he takes me in. When I reach the bottom, I release the front of my skirt as Olive lowers the back, arranging it perfectly so it pools the floor at my feet.

As Haydon moves in to greet me, I catch Damon by the door watching me as I start to tense up. "Gorgeous." Haydon takes my hands and kisses my cheek, taking full advantage of his immunity from protocol. As my husband, Haydon will never have to wait to be invited to touch me, and, terribly, I hate that.

His lips linger and my eyes close, wishing them off me. And with my eyes closed, I leave myself vulnerable to the locked images haunting me, flashes of Josh's toned body coming on with an onslaught of pain as well.

I jolt, my eyes springing open. "Better go," I say abruptly, my legs carrying me away from the source of my distress without waiting for Olive to help me with my gown. As a result of my hast, my feet get tangled up in the excess material, and I stagger, being caught by Damon before I tumble to my knees.

"Careful, ma'am," he says softly, righting me.

"Darling, are you okay?" Haydon rushes over and fusses over me, righting my already righted position. Darling. Not darlin', but darling.

I reach down and yank up the skirt, carrying on. "Silly me." I push away every thought plaguing me, every image too, and work hard to empty my mind once again. Lowering into the car, I smile when Damon moves in and blocks Haydon's path to me, gathering the bottom of my dress and setting it around my feet. "Thank you," I murmur, not for his help, but for his intervention.

"Welcome." He straightens and closes the door, turning toward an indignant Haydon. "This way, sir." Damon indicates around the car where the other door is held open for my husband-to-be.

"It should be *me* helping my fiancée, thank you," Haydon grumbles, giving Damon a death stare.

"Sorry, sir." He shrugs. "Habit." Damon isn't sorry at all, yet I'm still annoyed he has offered an apology, albeit fake. He's been with me for years, always there to catch me when I fall, in more ways than one. He should never have to apologize.

"He was only trying to help," I say when Haydon drops heavily onto the seat beside me. It's not Damon's fault that Haydon isn't quick enough to be there first. "He has been close by my side for years. He can't switch off his instinct." I wince at the sound of my own words, which are indirectly suggesting that Haydon doesn't know me well. But he doesn't.

"He's always overstepped the mark," Haydon mutters, yanking his seatbelt on. "It's high time someone put him in his place."

I turn an incredulous look onto him, astounded. "And that

person will be you, will it?" I am very protective of my staff, and I do not take too kindly to others intervening. My *husband* will be no exception.

Realizing he has annoyed me, he quickly corrects his affronted state, his face softening. "I'm sorry, darling. I guess I'm nervous."

Darling. I want to shove his term of endearment down his throat, more so than when I am addressed by my title. Hearing people refer to me as expected is simply a reminder of who I am. Hearing Haydon call me *darling* simply reminds me of someone I wanted to be. *Josh's.* I already question my ability to forget about him, but with that word being used on me every day, it will be a continuous reminder of my foolishness. Of my loss. "If you must insist on a pet name for me, please find something else," I grate, going on before he can question me. "And why ever would you be nervous? We are attending the ballet." I face forward again and speak to the back of Damon's head. "Let's be going, then."

Let's get this horror show done with.

≈

IF HE KISSED me once, he kissed me one hundred times during the short walk from the car to the doors of the Royal Opera House. Every opportunity, everytime someone congratulated me on my recent good news. Major Davenport was horrified each time, the displays of public affection from any Royal very much frowned upon. But the Queen? Unheard of. I felt like I was being constantly pissed on, for a lack of a less uncouth term. I have always been quite fond of Haydon, despite his thick skin. He isn't a terrible person, not unkind or rude, if a little suffocating, but tonight he is very different. Bold, loud, laughing at the silliest of things. He's lording it up, thriving on the attention, and it is irritating me to high heaven.

Every member of the dance troop we meet on arrival is gracious and polite, though Haydon finds fault in their lack of conversation. He hasn't yet perfected the art of putting someone he's meeting at ease. But is it an art? Or is it natural?

"They may be nervous," I whisper as we walk away from the line of people who were waiting to greet us. "You have to make them feel comfortable."

"They should be falling over themselves to please us." He snaps his fingers to get the attention of a waiter. "Hurry up, chap."

I stare at him like he must be an alien. "What has gotten into you?" I ask, so embarrassed.

Haydon pauses mid-swallow of his champagne, obviously taking a moment to think about what I mean. "Oh." He chuckles a little, snapping his fingers again. "Sorry, darling." He takes another glass and places it in my hand. "Nerves getting the better of me again."

I don't recognize this man. Has it really been argued for all of these years that he is suitable? I don't think his nerves are getting the better of him at all. I think his buried ego is. It doesn't suit him in the slightest. I look across to Kim and Davenport, who are obviously as staggered as I am. "Help," I mouth, prompting them both to come rushing my way.

"Mr. Sampson," Kim says, all smiley. "I believe there is someone who would like to meet you."

"And whom might that be?" Haydon gazes around, most likely looking for the lucky person. There is no one. Kim's being clever, and I can't thank her enough. I need him away from me for a second, so I can at least breathe without feeling like my heart is being squeezed.

"This way, sir." Kim ushers Haydon away toward a crowd of men in tuxedos—politicians, I think.

"Well," Davenport says, joining my side. "That was extremely painful to witness."

"Which part?" I ask, sipping some champagne as I glance over my shoulder. Olive is on my dress again, ensuring it is splayed perfectly, showcasing it to its best. I almost don't want to move again. Every step I take she is rearranging it. "Olive."

Her hands stop, and she looks up at me. "Yes, ma'am?"

"Leave the dress," I say on a smile. "Or you will be crawling around on your hands and knees all night, and we can't have that now, can we? Someone may step on you."

She giggles but gives my dress one last tweak before she rises. "Can I get you anything?"

A cage to put my fiancé in? "I'm fine, thank you."

"Your Majesty," Davenport steers me toward a man in a dashing tuxedo and a fair beard. "Allow me to introduce you to the Royal Ballet director, Mr. Hinde."

"How wonderful," I say, offering my hand. "I am very much looking forward to tonight's performance."

On a friendly smile, he accepts my hand and dips. "Such an honor to receive you, ma'am. The troupe has been rehearsing through the night to perfect their performance."

"Not on my account, surely." I laugh.

"Night-time practice is certainly not out of the ordinary before opening night, but I have to admit, the new queen's presence has added to the pressure."

"I'm sure I will be dazzled." I withdraw my hand. I can do this dance. I've had years to practice being warm to anyone in my presence, so despite my emptiness, I will never allow anyone like Mr. Hinde to feel beneath me. Unlike Haydon. *What has gotten into him?* "Would it be too—?" All words are sucked back, and my veins freeze. I find myself blinking, certain I must be seeing things.

"Sorry, ma'am, I didn't catch that," Mr. Hinde says, moving slightly to the left and blocking my view to the bar area. I look at him blankly, and he smiles, though it is unsure.

"I do believe I have lost my line," I say like a fool, wishing I had X-ray vision so I could see straight through Mr. Hinde to confirm I am mistaken.

"Happens to me all the time." He chuckles. "Enjoy this evening, ma'am." On a nod, he moves away, and like a brick to my face, I see him again, leaning against the bar, a few people around him, two of which are security and his publicist. He's in a tuxedo. His eyes are narrowed, but dazzling. "Oh my God," I whisper.

"Indeed," Davenport says dryly, and I look at him. He has found what I have found. "This is slightly inconvenient. Am I to assume Mr. Jameson is here to see you, ma'am?"

"No, you are not to assume that." I feel Josh's angry blue eyes burning into my profile, and through my internal meltdown I manage to wonder what on earth he has to feel angry about. And that, in turn, stokes my own anger. "Get rid of him."

"I'm afraid that won't be possible without causing a scene, ma'am. Something tells me Mr. Jameson won't take too kindly to being asked to leave."

God, he's right. I know Josh, and he'll kick up a stink of epic proportions. He has no regard for my status. Never has. I don't expect now to be any different, especially when I know he has tried to contact me. "I suddenly feel a little squeamish." My stomach does a cartwheel, swishing the champagne around.

"Me, too," Davenport counters seriously, and my hand pauses on my stomach, my surprised eyes looking up at his wooden form. He doesn't look at me, but keeps his shrewd eyes on Josh. My face wrinkles, and a flurry of giggles capture me, making me laugh much louder than I intended.

"Don't snort," Damon adds as he joins us, he too looking toward Josh. Of course, Damon's instruction only makes me laugh all the more, and before I can stop myself, I have tears streaming down my cheeks. "Okay, ma'am?" Both men look at me with the concern I deserve, and my laughs soon become sobs. My emotions are all askew, and this really isn't the place for it. Keeping my head low, I wrestle with my unrelenting need to cry and wail and scream. To march up to Josh Jameson and slap him. To yell to the world that I was ready to rewrite history to be with him, but he betrayed me. He is a bastard—a lowlife, narcissistic bastard.

"Oh no," Davenport sighs. "This way, ma'am." He takes my elbow as Damon flanks my other side, hurrying me along before I'm spotted being tearful in public. Showing emotion. However would that be explained? My steps quicken when the most horrific yet perfect excuse for my public crying episode manifests in my head. Oh God. They will be declaring me with child. Claringdon will choose their moment and announce that I am expecting the first heir. But that would make my wedding even more shotgun than it already is, and we can't be having that. Oh no. Queens don't get themselves pregnant before marriage. *Off with my head.* "Oh my God," I mumble to myself, my thoughts going into overdrive. What on earth am I thinking?

"That man certainly chooses his moments," Damon grunts, bringing us to a stop at the restroom door.

"Adeline," Davenport sighs. "It would be very helpful to be furnished with the details of your departure from Mr. Jameson's company, if only to know what we are dealing with."

"You are dealing with a lying, cheating pig," I snap. "That is what you are dealing with."

Davenport recoils, yet Damon expresses no reaction. Because, of course, he already knows.

"Excuse me." I rush into the restroom and close the door on poor Olive's face. "Sorry," I call, hurrying to the toilet and bracing my arms on the side. I really do feel nauseous. Sick to my stomach, but nothing wants to come up. Look at me. I turn toward the mirror as if obeying myself. Yes, just look at me. My eyes are glass—big round balls of unnerved glass. How am I expected to endure this? How can I get out of it?

"People are taking their seats, ma'am," Davenport calls through the door.

I *can't* get out of it. Simple. God damn him, how dare he show up like this? How dare he have this effect on me? "Urhhhhhhh!" I slap the edge of the sink and immediately regret it, pain bolting up my arm. I need to pull myself together. Show him what I am made of. "Coming," I call, opening the door and virtually dragging Jenny in to fix my disastrous face.

"What happened?" she asks, looking at the mess of me—tramlines from mascara, tear streaks through my beautifully contoured cheeks.

"I saw someone I wasn't expecting to see." I'm direct, since the moment Jenny sees Josh for herself, she will know the cause for this serious makeup malfunction.

I see comprehension dawn in her, though she chooses not to say anything and begins fixing me. She is swift, tidy, and accurate. "Perfect again," she says, popping the lid on her highlighter powder. "You show him, ma'am."

"I plan to." Swinging the door open, I declare myself ready. So bloody ready.

I link arms with Haydon when he approaches, and I don't question why. I smile, and though it is still painted on, it isn't as hard to keep in place. I keep my back straight and my neck long. *Fuck you, Josh Jameson.*

We are shown to our seats as everyone applauds my arrival to the Royal balcony box, and I wave, soaking up the sea of standing people before me, all looking this way.

"What a lovely warm welcome," I say, taking my seat and accepting the program from Kim. Haydon remains standing, smiling at the crowds. "Will you sit down?" I order shortly, tugging on the bottom of his suit jacket. He's like a toddler who needs constantly watching. I look to Damon, giving him view of my tight, impatient jaw. I'll be sending Haydon home soon. He's being ridiculous.

Once my husband-to-be has decided he's had enough basking in the limelight, he sits and flicks through his own program, then stuffs it under his seat. It's getting to the point that I can't even look at him. I feel like the past thirty years have all been a huge show, and now he supposedly *has* me, there's no need to keep up the act of Mr. Good Guy. He's more like his father than I realized.

Focusing on the stage, I let the dramatic start of the orchestra draw me in and the dancers mesmerize me. I may not be myself right now, but I can certainly appreciate the enchanting performance of Tchaikovsky's magnificent classic, allowing myself to be swept away by the beauty, if only for a short while. To concentrate on another tragic love story. To see two people fighting all the odds to be together. To watch them die. My heart slows its beats as I fall into a trance, my eyes gliding across the floor with the graceful ballerinas.

To be that free.

"Apologies for disturbing you during the performance, ma'am." Davenport is crouched behind me, his mouth close to my ear.

"What is it, Major?"

"Can't it wait?" Haydon grumbles, scowling at the stage.

"Afraid not, sir." Davenport doesn't grace Haydon with his attention. "We have a situation."

I'm immediately as stiff as a board. "What kind of situation?" I look past Davenport to the door of the box, seeing Damon guarding it. *Oh goodness, no.*

"Well, answer her, you old fool," Haydon snaps under his breath. I would shoot him down with a filthy glare if I could find the will to remove my eyes from the doorway. I get the feeling Damon is filling it in order to stop someone from entering.

"We've had a call from the Prime Minister, ma'am."

"Oh for God's sake." Haydon sinks into his chair, completely uninterested. "The man is a moron."

"The Prime Minister?" I question, a little taken aback.

"Yes, ma'am. I'm afraid there is news you need to be informed of immediately before it breaks publicly. If you wouldn't mind coming with me. He is waiting for you in a private room."

"Oh?" I stand, mystified, and let Davenport lead me away. If the Prime Minister is here, then I can only imagine the country is dealing with some kind of crisis. It's rather amusing that when there is such a crisis, the government's priority is to advise the Queen. It is a little backward, since, even as Head of State, I am powerless to do anything about the crisis. But, like most things, it is tradition, therefore expected. Plus, I'm rather curious as to what would warrant a personal visit from the PM while I am on an official engagement. War? It seems like the only explanation. "What's going on, Davenport?" I ask as he leads the way across the carpet. He looks worried himself, and that isn't aiding my own. "Major?"

"This way, ma'am." He opens a door. "We found somewhere private for you to speak."

"Lovely, but I am completely bewildered," I inform him, hitching up my dress some more and entering the room. It's empty. No Prime Minister in sight, not to mention any of the men who follow him around. "Now what on earth is the meaning of this?" I ask the empty space.

"Hello, Adeline." The smooth, American accent smacks me in my back, and my lungs squeeze with my sharp inhale.

29

I WHIRL AROUND, finding Josh behind the door. My body goes into shock, immobilizing me, as Josh takes control of the door from Davenport and starts to close it with Davenport on the wrong side.

"What's going on?" I ask Davenport, panic building and gripping me. "I demand to know."

"I'm sorry, ma'am." Davenport looks truly remorseful. "But Mr. Jameson came armed."

"Armed?" I question. "What? He's carrying a gun, is he? He held you at gunpoint?"

"No," Josh cuts in. "I told him if he didn't get you to this room, I would get on that stage and tell the world about his love child." Josh is so serious, I almost believe him.

Disgusted, I make sure Josh knows it with my most derisive expression. "You blackmailed my private secretary? Are there no boundaries on how low you will go?"

"No. Not when it comes to you." The door shuts, and we are alone in this big room. And then he turns the lock. And we are alone *and* locked in.

He slowly pivots to face me. His face. It arrests me, pumps my heart faster. "This wedding business is getting out of hand," he says seriously, moving in.

"Out of hand?" I start taking backward steps, annoyed with myself. But distance is paramount. He looks angry, the amber in his eyes fiery. He's angry? He has no right to be angry. All of that privilege is reserved for me and me alone.

"Have you slept with him?"

My steps halt, my mouth falling open. "That is none of your business."

His jaw ticks. "On your knees."

"Excuse me?"

"Get on your fuckin' knees, Adeline," he yells, stalking forward. "Your king is demanding you to kneel, so you will fuckin' kneel!"

I stare at him, lost in a moment of utter disbelief. And fear. Because my legs are trembling to keep me upright. To keep me from bowing to his command. He's livid, vibrating violently before me. He looks about ready to come out of his skin. "I bow to no one," I say clearly, every ounce of my strength being injected into my words, making sure they sound as even and strong as I mean. "Especially not *you*." I shove him from my path and storm away. I shouldn't have made contact. Why would I make contact? I jolt, energy surging through my nervous system viciously, trying to claim me, trying to force me to my knees.

"No." Josh grabs my wrist, one effortless tug yanking me to a stop. And then panic clouds everything, tossing me over the edge of sanity and into a tornado of madness.

I swing around aggressively, sending my tiara sailing across the room as I do. "Don't you dare touch me," I shout, hauling myself back, trying to escape his viselike grip. "You don't get to touch me ever again!" The drag of my flesh through his hold burns my skin, my free hand trying in vain to pry his clawed fingers away. The ground disappears from beneath my feet, my head suddenly on his chest. He holds me so tightly around my torso, squeezing me to him, my arms trapped between us to restrain me. I'm heaving madly, short of breath, but I find energy in my legs, kicking and lashing out. "Get off."

He loses his grip, hissing when I catch his shin. I use his lapse in focus to my advantage, breaking away and running for the door. I place my hand on the handle. I turn the lock. "No," Josh roars, grabbing me and hauling me back. "You're not leaving me, Adeline."

We become a messy, deranged tangle of bodies, tussling and yelling, my hands flailing wildly as Josh fights to get me under control. My vision is blanketed in a crimson haze, anger dominating me. Every tiny shitty thing I hate about my life, present and past, is pouring out of me now, the pressure pot exploding, and Josh is bearing the brunt of it all as I shout and lash out at him. I hate everything. Especially myself. But most of all, I hate him. For making me feel what I could have had. For showing me what love is, and then cruelly snatching it away. For being my hero and then the villain.

"I hate you," I yell, smashing into his chest. "I fucking hate you."

"There she is," he growls, spinning me around and slamming my back into his front, crossing my arms over my stomach and holding them, restraining me. I'm trapped. My lungs are burning. Exhausted. My body is rolling against his, violent waves crashing against each other. His mouth falls to my ear, nuzzling close. "There she fuckin' is." He blows the words across my skin. "My queen."

Adrenaline makes way for tears, my attempts to find air making me choke. "How could you?" I ask, my question broken by emotion. "How could you do that to me? After everything we've been through."

"You have to listen to me, Adeline." He doesn't ease up on his hold. "Please, just tell me you will listen to me."

"I'm not listening to anymore of your lies."

"Fine." In one expert move, I'm on my back on the floor, Josh blanketing me, my hands trapped. The second I register his face, close and cut with frustration, I snap my eyes closed, unwilling to allow anything to breach the chinks in my armor. Because there are chinks. Lots of chinks. Josh created those chinks. He broke down my walls. "I'll make you listen." He gets comfortable, spread over me, ensuring I'm going nowhere. "You may not be able to see me, but you can hear me."

There is nothing I can do to block that sense, no matter how loudly I scream in my head.

"That woman—"

"Shut up!" I yell, my distress growing.

"She was paid, Adeline."

"By you?" I wriggle beneath him.

"No, for fuck's sake." Josh jerks, nudging me, though I keep myself in my darkness. "I was drugged. I woke up with not a fuckin' clue where I was. I saw the woman in my bed. I saw your earrings on the nightstand. I thought I was losing my fuckin' mind."

Is he for real? No, he is an actor.

Am I expected to let him brainwash me with this rubbish? I will never be fooled by him again.

"She was naked. You were naked." I can't help it. I open my eyes and fire daggers at him. "You had a condom on." I wince at my own words, my throat swelling to the point I'm scared I might stop breathing.

"No." He slams my arms back to the floor above my head when I manage to lift them an inch. "I have spent these past two weeks trying to find out what the fuck happened. I needed the facts, anything to make you believe me. I knew what it looked like. I knew you would never trust my words alone."

"And you think I will now?"

"Yes. I had a drug test, Adeline. Positive. Those drinks were laced, for fuck's sake. The woman who was *paid* to get in bed with me took some persuasion, but she admitted it. She confessed to Bates that she was told to find a way into my suite. She and her friend did that by seducing some of my men. They ordered room service. I had two drinks and felt like shit, so I went to bed and left the others to party."

I stare at him, trying to let it all filter into my warped mind. *No.* Don't believe him. I mustn't believe him. I can't expose myself to more hurt again.

"Are you hearing me? Are you hearing how messed up this is? Adeline, I love you. I would never, *ever* betray you." His eyes cloud, his hurt pouring down on me. "I would kill myself before I hurt you. You're the beginning and end of everything. Why don't you see that?"

"I saw you in bed with another woman," I choke, looking away from him, my mind a tatty tangle of deceit that I can't get my head around. "What else would you expect me to do when my mind is tormented with that and that alone? I saw it, Josh. You and her." It's crowding my headspace. Consuming me. "Naked. Your . . ." I fade off, swallowing and shaking away the mental flashback. "I can't unsee it," I grate. "How do you think that made me feel?"

"About the same level as crazy as I feel when I see pictures of you with another man." He dips and nudges at my cheek, turning my face to him. "I'm devastated. But not as devastated as knowing you thought I could do that to you."

I swallow and press my lips together. "What did you expect me to do?"

His eyes close, the hollows of his cheeks pulsing. "Tell me you believe me."

The flashbacks come back with a vengeance, and I squeeze my eyes shut as well. They're all so clear. Josh in bed with another woman. My stomach turns, and I gulp down the devastation. Then I see Sir Don. I see David's smug face. I see satisfaction in them. *Accomplishment.*

I see the enemy. Could they really have been so intentionally cruel to me?

Then I see Josh and me. I hear every word we've ever spoken to each other. I see the way he looks at me with complete and utter adoration. How tormented he's been when he's struggled to accept our reality. He could have simply walked away. He could have simply left without a goodbye.

And then I feel.

I feel his love. I feel his devotion. I feel what I have never felt until Josh came into my life.

Appreciated.

Loved.

I open my eyes and stare at his handsome face. A face pouring with desperation. Desperation for me to believe him. He isn't my enemy. He wouldn't intentionally hurt me. He loves me.

What has happened, what he's saying to me, it's unbelievable. But . . ."I believe you," I whisper, and he exhales, his whole body softening.

"Tell me you've not slept with him. I beg you." He frees one of my hands, my left one, and takes my engagement ring off. "Tell me." He tosses it across the carpet like it is rubbish.

"I haven't slept with him," I admit, feeling his body going heavier over me. "Haven't even kissed him properly."

"Your kisses are mine, Adeline. Your love is mine. *You* are mine." My other hand is freed, though I keep them at my sides, unable to comprehend what any of this means. "And I am yours, Your Majesty." He takes my cheeks and forces his forehead to mine, drilling into me with a determination so strong, I start to feel it seeping into me. "Let's put an end to this madness and just be happy. Together. Me and you. I don't care where, how, why, so long as I'm with you."

"Even if I am still Queen?"

He smiles, rolling his forehead across mine and catching my lips. "As long as this country remembers whose queen you are first, then yes."

My arms come up, my mouth following his, so relieved. Then

just as fast as relief finds me, something awful comes to me, misery amid my newfound happiness. "Haydon."

The growl that hits my ears is fierce. "Don't mention that name when I'm kissing you. Don't ever mention that name again."

"What am I going to do?"

"Ditch his ass."

"You don't just get to call things off when you are me, Josh."

"Then I'll do it for you." He pushes himself up from the floor and pulls me to my feet. "I promise it'll be quick, but I can't guarantee it'll painless."

"Josh, I'm being serious."

"So am I." Moving in, he pulls me in for a cuddle. "He's a jerk."

I keep from challenging him this time, because after Haydon's performance this evening, I am inclined to agree. "Josh," I speak into his shoulder, reality once again raining down on me. "I need to handle this carefully."

"You mean you need to handle this *now*." I feel his head move to look at the back of mine. "Don't you? No more stalling so someone else has the opportunity to derail us."

Speaking of which . . .

"I need to know who did this. So I can deal with them."

"I'm working on it. The CCTV footage is hazy at best. The only concrete evidence Bates has is the call girl and her list of instructions from an anonymous payer. But still, they were banking on you finding me in bed with her." He frowns, and my head starts to spin. "Did you tell anyone you were planning on coming to see me that night?"

"Only Damon," I breathe, stepping away from Josh, leaving his frown deepening. "And I wasn't planning to. I came because I couldn't call you."

"Why?"

"Because my phone went missing." I drop my eyes to the floor, a few mysterious pieces of the crazy puzzle dropping into place. I turn and start pacing the room. "They took Damon's phone, too. I had no way to contact you other than to call the hotel directly, and of course they wouldn't put me through to you. I had to physically go to the hotel." I turn to face him, disturbed by the calculating tactics this person has taken. "Whoever did this knew I would come to the hotel." They knew I'd be desperate to see Josh. There is only one explanation. "It has to be David Sampson. Or Sir Don." Either are capable, desperate, and cruel enough. I'd just fired them both that very day. News of our relationship was imminent. I approach Josh and fist the front of his tuxedo jacket, looking up at his face that is distorted with disgust. "Get me the footage from the hotel."

"It's being analyzed." Josh takes my wrists and pulls my arms down. "You're not surprised, are you?"

Am I? I shouldn't be; I know the lengths these people will go to, but drugging someone? Hookers and stolen phones? "No," I sigh, letting my forehead drop to his chest. "I'm just tired of it all."

"Me, too, baby." His fingers find their way into my hair and massage at my scalp. "So get your ass out there and do what you need to do."

"Now?" I ask, springing out of his chest.

"Yeah, now. Don't think I'm letting you leave this joint with another man. Forget it, Adeline."

"Josh, you have to be reasonable. I can't very well stride out of here and declare during the ballet that I am not marrying Haydon Sampson and am, in fact, in love with a hot American actor."

"Why not? Isn't that the truth of it? And you got the hot part spot on."

"You're impossible."

"And you, my queen"—he plants a light kiss on my nose—"are coming home with me tonight."

"You have to give me until morning, at least." Goodness, there will be crisis meeting after crisis meeting. But then, given what I know, I don't know how I feel about letting Josh out of my sight.

"Actually," I say, looking at him, "you are coming home with me." What they might try to do next in their relentless mission to keep us apart is a frightening prospect. I thought I made myself clear before. I obviously didn't.

"What?"

"You and I aren't leaving each other's sights until I've done what needs to be done. At the palace, you'll be safe." God knows what could happen between now and morning if I leave him.

He reaches up and pinches the bridge of his nose. "Aren't all the enemies inside the palace walls, Adeline?"

"Yes, but they're not inside my private quarters. You are coming home with me, and that is the end of that. Like I said, you're not leaving my sight."

"Great," Josh chirps. "I'll just take a seat between you and Haydon in the Royal balcony, shall I?"

"Bloody hell," I curse. I forgot about the small detail that is my fiancé. I quickly run over my options and come up with only one. "Damon." I go to the door and pull it open, boldly and with no consideration for who may be on the other side. I couldn't care less. My bodyguard and Davenport are waiting. I only mildly cringe with the thought of what they may have heard. Shouts. Screams. Cries. Which begs the question . . ."Why didn't you come in?"

Damon's eyebrows rise, as if that is a stupid enquiry.

"He knows everything," Josh confirms, explaining Damon's lack of intervention. "Thumbs up all the way."

"Oh. Then you will watch Josh, Damon. Everywhere he goes, you go." I look on as my bodyguard casts an interested look across to Josh.

Josh simply shrugs. "She's cute when she's bossy, right?" He stuffs his hands into his tuxedo trousers.

"Ma'am," Damon says on a shake of his head. "I must advise—"

"That is a direct order, Damon. You will take Josh to Claringdon Palace immediately."

He sighs. "Adeline—"

"You know what happened, Damon. What they—"

"Yes," he says on a grind of his teeth. "But—"

"Then you will appreciate my anxiousness when it comes to Mr. Jameson."

"Did I say cute?" Josh asks, his blazing eyes on me. "Change that to fuckin' hot." His arm falls around my shoulder, his lips mauling my cheek for all to see. I watch as Davenport closes his eyes and breathes in, undoubtedly thinking he's got his work cut out. "Baby," Josh whispers, "you can take the reins all day every day."

I pull off an eye-roll that would give me an instant headache if it weren't aching already. "Stop it."

"I'll have one of my men assigned to Mr. Jameson," Damon tells me, giving me the rare look that tells me I am not winning this argument. "That is final." He transfers that look to Josh. "You're important, but not as important as she is."

I shake my head in objection. No. I only trust my head of security with Josh. "Damon—"

"He's right, Adeline." Josh places his palm over my mouth. "So shut up."

"Excuse me?" I mumble into his hand, ignoring the look of amusement from Damon, as well as Davenport.

"And Mr. Sampson?" Davenport asks, throwing that unwanted spanner in my works.

I pull Josh's hand away from my mouth. "I don't know yet."

"Then in the meantime, may I suggest Your Majesty might return to the performance?" Davenport asks.

"Right." I make to step forward but get tugged back into the room on a yelp.

"One moment, guys." Josh slams the door and thrusts me up against it. "You forgot something," he purrs, brushing his lips across mine.

"Josh, I really should go."

"Kiss me." He licks a precise line across the seam of my lips. And I'm his. His hands caging my neck, he holds my head still and we kiss the kind of kiss you never want to stop. Because it's blinding. Because it's so full of feelings. So full of love. It's deep, controlled, and passionate, the swirl of silent feelings and emotions between us capturing us both completely. And it's when I feel the fire return. But not simply lust-fueled fire. My light has returned in more ways than one. My heart has been kick-started, ready to do what I was destined to do. Fight. Rule. Reign.

Josh's throaty growl expresses his fulfilment. My whimpers express my bliss. "I don't want to let you go," he whispers into my mouth, his hands tightening on my neck.

"It's only for a few hours."

"Too long." He finishes with a wide sweep of his tongue around mine, withdrawing and dotting kisses across my lips, from one corner to the other. "Be careful, okay?"

"It is you who needs to be careful." Something glimmers in my side vision. "My tiara." I point across the room where it is on the carpet, making Josh look over his shoulder. He leaves me at the door to collect it, bringing it back and setting it neatly on my head.

"And my ring," I say quietly, and his hands pause while rearranging my hair.

"You're not putting that ring on. You're no longer engaged."

"But Haydon doesn't know that yet," I point out a little timidly. "And neither does the rest of the world."

The expansion of his broad chest is patience being breathed in. "I can't let you do it. I'm sorry." He shakes his head as if to affirm it. "Actually, I'm not sorry. You're not wearing it." A chaste, teasing kiss is placed on my cheek. "And that is the end of that."

I give up trying to protest. I can't blame him. Besides, I feel like I need to reserve my grit and fight for later when I find Sir Don and David Sampson. So I guess that really is the end of that. "Fine. But I can't leave it in here."

"Of course." Josh goes and collects it from where he threw it earlier. "I'll take it." In his pocket it goes, a guarantee that the ring will never make it back onto my finger. It may be noticed, but . . . so what? "I'll see you back at your place," he says on a grin, and I smile, pulling the door open behind me.

"My place," I confirm, turning to exit. The first thing I notice is Damon's wild eyes. Then Davenport's despair-filled gaze. And then . . .

"Haydon," I breathe as he appears from nowhere, his eyes lasers of hatred burning past me.

Into Josh.

I look over my shoulder and see Josh mirroring Haydon's threatening stance, two men boring holes of abhorrence into each other. *Oh God.*

"This doesn't look like a very political meeting," Haydon says, throwing Damon and Davenport a derisive look. Both men remain silent as Haydon steams forward and claims my arm, provoking Josh to lunge forward on a growl that could bring down the Opera House.

"Josh," I yell as Damon intercepts him, pulling him back. I give Damon a look he reads well. Haydon could very well tell Sir Don and Sampson about this little showdown. I have to make sure Josh gets to Claringdon and stays there.

"Easy, mate," Damon says, looking at Haydon like he might kill him. "Just let her go."

Haydon manhandles me to the door, and though shocked, I do nothing to stop him. "You stay away from my fiancée," he hisses, shoving Davenport away when he tries to intervene. "You should be dealing with him," he yells, moving his hold to my hand. His grip is tight. "I can *deal* with my fiancée."

The sounds of Josh's struggles sound out behind me, and I look over my shoulder as I'm dragged back to the theatre, seeing Damon working hard to placate him. "No scenes, Josh," Damon says. "Calm it down."

"I'll fuckin' kill him."

"You and me both," Damon mumbles, his death glare on Haydon's back.

As Davenport trails us and we get farther away, Haydon loosens his grip of my hand and I flex it, grimacing at the crack of my bones. He leads me to our seats. "Sit," he orders, more or less pushing me down. I scan our surroundings, hyper alert and worried about anyone who could be watching us. "You will not see him again," he says quietly as he lowers to his chair, but there is no mistaking the threatening edge in his tone. "I am your husband, and you will obey me. Your status doesn't affect your obligations to me as my wife."

I stare at his profile in absolute astonishment. I hold my tongue, but not in alarm. Or fear. Or in submission. Now, he has only my contempt. The man is a leech. And if it's the last thing I do, I will make *him* yield. He will damn well capitulate his fantasized throne.

I don't tell him I am not his wife. I don't point out he is ahead of himself. And I don't tell him I will never obey him.

I simply consider how wrong I was to ever fear hurting Haydon's feelings. The man has his father's blood running through his veins. And now he can go to hell with him and stay there.

30

AS SOON AS the opera finishes, I'm the first to the car with Damon, Haydon following not far behind. Once I'm comfortable inside, my bodyguard turns back from the driver's seat to find me. "Okay, ma'am?"

"I will be."

He nods, checking out the window. "I think the power has gone to his head."

I laugh under my breath. "Quite."

Davenport opens my car door and bends to get to my seated level. "Am I to assume a meeting is to be arranged for the morning?"

"No," I say, looking past him to see Haydon coming down the steps with Kim. "There will be no meeting with my council on this."

"Ma'am?"

I return my attention to Davenport. "Telling them what I am going to do will only give them another opportunity to stop me. No." I'm not making that mistake again. "Please draft an announcement about my canceled engagement and have it ready for the morning."

"And your relationship with Mr. Jameson?"

I breathe in deeply. "Tell the world."

"Very well." Davenport closes the door and walks around the back, opening the other for Haydon.

He falls into the seat without so much as a thank you, turning his angry eyes onto me. "I hope you got a thrill out of humiliating me."

"You humiliated yourself," I spit back. "Drive, Damon." I turn away from him, disappointed I once thought more of the man who seems to have fooled us all.

The journey is drenched in an unbearable atmosphere, Damon constantly checking me in the rearview mirror. When Haydon's hand falls onto my knee, I stare at it silently, knowing he'll want to get me into bed tonight. Claim me.

Too bad I am already claimed. I peel his hand away and shove it back at him. "Don't touch me." I make myself as small as possible, pushed against the door.

When we pull up outside Claringdon, I don't wait for the footman to open the door. I do it myself. "Please take Mr. Sampson to his residence," I tell Damon.

"I'm staying here," Haydon declares, getting out the other side.

I shoot Damon a panicked look. I knew it. "Thumbs down," I murmur, though my head of security is already on his way out of the driver's seat, not needing to be told. He meets Haydon at the front of the car, chest to chest. "I don't think so," Damon says menacingly. "Turn around and get back in the car."

"Get out of my way." Haydon's chest puffs out, his shoulders pulled back, though his attempts to look bigger, more imposing, fail miserably. Damon is inches above him, his stance threatening.

He looks homicidal. "Get. In. The. Car."

"Who do you think you're talking to?"

"You."

"Adeline," Haydon yells, throwing me an expectant look. "Call off your dog."

"Get in the car, Haydon," I tell him calmly. "Don't make a scene." I'm aware of the staff behind us, as well as the car up front that carried Davenport, Kim, Olive, and Jenny, who are all silently looking on.

Haydon laughs at me, trying to push his way past an unmoving Damon. "Get the hell out of my way. I am staying here with my fiancée."

That word from his mouth makes me want to throw up. "I am not your fiancée," I spit. "I am not your anything." I pick up the bottom of my dress and take the stairs to the door, stopping halfway when I hear a thud. I turn and find Haydon wrestling with Damon, throwing punches like a madman. "Haydon!"

Damon ducks once and swings his fist, catching Haydon on the jaw with a deafening crack, sending him flying back onto the bonnet of the car. "I warned you," Damon hisses, shaking his hand. "All you had to do was get in the fucking car."

Haydon holds his face, flexing his jaw as he scrambles off the bonnet. "You're fired," he yells, and Damon laughs, so hard I'm certain he'll fall over.

"Shut up, you prick." Grabbing Haydon by the scruff of his suit jacket, he manhandles him around the car and throws him into the back. "Ever lay a finger on her again, even a touch, it won't just be a jab to the jaw next time." He slams the door and roughly pulls himself back together as he stamps his way back to the driver's side. "Posh, entitled twat," he grunts, throwing himself in the car.

The roar of the engine jerks me out of my inertness, the tires skidding away. "Ma'am?" Olive asks quietly, resting a hand on my arm.

I look at her, and though my vision is a little hazy from my welling eyes, I see sympathy. I turn to find a dozen other members of my staff standing in stunned silence, waiting for me to move. "I think I'd like a drink," I say to no one in particular. "A stiff one."

Olive nods to one of the footmen, who darts into the palace like a whippet. "I'll have one, too," Davenport calls to his back, brushing over his tired face with a rough hand.

"Make that three," Kim shouts, coming to collect me. "I'm in shock."

"Aren't we all?" I ask, continuing up the steps with her help. "Would anyone else like a drink?" I gaze across the faces of my staff, who are all looking out the corners of their eyes to each other, obviously wondering if it is a trick question. "Stiff drinks all round," I answer for them, letting Olive take my purse as we breach the entrance.

"I think I might have one, too." Mother appears, her face grave, and I know it is because she has just witnessed everything unfold. She comes straight to me and takes me in a hug that both surprises me and comforts me. "I didn't know what to do with the American that Damon's men brought back, so I put him in the Claret Lounge."

I have not the faintest idea why I laugh lightly. There is really nothing funny about any of this. "I'm not letting him go this time."

She pulls back and gives my face a soft stroke. "You should not have the first time. I realize that now."

My lip wobbles. Stupid lip. But this evening has been an ambush of eye-openers that could curl my body into a ball of anxiety. "I need to see him."

"He's here," Josh calls from the doorway. My eyes shoot to him, my breath gone at the sight of him here. In my palace. Among my people. My American boy. The window to the Claret Lounge looks out onto the front courtyard. Did he see? A small nod confirms he knows what I am thinking. "I decided brawling in front of the Queen Mother wasn't the way forward," he says, and I wonder just how hard it was for him to fight with his instinct to run out and give Haydon a thump.

I laugh through a sob, taking the bottom of my dress and going to Josh. In front of everyone standing in the foyer.

He throws his arms around me, and tears tumble unstoppably down my cheeks as he hushes me quietly. "Okay?" he asks on a whisper, to which I can only manage to nod. Now, yes. Everything is so okay. "Hey," He tries to wrestle me away. "Let me see you." A firm hand grips my loose hair and tugs back, forcing me to obey. When he finds my eyes, he smiles lightly. "I love you."

My bottom lip quivers once again, it all becoming too much. "How much?" I want to hear it, hear if it's as desperately as I love him. Hear if it hurts as much. "Tell me how much."

Stroking down my cheek, he smiles, oblivious to the spectators behind us. "More than I will ever be able to show you during our lifetime. But you bet your queenly ass I'll try, Your Majesty."

I look at him, using this precious time to absorb him, feeling his face, his lips, looking into his eyes. "My king," I whisper, and he kisses me, taking us away from this life and transporting us to the clouds.

A small cough.

Our tongues dance and glide, roll and explore.

Another cough.

I breathe out on a sigh, feeling his hair, silky and soft through my fingers.

A loud cough.

Josh pulls away, and for the first time since I have known him, he looks awkward. And there is definitely a tinge of color in his cheeks. "Are you blushing?"

He clears his throat and drops his mouth to my ear. "I think I just violated the Queen of England in front of her loyal subjects."

I grin and look over my shoulder, finding an audience, most holding their smiles in check. Because to be pleased about this would be to defy royal law. "That drink," I say, and a tray is under my nose within a second, the footman clearly not wanting to interrupt us. "Thank you." I take one for Josh, too. "Davenport, is everything in hand?"

"Absolutely, ma'am."

"Very good." I take a sip of my drink. "Please do let me know when you are finished. If I'm needed, I will be in my private quarters." I take Josh's hand and pull him along beside me. "Good evening."

A flurry of murmured words follows us up the stairs, and Josh constantly looks back over his shoulder as we go. "They're all staring at us."

I look, too, seeing Davenport move in, ready to reinforce their oath of silence. Not that it matters. By tomorrow, the world will know. And this time they really will. "They will go about their business once we're gone," I assure him, my steps hurrying.

"Slow down, woman." Josh trips up the last step and sends his drink flying, the glass hitting the carpet, the contents spilling everywhere. "Oh shit."

"Leave it," I order, pulling him up and on.

"You're certainly throwing your weight around today."

"I'm about to throw my weight on you," I say, laughing when he speeds up, overtaking me so it is now him dragging me along.

"Josh!" I yelp, my legs getting tangled in my dress. "I'm going to fa . . . oh!" I'm tossed over his shoulder like a sack, my drink joining his on the carpet. He runs full pelt across the gallery landing. Then he stops abruptly. "Shit. Which way is it?"

"That way," I laugh, pointing, though of course, he can't see in which direction I'm pointing because he can't see my arms.

"Which way?" He turns on the spot a few times, making me dizzy.

"That way." I can barely talk through my giggles.

"Adeline, I'm about to come in my pants. Which way?"

"The portraits."

"I take it you mean through the pictures of old people hanging every two yards?" He's off without confirmation, running with me over his shoulder before every king and queen that has ever lived. What would they think? What would they say?

"Faster." I slap his arse like I could be egging on a horse, my stomach aching from tensing where it's bent over his shoulder.

We're through the doors at lightning speed, and I'm tossed on the couch clumsily, Josh landing on top of me. I get him in my sights, brushing my hair from my face, feeling him resting perfectly between my legs. "I couldn't wait to get you into bed," he declares, banging our mouths together. "You've lost your tiara again."

"Don't care." I attack his mouth savagely. Everything I need is here right now, and I start to wrestle his jacket from his shoulders, not releasing his mouth to see what I'm doing. He helps, albeit clumsily. Our clothes are ripped off piece by piece and tossed blindly away, my feet taking care of his trousers and boxers, my foot hooking into the waistbands and pushing them down his legs. He gets to his knees, reaching back to push his shoes off and get his trousers and boxers past his feet. Then he rips off my knickers.

"Bra," he says urgently, reaching under my back as I arch. One flick has the clasp undone, and one yank has if off and on the floor with the rest of our clothes. "Let's call that foreplay," he declares, taking his arousal and guiding it to between my thighs. "Does my queen object?"

"Nope."

"Good." He sinks in smoothly on a ragged exhale, right to the root. "Oh . . . yeah."

I sigh, and he settles, hands braced above my head on the arm of the couch. "I'm just gonna stay here for a few moments, so you know." He kisses my cheek, the swell of him inside me sparking spasms in my muscles, making me clench. "Stop it," Josh warns.

"I can't help it."

"Adeline, I'll come."

"I'm not doing anything."

"Yes, your pussy is squeezing my dick. Stop it." He looks at me, his jaw tight as he fights to find control.

I flex my hips, encouraged by the surges of pleasure pulsing throughout me. "I have no control with you."

"God damn you, woman." His groin rolls, meeting my flex,

taking his depth to its fullest. He starts pumping, abandoning trying to find that control. But though we are both so desperate, we are both very measured. Every stroke is incapacitating, my hands scratching at his back as I lazily toss my head from side to side. Straightaway, it's there, a climax brewing, my groin heavy with the pressure of the pleasure. In and out, slowly and exact, his skin wet, my muscles hard. "We're so fuckin' good together." He can hardly talk, his cheeks puffing out on every drive, pushing me up the couch. It's clear neither of us will last long, but for the first time, I don't let that stop me from claiming my climax. I'm not worried about making it last. Not worried about when the next time will be.

I buck beneath him, closing my eyes and throwing my head back. The heat of his mouth finds my breast, my hands finding his arse and following the motions of his swaying hips.

"Yeah?" he asks, driving on, sending me wild. "That good, darlin'?" He picks up his pace, nibbling on my nipple, and I drop my head, finding his eyes watching me coming undone. His face is pure, exquisite indulgence. "You comin' for me?"

I nod, scraping my way up his back to his hair, clinging on, knowing I'm about to be bent with the intensity of my release. Josh moves up and punches his fists into the couch, bracing himself and slamming home.

He goes first, his chest concaving, his last drive a long, circling grind, as he moans a broken, strangled moan. And the look on his face sends me over. My arms fly up to the couch behind me, my back arching, as my orgasm tears through me, taking everything out of me until I break and sink into the cushions, my breathing gone.

"God save the fuckin' Queen," he mumbles, falling down on top of me. "I'm fucked."

Unable to respond, I close my eyes and let my mind shut down with my body, blindly grabbing the throw from the back of the couch and pulling it over us. And we doze off. Together. Always together.

31

"WHY AM I so nervous?" I ask, pacing in front of the fireplace, up and down, up and down.

"Oh, I don't know," Kim muses, very casual-like. "Because you're about to change history?"

"Possibly." Or it could be because I am worried about Sir Don and David Sampson throwing a spanner in my works. Again. I'm certain Haydon will have told them about Josh. I'm certain they must be waiting for a call summoning them to the palace. They could already be hatching their plan to derail me. My eyes fall to the couch where Josh is asleep, just to remind myself he is here and we are safe from any attempts to rip us apart. We didn't make it to bed last night, because neither of us woke up after dozing off. Josh still hasn't, mumbling sleepily as I peeled my way from beneath him to answer the door to Kim. Once I'd made sure he was covered, of course. That throw is slowly making its way down to his waist with each cute little stretch or move he makes. Wandering over, I pull it up to his chest to reduce the risk of giving Kim an eyeful of something she probably won't appreciate like I would. I smile when he nuzzles his face into the cushion. He's dead to the world.

"He's cute when he's asleep," Kim says from the chair opposite. "Even covered in a floral blanket."

I grin as I walk to the tray Olive delivered, taking the coffee she poured. "He's cute all the time." I sip, smiling as Kim rolls her eyes at me.

"You sound so in love, I want to vomit."

I settle on the chair next to her. "I want Sir Don and Sampson summoned, but only once the statement about Josh and I has been released. I don't trust those two as far as I can throw them. I want them gone."

"Wow. You mean business. I've missed this Adeline."

I smile. I've missed her, too. "I want to get the inevitable done with." My phone rings from across the room, but I don't rush to answer. "Leave it," I say when Kim makes to stand. "It will be Haydon again."

She lowers, looking awkward. "What on earth got into him last night?"

I sigh. "I have no idea." Was he showing his true colors for the first time in thirty years? If so, he has done a marvelous job of hiding them for so long. Or was that simply the behavior of a desperate man?

"And what are you going to do with the American on your couch?"

"Really, Kim?" I set my cup down and stand, pulling in my robe. "You talk about him like he's a vagrant I found on the streets."

She shrugs. "You can't keep him locked up in here forever."

"Watch me," I joke, just as Josh groans and turns to his back, his naked arms stretching above his head. It's a long stretch, one that nearly has me moaning in appreciation. His taut arms form waves of muscles, his stomach rippling gorgeously. He opens one eye and looks around the room, finding Kim first and bolting upright. "Morning," I chirp, pouring a coffee for him.

He relaxes when he sees me, dropping to his back again.

"Morning." His voice is low, rough, and lovely. If Kim weren't here, I'd be on him faster than I plan on firing Sir Don and David. Pretty bloody fast. "What time is it?" Josh asks.

"Nine."

"Nine?" He's back up again, but not sitting this time. He's standing, and the blanket falls to the ground at his feet. "Fuck, I have a meeting at ten." He swipes his trousers up from the floor and starts rootling through the pocket. When he finds his phone, he curses at the screen, cringing as he dials.

"Um, Josh?" I call, pulling him back around. I purse my lips and nod at his groin, prompting him to glance down.

"Fuck." He drops to the couch and pulls the blanket onto his lap, and I laugh, looking to Kim who has her eyes covered. "Sorry."

"Things have seriously changed around here," she mumbles, getting to her feet as she peeks through her spread fingers. "Is he decent?"

"He's decent." My grin is colossal. "Who are you calling?" I ask Josh.

"Tammy. She's seriously gonna kick my ass." He shrinks where he's sitting, his face screwing up as the sound of a very displeased female filters down the line.

I leave him to it and walk Kim to the door. "Have you seen Davenport this morning?"

"He's in his office finalizing the announcement. All I keep hearing is the sound of keys being smacked hard and a few curse words thrown in here and there." I laugh to myself. I can imagine. I also feel a tad guilty. I expect he's been holed up in his office all night attempting to write the announcement that will change British history. "I think he might be a few hours yet," Kim goes on. "So you have some spare time this morning."

"I do?" What a novelty.

"Don't worry, I have something to keep you occupied."

"Who said I needed anything to keep me occupied?" I ask coyly, looking over my shoulder to Josh.

"Me. It looks like he's got plans, anyway."

"Not if I have anything to do with it." I let Kim hand me a folder stuffed full of photographs. "What's this?"

"The BBC is working on a documentary about the Royals," she says, and I look at her, worried. "It's fine. We've negotiated consultation rights."

"Thank goodness," I breathe, dreading what they may have dug up. Because that would be frightening. "So these are . . . ?"

"Photographs from the Royal archives going back seventy years. You need to let me know which ones you're happy to have released."

I flick through the first few, smiling when I see me as a baby. I'm sitting on a blanket in the grounds of Farringdon Palace, the place that was our home before my grandfather died and my father became King. Eddie and John are running around me. My smile turns sad. One brother dead, the other seemingly on a mission to kill himself. I snap the folder closed. This could be hard, all these memories, happy faces, and scenes masking secrets and lies. I clear my throat of the unexpected lump that has found its way there. "I'll do it as soon as I have showered."

"Okay. There's also some video footage."

"There is?"

"Old VCR tapes. Loads of them. I've put them in a box on your desk."

"Do we even have a VCR player?"

"I'll find one." She heads off, and I close the door, placing the folder on a nearby table. Josh's head is in his hands when I turn to find him. "Everything okay?"

"I'm in deep shit." He stands and starts tugging on his boxers. "She's managed to postpone my meeting by an hour."

Wait, what? "Josh, you can't leave." I go to him, stopping him from pulling his trousers on. I'm not taking any chances. I'm not foolish enough to think Haydon has not told Sir Don and David

Sampson about Josh being at the Opera House. "Just wait until the announcement has been released."

"That could be hours. I have to go."

"Josh, you can't." I swipe up his shirt and move away, and he drops his chin to his chest, looking at me seriously.

"Is that a direct order?" he asks.

"I'm not playing."

His shoulders drop. "It's an important meeting with my UK agent, Adeline. I have to show up."

"Aren't we important?" I feel awful for more or less emotionally blackmailing him. But . . ."Please," I beg. "Just stay with me."

"I can't miss it." He reaches for his shirt and snatches it from my hands. "I'll have Damon call Bates." He buttons his shirt and throws on his tuxedo jacket, and my anxiety grows with each piece of clothing he puts on. "I'm not putting my life on hold for those two assholes." He marches to the door.

"I demand you stay," I shout at his back. "I am the Queen and you will do as I say." I snap my mouth closed the second the disgusting words have fallen past my lips, watching as Josh comes to a gradual stop by the door. I squint, my face screwing up. I'm so disappointed in myself. But I'm desperate. And stupid.

Trepidation rolls through me as he slowly turns toward me, his face a picture of repulsion. "You know, if we're going to have a future together, you can't throw that line at me every time you don't get your way." He takes the handle. "And you're *my* queen, not *the* queen." Pulling the door open, he leaves. And my panic rockets.

"Josh, please!" I don't mean to sound so frightened, but I truly am. I would put nothing past them now. God knows what they will do next to derail my plans. "Please," I murmur, blinking back my tears.

Stopping in his tracks, Josh's entire body deflates under his crumpled tuxedo. "God damn it," he sighs, turning around and pacing to me, taking my quaking body in a hug. He shushes me, cupping the back of my head. "Okay. Don't get your panties in a twist."

"I don't wear panties," I sob into his chest, and he laughs, burying his face into my hair.

"I'll stay."

I puddle in his arms, my relief great. "Thank you."

"Don't thank me." Kissing my hair, he pulls back and wipes under my eyes with the pads of his thumbs. "But don't you ever throw that line at me ever again, do you hear me?"

I pout on a nod, pretty ashamed of myself. And with nothing else to say in my defense, I reach up on my tiptoes and bring our mouths together. If only to remind me—to reassure me—that he's still here. I didn't intend for it to be a full-on, hot kiss, but Josh soon turns it into that, growling deep in his throat as he explores my mouth with a keen, firm tongue. "I said I'd stay," he mumbles, and I smile against him, breaking our kiss and sinking my face into his neck, my arms locked around his shoulders. His heartbeat is strong. My tummy swirls, a mixture of happiness and anxiousness. "So since I'm staying at Her Majesty's pleasure, what is she going to do with me?"

I break away reluctantly and let Josh sweep my hair from my eyes. "I have a ton of photographs and video footage to look at."

"What for?"

"A documentary that's airing on television about my wonderful family and me." Thunder rumbles within me, my heart splitting a little with the thought of what I must do. It will be impossible to look at those photographs without pairing them with this lie or that. Without sinking into a black pit of sadness. "Will you help me?" I ask, hopeful. Josh makes everything easier to tackle, and this will be no exception.

"Would love to." My cheeks are squeezed, a kiss planted on my squished lips. "Shower first." I'm turned by the shoulders and directed into the bathroom, and that wonderful sense of serenity takes me in its arms and dulls the thunder. Soon, Josh will have chased the storm away completely.

I let him dictate the pace. I let him push my robe from my shoulders slowly. I let him strip himself while I watch, quiet and content. I let him walk me backward into the cubicle. I let him pick me up and direct my legs around his waist.

And I let him push me up the wall on a muffled cry of ecstasy.

Everything about this moment is calm and peaceful; the only thunder now is that of the spray hitting our bodies and the flames raging within me. "I love you so much," he whispers, rearing back and gliding home.

I push away the water pouring down his face and look at him. Look at the man who is not only changing *my* story, but changing history's story.

32

"HOW DO YOU find your way around this place?" Josh asks as we wander the palace rooms, taking the long way around to my office. I smile at his amazement, his eyes always high, taking in the grandeur that runs to every corner of each space. He looks utterly adorable with his damp hair, his shirt hanging out, and his bow tie hanging around his neck. Perfectly messy and ruggedly adorable in my perfect palace.

"Years of exploring." We pass a footman who stops and takes position, nodding his head respectfully. "Morning," I chirp.

"Morning, ma'am." His curious eyes follow us all the way to the Throne Room, where two members of the household stand, guarding the doors. I can see the effort it's taking them not to gawk at Josh.

"Why don't you take a break?" I ask, as one of them pushes the doors open for us. "I'm sure Dolly will fix you some brunch."

They look at each other briefly, bemused. "Ma'am?" one questions.

"Chop-chop," I prompt, and they make tracks, leaving me to close the doors with Josh and me inside.

Josh's hands slide into his pockets, and he takes slow steps to the center of the room, circling on the spot, looking around him. "Jesus," he all but breathes, taking in the lavish gold and crimson décor that reeks royalty. "I don't think that chandelier is big enough."

I chuckle when he points to the ceiling. "It's a showpiece, I know."

"What lucky person gets to polish that beast?"

"Someone who doesn't have butterfingers."

His eyes fall to the thrones on the far side of the room, and he looks over his shoulder on a little smirk. I roll my eyes, knowing exactly what is currently whirling around in that gorgeous head of his. Passing him, I take the few red-carpeted steps to the two red velvet chairs, turning when I'm in front of them. I cock my head on a smile that Josh matches, if mild, as he lazily strolls toward me, coming to a stop at the bottom of the steps.

Maintaining his grin, he lowers to his knee and bows his head. "Your Majesty, I am here to serve you." He peeks up, now a full-on, dashing grin splashed across his face. "Or service you. Whatever."

I laugh and take a couple of the steps down, crouching to get myself at his level. I raise my imaginary sword and lower it onto his shoulder. "Joshua Jameson, you have undertaken to accept the accolade of Queen Adeline of England's boyfriend." I press my lips together, trying to remain serious.

"What am I supposed to say now?" he asks on a whisper, as if the Throne Room is full of watchers. As if this is official.

"You say, 'I have'," I whisper back.

"Oh," He clears his throat. "Too fuckin' right I have."

My smile could not be contained if my mouth was sewn shut. "Joshua Jameson, you have been deemed fit for this high estate by your peers, and have indicated your willingness to accept this honor . . ." I fade off, still smiling, when he cocks an eyebrow.

"Honor?" he asks.

"Yes."

"Okay. Continue."

Amusement overwhelms me, yet I push on through it. "Do you now swear by all that you hold sacred—"

"I hold only *you* sacred"—he blows me a kiss—"for the record."

"Let me finish," I admonish, no matter how thrilled I am to hear that. I continue when he nods. "Do you swear by all that you hold sacred, true, and holy, that you will honor and defend your Queen and her kingdom?"

"I couldn't give a fuck about her kingdom."

"Josh," I say on a laugh, falling to my backside on the step. "This is serious business."

"It's a bit verbose, isn't it?" He moves from one knee to the other and gets comfortable again, as I right my own position, crouching again and realigning my pretend sword on his shoulder.

I clear my throat. "This is the shortened, ancient version."

"In that case, don't ever make me a knight for real, okay?"

"Okay. So, will you?"

"What?"

"Honor and protect me?"

"Oh, yes, of course. And fuck you blind every day for the rest of our lives together."

"How thrilling," I reply, and he winks. "Then having sworn these solemn oaths, I, Queen Adeline of England, by right of arms, do dub you with my sword, once for honor"—I move my imaginary sword to his other shoulder—"twice for duty"—I take my sword back and forth as he smirks at my poor attempt to keep a straight face—"and thrice for chivalry." I stand and look down at him. "Arise, Prince Charming."

"No." He shakes his head.

I frown through my smile. "You must."

"Nope." He reaches for my hand and pulls me down so I'm sitting on the step before him again.

"What are you doing?"

He shrugs, a little nonchalant. "Shouldn't a man kneel when he's asking the woman he loves to marry him?"

Air leaves my lungs so fast, I'm sure the release of pressure would have me flying around the room if I was not sitting. I look into his eyes, my tongue thick, no words coming to me.

"I don't have a ring." He takes both of my hands and holds them so very tightly. "Not right now." Abandoning my hands, he walks up a step on his knees and takes my face in his palms. "But I have a heart bursting with love for you, my queen." My hands find his on my face, holding them there as he kisses each corner of my mouth. "I will love you. I will honor you. I will kiss the fuckin' ground you walk on for the rest of my life." A small snivel tumbles past my lips unstoppably, my eyes stinging. "But I will never obey you."

"I don't want you to," I more or less sob.

"And you will only ever bow to me."

"I will."

He pushes his mouth to mine, sending me back against the steps, and ravishes me completely, here in the Throne Room of Claringdon Palace. "That's a yes, right?"

"Yes." I laugh, trapping him in my arms, happiness like I have never felt before claiming me, and I know it will never let me go. Not even the inevitable reaction of my advisors can tarnish it. The rebellious queen will go down in history. Whether that be in good standing or bad is not something I can bring myself to care about. Because right now, love truly does conquer all. Even the British Monarchy and its obsolete customs. I will marry the man I love, the man who is the very essence of the pulse in my veins, and no sense of expectation will stop me. "I hope you are ready for this," I murmur across his mouth, gorging on the taste of him.

"I've been ready since I rescued you in a helicopter, Adeline. Your status has never changed to me. You've always simply been mine."

His ardent words only increase the tears. I feel so lucky in this moment. So blessed to have found a man who is so fiercely determined to have me, no matter the cost, and more than that, one I am so incredibly in love with. "You make me so happy." Josh's love serves like an invisible force field, protecting me from anything that could damage me. Hurt me. Only he has that ability now. Only he can hurt me. Everything else is inconsequential.

"Good." He helps me to my feet and smothers my damp face with his lips before gently wiping under my eyes. "Okay?"

Okay? I'm walking on clouds. I nod, and he takes my hand with a solid grip, taking the lead out of the Throne Room. "I can't look at those thrones without thinking how much better you look on mine."

A burst of laughter escapes me, and he gives me a devilish smirk as he looks back at me. "You are terrible."

"Which way to your office?" he asks when we come to a crossroads of corridors. I go to overtake him but get tugged back. "No, I'm fed up with you leading the way around here. Which way?"

I point, and he gets us moving again. I smile at his back, letting him lead. The man I'm going to marry. My American boy.

He motions to the double doors on the gallery landing when we make it there, and I nod. Josh lets us in, drops my hand, and takes himself straight to the large, important-looking chair on the other side of my desk. The Sovereign's chair. The chair that has only ever had royal backsides sitting on it. I think he must know this if the mischievous grin on his face is anything to go by. Brazenly, and on an extravagant sigh, he lowers and stretches out his body, kicking his feet up onto the desk. "Off with my head?" he asks, folding his arms behind his head.

"Which head?" I quip, doing what no king or queen has ever done before; sit on the wrong side of their desk. "Comfortable?"

"Yep." He looks around, his lips twisting in contemplation. "Can you imagine the conversations that have happened in here?"

"Yes, I can." I laugh, reaching for the box of tapes Kim has left for me. Those conversations will have shaped history, and I'm about to have one myself. Probably one of the most momentous conversations this room has ever heard. Just as soon as the announcement has gone out and the people with whom I need to have that conversation arrive.

I pull out a few tapes, looking through the labels on the front telling me what I will discover when I find the strength I know I will need to watch them. John's tenth birthday. Eddie's baptism. My grandfather's silver jubilee. I inhale and set the tapes back in the box.

"What's up?" Josh asks, taking his legs down and resting his elbows on the wood, leaning in.

I shrug, blasé, though it doesn't wash with Josh. "I'm not relishing the thought of sifting through decades of my family history in photographs and videos."

"Then don't do it."

"It's a lovely notion, but part of our relationship with the media is give and take. I give them something to work with, something I'm comfortable with, and they don't take liberties."

"So what do *we* give them?" He reaches for my hand and strokes over my finger where soon he will put a ring. His question is a good one, and though I am steaming ahead, guns blazing, if you will, I appreciate that this will have to be handled delicately.

"Davenport is still in his office working on the statement. As soon as he is done, we will discuss with the PR team."

We both look up when we hear a knock on the door. I don't feel it necessary to eject Josh from my chair. Everyone around here will have to get used to his presence, no matter where he decides to put himself. "Come in," I call, dropping Josh's hand and resting back.

Kim enters, her eyebrows arching sharply when she finds Josh and me in the wrong seats. "You left this in your private quarters." She sets the folder full of photographs on the desk.

"Thanks, Kim."

"And you have a visitor."

I feel my heart pick up pace. "Oh?" Please, not Sir Don or

Sampson. I need that announcement approved and sent before they can stop it.

Her head tilts, as does mine. "His Royal Highness Prince Edward, ma'am."

"Eddie's here?" I'm up out of my chair quickly. "Is he sober?"

"I believe so."

That simple confirmation makes me happy. "Please, send him in." I start pacing the room, feeling nervous to be receiving my brother. What is the meaning of his visit? Will he be hostile? Sarcastic? Bitter? Has he seen Davenport or our mother since he arrived?

"Sit down, Adeline," Josh says softly, interrupting my mounting silent questions. "I'm sure it'll be fine."

I lower to the chair. "I'm nervous."

"You should be. He might ask you if he can marry that porn star he's been shacked up with."

"Oh, behave." My fingers twiddle apprehensively in my lap. Good Lord, what if that really is why he's here? I have just accepted a proposal from Josh, an entirely different breed of unsuitable, but unsuitable nevertheless. "And she's a model, as I understand it. He's just rebelling." I'm telling myself more than Josh.

"Like you?"

"I'm not rebelling. I'm dragging the Monarchy into the twenty-first century, albeit kicking and screaming."

"So does this lowly American actor get a title?" he asks, hitching a cocky eyebrow. "Because I think Prince Charming suits me well."

"You are, as ever, incorrigible."

"Actually, scrap that. I'm leaning more toward *King*."

"King of cocky?"

"No, King of *you*," he says simply, and I don't argue, because he is absolutely correct. But declaring him officially my king may be a step too far for the institution. One shocking step at a time. "Let us keep that as a personal joke."

"I'm not joking. Hey, are you going to be shoving a plum in my mouth?"

"Absolutely not." Goodness, stripping him of that rough American southern drawl? Out of the question. "I love the way you speak." I love everything about him, and I would never try to change that. And if anyone else tries to, they will face my wrath. "I'll keep you just the way you are, thank you very much."

"Honored."

"You should be." Our grins collide across the desk, but mine falls the second the door knocks. "Oh, heck," I mumble, standing and rearranging my pencil skirt and blouse. "Do I look okay?"

"Adeline, chill out."

That is easy for him to say. "Come in," I call.

Kim lets herself in, and my eyes fall straight past her to my brother. "Oh, Eddie," I whisper in despair. I almost don't recognize him. The Playboy Prince, with the cheeky twinkle in his eye, has been replaced by the Fallen Prince, with black, empty holes for eyes.

"His Royal Highness Prince Edward," Kim declares softly, and Eddie's eyes fall closed, as if hearing his title pains him. Painful for me as well, I know it does. He shows no attempt to enter, just hovers on the threshold of my office, scared to come in. So I go to him, doing what instinct is telling me and what my heart cannot stop. I throw my arms around his weak body and cuddle him as tightly as I think he can stand, so thankful when he doesn't object or push me away.

Like he needs me to hold him up, he clings on, a lost little boy trying to navigate the cruel blows that have been thrown his way. "I don't want to feel this way anymore, Addy," he croaks into my neck, burying himself deeply to hide. "The bitterness, the hurt, I can't stand it anymore."

Devastated by his words, I close my eyes, feeling the river of tears pour down my cheeks. My beloved Eddie, so broken and scared.

"I'll fix you," I assure him. "I promise I will fix you." Whatever it takes, I will reinstate that twinkle in his eye, find the man he has lost during this torrid time in our lives.

I hear him sniffle and feel him pull away, clearing his throat. I quickly brush at my cheeks and then his, linking arms with him and pulling him into the room so Kim can leave and shut the door.

"Shit," Eddie curses, finally finding Josh at my desk. "Mr. Hollywood." He turns a questioning look my way. "What's going on?"

"That is a story for another day," I assure him, my focus now on Eddie. "Sit down."

"I'd do as she says," Josh pipes in quietly, a sympathetic smile pointed Eddie's way. "She's in a seriously officious mood today."

"Why are you here?" Eddie lowers, casting his eyes between Josh and me. "The last I heard my sister was engaged to Hayd—"

I cough, stopping Eddie from uttering the name that'll likely send Josh into orbit.

I feel more than see his hackles rise, Eddie's words igniting his temper. "Momentary lapse of sanity on her part," Josh bites back, making Eddie raise his palms in surrender.

"Hey, we all have those." He laughs a little under his breath, resting back in his chair. "That's why I came."

"Sorry?"

"I saw you on TV last night at the Royal Ballet. With Hay . . ." Eddie drifts off and gives Josh a sorry smile. "With *him*. Addy, you were miserable through that smile. I had to come and tell you not to do it."

I could cry. I knew Eddie would see the turmoil inside me. And though he's a little late—I was hoping for his intervention way before now, to talk some sense into me—I feel overcome with comfort that he is now here. "I'm not doing it."

"She's *definitely* not doing it," Josh clarifies.

"Well, I guessed that, since you're sitting here looking all sexed-up." Eddie takes his eyes from Josh's *sexed-up* form and finds me. I fight my blush back. "So what happened?"

"Don't ask."

"He got a little physical with your sister." Josh is positively buzzing with anger again.

"What the hell?" Eddie balks. "He hit you?"

"No." I wave a flippant hand that I know provokes Josh's anger further. "A little rough, maybe."

"I'll kill him," Eddie declares.

"Get in line," Josh spits, standing, like he could do with walking off some of his rage.

Goodness, I need to defuse this quickly before my brother and Josh go on a manhunt. This isn't about me. This is about Eddie. Yet hearing that protectiveness in him after so long fills me with joy. "How—"

"So now you are with Mr. Hollywood again?" Eddie, clearly not done with this subject, interrupts my attempts to steer us away from it.

"Will you stop calling him that?" I huff, annoyed. "And yes, I am." My eyes are quickly thin slits of irritation when Eddie laughs.

"Oh, Jesus. Do they know?"

"Officially, no. But they will do, just as soon as we release the announcement."

"Bloody hell, Adeline, you're going to send them off the deep end."

"I am aware of the repercussions, Edward." I've been dealing with them for months now, and Eddie would know all about the latest, had he not been drowning his sorrows in alcohol and women.

"Edward." He chuckles, thumbing at me as he finds Josh at the window. "She only ever calls me Edward when she is on the defense."

"I am not on the defense," I snap indignantly. "I am merely—"

"Marrying me." Josh throws our news out there like a bomb, and I'm quite sure Eddie's brain just blew up. His entire form convulses in his chair, his weak, tired, abused body moving more in that one jerk than he has since he arrived.

"Say what?"

I close my eyes, hiding from Eddie's astonished face, and breathe in some patience. "Thank you, Josh," I say tiredly. "Thanks a bunch." Firing a glare his way, I note he is expressing no remorse. He just shrugs unapologetically as he continues to pace the room.

"When did all this happen?" Eddie asks, his head swinging back and forth between us. "Shit, I've come on a good day for entertainment."

"Damn it, Eddie, won't you just stop?" I stand, joining Josh in walking, yet I am walking off my nerves once again, my beloved brother kindly reminding me of the enormity of what I am about to do. I have been here before, granted, yet this time seems so . . . final. Like I really am on the cusp of something groundbreaking. There is nothing to stop us now. I know in my heart of hearts. Every obstacle that has been thrown at us we have managed to duck, with only a few little scrapes. Kind of. "Anyway"—I shake off the dreaded apprehension and refocus on Eddie—"whatever am I going to do with you, dear brother?"

He snorts, and Josh chuckles. It earns them both an indignant glare. "Well," Eddie says, "I'm not so worried about causing a scandal now. You are doing a stellar job of that yourself."

"Hey, dude." Josh falls back into my chair and picks up a pen, tossing it at Eddie's head. "Don't be an asshole."

The pen ricochets off my brother's head. He's too tired to duck it. "It's not personal, Mr. Hollywood. I'm just saying it like it is."

Losing my patience, I toss the word out there and wait for the explosion. "Rehab."

Eddie stills in his seat, and Josh shrinks somewhat. That's more like it. Men who know their place. I nod to myself and lower to the chair next to Eddie. "Now that I have your attention—"

"Or stabbed it with a bloody bread knife," Eddie grunts, shifting uncomfortably on a bit of a scowl.

I pout on a shrug. I recall the last time I suggested rehab over dinner the night before I vacated Kellington. Eddie stormed out on me. Well, at least he's still here. "What do you think?"

"I think the news of the prince in rehab will cause a media shitstorm."

He doesn't want anyone to know. Not because he is a prince, and he *is* a prince, no matter what our history says, but because he is a proud man. "No one will know, Eddie," I say. "Besides, news will soon break about the Queen marrying some lowly American actor. That will overshadow everything."

"Full of compliments this morning, aren't we?" Josh mutters, picking up another pen and flicking it as if to throw it at *my* head. He won't. I smile and reach for Eddie's hand. "You can't go on like this."

"I know, Addy." He rubs at his forehead with the tips of his fingers. "I know." On a sigh, he looks to the ceiling and closes his eyes. "Drink is the only thing that makes me forget what a fuck-up my family is."

"When was the last time you had alcohol?"

"Thursday."

"That's three days," I exclaim, encouraged by the news. Three days is an excellent start.

"Yes, three days of hell. Three days of watching the news, seeing you looking so misplaced, and realizing that you were feeling the exact same way as me. Lost."

My excitement fades, blanketed by a horrid sense of sadness. "But I am now determined to find myself, Eddie," I tell him, looking to Josh. "We should not allow our unfortunate lineage to command our fates, not even for the throne." The fact that Eddie is not my father's biological child is a moot point. He has been raised as a Royal, and the way I see it, he has earned the right to decide his fate for himself. He must not allow himself to be told what his fate should be. "If you want out of this melting pot of lies, I won't stop you. I will find a way to make it happen." I will also try my hardest not to envy him. I can't say I wouldn't do the same if it were me in his position. "But whatever you decide, please do remember you must do it for yourself, and not allow bitterness and hatred to fuel your decision."

"I'm not sure the Head of State is supposed to speak with such selfless reason." He reaches for my cheek and strokes it fondly. "Despite what you and many others think, little princess, you will be a queen this country can be proud of. Real, rare, and precious."

"Oh stop." I take his hand from my face before I wet it with my silly tears. "I highly doubt the Privy Council will see it that way." Clearing my throat, I stand and brush myself down, sniffing back my emotion. "Now, I believe I have—"

The door swings open, and I whirl around to see who has had the audacity to barge in without being announced. "I tried to stop him, ma'am." Sid looks thoroughly exhausted by the door, his hand propped on the frame to hold himself upright.

Haydon takes in the scene, notably Josh in my chair looking extremely comfortable. And now hostile. *Oh dear.* Eddie shoots up from his seat, his weak body moving surprisingly fast. "You have a bloody nerve," he scathes, bristling terribly.

"Damn straight." Josh rises, too, though more slowly, more threateningly.

Haydon ignores both men and approaches me, snatching up my hand. His nose is a bruised mess, black rimming one eye. *Oh, Damon.* "Adeline, please, I wasn't myself last night."

"You don't say," I quip sarcastically, removing my hand from his. "I think it's best you leave."

"Please stand aside, Addy," Eddie requests politely, his fists clenching at his sides.

"No, Edward, there really isn't—"

"Move, Adeline." Josh's demand is a far cry from a polite request, his jaw rolling. "Now."

"Oh dear," Sid sighs from the door, watching the wolves move in on their prey. "I shall get Damon, ma'am." He scuttles off, leaving me to deal with the impending explosion of tempers.

"Haydon, please go."

"I need to talk to you." He's on me again, begging. "I can make it right. Just give me a chance."

"Get your hands off my woman," Josh growls, his referral as animalistic as his tone.

"Get your hands off his woman." Eddie backs him up, snarling at Haydon's back.

"Will you both shut up?" I snap, shrugging Haydon off. "I am perfectly capable of dealing with this myself." I throw an arm out to the door, squaring each of my protectors with a determined look. "Leave."

"Not on your life." Josh more or less laughs. "Not a fuckin' chance."

Haydon's face scrunches in disgust. "You would sacrifice a life with me to be with that uncivilized ape? It's laughable."

Oh boy.

Josh is across the desk in a second, tackling a startled Haydon to the floor. He sends the entire contents of the wooden top sailing in all directions as he does, and I jump out of the way on a startled yelp when the folder holding the photographs of my family lands at my feet.

"You fuckin' jerk," Josh growls, pinning Haydon to the carpet and drawing back his fist, sending it sailing forward on a roar. The connecting crack is cutting, both Eddie and I hissing on a wince.

Oh good Lord. "Josh," I cry, but Eddie seizes me as I go to split them up, pulling me back and keeping me there. "Stop them, for heaven's sake!"

"I think we should let them get it out of their systems," Eddie argues. Is he smiling? Smiling while he watches them roll around on the floor of my office like animals? "Josh will kick his arse.

Someone needs to."

"Fat lot of help you are," I snap, jumping when I hear another punch connect. With one eye closed, I peek across to where they are brawling, finding Haydon being completely overpowered by Josh. I can't watch this. I may not like Haydon, but I don't relish him being pummeled to death. I think Damon delivered a good enough message last night.

As I think his name, he comes crashing into the room.

"Oh, thank God," I breathe, watching as my head of protection puts himself straight in the mix and rips Josh off Haydon's squirming form, holding him back at a safe distance.

"You're an animal," Haydon cries, scrambling to his feet. Looking at me, he sneers, and that alone could be like a slap to the face. "You are perfect for each other."

"You fucker," Josh wrestles and worms in Damon's hold, fighting to get at him again. He soon realizes he is going nowhere and calms, though his next words could hurt Haydon as much as another clean, powerful crack to his chin. "Good fuckin' thing I'm the one marrying her then, right?"

Oh, shit.

"What?" Haydon asks, bemused.

"What?" Damon coughs, swinging a wide-eyed look my way.

"What?" comes a voice from behind. I cringe, turning to find Sir Don and Sampson on the threshold of my office. My entire body goes lax. This isn't how I planned for things to go. Kim appears behind the men in the doorway, out of breath. She shakes her head at me, obviously in apology for not managing to stop them from entering my office, or for making it to me in time to warn me they're here.

I can't hold it against her.

"You heard," Josh spits, yanking himself free from Damon's hold and wrestling his jacket back onto his shoulders. His labored, loud breaths are quickly killed by the deathly silence in the room.

"She's marrying me."

"I think they heard," I say, taking myself to my chair and dropping into it. "Damon, please, see Mr. Sampson out." He goes straight to Haydon, leaving me with his delightful father. "Sir Don, David, please sit." I look to Josh, expressing my displeasure through my scowl.

He huffs. "I'm not sorry."

"I didn't expect you to be."

"Whatever is going on?" Sir Don asks, looking at Josh like he's an alien.

"She's marrying him," Haydon yells as he's manhandled from my office. "She's marrying a bloody American. Father, you have to do something."

"I think your father has done more than enough," I retort, tight jawed. So Haydon didn't go squealing to his dad and Sir Don last night? I'm surprised. Or maybe I'm not. Maybe Haydon thought he could fix his mess before these two pigs found out he'd screwed up their hard work.

"What the hell is going on?" David asks, not bothering to go to his son's assistance, too concerned with what he's missing.

"What is going on?" I muse, thoughtful. "I think we will wait for the PR team and Major Davenport before I furnish you with all the details." I sit back and nod to Josh to take a seat on the couch by the fireplace, which he does on a wary look, adjusting his groin area as he lowers. Is he hard? I drop my eyes there, and quickly back up to his when I find he most definitely is. He nods. I blink rapidly, turning back to Sir Don and David Sampson on a swallow and a nervous laugh. Bloody hell, will it always be like this? Fighting to maintain authority and composure while fighting not to jump him? I peek out the corner of my eye. He's grinning. I cough and shake my head clear, grateful when my PR team march in, followed by a stiff-looking Davenport. The second he cocks his head at me, I know he's finished the statement. Good. As Eddie joins Josh over on the couch, I faff with the few things that Kim has kindly picked up off the floor and replaced,

"What was I saying?" I set my red box to the side, just so. "Ah, yes, whatever is going on?" I give David the sickliest smile I can muster. "You mean aside from the malicious attempts to turn me against Mr. Jameson?" I ask, tilting my head in question. Both he and Sir Don just stare at me. Of course, I never expected them to admit it. "Well, aside from that, which I am pleased to report was a terrible misunderstanding between Mr. Jameson and myself, now resolved, we are getting married."

"Preposterous." Sir Don dismisses me once again. "A misunderstanding? Mr. Jameson has proved time and again he is a womanizer. You are blinded by lust, Your Majesty."

I see Josh twitching in his seat, ready to explode. "No, I was blinded by your attempts to destroy him," I retort.

"Rubbish! Mr. Jameson's behavior was nothing to do with me. He's brainwashed you."

"Sir Don, your opinion is neither here nor there. I don't believe you wish to work for a Monarchy that you do not have full control over when it comes to decision making, am I right?"

"I have told you a thousand times, such a reckless move will cause ructions across the country."

"You mean the secrets we all keep?" I ask.

"Indeed."

"You and your family have been protectors of the realm for decades, Sir Don." I lean forward and smile sweetly. "Do you want to protect it now?"

"I can't possibly be involved in such absurdity. It's unspeakable."

Of course he can't. He only returned to royal employment after setting up Josh with a hooker. After turning me against him. When he was back in control. "Then don't be," I retort. He's just saved me the unpleasantness of firing him. "I accept your resignation." Turning my attention to Haydon's father, I tilt my head. "You are rather quiet, David."

"Shock will do that to a man," he admits, blinking, as if confused.

"I expect so." He thought he was on the home straight. I do so hate disappointing people. "Now listen, and listen carefully. I will be announcing my relationship with Joshua Jameson today." Both men balk, probably irritated to high heaven because it narrows their scope for intervention. "Not that it's something you should be concerned about, since neither of you are advising me any longer. But, rest assured, it will be carefully coordinated by the PR team, handled tastefully, and when the time is right, we will announce our engagement."

Josh bolts forward to the edge of the couch. "Adeline, hold up—"

I shut him up with just one look. A look that dares him to undermine me in front of these two men. Anyone else, I can stomach. But these two? Never. I'll take Josh's wrath later if I have to. What does he want me to do, anyway? Announce a canceled engagement, a relationship with an entirely different man, and another engagement? All at once? The world with pass out. I'm already pushing the boundaries of breaking news. "You and I will discuss in private."

His face. God, his face. It's telling me that my arse is seriously getting it once we are alone. Is it terrible that flames lick up my spine at the very thought? I quickly realign my mind and face my adversaries.

Sir Don is waiting for my attention before he goes on. "And what reason do you suppose you will give the world for your parting of ways with Mr. Sampson?"

"What do you think, Sir Don? I'll tell them the truth for once. Tell them that I tried to follow tradition, but in the end I had to follow my heart." I know this could go one way or the other. Be received with praise for my bravery, or distain for my selfishness. Either or, I am ready.

"Utterly ridiculous," Sir Don snorts.

"No, Sir Don, it is actually ridiculous that you have failed in your duty to protect the Monarch. It is ridiculous that I have spared you from being dragged over the coals for your insolence and betrayal. You wanted to take me on? You stupid little man. I am the damn Queen of England, and you were a mere servant. Now, you are nothing. Now, you can scurry out of my palace like the rat you are and live the rest of your days knowing you failed me." I take in air and calm my quaking body. "Now pack your offices and get out of my palace before I have you both arrested for treason."

David Sampson slowly casts his eyes across to where Josh is sitting, his silence speaking volumes. He is wondering how. How he convinced me he was set up. How he got to me. How he made me believe. Without any of the evidence, which I really don't think I need, I believe. My heart believes. My faith believes.

"Your father would be ashamed," Sir Don hisses.

"My father is no longer here, Sir Don. You are sitting in *my* office. Your *Queen's* office. Your superior. And now your nemesis." I stand, my way of telling them we are done. "I don't ever want to see your betraying faces ever again. Your titles have been stripped. Your privileges revoked. Get out."

I watch as both men drag themselves up from their seats and turn slowly without another word. "And just so you know," I say to their backs, low and calm, "Mr. Jameson will be staying with me here at the palace for the foreseeable future." I smile as they both look over their shoulders. "Under the Palace's protection. I think it's only wise. It's a jungle out there, after all. All kinds of dangers ready to pounce."

I get no response, from *either* man. They look somewhat stunned. I give Damon a flick of my head when he appears at the door, having disposed of my last piece of rubbish, and he nods his acknowledgment, following on behind Sir Don and Sampson.

Kim sees out the PR people, too, and as soon as the door closes, I brush my hands off, as though I have just dealt with some dirty business. "Well, that wasn't so bad, was it?" I find Josh on the couch.

402   JODI ELLEN MALPAS

His eyes are burning into me. Full of fire. He shakes his head and glances away, discreetly adjusting his groin area on a puff of breath. I bite my lip, a little amused by his condition.

Leaving him to gather himself, I cast my eyes around the rest of the room. Eddie is staring at Davenport, though not with an angry glare, but with quite an impassive expression. Nervously, I turn my eyes to the major. Or Eddie's biological father. I'm certain this is the first time they have been in each other's company. He's staring at Eddie, too, his usually stony face now soft. "The announcement?" I ask Davenport, and he slowly looks at me.

"Married?" he asks in return, and I shrink a little, forgetting it was news to him, too. He didn't question it before when Sir Don and David were in here. He wouldn't destabilize me like that, and he would not have wanted them to know he was in the dark.

"It came as a bit of a shock to me, too."

On a mild, disbelieving shake of his head, he stands and leaves, not wanting to outstay his welcome while Eddie is here. "I will print off the statement for your signature."

"Okay," I call. "Thank you, Major."

Eddie jumps up from the couch. "Davenport," he calls, a little awkwardly, making him stop at the door. He doesn't turn around. "I wondered if we might talk?" Stuffing his hands in his jean pockets, Eddie, like me, waits with bated breath for Davenport's reply.

"I believe I would like that," he says. "I'll be in my office."

Eddie follows, and I smile, so hopeful. I pray they can make amends.

Then Josh and I are alone. Everything is falling into place. Josh is here. I am here. The announcement will be sent imminently. Nothing can happen. But my stomach refuses to stop turning in apprehension. I grab my phone and text Damon, telling him to advise me the moment Sir Don and David have gathered their belongings and left the palace. He confirms he will immediately, also adding that Haydon has been escorted out by one of his men.

I need to distract myself. Forget about the impending explosion of news. "Are you ready to look at some photographs?" I ask Josh, keen to find something to do to pass the time.

"Stop worrying," he orders.

"I can't help it. After everything, I think being prudent is wise."

"You need to relax."

"Easier said than done."

"Is it?" His head cocks, and I find mine slowly tilting, too, curious. "Stand up and brace your hands on the edge of the desk."

"What?"

"I believe I owe you for cutting my balls off in front of your minions. And you need to forget for a short while, no?" He stands. "Do it."

I'm on my feet with a few skips of my heartbeats, my hands wedged on the edge of my desk. There is no hesitation. No question. He knows what to do with me, and I am more than happy to let him do it. That was an exceptionally hard task, maintaining my resilience. I could do with a nap. Or . . .

I walk my legs back and look at him through lusty, pleading eyes as he strolls casually to the door and locks it. And it feels like it takes him years to make it to me by the desk. On a thoughtful pout, he picks up a ruler from the desk tidy, inspecting it before lashing it across his palm on a tiny smirk. "Perfect," he declares, moving around the back of me. I close my eyes and suck in air, holding it as he lifts my skirt up to my waist. "You are so fuckin' hot when you're in command," he says, smoothing a palm over the peak of my left cheek.

Thwack!

The lash takes me by surprise, the wood stinging far more than his palm. "Fuck." I jolt forward as flames spread like cracking glass across my backside. I pant, trying to right my position, knowing he is far from done. Like I could be in a trance, my breathing slows, and I smile as the pain transforms into a wonderful kind of pulse between my thighs. "Again," I demand, grunting when he whips across my flesh brutally. More pain, even more pleasure. I'm vibrating, my clitoris buzzing uncontrollably. One touch, and I will be gone. Moving in, Josh lays his torso on my back, reaching around my stomach, feeling his way down to the juncture of my thighs.

He hisses as his fingers glide past the seam of my knickers into my wetness, scissoring, my arse pushing back into his groin. "God, yes," I breathe, rolling my hips to get the friction I need.

"Is that good, Your Majesty? Me fucking you with my fingers, is it good?" His touch works easily, each slide back and forth pushing my pulse to the next level until it's pounding.

"Oh, God, yes," I choke, balling my hands and slamming them into the wood. "Faster."

I feel his smile as he bites into my shoulder, and with a few more body-bending slips, I go, my head dropping, my eyes rolling in the back of my head. "Shit," I mumble, free-falling through my pleasure, waiting for the convulsions to claim me. My body locks when they do, the intensity making me shake. "Stop," I beg, the pressure too much. "Please, stop."

"I will never stop, Adeline." He sinks his fingers into me, high and deep, my muscles curling around his touch possessively, telling him I never really want him to. I pant, blinking back the stars, riding through the intensity of my orgasm until he slowly pulls his fingers free.

Josh pulls away and turns me, pushing me down to the desk and spreading himself on me. As I breathe into his face, he does nothing but smile. "Feeling better, my queen?"

"Much," I gasp, the weight now gone from my shoulders, my mind fuzzy for a far more satisfying reason. "Thank you, kind sir."

"I'm here to serve." He kisses every part of my hot face before helping me to my wobbly legs and pulling down my skirt. "I can't decide if I love the pre-orgasm look on you more, or the post-orgasm." My hair is pushed over my shoulders and a kiss landed on my lips. "Photographs?"

My eyes fall to the box of videotapes, my rush of contentment receiving a prod of dejection. "I suppose I ought to get it done with."

"C'mon." Josh collects the box as I get the file of photographs. "I'm looking forward to seeing if you were as cute then as you are now."

"Cute?" I ask as he slings an arm around my shoulders and walks us to the door. Unlocking it, I pull it open and find Kim on the other side, her arms full of . . ."What is that?"

"This is a VCR player for all those tapes." She hoofs it at Josh, dumping it onto the box he's carrying. "Any good with obsolete technology?"

He looks at the huge machine with skepticism. "I'll give it a go."

"Thanks, Kim," I call as she goes, leaving Josh and I to fend for ourselves. "We'll set it up in the Wendsley Lounge."

"How many lounges are in this joint?" Josh asks as we walk across the landing and down the stairs.

"A few."

"Hundred?"

I push my way into the Wendsley Lounge, holding the door for Josh with my back. He sets the box next to the television and pulls the leads from the back of the machine, scratching his head. I leave him to figure it out as I kneel by the coffee table and pull out all the tapes from the box, stacking them neatly in date order. "My baptism," I muse, only just making out the faded print on the sticker of the tape. "And my first birthday." I hold it up for Josh to see, laughing when I find his face wedged against the television as he stretches around the back to connect a lead. "We'll start with this one. Is it working?" I crawl across to the video player, searching for any lights that will indicate power.

"Give me a chance," Josh mutters, fiddling and faffing. "Fuckin' hell, where did she even find this thing?" He turns his face to try and see where his blind hands are working, cursing and muttering under his breath. "There. Is it on?"

"Wait." I grab the remote control and switch on the television, looking for a light on the VCR player. "Yes!" I shove the tape into the slot and wince at the sounds of crunching and mechanisms turning. "Should it sound like that?"

"Who knows?" Josh joins me on the floor as we wait for the screen to come to life. "Oh my God." He laughs when the screen is suddenly full of a chubby baby's face. "Is that you?"

"No," I protest indignantly, praying it isn't. Though the elaborate christening gown the baby is wrapped in like a present tells me otherwise. Goodness, I look like a baby bride. "Shit, it *is* me." I throw a disgusted look at Josh's jerking body, fast-forwarding the tape through the close up of my chunky cheeks. "There." I play and let the tape roll, watching as I'm passed from my mother's arms to . . ."Oh my God, look at Sabina."

"I'm too busy looking at your mother," Josh says, settling on his arse and pulling me to between his legs. I wince as my sore bottom meets the carpet. He rests against the couch, and I rest against him. "Fuckin' hell, it's you."

I smile. It really is, her hair as long as mine now, though a bit bigger and set with what is possibly an entire tin of firm-hold hairspray. "And Eddie." I point at the screen as my brother, just a toddler, tries to crawl up our mother's body. She picks him up, letting him smother her face with wet kisses.

"And is that John?" Josh asks, sending my eyes to the other side of the screen.

"Yes." He looks utterly unimpressed by the fuss being made of me. "God, he was uptight even then." An edge of sadness washes over me. "But he was born to be King." I feel Josh constrict his arms around my shoulders, a silent sign of sympathy. With a lump in my throat, I fast-forward again, speeding through the footage of me as a baby being fussed over by everyone. "There's my grandfather," I say, playing the tape again for Josh to see. My father's father is holding me now, my tiny body looking awkward in his big kingly arms.

"The stone dude in the maze." Josh recognizes him.

"He was stony in real life, too." My grandfather passes me back to Sabina, his crabby face rather indifferent, and then, out of nowhere, he smiles. But not at his granddaughter in his arms, but at Sabina when she says something. I quickly rewind and turn up the volume, wondering what provoked such a beam from the notoriously compassionless man.

"What's up?"

"What does she say?" I ask, leaning forward, listening carefully, but the surrounding bustle blankets the words being exchanged.

"I can't hear," Josh says.

"Me either." I settle back on a little shrug and fast-forward again. "Sabina is honored. He smiled for no one." The screen goes blank, the tape finished. "Next one?" I ask, breaking away and collecting another. I flash it to him on a grin. "My second birthday."

"Do you think your cheeks will have deflated?" It's a serious question I shouldn't entertain, but his cheeky grin is too adorable. I roll my eyes as I eject the tape and pop the next in, crawling back over to Josh. "I hope one day I get to see you as a baby."

His grin drops like a stone, and I quickly scold myself for unwittingly bringing up his less than happy childhood. "I'm sorry."

"Stop it." He encourages me back into my place between his legs, wrapping me up tightly in his arms. "I wish there were pictures to show you, 'cause I'm damn sure I was cuter than you."

I nudge him playfully, eliciting a small chuckle and a nip of my earlobe. "With no evidence, I guess we'll never know." I press play and wish I hadn't. "Urghhhh."

"Fuckin' hell, what's going on with your hair?"

I immediately hit the fast-forward button with my thumb, looking at the screen through squinted eyes as it skips past the frightful sight of me. "Mother clearly hated me," I mutter. Lord, I look like a boy. When the scene changes to the gardens of Claringdon, I resume playing. There's me again, waddling around the legs of my nanny. "I can't believe I have never seen all these before." I've seen some photographs, yes, but never any footage. "Look, there's Davenport."

"As happy as ever." Josh laughs, though I don't. The old stickler looks as stiff nearly thirty years ago as he does now, but now I know why. He's watching Eddie, and my heart cracks a little as my brother zooms around on his little push-along bicycle. How much did he want to go to him? How much did he want to be the one to teach him how to ride it?

Sadness crashes through me, even more so when Eddie falls off and starts wailing. I watch as Davenport's body twitches, his instinct telling him to go to his son.

"Fuck," Josh breathes, telling me he is thinking the exact same thing as I am. I should show Eddie this. Would he want to see?

I shake my head, so overcome as I watch the scenes playing before me. Scenes from a time gone by; scenes that are so very damaging. Truths that have been masked by lies for decades. "It's all rather obvious now, don't you think?"

"Yeah." Josh drops a chaste kiss on my cheek as I wonder if what I'm looking at now is the very reason these tapes haven't seen daylight in nearly thirty years. Undoubtedly.

I watch on, rapt, as a younger Davenport wrestles with his instinct, looking on while Mother goes to Eddie, collecting him up and brushing him down. My father is in the background with my grandfather, oblivious to his injured *son*. "If this is too hard to watch, you should stop," Josh says, taking the remote control from my hand.

"No." I claim it back. All the lies playing out before me, seeing it first-hand, is like substantiation that what I am doing is the right thing to do. Mother looks thoroughly lost as she tends to her son, everyone around her ignorant to her turmoil. As she scoops Eddie up, she turns, seeing Davenport. There's a moment between them, a few seconds of them both frozen and staring at each other. Then she hurries the other way, handing Eddie to our nanny. I look past her, seeing me, a toddler, waddling across the grass in the background. It's my turn to have a fall, my little legs moving too fast for my little body as I chase a ball across the lawn, beyond the focus of the camera, which is still on Eddie wailing. I go down with a crash, my arms not strong enough to stop my face from hitting the ground. I wince.

"Ouch," Josh says, as my toddler-self starts to scream to high heaven. I'm utterly stunned when Davenport moves in and scoops me up from the grass, holding me tightly against his body and soothing me until I stop crying. Then he kneels and sits me on his knee, inspecting my hands. He's talking to me as he dusts off my palms, his face soft and loving. My shoulders drop a little. The poor man. How much would he have loved to tend to Eddie like that? To pick him up when he fell and dust him off? Setting me on my feet, he sends me on my way and slowly rises, taking his place back on the outskirts of my family.

"I feel terrible for him," I whisper. "I've always loathed his intrusion on my life, and now I feel terrible." He didn't hate me like I thought. He could have, given I was born in some sick kind of revenge, but he didn't.

"You didn't know."

Unable to bear watching anymore, I fast-forward again, skipping through the footage of Mother helping me open gifts and blow out the candles on my birthday cake. When my father comes back on the screen, I press play, grimacing when I see him with David Sampson. He hasn't changed a bit. His face back then is as slap-worthy as it is now. They're chatting, utterly uninvolved with the celebrations. As is my grandfather who is in the background with Sabina.

My attention diverts to them, seeing Sabina's arms flail a little, as if frustrated. My grandfather pulls her aside, looking around. What for? Listening ears? They're hardly noticeable in the distance now, but I can see them. Are they arguing?

Josh's phone starts ringing, and he disappears from my peripheral vision to answer it. I'm aware of him talking, to whom I don't know. My focus is on the small bodies of my grandfather and Sabina at the back of the television. They're definitely having words, and my thoughts are only confirmed when my grandfather walks away, forcing his stressed expression into something close to calm as he takes himself back into the celebrations, and closer to the camera. He approaches my father and David Sampson. He looks to my father first, and then to David, resting his palm on his shoulder and giving it a light squeeze. I'm not the only one to find my grandfather's move odd, my father and David both frowning. I pause the tape, freezing the screen. The still image is haunting. It speaks a thousand words. Or secrets. Leaving Josh talking on the phone, I scramble across to the file full of photographs and flick though them urgently, looking for . . . something. Years of pictures, but the focus of the shots isn't what I'm interested in. It's the photographs with backgrounds, pictures snapped catching people unaware.

There are endless, ones of my mother always looking so absent in the background, of Davenport appearing his usual blank self. I pause when I find a picture of my father holding me, and David Sampson holding Haydon. I look past them, seeing my grandfather on the edge of the scene. With Sabina. His hand on her arm. Her hand on his. I move to the next picture. It's the same scene, but there's another person captured in this one. Someone watching the King and Sabina. His expression couldn't be mistaken as anything less than angry. Dr. Goodridge. I flick through a few more, finding a black and white picture of my grandfather and Dr. Goodridge. I drop every other picture from my hands and stare down. Dr. Goodridge has his arm around my grandfather. They're both standing in front of a helicopter. Smiling.

No.

I rummage through some more pictures and find one of Sabina,

Dr. Goodridge, and my grandfather. Sabina is in the middle of them. The two men have their arms around her. Dr. Goodridge is looking at Sabina fondly. But Sabina is unaware, as she is staring fondly at my grandfather. *Oh my God.*

"Adeline?" Josh says, pulling my face up from the pictures. He visibly recoils. "You look like you've seen a ghost."

"I think I have," I murmur, dropping the damaging pictures like the poison they are.

"What's—" His phone rings, and he curses. "Bates, I'll call you ba . . ." Josh fades off, and I look at him. "Send it through." He hangs up and goes straight to his messages, opening it up. "Bates has a visual of someone talking to a member of staff of The Ritz at the delivery entrance."

I stare at Josh as he opens the picture that Bates sent him, his forehead creased. "Hey, I recognize him."

"Overweight?" I ask.

"Yeah." His frown deepens.

"A tweed suit two sizes too small? Silver hair?"

His phone slowly lowers. "Yeah."

"A slight hump on the right side of his back? A black leather bag?"

"For fuck's sake, Adeline. What's going on?"

"Am I right?"

"Yes!"

I jump up, grab the pictures, and run to the door, yanking it open. "Kim," I yell, wandering out, looking around, waiting for her to appear. When she does, she looks alarmed by my agitation. "Tell Davenport we're holding off on the announcement," I say, marching across the foyer and taking the stairs quickly. "And send him to my office."

"What's going on?" Josh yells after me, his feet thundering up the stairs behind me. "Why are we stalling the announcement?"

"Because it might change."

"No, Adeline." He overtakes me and blocks the door to my

office. "No more waiting. We agreed."

"I'm not waiting," I assure him, muscling my way past him. I look up at the picture of my father hanging over the fireplace, and just as quickly look away.

"Will you please tell me what the fuck is going on?"

I pace up and down in front of the window. "I can't believe I have been so stupid."

"Adeline," Josh yells, his impatience growing. "Tell me what—"

"Your Majesty?" Davenport presents himself at the doorway of my office, taking in the scene of Josh looking irate, and me looking what I can only assume is haunted.

"I need to see Dr. Goodridge."

"Are you ill?"

"Yes," I confirm, sitting down and rubbing at my turning stomach. I could honestly throw up at any moment. "Has Sir Don and Sampson left yet?"

"They're still collecting their belongings."

"Good. I want to see them. And please summon Sabina and Haydon Sampson."

Davenport takes a brisk walk off, and Josh comes to my chair, turning it by the arms until I'm facing him. He bends, his barely contained temper cutting his handsome face. "What the fuck is going on?"

"It's all a lie," I whisper raggedly. "Every single thing about my life is a lie."

His forehead furrows deeply. "What did you see in those pictures?"

"The truth," I breathe, my head set to explode. "For the first time, I think I saw the whole truth."

33

ALTHOUGH AGITATED, JOSH backs off and leaves me to think once I've begged for a little space, my mind swirling, as I break down everything hurting my head and rebuild it again, making the picture clearer. Uglier. I rewind through time, finding clues everywhere. It's frighteningly clear.

I get up, I pace, I sit back down, and I drop my head in my hands a few times when more of the picture I build becomes frighteningly real.

"Just tell me everything is going to be okay," Josh says quietly from his place on the couch, disturbing me. I glance up, hating to see him looking so lost and helpless.

My intention to assure him as best I can is halted when I hear a knock on the door. We both swing our stares to the wood, my heart rate rocketing. "Come in." I can hardly talk through my apprehension.

Entering gingerly, Davenport finds me and runs a quick eye over my seated form. "Dr. Goodridge, ma'am," he announces, opening the way for my private physician. The short, round man who has served us for decades, enters, his suit as ill-fitted as always, the buttons pulled taut over his potbelly. I flick my eyes to Josh when I hear him inhale. He's clicked. He recognizes him now.

"Your Majesty." Dr. Goodridge approaches and sets his leather bag on my desk, assessing me.

"Sit down, Doctor," I say, ignoring his frown and stopping Davenport as he backs out of my office. "You should stay, Major."

He stalls, unsure, before slowly closing the door. "As you wish." Rather than join Dr. Goodridge on the other side of my desk, he takes a seat beside Josh on the couch, their wary expressions colliding.

"How can I help you, ma'am?" Dr. Goodridge asks, undoing his buttons before they give in and pop off.

"Tell me, Doctor. What did you do before you took the position of private doctor to the Sovereign?"

He frowns on a smile, a little bemused. "I was in the RAF, ma'am."

"A doctor in the RAF?"

"Indeed." He smiles as if reliving fond memories.

"So you spent a lot of time around helicopters, yes?"

"They're a passion second only to medicine." He shifts his old body in the seat. "Did you summon me to discuss my military career, ma'am?"

I smile sweetly. "Of course not. I was just curious."

"Then I'm glad I've curbed that curiosity. Now, what can I help with?"

Oh, doctor, you've helped with more than you know. "I'm feeling a little under the weather,"

"And what are your symptoms?" He reaches forward and undoes his bag, taking a thermometer from inside.

"Nausea, mainly."

"Shall we take your temperature?"

"I don't think that is necessary," I say, keeping my eyes closely on him. "Maybe a blood test will reveal what is wrong with me."

I don't miss the slight falter of his hand as he places a protective wrapper on the end of the thermometer, no matter how hard he tries to disguise it.

His nervous laugh only confirms my suspicions. "A little extreme at the moment, ma'am."

"Hmm," I hum, standing from my seat and rounding the desk. I sit myself on the edge and offer my arm to Dr. Goodridge. "Better safe than sorry, though, yes?"

He stills, his old eyes creeping up to mine. "I'm afraid I don't have the correct equipment with me."

"Dr. Goodridge, you have been the royal doctor for decades. You and I both know the equipment you require to draw my bloods are in that bag." His reluctance is only strengthening another part of this awful puzzle.

"Adeline, what are you doing?" Josh asks, sounding more worried than he should.

"I'm asking my doctor to do a blood test, except this time I would like him to give me the correct results." I tilt my head as Dr. Goodridge's eyes widen. And there it is. Guilt. I almost lose my breath with the confirmation that I'm not losing my mind.

Davenport stands from the sofa. "What?"

"Can you do that?" I ask the doctor. "Share the correct results of my blood test?"

"I'm not sure what you are suggesting, ma'am."

I sigh. "It seems you are struggling with that question, so let us try another. When I was born, you were there for my birth, yes?"

"Of course. I have been present for every royal birth during my service."

"Indeed. And tell me, Doctor, did my brother John have a blood test at birth?"

"No, ma'am."

"Did Eddie?"

He coughs his throat clear. "Yes."

Of course he did. My father only stopped Mother and Davenport's affair the year before. "And you took those results straight to my father, yes?"

He nods.

I hear Davenport breathe out, obviously finding this hard to hear. I'm afraid he is going to have to hear more. "And when I was born, did I have a blood test?"

A swallow. "Yes."

Naturally. "But you didn't take those results straight to my father, did you? You didn't take them to the King." He doesn't answer, leaving me to continue dictating what happened on the day I came into this world. "You took them to someone else before you took them to the King. Someone who told you to tell the King I was his blood, and not that of another man."

"What the fuck?" Josh is up now, though Davenport drops back to the couch heavily in a state of shock. He knows who that other man is, just the same as I do. After the scandal of Eddie's illegitimacy, when I was born, my father demanded a blood test to check I was his. I wasn't. But someone didn't want him to know.

"You lied to the King," I state it as a fact, since it is. "Why would you?"

Dr. Goodridge's head drops. "I loved her."

"Who, Dr. Goodridge?"

"Sabina Sampson," he sighs.

His answer cements everything. "She told you to tell the King I was his blood."

He just nods, shame rife in his meek action. I stand and walk away. "So when a blood test was demanded by my council before my recent succession, you had no choice but to lie again or have your secret discovered." I can't even bring myself to be mad. I don't feel like Eddie did when he discovered he wasn't who he thought he was. I don't feel betrayed and lost. I feel only relief.

Davenport stands, looking a little stunned. "I don't understand."

"I didn't either," I admit. But those photographs brought too many things together, and now it is crystal clear. I go to the door and open it, finding all three members of the Sampson family–David, Sabina, and Haydon—sitting on a roll-top couch across the landing, as well as Sir Don. I force a smile, one that I hope seems genuine. "Please," I say, turning and wandering back to my desk.

They file in and tentatively sit, the atmosphere thickening by the second. "What's going on?" Sabina asks, her eyes on Dr. Goodridge, obviously surprised to see him.

"I know everything, Sabina." I don't beat around the bush. I cut straight to the chase. Too much of my life has been wasted on these lies already. "Why?"

Her eyes shoot to me. "I don't know what you're talking about."

I throw one of the pictures on the desk before her, and she glances down. "Every picture tells a story, Sabina. Dr. Goodridge was in love with you. But you were in love with my grandfather," I say, not taking any pleasure from the flinch my declaration draws from her. The pictures tell a story. Perhaps seeing the photographs of Josh and me on the dance floor of the White House has helped me—photographs of two people who have so clearly got something to hide. And I remember finding her in the maze on the day of my father's funeral, staring at the statue of my grandfather. She was looking at the memorial of the man she loved. I cast my eyes to David. "You're not who you think you are." He says nothing, just stares at me. "You are my grandfather's first born son, David. The true heir to the throne. Everything that has happened is because of your mother's bitterness. She has slowly but surely worked her way through my family, all the way down to me. But you won't get rid of me, will you, Sabina? Because I am your last chance to get back the throne you believe your family should have. By marrying your grandson." She's been so calculating. So scheming and manipulative. Every single thing that has happened has been because Sabina made it happen. "You knew Eddie was illegitimate. You knew John was infertile, but you made sure Dr. Goodridge declared him otherwise when he and Helen were to marry." It was Sabina who told my mother the unborn child wasn't Royal. "So when Helen eventually fell pregnant, you knew it wasn't my brother's child." I breathe in, shivering at the sound of my words. "And Eddie's incident in the countryside was no accident. It was you who fired at him while he was riding that day." Her eyes widen. I'm smarter than she thought. "Why not just expose his identity?"

"What good is the throne to me if it's tarnished with scandal?" Sabina's usually soft, friendly face is far from it now. Now, every ounce of bitterness and resentment is emblazoned all over it. "Revealing his identity to the world would have smeared the Monarchy. He had to go."

In stunned disbelief, I look to Dr. Goodridge. The old doctor looks ancient all of a sudden. Grey and tired. He's shaking his head, his eyes on his lap. "I loved you," he says. "Would do whatever you wanted in the hopes you would return my love. I was a fool. Still am a fool. You never loved me. You used me. It's been like a damn domino effect. One little white lie led to another and another and another." His arms go up into the air heavily. "I'm done. I'm glad it's over."

"A little white lie?" I balk at Dr. Goodridge. "I've lived a lie for thirty years because of your *little white lie*. The King died. My brother died. A little white lie?"

He shrinks. He's a man out of his depth. I return my attention to Sabina. "When your attempt to get rid of Eddie failed, you had no choice but to reveal my mother's affair and Eddie's identity if the crown was going to bypass his head and land on mine. You exposed the letters. Everything the King tried to hide was going to be exposed. That is why he traveled home from Scotland early. Not to stop me from being with Josh, but to stop the letters between Davenport and my mother being leaked. But you would never have publicly leaked those letters. Because it would have tarnished the crown you so desperately want. You just needed to get my father on that helicopter." All this time I have blamed myself. Have been dictated by guilt. "And you needed help." I turn my eyes onto Dr. Goodridge again. "You were in Evernmore, you sabotaged the royal helicopter, and you stopped Sir Don and David from reaching my father and John before they took flight."

Sir Don throws his eyes toward the doctor. "You? You were stalling us? You weren't ill?"

"Oh my God," Haydon breathes, staring at the floor at his feet.

David looks plain shocked. He never knew of all this madness. The reason he was so angry with Sabina after his father died was because he discovered she knew about my mother's affair and Eddie's illegitimacy. His ego was put out. The fact that it probably only accelerated his desire to marry me off to Haydon is a moot point now. Because, in fact, it is David who should have been King. Not my father. His family should be Royals, not servants.

He slowly casts his eyes to his mother. "You told me to go to Evernmore when Adeline fled."

"Of course I did," Sabina says. "It was the perfect opportunity to get rid of the King."

"And you told me to advise him the letters had been leaked. You knew he'd fly into a rage. And Dr. Goodridge made sure none of us made it to him before he and John took flight back to London."

"The King was a predictable man." She shrugs, rather nonchalantly. "The kind doctor made sure John was on the flight, too. No pilot, a mechanical fault. Oopsy."

I can only stare at her. She's a wolf in sheep's clothing.

"Why didn't you tell me?" David asks. "I should have known."

Sabina snorts. "Tell you that you were the true heir? Really, David? Your ego is too big to let that pass. You would have ruined everything. You weren't born to be King. You were born to be a puppet. It was always supposed to be Adeline and Haydon," she spits. "The beautiful little princess and my beautiful grandson."

"Is that why you told Dr. Goodridge to lie about my blood tests when I was born?" I ask, thinking how outraged she must have been to discover that I was illegitimate, too.

"You were my last hope. After you, the dynasty dies, and so does my family's claim to the throne. It doesn't matter that you aren't of true British Royal blood. Because my grandson *is*."

Why she would want the throne is beyond me. The lengths she has gone to are mind-blowing. "You made me feel like I had a friend," I say. "You have manipulated me at every turn."

"I haven't manipulated you. I didn't need to push you into marrying Haydon. My son did that all by himself. I just needed to ensure there was no one in the way." Her glare points to Josh. "You just couldn't stay away, could you?" She stands. "My Haydon should be with her." She throws an arm out to me. "It should have been *you* begging to marry my grandson, and instead I have been forced to these lengths to get my family what it should rightfully have." Her body vibrates as years' worth of frustration pours across the desk at me.

"You're crazy," I murmur, so utterly shocked. "You have single-handedly destroyed everything."

"No, your grandfather did that, Adeline. When he dumped me as a seventeen-year-old girl, pregnant and poor." She laughs coldly. "Handing me over to one of his blue-blooded friends as a wife. Giving me shelter and a job at the stables. All of this was supposed to appease me? I watched as your father came to the throne, as your mother cheated on him and birthed two illegitimate children. It was farcical."

"I agree," I say, making her recoil. "Everything about this family, about the Monarchy, is a farce." I stand, giving everyone in the room a moment of my eyes. "These secrets will die with my abdication."

I round the desk and walk out on a collection of gasps, my legs working of their own volition, taking me away from the poison that has shaped my life. I meet my mother just outside the door.

I see Damon a few paces behind her with Kim. Their faces are a picture of shock. They heard.

Mother steps forward, and I beg her not to make me reconsider. "Adeline—"

"It was Sabina who told you my brother's unborn child wasn't his."

She nods, her eyes flicking past me into my office. "I believed she was acting with integrity."

Integrity? No. She was simply ensuring all obstacles were out of the way. "And did you believe I was the King's child?" I ask.

"I had no reason not to."

I guess she didn't, other than the fact that she had clearly slept with Davenport again. Yet blood tests *confirmed* I was the King's child.

My head hurts. The way the King treated Eddie and the way he treated me is making it spin. Was he kinder, more loving toward Eddie simply to hurt Davenport? Was he heavy-handed with me because he was worried that someday Eddie's true identity would be discovered and I would be one step closer to the throne?

I shout at myself on the inside. Why do I care? I've spent my entire life caught up in the Royal web of lies. I've been as fooled by the smoke and mirrors as everyone else. What does it matter now?

I continue on my way, my head high, my strides determined. There is so much to do, so much to deal with. But right now, it is just about me. I need a moment alone. I need to wrap my head around what is happening.

When I arrive at my private quarters, I go straight to my bed and collapse onto it, curling myself into a little ball and staring ahead at the huge window looking out onto the grounds. I'm not hurting. My heart doesn't ache. Maybe I have become immune to the toxins I've been swimming in all my life. Or maybe I don't have the energy to hurt.

When I hear the door open, I know it is Josh, but I remain where

I am, bunched up tightly. The bed dips. His body moves in close, curling around mine. His face goes into my hair. Josh is the only true thing I have in my life. He doesn't wear a mask. He doesn't live on lies, and I very nearly dragged him into a damaging life of deceit.

Reaching for my hand, he weaves his fingers through mine and squeezes.

My American boy.

34

July 2018

Official statement from HRH Queen Adeline Lockhart I.

Ever since I was a little girl, my father fondly called me spirited. He used to say my heart was much bigger than my brain, and in the end, it was that big heart that brought me to this point in my life. I have never wanted to withhold anything from my people, but it has been inappropriate for me to speak until now.

You see, my big heart has led me down a path of which I should not have gone. Not as a Royal. Not as a princess. And most definitely not as your Queen. Now I find myself unable to divert from that path, as it has led me to a man who has stolen my big heart. If I were to turn back now, I would return to my duties with no heart at all. The spirit you all so love in me will be lost forever, and a mere shell of a woman would be ruling this glorious country. My people deserve more than that. They deserve a devoted Sovereign, one who can commit themselves entirely to the task. I no longer own myself in order to commit fully to my duties, and the man I love does not deserve the constraints my life as Queen will impose on him.

I fear it will change him. I fear it will strip him of the qualities I so love about him. I fear he will be lost. I can't lose him.

This morning I completed the last of my duties as Queen. After the loss of my father and my dear brother, as well as coping with His Royal Highness Prince Edward's battle scars after he served our country so bravely, my beginning as Head of State was saddled with sadness and confusion. I have only been able to overcome these tragedies because of the love of one man. I owe him everything. He helped me navigate the dark times. He showed me what hope was. I will never be able to repay him, but I will die trying.

I have been succeeded by Her Royal Highness the Duchess of Sussex, and I swear my allegiance to her. She will serve you well, far better than I ever could. I believe one must carry the title of Sovereign with unrelenting desire and commitment, and I trust my aunt will not fail in that.

You must understand, this is not a decision that I have made lightly. My family has been burdened with tragedy and sadness, and I believe it has weakened us a people, as well as Royals. It is the end of a dynasty, but the end of a dynasty that I am proud of. I will not abandon my country. My reasons for renouncing the throne are somewhat personal, not political, and I will serve your new Queen loyally and devotedly. This decision has been mine alone, the biggest I am ever likely to make. For me and for you, I believe it to be the right decision. I have received endless love from my closest family, and invaluable advice from my trusted council, all of whom are supportive of my decision to step down as your Queen and revoke all royal privileges.

Now I pray God will forgive me for choosing love over duty. And you, my people, will understand that when it came down to it, I really didn't have a choice.

Love always wins.

Miss Adeline Catherine Luisa Lockhart

35

WHO IS THE man she gave up her throne for?

It's the most anticipated question in history. My abdication has been met with shock and sadness. But no one is more shocked than I am. The reaction of people from around the world has truly been humbling, supporters rallying and protesting the sacrifice I have made. If only they knew they are wrong in their assumption that I was pushed out. I walked away from the throne and did not look back. I left behind the secrets, too. I left behind the task of concealing the lies, of creating more smoke and erecting more mirrors to deflect the deceit. It will no longer play a part in who I am or where I am going.

I am free.

Well, I will be, when the dust settles. Right now, I am lying low in the very apartment Josh hid me in after he rescued me from a field in the middle of the countryside. My arms are folded over my chest as I stare out across the London skyline, my eyes rooted on Claringdon Palace. I wonder how Aunt Victoria is settling into her new job. Rather well, I expect. I haven't heard from her, though Matilda has called me frequently over the past few days since I walked out of Claringdon. She is in Argentina meeting Santiago's family. Eddie is in rehab and doing "okay" according to the support workers, and the Sampson's and Dr. Goodridge have all but disappeared off the face of the planet, banished in shame and disgrace. I expect they were told to go quietly, or face prosecution. They were undoubtedly dealt with by Sir Don. He stayed at Claringdon under Victoria's reign. Of course he stayed. The man is committed to the core, and a new batch of secrets will keep him busy for the rest of his time in royal duty. I expect he's thriving.

I'm still stunned that he asked me for an apology before I walked out of my palace. I laughed in his face. He may not have been entirely responsible for trying to discredit Josh and sabotage our relationship, but he didn't do anything to protect me from Sabina's malicious tactics, either. He let it happen, probably willed it on. His first job was to serve his Queen, to protect her. And he didn't.

I shudder, not for the first time. It's ironic how after all these years, it is in fact Haydon who was royal blooded and not me. Not that the world will ever know. The world will know nothing of the corruption within the royal circle. Of the murders and affairs. Of the illegitimate babies and sabotage between families. All of that will remain safe behind the smoke and mirrors.

So lost in my thoughts, I startle a little when Josh wraps his arms around me from behind. He has been so patient these past three days while we have been held hostage by the media. He hasn't protested having to remain within these four walls, and he hasn't made me feel guilty. He's missed two interviews. He's also had to postpone filming on his current project. All because of me.

"Wouldn't it be lovely to go for a stroll in the park?" I muse, clinging onto his arms around my shoulders as I look at the dots of people wandering freely, enjoying the fresh air and beautiful scenery.

"Shh." He kisses my hair and turns me away from the window. "Come have some coffee."

The cool material of my silk robe slips across my legs as I walk, then separates when I lower to the chair, revealing my bare thighs. I don't right myself. Josh's appreciative eyes are too lovely to deprive myself of them. When I catch sight of a newspaper, I push it away, ignoring the headlines.

"Your mother has been calling." Josh pours my coffee, looking up at me as I stir the dark liquid, absentminded. "Are you going to avoid her forever?"

"I just need time," I say, not for the first time. Finding out you have lived a lie isn't an easy pill to swallow. I'm not mad. Not really hurt either, but I am a little disconcerted by it all. I don't feel like I can face *anyone* right now. Only Josh. I want to cement my future in this world with him before I face my past.

I look up and smile, taking a sip of my coffee. I wonder if I would have found him had I not endured a thirty-year lie. Did all this happen for a reason? I have to believe it did, or I might be eaten alive with bitterness.

"Are you nervous about later?" he asks, lowering his arse to the edge of the table. His taut stomach ripples a little as he leans toward me, offering up his lips. I move in and give him what he wants. Always.

I shrug, so nonchalant. "I need to give the world what they want and then move on." My eyes drift over to the window again. "I will be sniffed out soon. Everyone is wondering where I am."

His eyebrows rise as he sits up straight again. "Imagine their reactions when they discover you've been shacked up with some lowly American actor."

"It's time they know who the mystery man is, don't you think? And your mystery woman, for that matter." A thrill mixed with apprehension tickles my insides. He doesn't answer. I know Josh thinks it is long overdue. "I should probably get myself ready."

"I'll watch." He lowers from the table and collects me. "Do I get to approve the outfit you wear when you tell the world about me?"

"And what would you have me wear?"

"I know just the thing." As we enter our temporary bedroom, Josh once again shakes his head at the masses of clothes spreading to every corner. "I'm going to have to extend the dressing room at my place."

I settle on the bed as I watch him rummage through the endless suitcases. "Or we could buy somewhere else," I suggest.

"In LA?"

"Sure." I place my hands in my lap, gazing around the penthouse. "An apartment like this would be nice."

"You don't want to live in my house?" There's no hurt apparent, just curiosity.

"Well, it's yours," I point out. "And I've never been house hunting before. It'll be exciting. I want to look for a ranch, too. Some place in the middle of nowhere with acres of land for me to roam on my horse."

"Whatever you want, baby." He pulls out a dress. "Found it." Looking pleased with his find, he holds it up to me. "My favorite."

I grin at the black satin number, the very dress I had on the day of my thirtieth. The day I met Josh Jameson. "That one?"

"Yes, this one." He wanders over and lays it next to me on the bed. "Perfect."

"Very well," I agree, hearing the front door open and close, followed by the voice of Kim calling me. "In here," I shout.

Josh snatches a quick kiss before Kim enters, her arms loaded with everything needed to make me look like the defiant queen I no longer am. "She's all yours," he declares, pulling on some grey sweatpants. "For now." On a wink, he leaves me to get ready for my interview.

"You have received a summons," Kim says dryly, holding up a letter that displays the coat of arms of Claringdon. "From Queen Victoria."

I scoff and get up, heading straight for the bathroom. "I'm disappointed it took so long."

"News of your live interview this evening was only made public a few hours ago. I'd say she's rather prompt."

"And wasting her time," I call, flipping the shower on before taking myself back to the door. Holding the doorframe, I lean out. "The Monarchy's power over me is a thing of the past. What does it say?"

"That they want consultation rights." She looks down. "That it must be pre-recorded."

"No can do," I sing, going back to the shower. "Part of the deal was live, and they are paying me millions for the exclusive." I step under the spray and start washing my hair. I don't need the money. The properties the King owned outside the publicly owned royal households would keep Eddie, Mother, and me going for ten life-times. Not to mention the fact that, though I am not technically British royalty anymore, my mother is still a Spanish princess. I'm still royal, as is Eddie. Money isn't an issue. But I have another good cause. Shockingly and very unexpectedly, my closest staff walked out of Claringdon three days ago with me. They left behind stable jobs, and whether that was a result of loyalty or that they couldn't bear the thought of serving my aunt isn't something that really matters. At the end of the day, Victoria is Queen because I abdicated. I put them in that position. So the money will go to them. It's the least I can do.

⁓

WHEN DAMON ARRIVES to collect me, I've bypassed the nervous shakes and gone straight to a trembling wreck. The closer the interview gets, the worse my shakes become. Josh and Kim have left me to pace up and down in front of the window, both of them quiet.

"Are you ready, Your Maj . . ." Damon drifts off, shaking his head to himself. "Sorry. It's taking some getting used to. Are you ready, Miss Lockhart?"

Now, I wasn't surprised to see Damon follow me out of

Claringdon. Even now, he's never far. "Or Adeline." I laugh, accepting my purse from Kim. "Do I look okay?"

"You look like Adeline Lockhart." She checks the zip of my dress. "You're good."

"Okay." *Deep breaths. Deep breaths.* I turn to Josh and press my lips together. He's sprawled on the couch, a bowl of popcorn in his lap. "Comfortable?"

"Yeah. I've heard it's a great night on TV." He grins around a mouthful of popcorn, and my eyes narrow playfully. Then he dumps it to the side and comes to me, taking me in his arms and kissing the living daylights out of me. "I know you're nervous, but try to be excited, yeah? After tonight, we get to start our lives together. Me and you. Everyday. No sneaking around, no sabotage."

"Stop, you'll make me cry, and I'll ruin my makeup."

"Be brave. Be honest." He rests his forehead on mine. "Just be the woman I love, and everything will be okay."

I nod, syphoning off some calm from him. "It's okay for you. You do interviews all the time."

He laughs, thoroughly amused. "Baby, ain't no one done an interview like this before, believe me."

"I do," I grumble as he passes me over to Damon, the only man I know Josh will trust with me.

"Keep her safe." But he has to reinforce it.

"Let's go." Damon takes the reins, and I'm led to the car with the backup of Bates and a few of Josh's other men.

I feel like I am about to take the biggest leap of faith any human could take.

36

WE CONTEMPLATED KEEPING the location secret, but that defeated the whole point of me being free of the clutches of the Royal Family. We didn't explicitly state where the interview was happening, either, but those in the know just know. So when we arrive, the area outside the TV studio is awash with press.

"Oh God," I murmur, feeling Kim take my hand and squeeze. Not to belittle Kim's act of comfort, but the only person who could possibly comfort me right now is Josh. It's a frenzy as Damon leads me to the doors, flashes blinding me, people shouting and hollering. My only relief is that they are friendly words being shouted.

I'm led through the corridors of the studio and into a room that has my name emblazoned across the front. I take a moment to read it. It's not a title. It's just my name.

ADELINE LOCKHART

I blow out air. That is me now. Simply Adeline Lockhart.

"Ma'am?" Damon asks, pulling my eyes up to him. He may as well physically kick himself. "Sorry." He opens the door and lets me wander into the suite, where couches form a square, a TV hangs on the wall, and cameras cover every angle.

A young girl comes to me, her face awash with awe that makes me feel somewhat uncomfortable. "Please don't curtsey," I beg, lowering to the plush sofa and helping myself to the jug of water on the table before me. My mouth is parched. I'm still trembling. Damn it, I need to pull myself together. I don't want the world to see me like this—a nervous, shaking wreck. I need to be strong. Sure.

I glug down a whole glass of water as I'm given direction. The papers handed to me are taken by Kim, a good job since my shaking limbs refuse to grant me control of them.

"Are you certain of the open-question policy?" Kim asks for the thousandth time. "I still have time to get approval."

I shake my head. "If I don't want to answer something, I won't." We're left alone by the studio staff, giving me time to gather myself. I'm just making progress in the relaxing stakes when I hear applause erupt. I look up at the TV on the wall and lose every second of the time I spent talking myself down as the camera pans across the audience, hundreds of people standing as they welcome the show's host. It's a good full minute before they settle enough for him to talk. The usual bubbly, vivacious man looks serious.

"Good evening." Graham Miles' suit is sparkling, new no doubt. "It isn't often in one's lifetime they are presented with an opportunity like the one I have been given this evening." I look up when the door opens, and the young girl who gave me directions earlier, all directions of which I have now forgotten, smiles as she rearranges her headpiece. "We're ready for you, Miss Lockhart."

Oh God, oh God, oh God.

Kim stands before me, and after I've displayed no signs of moving, Damon helps me up. I breathe out, my heart going crazy in my chest. For a moment, I question why on earth I decided to do this. How I thought I would ever get through it. But my self-doubt disappears in a puff of dust when a solid, vivid vison on Josh invades my mind. For him, I can do anything. For us. For *me*.

Making sure my strides are sure and steady, I follow the young girl through a maze of corridors until we reach a screen. My makeup is checked. Kim faffs with my hair. Damon gives me a wink.

"Ladies and gentlemen, Miss Adeline Lockhart." Graham Miles's announcement is spoken calmly, but the clapping and cheers reach unspeakable levels. I'm indicated to proceed. I could be carrying iron in my legs. I have to tell myself to smile. All those years I spent summoning my mask so easily, and now it is so hard to find. But I don't need my mask. I don't need to fool anyone. This is me. The *real* me.

I take the stairs to the studio floor, praying I don't tumble, and make my way to the couches, thankful when Graham meets me halfway and takes my hands, kissing me like he never could have before. Because I was Queen. Because no one must touch me. Now, I am more thankful than he will ever know for his support.

"Absolutely ravishing," he says, holding my arms out to the sides to take me in. "Please, come sit." I'm helped to the couch, taking my seat as I gaze into the crowd, trying to disregard all of the cameras dotted around. Trying not to think about the entire world watching me.

I lose myself in time, waiting for the deafening sounds to die down so Graham can speak. "Comfortable?" he asks, getting comfortable himself.

I pad the cushions with my palms before edging closer to the arm and resting an elbow on it. "It'll do," I say, and he laughs, along with everyone else in the crowd.

"Now, before we begin,' he says, 'I have to ask the most important question."

"Which is what?"

"Since you are no longer the Queen of England, does that mean I should disregard that official letter I received from yourself awarding me a knighthood?"

I laugh, my head thrown back a little, feeling a little bit of my stress leave me. I spent years adopting this tactic with the people I met, trying to ease their nerves by making them laugh. Am I that obviously terrified? "I believe the New Year's Honors list still stands." I smile madly when he places his hand over his heart as if thanking God.

"Then with that confirmed, I can move on at ease." He sits back, the crowd now deathly silent, waiting for his first real question. "Why?" he asks simply.

"I'm afraid you will have to be a little more specific," I say on a smile. "I'm sure there are many answers to many whys."

"Why this?" He motions around the studio. "Live, an audience, and me of all people. I'm certain there are many more qualified people who could interview you, but you personally selected me."

"Well I rather like you, Graham," I reply simply, stirring a few chuckles from the crowd and a lovely smile from my host.

"But this?" he asks again, looking to all of the cameras. "Why this way?"

I inhale and breathe out. "Because I can," I say simply. It's all I really need to say, and he nods, as if he gets it. I just hope everyone else does, too.

"Because you are no longer under the control of the British Monarchy?" he counters nevertheless, a little cheekily, raising my eyebrows.

"I don't think it is a big secret that I struggled with my role within the institution."

"As Princess or as Queen?"

"Both, of course. I never expected to fall onto the throne. I suppose the circumstances of my succession made it somewhat more difficult to come to terms with."

He nods. Whether that is understanding or simply an acknowledgement, I don't know. "Indeed, we can't very well avoid the tragedy that you and your family have suffered in recent months.

The world's media has been gripped by the shock of your father's death, as well as your brother's. Tell me about that. As mere mortals, we only got what the media reported."

I beg the growing lump in my throat to shrink so I can speak with some kind of stability. "I think the whole horrific matter proved that the Royals are simply mere mortals, too." There are cracks in my voice that cannot be concealed, not with any amount of determination. Proving I am right. We're mere mortals. "My father was a good man. A good King." I clear my throat, ignoring that I am adding more smoke and more mirrors. But it is for the greater good. The secrets are no longer mine to keep, but they are also not mine to tell. Besides, I still need to protect my mother and brothers. "He followed my grandfather and set an example to myself and my brothers that was always going to be hard to fulfil. When Edward stepped aside, the pressure fell onto my shoulders, and I am not ashamed to say that I doubted myself more than anyone else doubted me. I have always maintained that such an important role should be driven by ability, desire, and commitment. I lacked those qualities. I also had a severe handicap in another form, and it was one of which there was no cure."

"The mystery man," Graham says, and the silence in the studio seems to become deafening. "We could talk all day about your life as a princess, and then as Queen, but I believe there is only one question unanswered. Your official announcement abdicating the throne spoke deeply of a man in your life."

I stare at him, flicking my eyes to a nearby camera, knowing Josh is watching. One question unanswered. If only they knew. "Apparently the world is rather curious," I muse, making Graham laugh along with the crowd. I smile coyly, reaching forward for my glass of water.

"Of course, because what kind of man could make a Queen give up her kingdom for him?"

"The kind the Monarchy doesn't approve of," I quip, and he

gives me a sideways grin. "Not to mention the kind of man who makes everything else in your life seem so pointless."

"Being the Queen was pointless?"

"No, being *anything* was pointless if I couldn't have him. He made the impossible seem possible, yet it was made abundantly clear to me that I couldn't have him."

"And so you got engaged to Haydon Sampson." He fires the statement and relaxes back, letting it explode and take the silence to an entirely new level.

I swallow and shift, crossing one leg over the other. "Unfortunately I was under a strong influence at the time. I was trying to be the Queen I was expected to be. I could deny my heart belonged to another to all, but not to myself. It was too painful and daunting to think I would live out my life without the man I loved. We faced numerous bumps in our road, but thankfully we have overcome them, and now there is nothing to stop us from being together."

He nods slowly, letting my answer settle with the audience. "So are you ready to tell the world who this man is?"

"Not really." I shoot back on a smile. "I've rather enjoyed having him to myself." Laughter erupts again, taking a while to die down. I purposely make sure there is silence before I go on. "But, if you must know . . ." I fade and draw breath, sure I hear millions of people do the same, bracing themselves for the name I will say next. I take the leap I've been bracing myself for. "His name is—" I snap my mouth closed when Graham holds up a hand, stopping me from uttering the words that will send the world into further media meltdown.

"Just one second," he says, standing. I look around the studio, worried, wondering what is going on. I imagine all kinds—the royal aides storming the studio to silence me, or maybe even the police.

"Don't look so worried," Graham says as I glance from one corner of the studio to the other. "I believe the mystery man would like to introduce *himself.*"

What?

My wide eyes dart to Graham, finding him smiling at me where I'm frozen on the couch, unable to talk, move . . . breathe.

"Ladies and gentlemen." He glides his arm out to the stairs that I descended, and I crane my neck to see, certain I am the butt of a terrible joke.

It's no joke. "Oh my God," I whisper as Josh appears at the top of the stairs, his hands in the pockets of his suit trousers. The suit he wore to my thirtieth garden party at Claringdon. He even has the pink handkerchief poking out of his breast pocket. I stare in complete shock as he smiles at the crowd and the audience go wild, standing and clapping, whooping and cheering. He looks out-of-this-world handsome, his smile dashing, his body confident.

"Josh Jameson," Graham yells over the deafening noise, the confirmation of his name sending the crowds into another dimension of excitement. And as if the masses of spectators aren't there, Josh turns to me on the couch. When our eyes meet, my entire world turns upside down again, and I cover my face with my palms, returning forward and bending my torso over my lap, my emotion too much to contain. I'm so overwhelmed. So . . . stunned.

Within a few seconds, I feel him before me, crouching, his knees either side of my legs. He takes my wrists. He pulls my hands away, revealing my stained face. And he smiles a smile that tells me everything is going to be okay.

"Hello, beautiful."

I let out a ragged sob and throw my seated body forward, grabbing him and burying my face into his neck. The noise around me disappears. Right now, there is only Josh.

He holds me tightly. So tightly. My hair is stroked, he hushes me gently in my ear. "I couldn't let you do it alone," he whispers, cupping my head and pulling me out of my hiding place, wiping my tears away with the pads of his thumbs. Then he drops a lingering kiss on my forehead, breathing me into him, as if the whole world isn't watching. "Okay?"

I nod, but it's jerky, lacking any control. I must look a fright, but I don't care. This is me. I'm just a woman. I'm not made of stone.

"Let's do this," he murmurs, breaking away, though keeping a firm hold of my hand. Taking a seat beside me, he wraps his arm around my shoulders and pulls me close. "Surprise," he jokes as the crowd roars on.

"I think the world just drowned in a tsunami of swoons." Graham's hand meets his chest, his body deflating with his sigh.

I laugh through another sob, squeezing Josh's hand, smiling up at him. God, he looks unimaginably gorgeous, so relaxed and content. And now, I am relaxed, too, and more content than I have ever been.

"So then," Graham says when the audience has finally quietened down, "they didn't approve of you?" He throws a disgusted look to the cameras. "The audacity."

"Well, I'm American." Josh shrugs. "I swear too much, and half the world has seen my bare ass. So no, I didn't get off to the best start with the British Royals." Josh's answer causes rip-roaring laughter within the audience, and I shake my head in utter disbelief, just gazing at him.

Graham eventually gets his own chuckles under control. "So there really was a story in that little dance you two had at the White House." He purses his lips, as if in disapproval, and I blush terribly, more so when Josh plucks his pink hanky from his top pocket and hands it to me on a cheeky grin. "And those Uggs plastered all over the Internet were yours," Graham adds.

"They were mine." It feels so good to tell the truth.

"So how did you meet?"

"Like many other couples might meet," Josh answers for us. "At a social event."

"Which one?"

"My thirtieth birthday." I watch as Graham shakes his head to himself on a smile, obviously recalling his interview with Josh some time ago when Josh played down the whole event. I stuff Josh's hanky back into his top pocket. "Our eyes met, and I did what any other woman would do when faced with Josh Jameson."

"And what's that?" Graham asks seriously, hiding his amusement. As if he needs to ask.

"I believe the term is *swoon*."

Graham nods, looking to the audience briefly. "But you were not just *any* woman."

"On the contrary, I am just that. A woman. Any other woman could have been in my position. It just so happened I was third in line to the British throne."

"And due to tragic circumstances, you became Queen."

"I did. But does that mean my heart shouldn't want what it wants anymore?" I ask, feeling Josh's hand constrict around mine. I look up at him and smile. "It just meant I wanted him more."

"Adeline was in an impossible position." Josh speaks up, reaching for his scruff and rubbing at his chin. "I fell in love with her fast." He shrugs, all nonchalant. "I know she did me, too."

"Ever so confident," I mutter, spiking chuckles all round.

Josh nudges me in the shoulder playfully, and I laugh as he pushes on. "Even as the Princess of England, being together was a challenge." He peeks down at me, nearly blinding me with his smile. "But we were ready to take on that challenge. After the events of a few months ago when Adeline lost her father and her brother and she unexpectedly took the throne, everything changed. She wanted desperately to do her father proud. She wanted desperately to prove the doubters wrong. And she wanted desperately to be with me." He swallows. "She didn't want to choose, but in the end she had to."

"And you chose Josh," Graham says, as if that needs clarifying.

"No," I counter quietly. "I chose love."

"Why?"

I look at the man sitting beside me, the man I know will always be here for me. The man who changed everything. He gives me that adorable, devilish smirk, his eyes flashing brightly. "Because he loves me for who I am. Because he saw deep into my soul and embraced me. Because he loves my fierceness but won't think twice about putting me in my place." I smirk when he lifts his eyebrow knowingly, mentally feeling his palm on my arse. "I was born to love Josh." I swallow, thinking about all of the love that's been lost over the years by so many people close to me. "Because," I whisper, "love should always win." I clear my throat on a little cough, letting Josh pull me closer.

Graham's face is almost dreamy as he observes us. "Some argue that you were born to be Queen."

"Oh, she was," Josh says, lacing our fingers tightly. "But she was born to be *my* queen." Bringing my hand to his mouth, he kisses the back. "And if you don't mind, there is something I'd like to do."

I tense as Josh smiles, breaking away from me.

He stands.

He clears his throat.

He reaches into his pocket.

I tense more.

"Josh . . ." I say, as the audience all draw breath, too.

Then . . . silence.

You could hear a pin drop.

He turns and drops to one knee, presenting me with a small black velvet box. My hand meets my chest. "Oh my goodness."

He smiles, quite shy, as he pulls it open, revealing a ring. A simple ring. A small diamond on a simple band. Nothing elaborate or showy. Just a simple ring. And I know he's chosen this simple ring on purpose.

"We both know the answer to this question," he says quietly as I blink my eyes clear and look up at him. His face. It's beautiful. "But I want the world to hear you say it." Dropping his other knee, he walks forward on them and places the ring on the sofa, taking my face in is hands. "Will you marry me, Miss Adeline Lockhart?"

"Yes," I sob, feeling his hands on my cheeks as my eyes explode. "Yes, yes, yes." On a smile as bright as mine, he dips, catching my lips, unbothered by the crowd, who are now applauding crazily in the background, stamping their feet, cheering and yelling. I laugh into his mouth, feeling his palm move to my hair and force me closer. And then I hear something over the applause, and I quickly rip my mouth from Josh's, finding his eyes. They're sparkling madly, his smile wide, as Estelle's and Kanye West's *American Boy* booms from the speakers all around us. "Oh my God," I laugh, falling into Josh's chest when he tugs me up from the couch.

He's looking down at me on an epic grin, his hands firmly on my arse. "This time when we dance, you can relax, you can smile, and you can let go." He gives me a hard, possessive kiss. "Because now the whole fuckin' world knows you belong to me."

I mirror his grin, and he starts twirling me around the floor, my head thrown back in pure, unimaginable happiness. I'm completely uninhibited, being watched by the world as I, the former Queen of England, dance with my American boy live on TV.

"There you are, ladies and gentlemen," Graham shouts over the ear-piercing cheers and music. "His true queen!"

EPILOGUE

JOSH

FUCKIN' HELL. I'VE never been so nervous in my life. I've attended endless press conferences. Done thousands of interviews. Accepted awards and given speeches. But nothing compares to the nerves I'm feeling right now. I'm perched on the front pew, bent over, hands clasped, palms sweaty, my knee jumping up and down. I blow out air.

Pull it together, Josh.

A light smack on my shoulder jolts me from my pending meltdown, and I look up to find Dad smiling fondly at me. "Don't," I warn. "I'm trying."

He chuckles and sits down next to me, reaching into the inside pocket of his suit jacket. He pulls out a hip flask and unscrews the cap. "Dutch courage." He passes it over and I swig more than I probably should.

"I don't need courage. I need calming the fuck down."

"You're in the house of God, boy. Have some respect."

"Sorry," I mutter, passing him back the flask. "Where's Eddie?" Adeline's brother is flighty these days at best. One second he's here, the next he's gone and disappears for days on end. He didn't last long in rehab. I'm sure he's getting worse.

"Restroom."

That means he's taking his own form of Dutch courage. Great. I need him like I need a hole in my fuckin' head. I glance behind me. The rows of pews are filling up, the church quickly getting full to capacity. Everyone who falls through the doors looks flustered, like they've just run the gauntlet. Because they have. It's fuckin' chaos out there, utter madness. Wedding of the century, they claim. Part of me is a little annoyed. Another part is enjoying the humongous *fuck you* this event will signify to those royal assholes.

"What's the time?" I ask Dad, returning forward.

"Two minutes later than when you last asked." He slips his flask back into his pocket. "Christ, boy, what's gotten into you?"

"I don't know," I admit. I've been desperate for this day to hurry the fuck up and be here. And now it is. And now I'm nervous as shit. I rake a hand through my hair, probably messing it all up. I don't care. What's a bit of mussed hair when you're sweating like a racehorse?

Dad smacks my jumping leg and stands. "I better go say some hellos." He smiles a shit-eating smile and leaves me to welcome some of the hundreds of guests. Me? I stay exactly where I am. Paralyzed by my nerves. *Breathe. Breathe. Breathe.* Shit, I haven't spent one night away from Adeline since she abdicated. That was until last night. I was twitchy. Restless. Not surprising given what we've been through to get to today. I had Tammy call her every hour. I called her mother myself a few times, too. She was fine. Of course she was okay. I, however, wasn't. Those royals. They're capable of too much shady shit, and they've made more than one summons on Adeline. I ripped up one. Adeline burned another. What the fuck has our wedding day got to do with those douchebags?

"Seriously, Josh." Eddie appears, refastening his fly. The man seems to have dropped all his royal etiquette along with his title.

"You look petrified."

"I am." Storing lines in my mind is my job. I'm one of the best at it. Today, I can't remember a fuckin' thing of what I'm supposed to say. I catch a whiff of alcohol and look to my soon-to-be brother-in-law. I'm in no position to judge since Dad just fed me some of the good stuff, but I can guarantee I haven't had as much as Eddie. "No more," I warn. The last thing I need is Adeline whittling on our special day. I promised I'd keep an eye on him.

He rolls his eyes, the condescending asshole. "We're celebrating."

"You've been celebrating for nearly a year."

"Too fucking right. I have a lot of lost time to catch up on."

I sigh but don't counter. He has a long way to go before he gets over the bombshells that were dropped on him.

"Just behave."

"Yes, bro."

I look back when I hear the sounds of people gushing. Adeline's mother appears, looking truly stunning in a pearl-blue gown. No mother-of-the-bride two-piece for her. I find the will and strength I need to get up and go to her, meeting her halfway down the aisle, my legs now surprisingly stable. Catherine is here, that's why. If Adeline wasn't okay or if something was up, Catherine wouldn't be here smiling that soft, reassuring smile.

She holds her arms out to me as I approach. "Look at you, you handsome thing."

"You look stunning, Catherine." I let her embrace me, grateful for her easy affection. "How's Adeline?" I ask.

"Worried she'll desert you at the altar?"

I scoff. "No."

She laughs lightly, patting my cheek tenderly. "She's wonderful. You're a lucky boy, Josh Jameson." Her eyes move up to the hair I just roughed up, and her hand faffs to coax it back into place. She's wasting her time.

"I know," I agree. So lucky.

"Oh, Edward," Catherine coos, spotting her wayward son over my shoulder. She looks so happy to see him. I know she doesn't often these days, their relationship far from fixed. Breaking away, she goes to him, taking him in a hug. He accepts, embraces even, but that edge of resentment still lingers.

Something catches my attention out the corner of my eye, and I look up to the balcony above the altar, frowning. *What the fuck?* "Hey!" I yell, just as a flash blinds me. "Bates!"

He's on his way fast, chasing the rogue pap down. The fucker. How the hell did he get in here? It's like fuckin' Fort Knox. I make tracks, following Bates up the stone steps. I find him manhandling the guy toward me when I arrive, his camera smashed to pieces on the floor. "Is that a tent?" I ask. It's like a fuckin' campsite—empty bottles of water, cans of . . ."Tuna?"

"Yeah, I think he's been staking the place out."

I throw the pap a look that could turn him to dust. "Get him out of here before I kick his ass."

Bates wrestles the asshole away as he yells in protest, trying to make it back to his smashed camera. I crouch and root through the pieces, finding what I'm looking for. I eject the memory card and slip it into my inside pocket.

"Josh, it's time."

I stand and turn, finding Catherine looking on in disgust as Bates disappears with the rogue photographer. "Time?" I question.

Adeline's mother approaches me, amused, taking my hands and squeezing them gently. Her hands are so soft. Her smile soft. Everything about this woman is soft and delicate. "You are getting married today, are you not?"

"I am." My pulse quickens.

"She's here."

And then my heart drops into my feet. "Already?"

"She didn't want to be fashionably late."

I release her hold and step back, my hand automatically running through my hair again. "Fuck," I breathe, and then immediately apologize for it. "Sorry."

On a sigh, Catherine steps forward and fixes my hair for the second time, but not for the last. "Are you going to keep *her* waiting?"

My eyes dart to the doorway that leads back down to the altar. My fuckin' legs won't work. "I can't move," I admit. This is it. She's here. The moment I've been waiting *too* long for. And I'm frozen. By nerves? By excitement?

"Josh." Catherine physically shakes me and snaps me from my lifelessness. I look at her blankly, my mind screaming at me to get my ass moving. "Go."

"Right."

She physically moves me along, and I rely on her to help me down the stone steps back to the altar. I only start to feel my legs once I breach the entrance into the church and the congregation comes into view, every available seating space taken, and some standing space, too. Spanish royalty, Hollywood royalty, friends, family, and world leaders. Even the damn President of the United States. I had suggested a small, intimate affair. Adeline had replied, "Screw that." I get my girl's point. We're no longer hiding anything.

"Oh boy," I whisper, every set of eyes on me. Another rake of my hand through my hair provides Catherine with the task of fixing me again.

"What's up?" Dad asks, approaching, a look of concern all over his face.

"I think Josh has had an attack of the nerves," Catherine says, straightening out my suit jacket once she's finished on my hair.

"I'm not nervous," I tell them, swallowing and breaking away, taking over Catherine in sorting myself out. "I'm excited." Let's get this show on the road.

I walk with purpose to my place, Dad following, and join Eddie. He's grinning. And he's definitely had a few more swigs of whatever he's hiding. His cheeks are flushed. "Ready?" he asks, slapping my shoulder heavily.

"When it comes to your sister, *bro*, I was born ready." I turn when I hear the organist begin, as does everyone else in the vast space. Two men reach for the handles of the sky-high double doors, and I take a breath as they slowly creak open.

The gasps of the hundreds of people must suck all oxygen from the room, because I suddenly can't breathe.

And I have not a fuckin' hope of regaining my ability to draw breath when I spot her.

"Oh, sweet Jesus," I murmur, every single detail of my world disappearing. Every single detail except for her. She's wearing her fuckin' tiara.

She stands on the threshold staring down the aisle at me. There's no veil covering her face. Nothing blocking my view to her beauty. She did that on purpose. I know she did that on purpose. And I'm glad. So glad. There's nothing between us.

Her gown is the simplest wedding gown I've ever seen. Simple and stunning. It's all she needs. Off-the-shoulder, satin, and straight to the floor. No train. No embellishment. Just the gown, her Spanish tiara, and her exquisite face.

My throat starts to swell, and my eyes start to burn with a mixture of pleasure and tears. And as she slowly starts down the aisle toward me—Davenport on one arm, Damon on the other—my mind seems to think now is a good time to remind myself of how I came to be here, in this spot, on this day, ready to swear my life to this woman.

Every moment from the very first second I encountered Adeline Catherine Luisa Lockhart, to just yesterday when she cooked me steak and washed my hair in the tub.

"Do you want to get into trouble with me?"

I smile to myself. Neither of us knew just how much trouble we were getting into. Not the kind of trouble we thought at the time.

"Maybe I want to violate a princess."

I didn't want to violate her. I wanted to cage her and keep her close forever. A rush of contentment washes over me, my body warm, as I run through the endless images of Adeline I have stored in every corner of my mind. The most special images are those of her sleeping. When she's naked, peaceful, and unaware of me studying her. When I spend a few minutes every morning tracing the line of her hip, up to her breast. When I move her hair away from her face, over her shoulders, so I can see all of her blinding beauty. When I trace her lips. When I kiss her forehead. And when she eventually stirs and sleepily crawls into my side. Mornings are my favorite times. Undisturbed. Quiet. Reflective. Simply . . . us.

My head lowers, and I drop my eyes to the floor, pulling in air slowly and steadily, my smile lazily creeping onto my face. I know she's getting closer, my body becoming more energized by the second, until every nerve ending within me is sizzling with her nearness and my veins are white hot. I look up through my lashes, biting my bottom lip through my smile. And when she smiles right back, my world goes up in smoke. The tip of her tongue trails across her red lips, her eyes falling to my chest, sparkling like crazy. I reach for my breast pocket and tweak the pink handkerchief, keeping my gaze on her. Always on her.

"Who gives this woman to be married to this man?" the priest asks as Damon gently breaks away, giving Adeline a soft kiss on her cheek before leaving her in the hands of her father.

Davenport swallows, his eyes glazed. "I do." His declaration is low, cut with every overwhelming emotion I know he's feeling today. He strains a smile through his overcome state as he unlinks Adeline's arm from his and turns into his daughter, taking her shoulders and kissing her lightly on the cheek. Shit, my own emotion fires up a few notches, and I'm forced to roughly wipe at my cheeks. She smiles and closes her eyes, taking a few moments with her father while I wait patiently. I'm happy to wait. He deserves his time. The world doesn't know of his status in Adeline's life. But Davenport does. And I know that is all that matters to him. I live in hope that Eddie will one day accept him fully, too. And then maybe Adeline will get back the fun-loving, strong brother she loves so much.

My attention jumps to Catherine, finding her discreetly wiping her own eyes with a tissue. And then I take in the rest of the church. Everyone looks as overawed as I feel.

"Josh"—Davenport takes Adeline's hand and extends it to me— "she's yours now."

I refrain from correcting him. She's always been mine. I nod and take her hand, moving in as Davenport moves away, joining Catherine on the front pew. He takes her hand. She smiles at him. It's a lovely sight.

I bring our chests together and look into Adeline's eyes. "Are you ready to get into trouble with me?"

Her hand takes mine and leads it to her stomach, and I glance down on a discreet smile. She's barely showing only being three months in. "That ship sailed the second I bowed to you."

I have to stop myself from dipping and kissing her midriff. That's news the world is yet to learn. "How crazy was it out there?" I ask, lacing our fingers together.

"Anyone would think I'm still Queen," she replies on a whisper.

I pull my gaze from her tummy, from my growing baby, and find her eyes. And the pad of my thumb finds her lips, dragging lightly across the red. "You are," I murmur, dipping and kissing the corner of her mouth, sliding my palm onto the column of her throat, thumbing at her lobe. I pull back and lift her loose hair, finding the earrings I had made for her. I smile. "You're *my* queen."

I turn us toward the patiently waiting priest and take one last deep breath.

"Marriage in itself is a blessing," he begins, "but doubly blessed is the couple who comes to the marriage altar with the approval and love of their families and friends." I look at Adeline, as she gazes at me, our smiles ironic as the man of God talks to the congregation. Neither of us sought to gain the blessing of anyone. But I know we have the blessing of the world.

"What are you smiling at?" Adeline asks quietly.

"I'm thinking," I whisper, "that I can't wait to violate my wife."

Her grin is demure as she returns her gaze to the priest. "I assure you, Mr. Jameson, your wife needs no violating."

"Is that so?'

"That is so," she counters, looking out the corner of her eye. I flash her my biggest smile, and she struggles to keep hers at bay. "I have just one vice, Mr. Jameson."

I cock my head subtly. "Hot American actors?"

"No," she muses softly, squeezing my hand. "My husband."

My smile turns into a smug grin. "God save the fuckin' Queen."

Ignoring the priest who is now mid-speech, she turns into me, ever the defiant, sassy woman I fell in love with, and throws her arms around me. "You already did, my gorgeous American boy."

THE END

ABOUT THE AUTHOR

JODI ELLEN MALPAS was born and raised in the Midlands town of Northampton, England, where she lives with her two boys and a beagle. She is a self-professed daydreamer, a Converse and mojito addict, and has a terrible weak spot for alpha males. Writing powerful love stories and creating addictive characters have become her passion—a passion she now shares with her devoted readers. She's a proud #1 New York Times bestselling author, and seven of her published novels were New York Times bestsellers, in addition to being international and Sunday Times bestsellers. Her work is published in more than twenty-three languages across the world.

You can learn more at:
www.jodiellenmalpas.co.uk

Follow Jodi:
Twitter @JodiEllenMalpas
Facebook.com/JodiEllenMalpas
Instagram Jodi_Ellen_Malpas

THIS MAN NOVELS
No other man compares . . .

    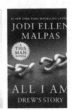

ONE NIGHT SERIES
Meet the mysterious, masterful M . . .

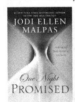  

THE SIZZLING STAND-ALONE NOVELS

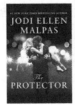 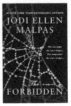